Gud

Timothy Top

BOOK THREE:
THE RED
PLUMBEE

Translation, Layout, and Editing by Mike Kennedy

ISBN: 978-1-942367-89-5

Library of Congress Control Number: 2019936690

Timothy Top Book Three: The Red Plumbee, published 2019 by The Lion Forge, LLC. Text and illustrations Copyright © 2016 Gud/Tunué S.r.l. First published by agreement with Tunué – www.tunue.com. All rights reserved. MAGNETIC™, MAGNETIC COLLECTION™, LION FORGE™ and all associated distinctive designs are trademarks of The Lion Forge, LLC. No similarity between any of the names, characters, persons, or institutions in this book with those of any living or dead person or institution is intended, and any such similarity which may exist is purely coincidental. Printed in China.

10 9 8 7 6 5 4 3 2 1

PROLOGUE
PLANET
SPERGENZIA

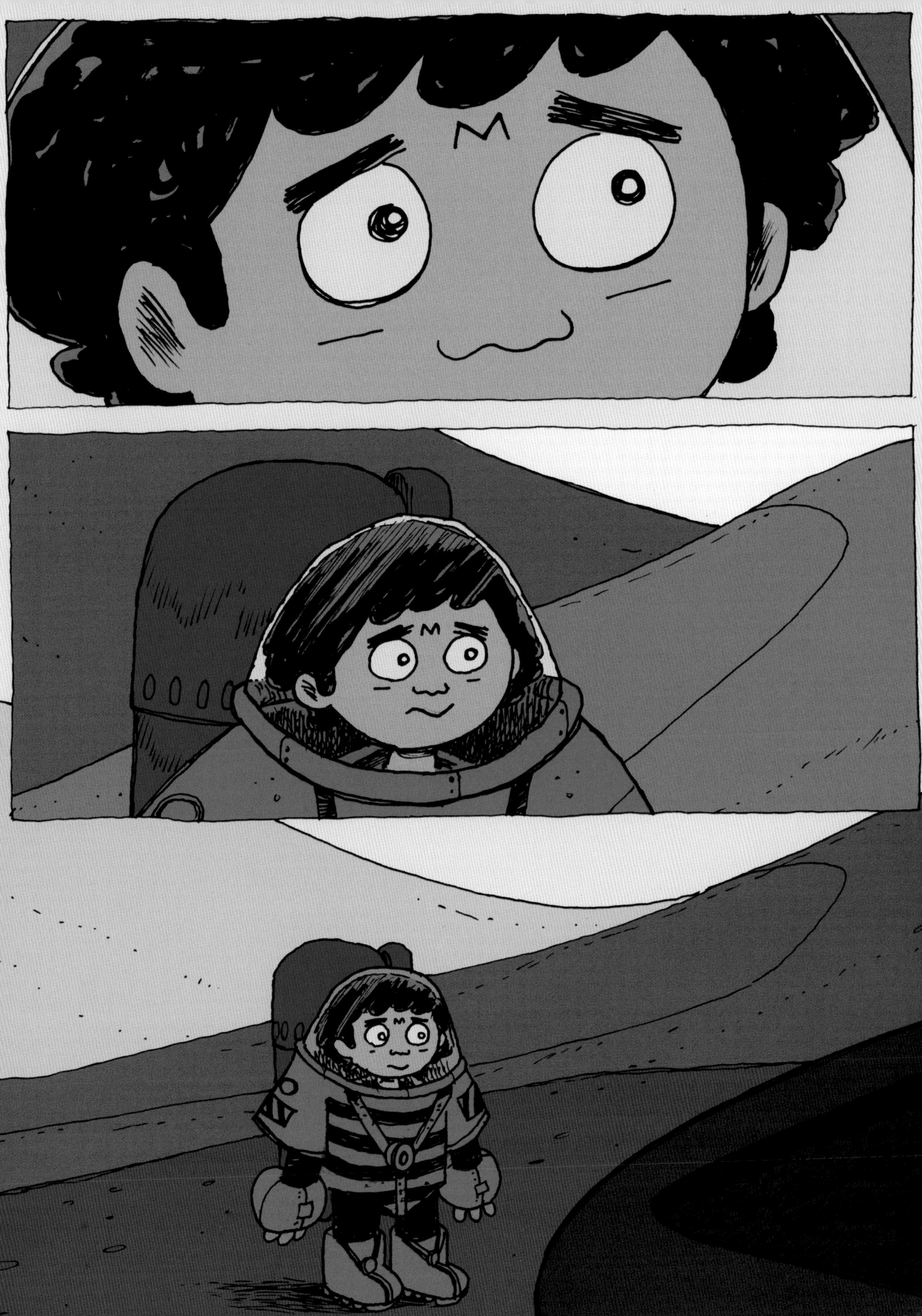

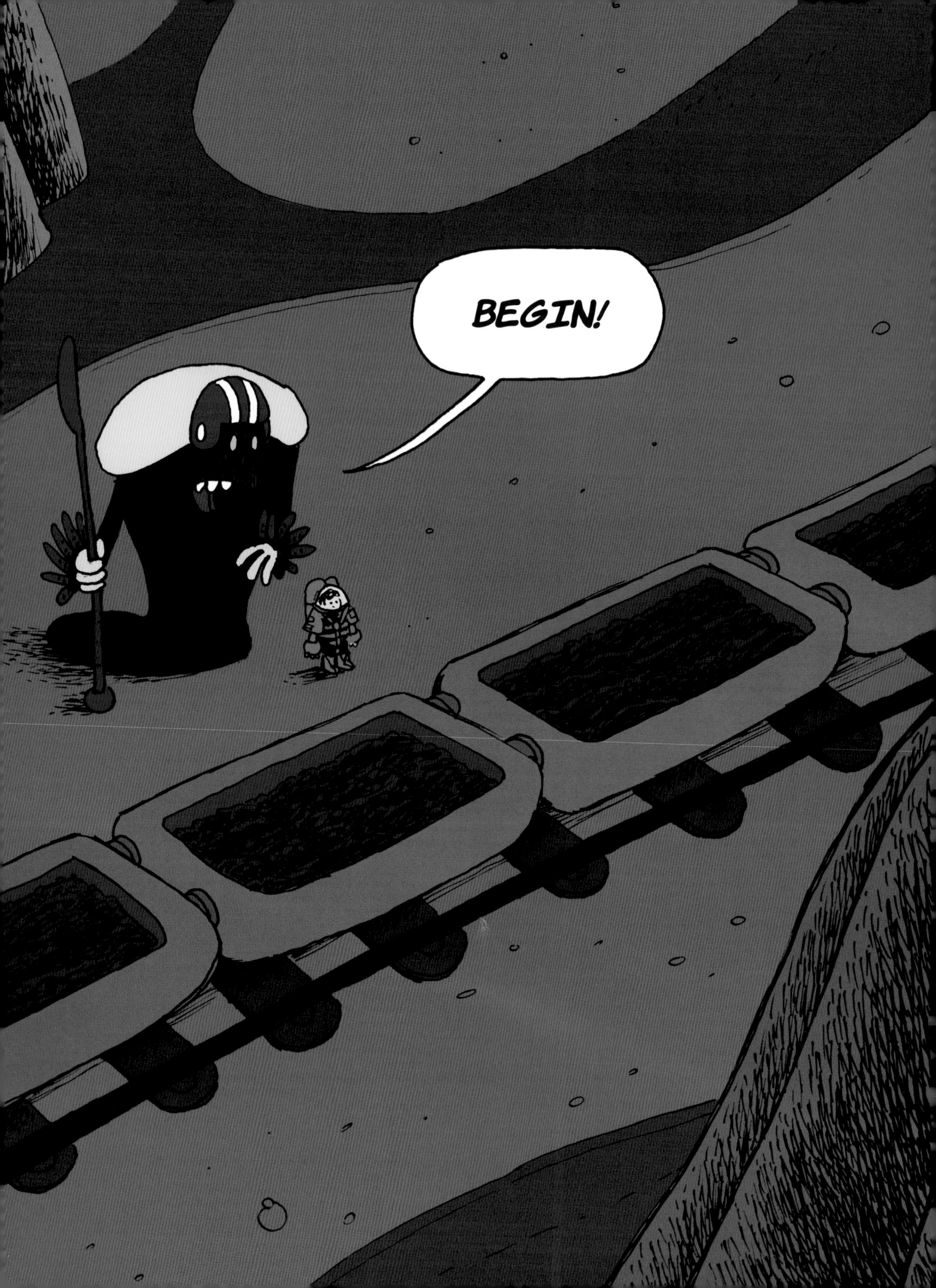
BEGIN!

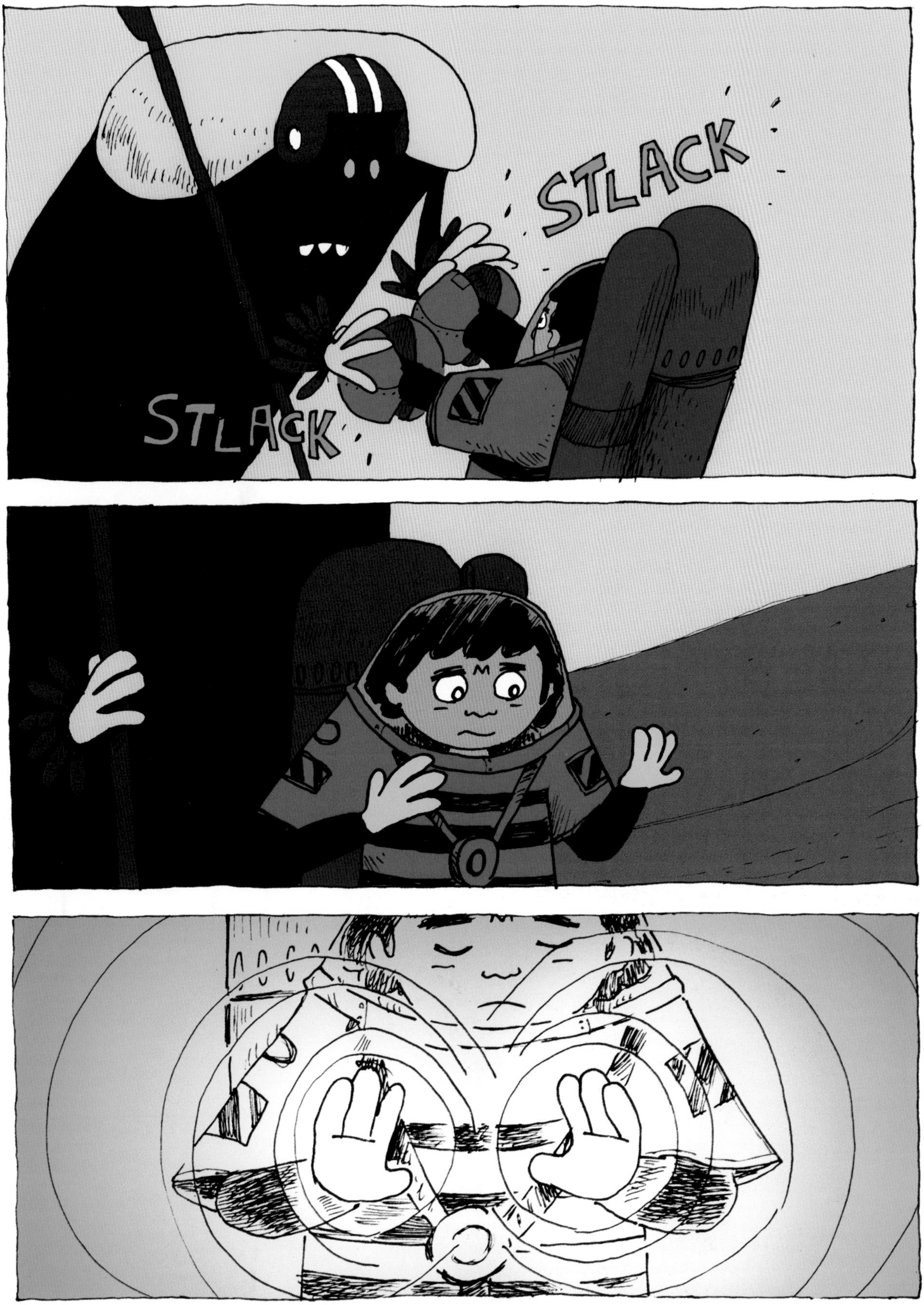
STLACK
STLACK

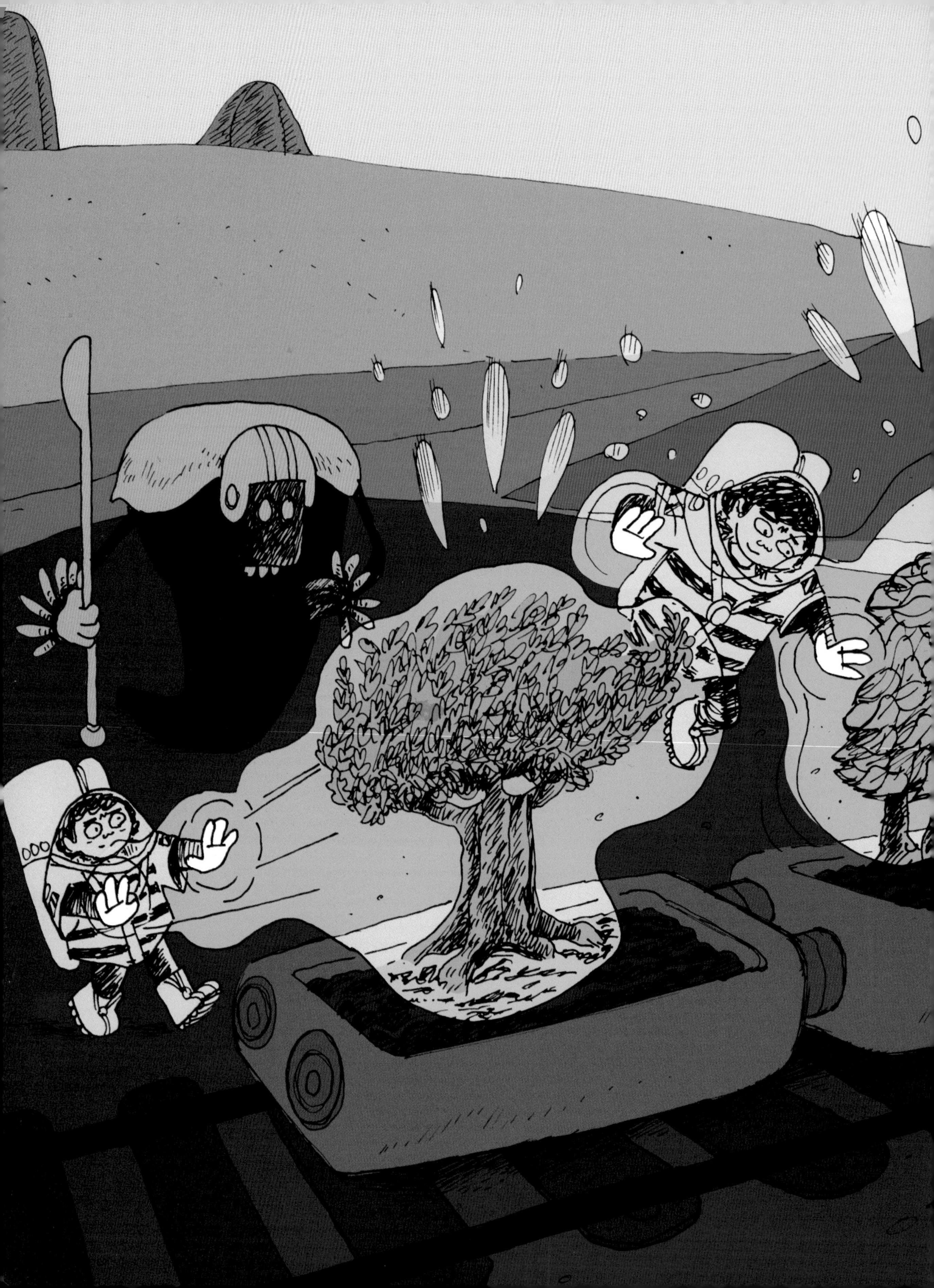

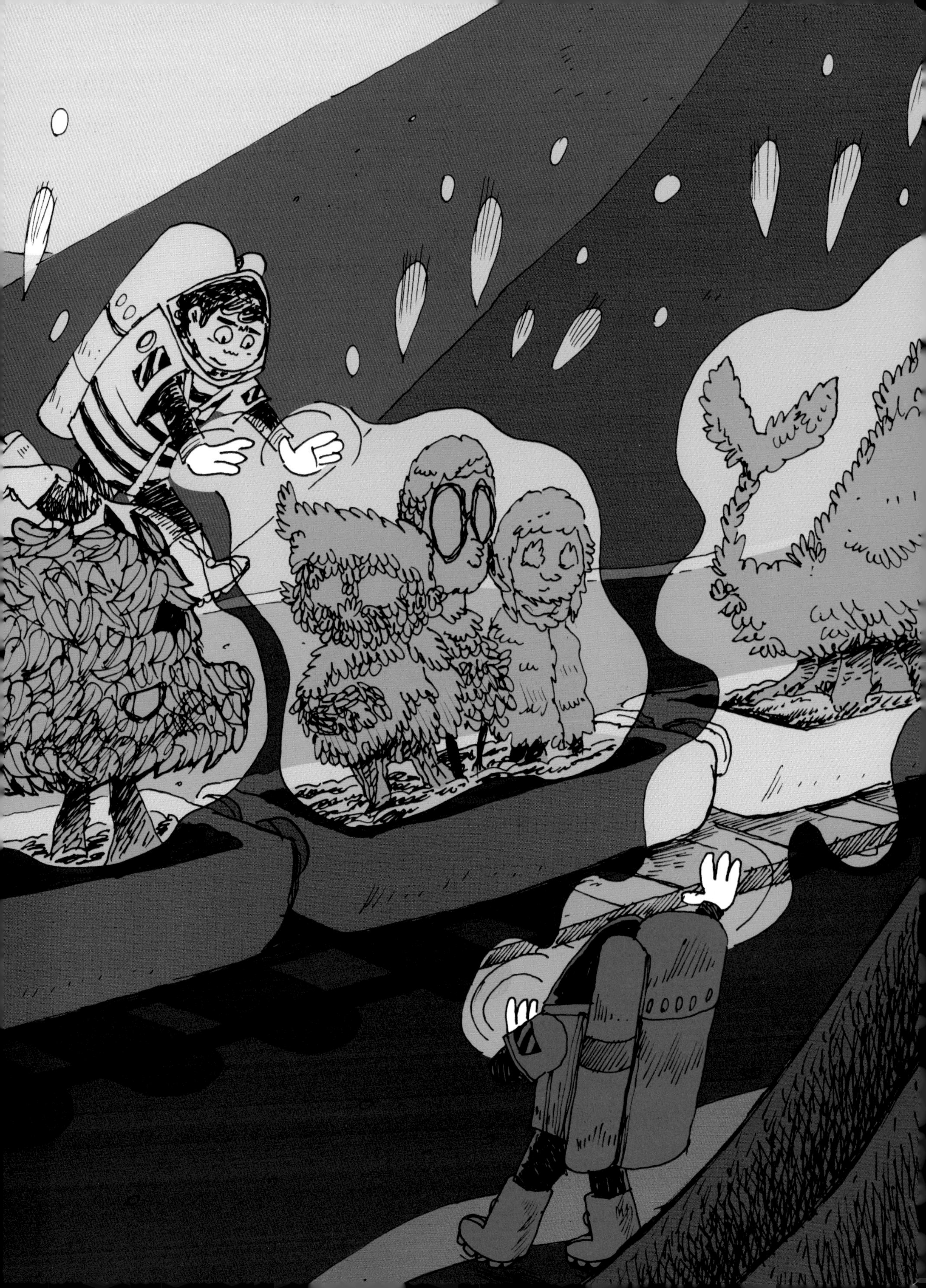

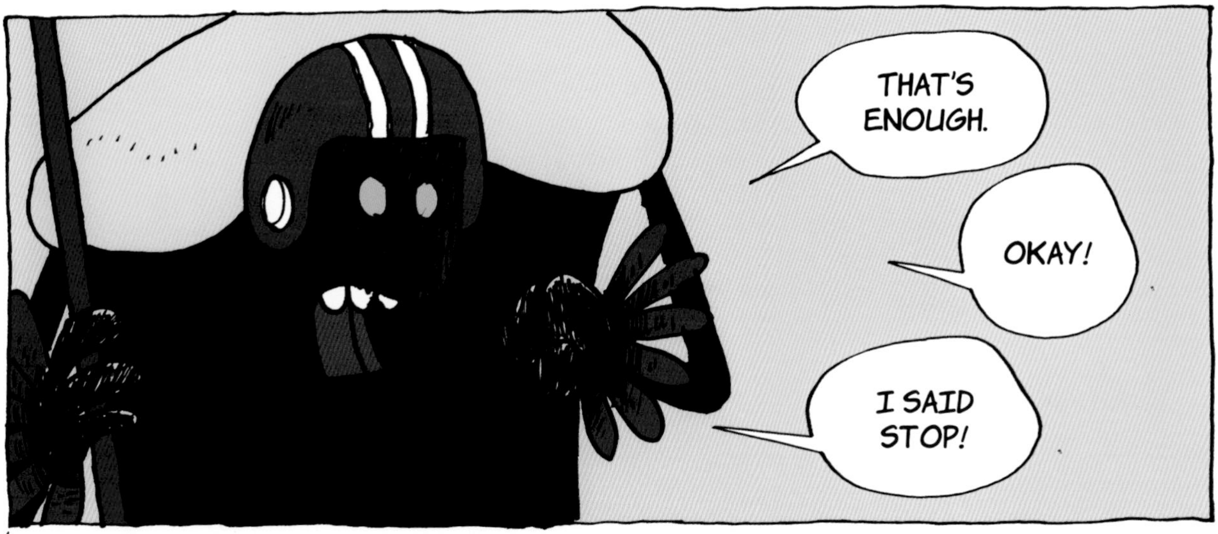
THAT'S ENOUGH.
OKAY!
I SAID STOP!

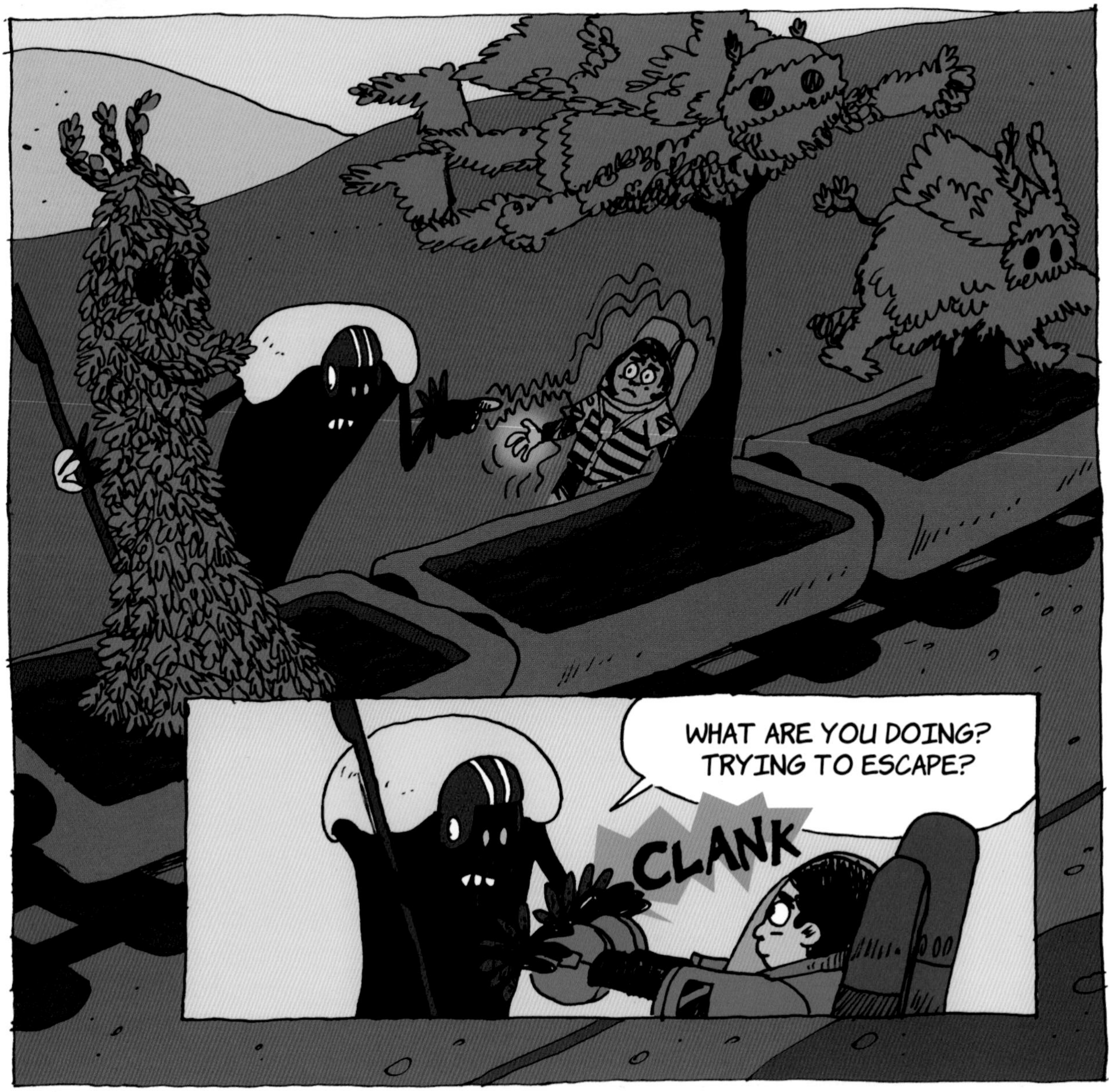
WHAT ARE YOU DOING? TRYING TO ESCAPE?
CLANK

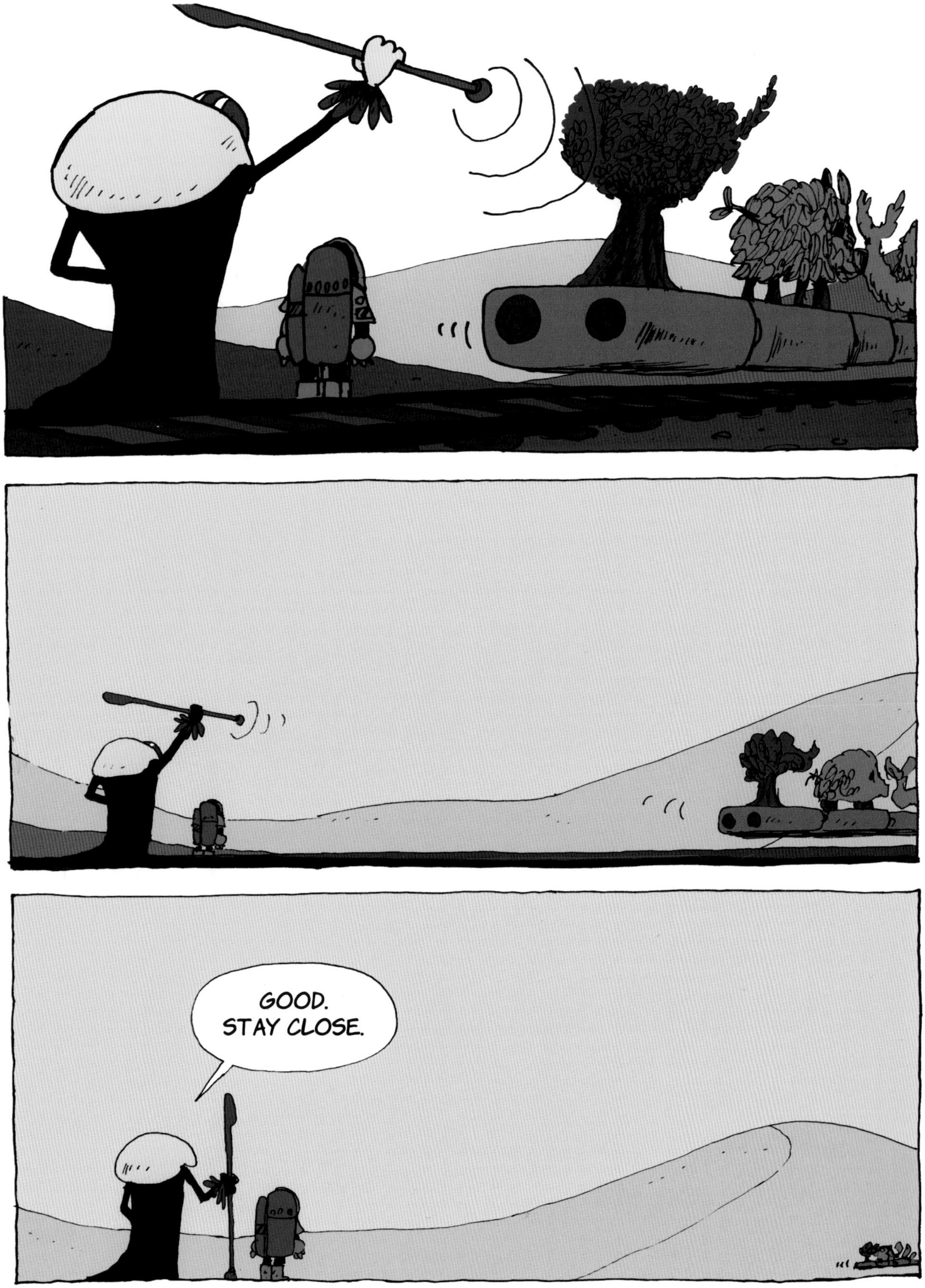
GOOD.
STAY CLOSE.

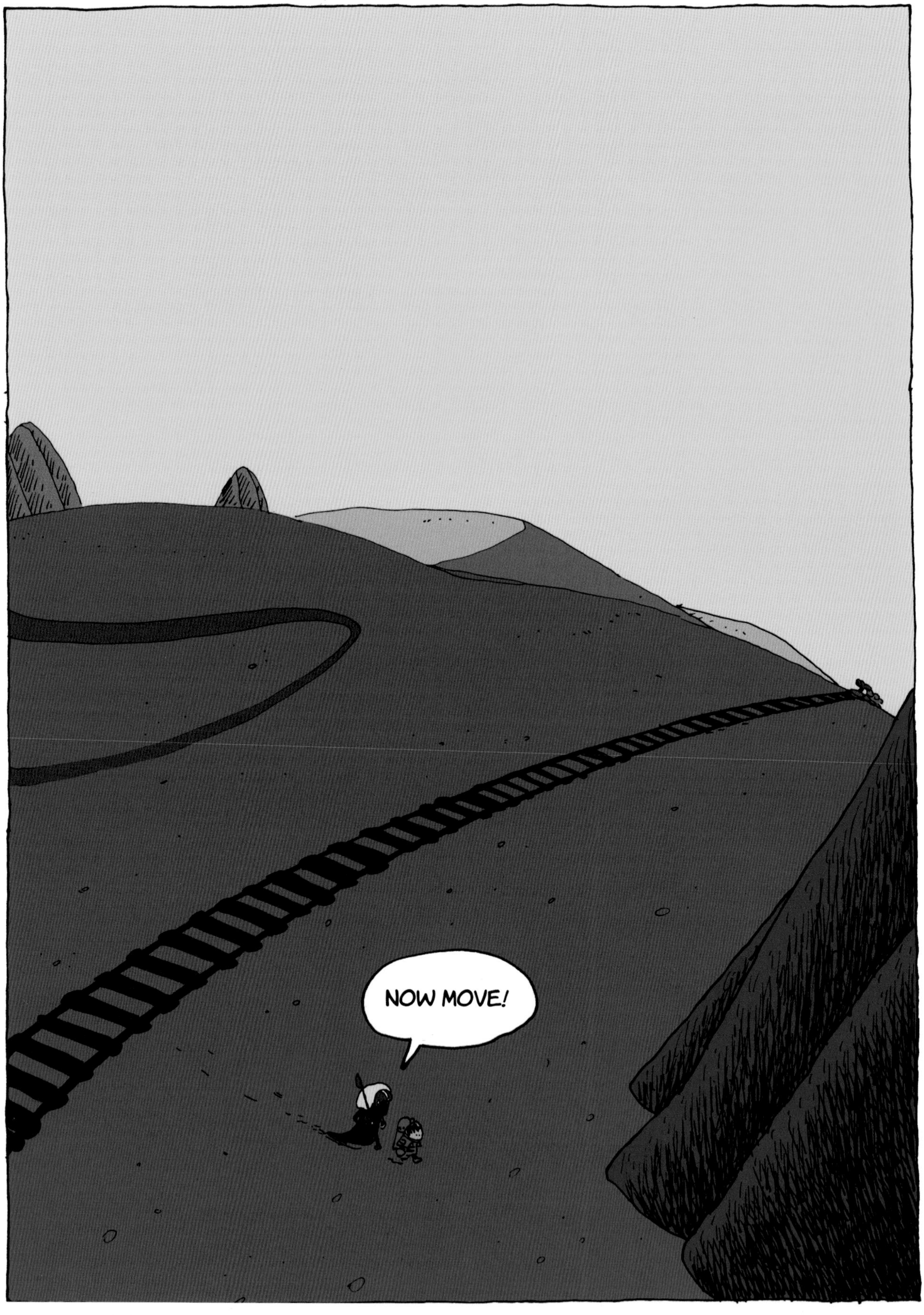
NOW MOVE!

CHAPTER ONE
BRATISBONA

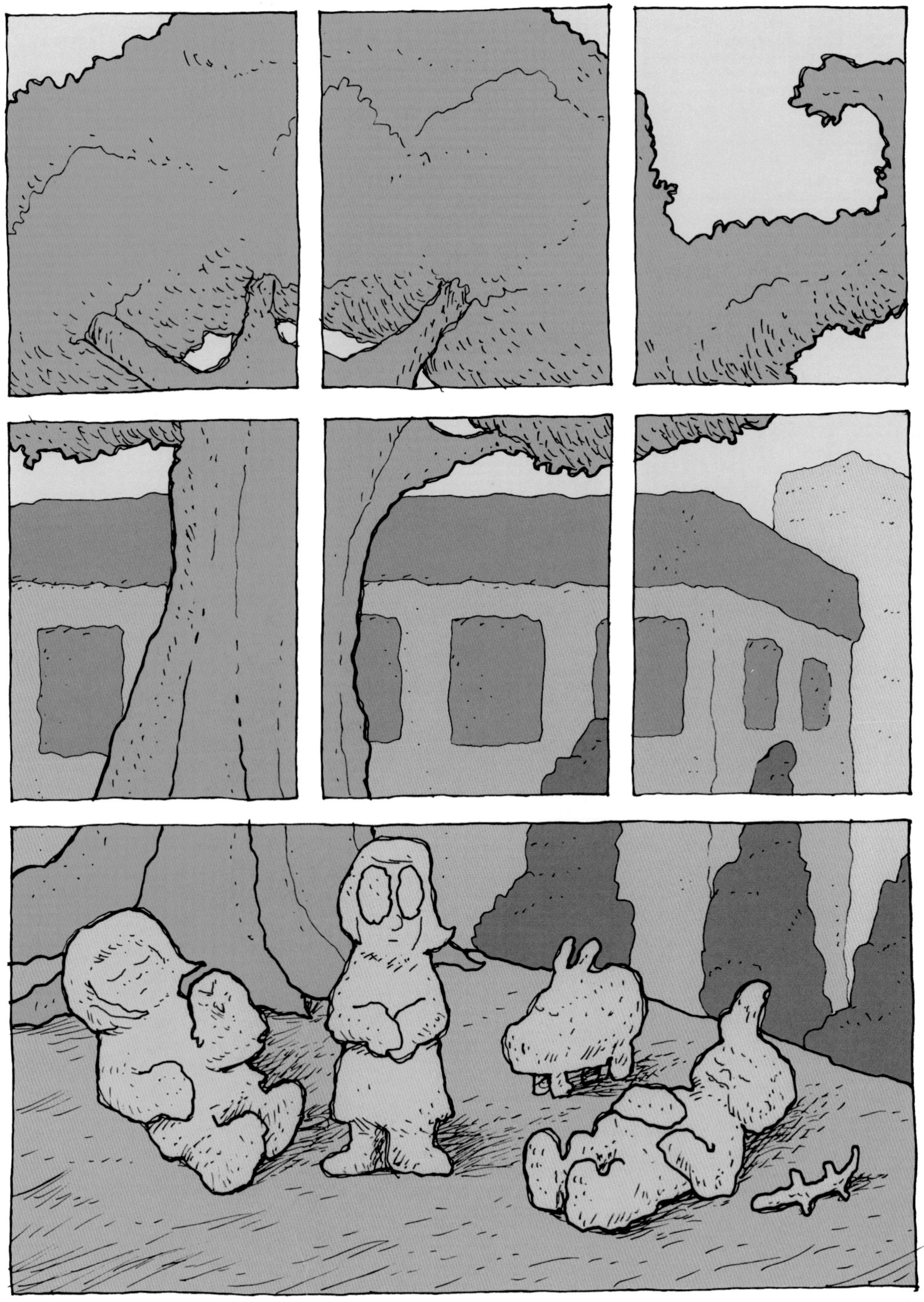

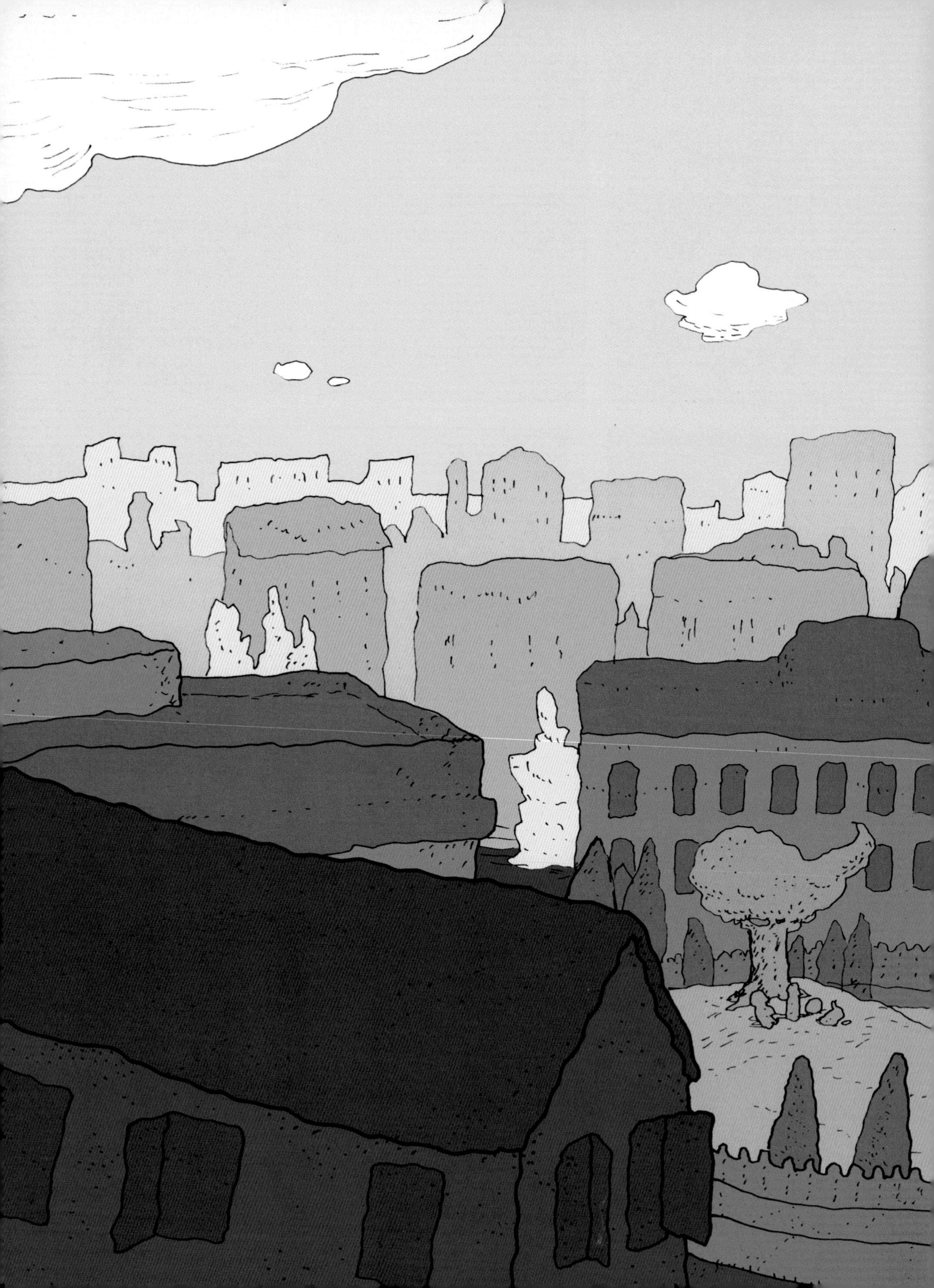

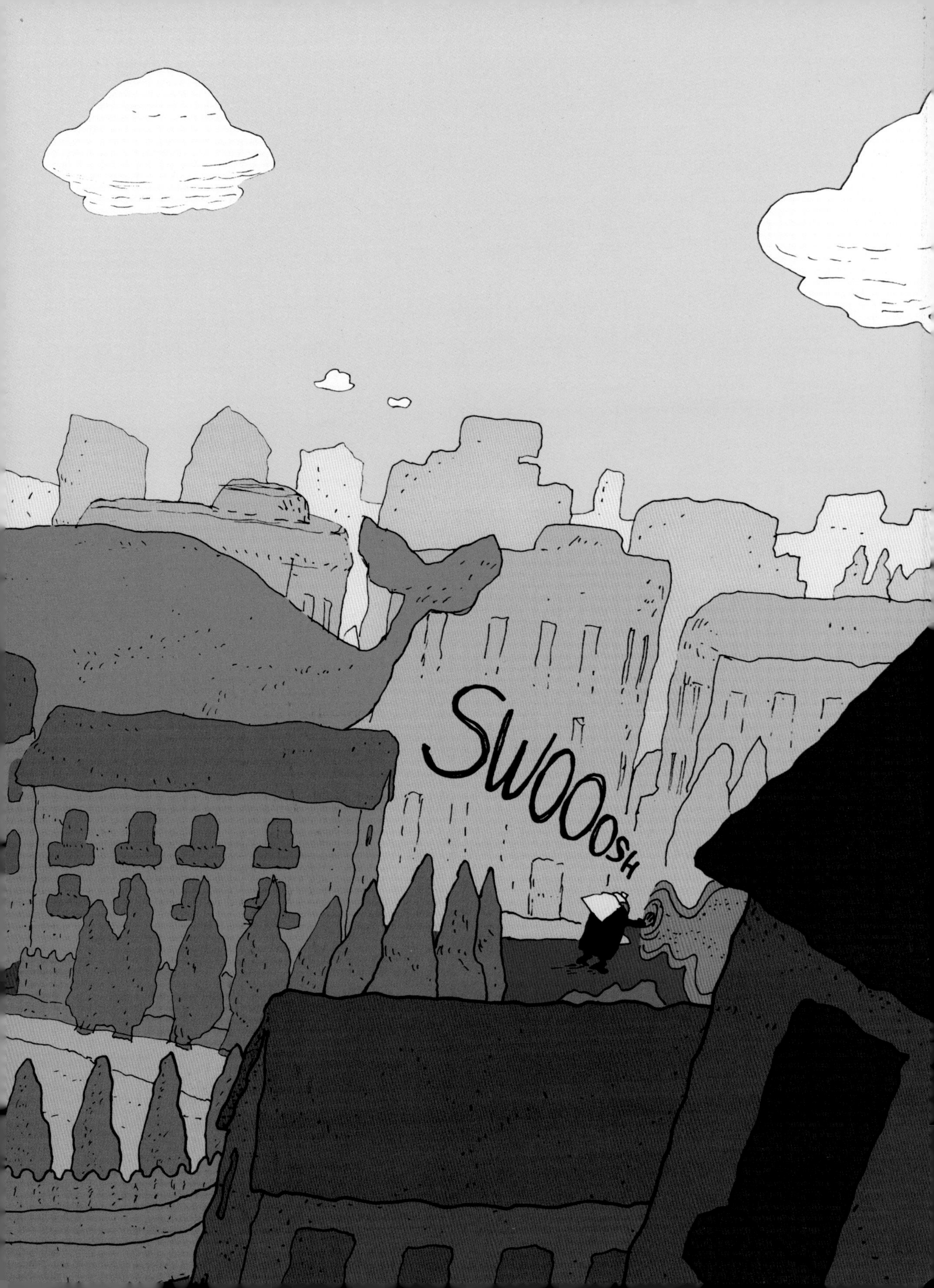
SWOOoosh

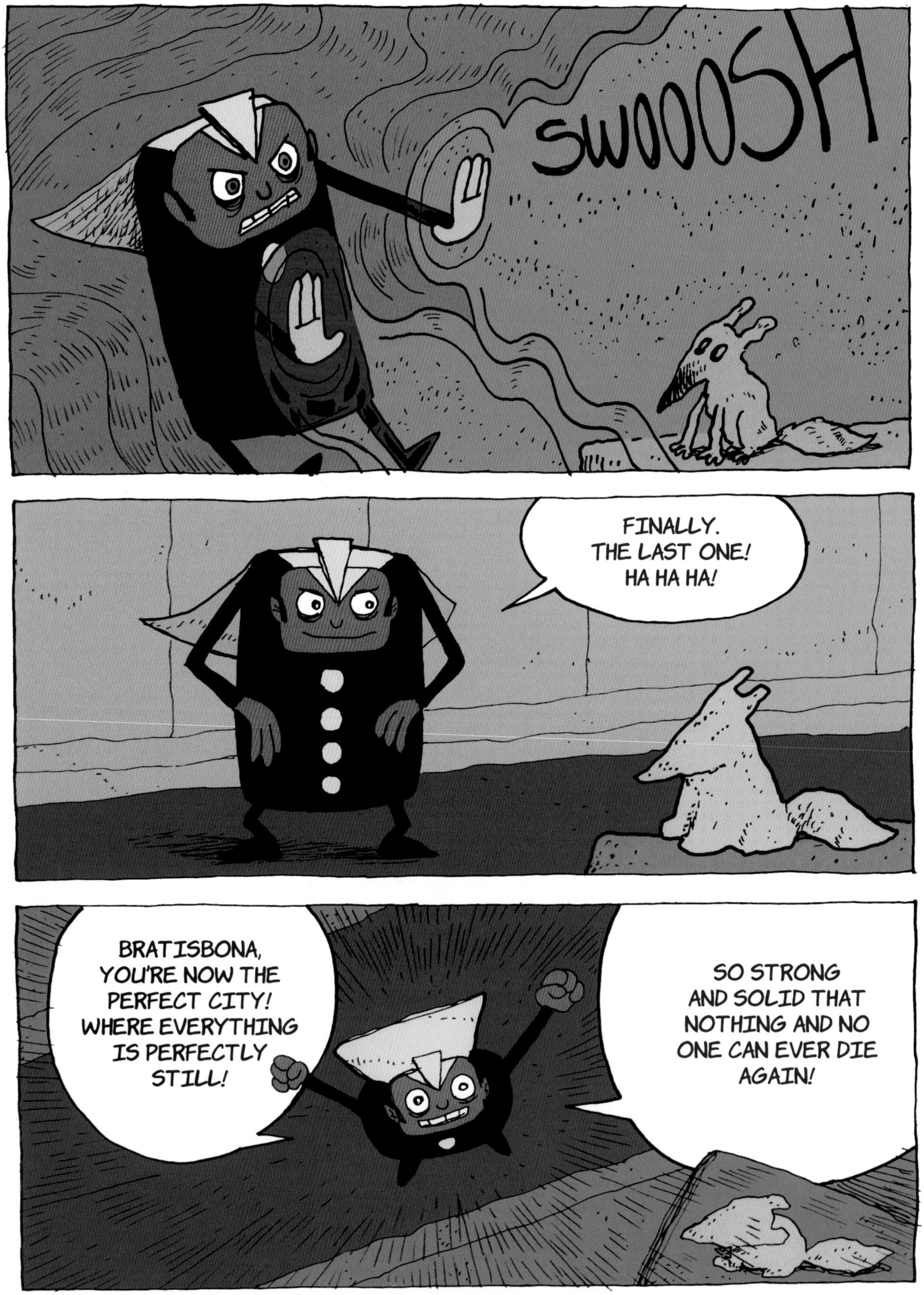
SWOOOSH
FINALLY. THE LAST ONE! HA HA HA!
BRATISBONA, YOU'RE NOW THE PERFECT CITY! WHERE EVERYTHING IS PERFECTLY STILL!
SO STRONG AND SOLID THAT NOTHING AND NO ONE CAN EVER DIE AGAIN!

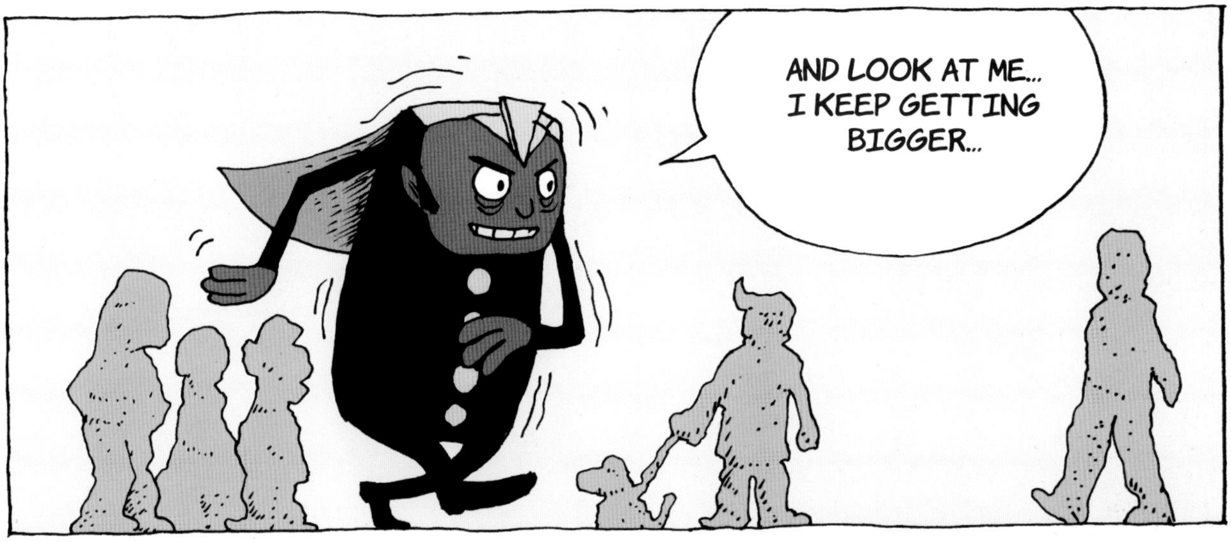
AND LOOK AT ME... I KEEP GETTING BIGGER...

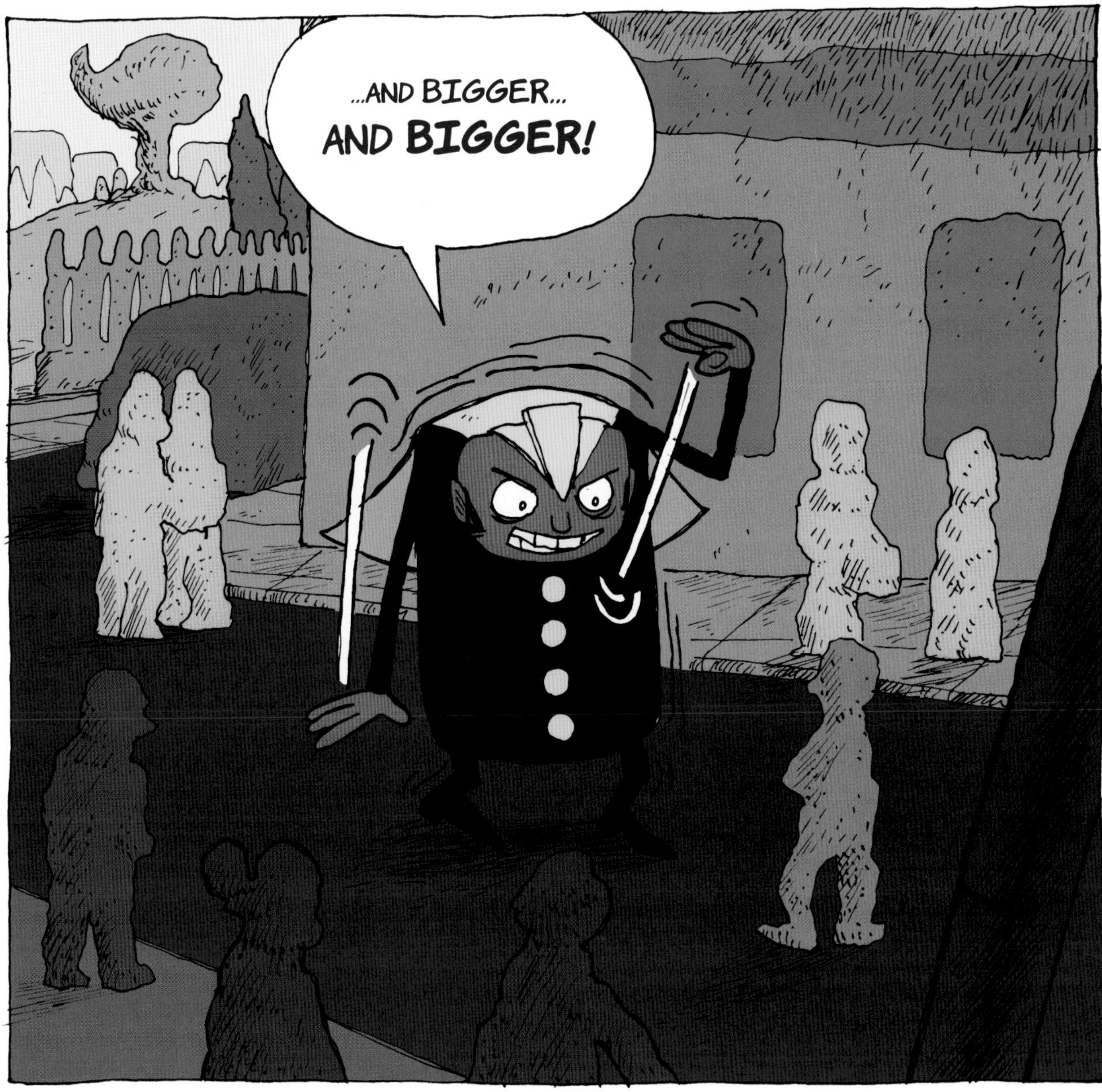
...AND BIGGER... AND BIGGER!

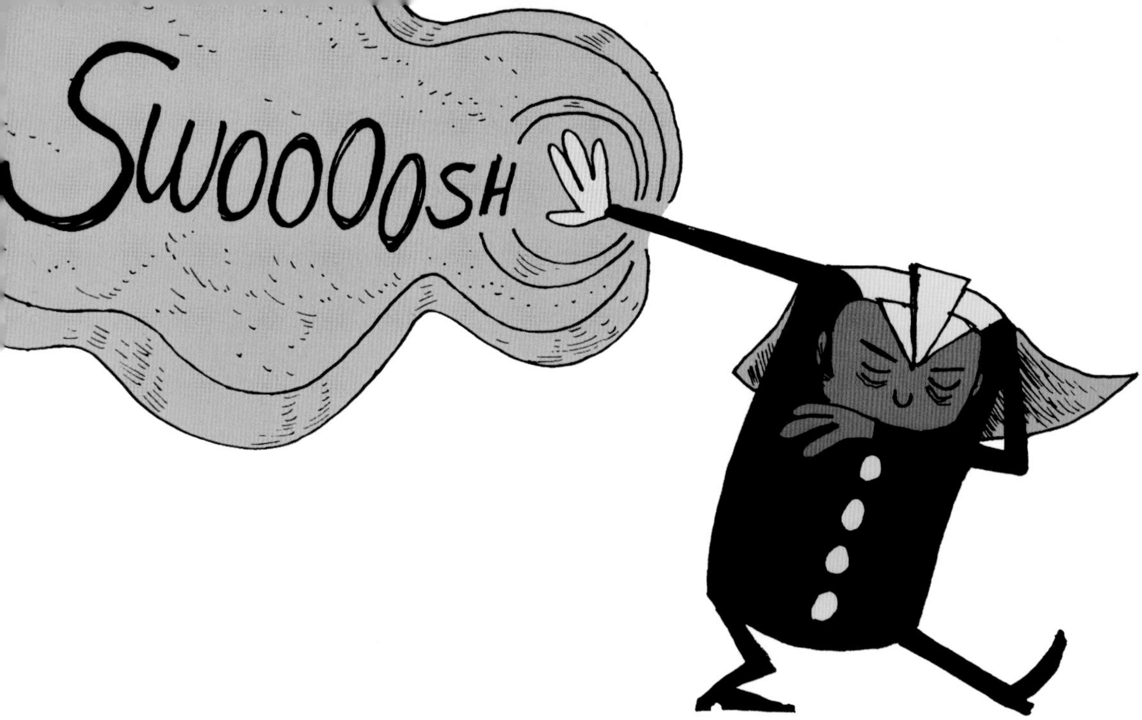
SWOOOOOSH

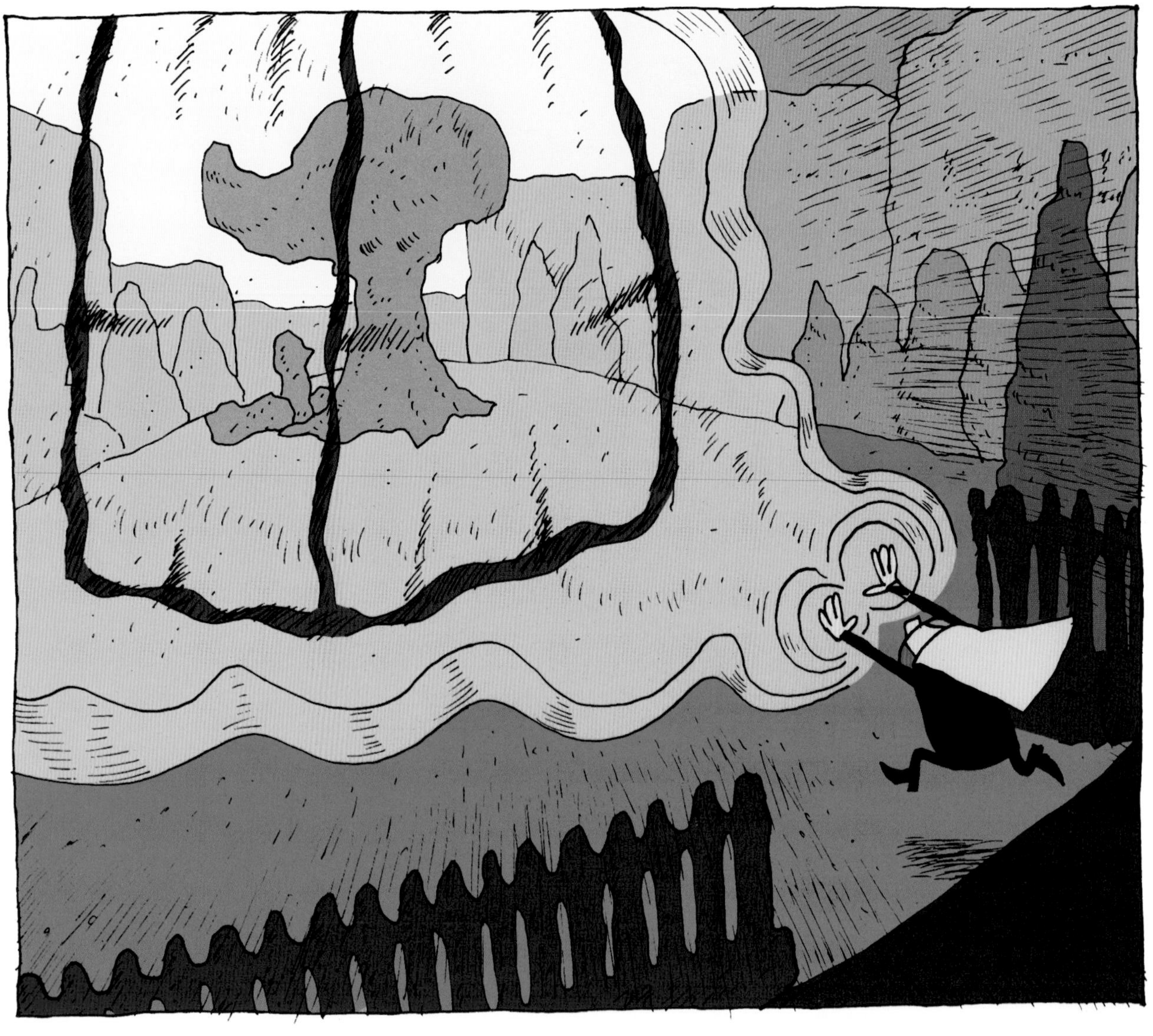

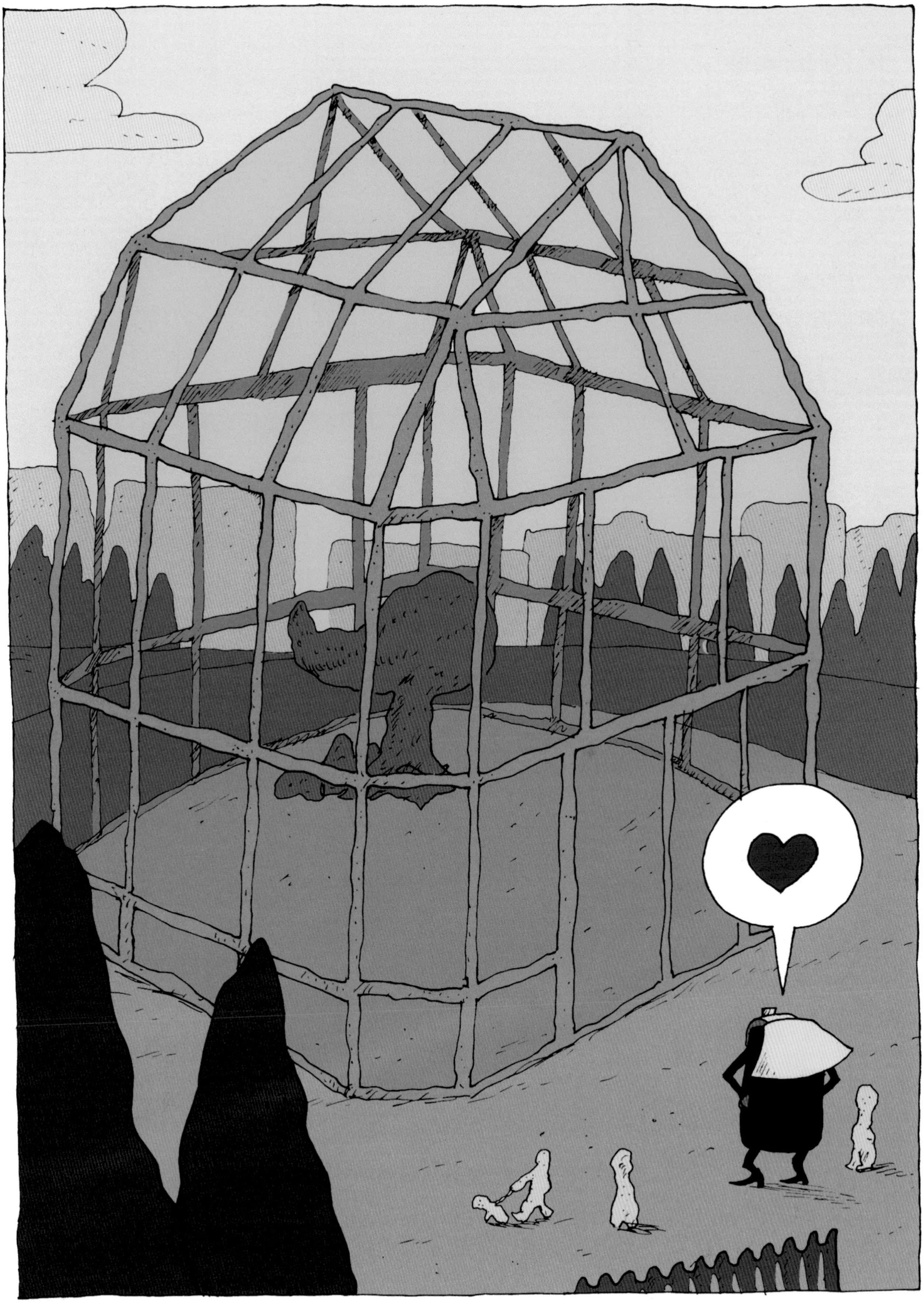

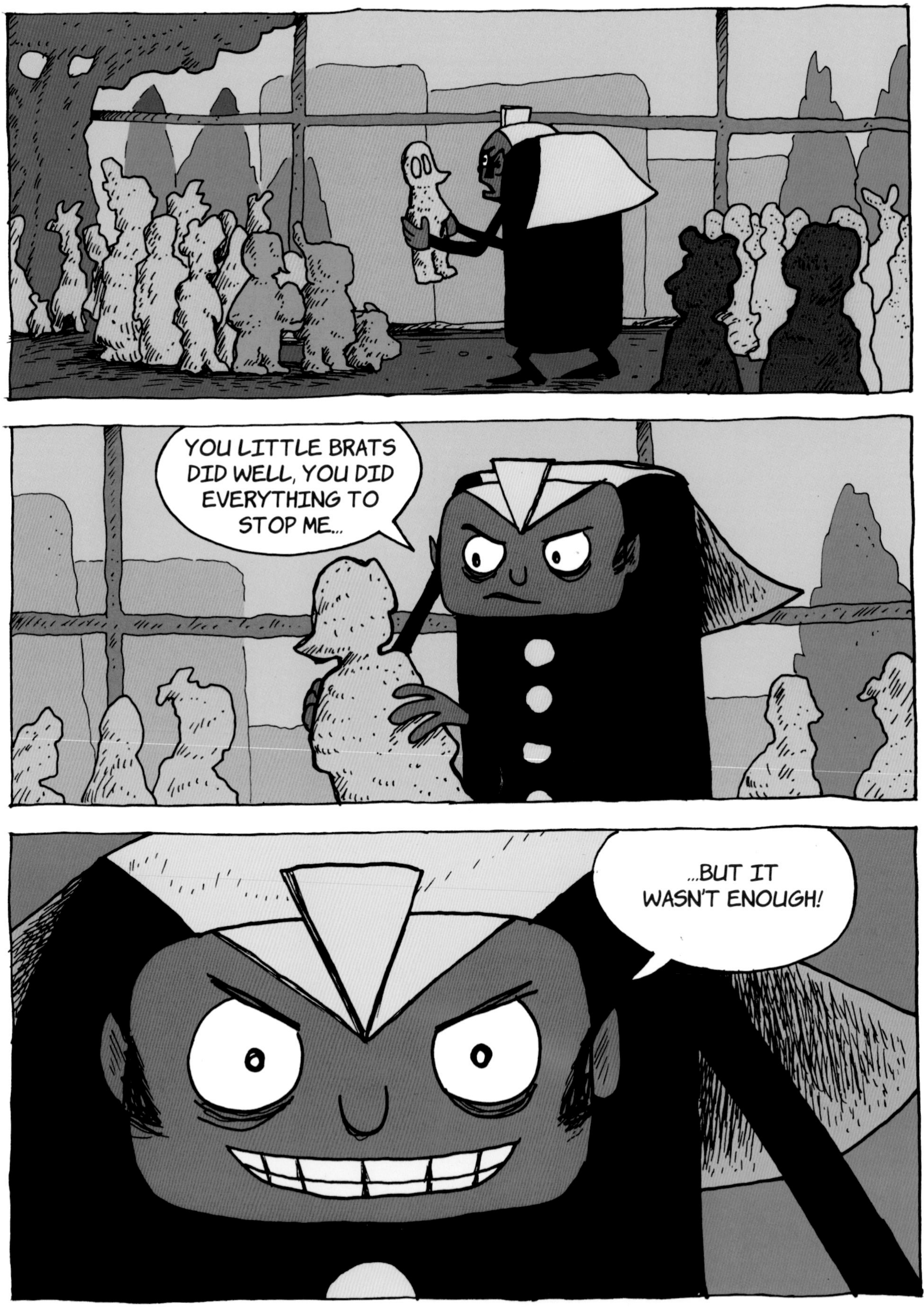
YOU LITTLE BRATS DID WELL, YOU DID EVERYTHING TO STOP ME...
...BUT IT WASN'T ENOUGH!

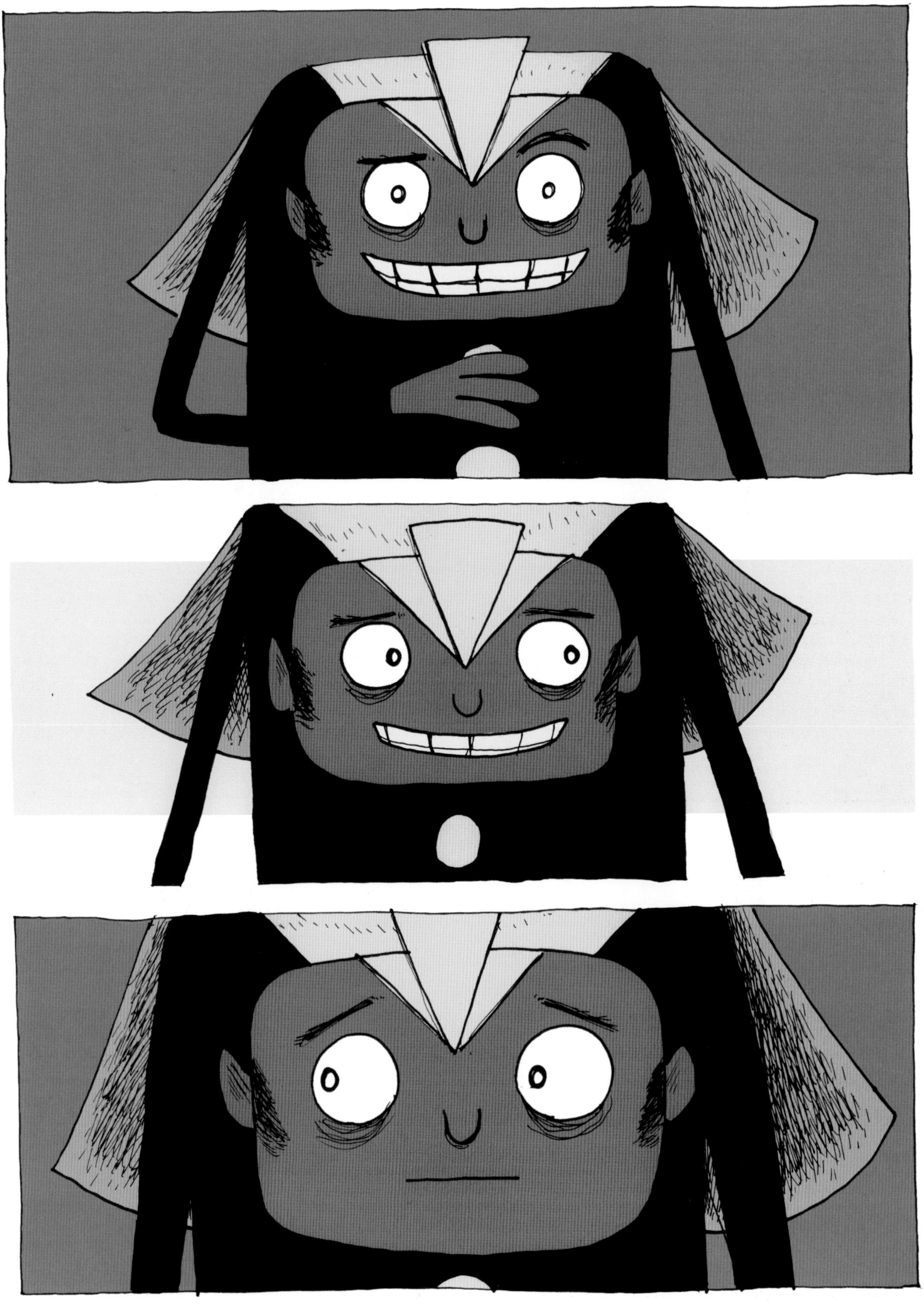

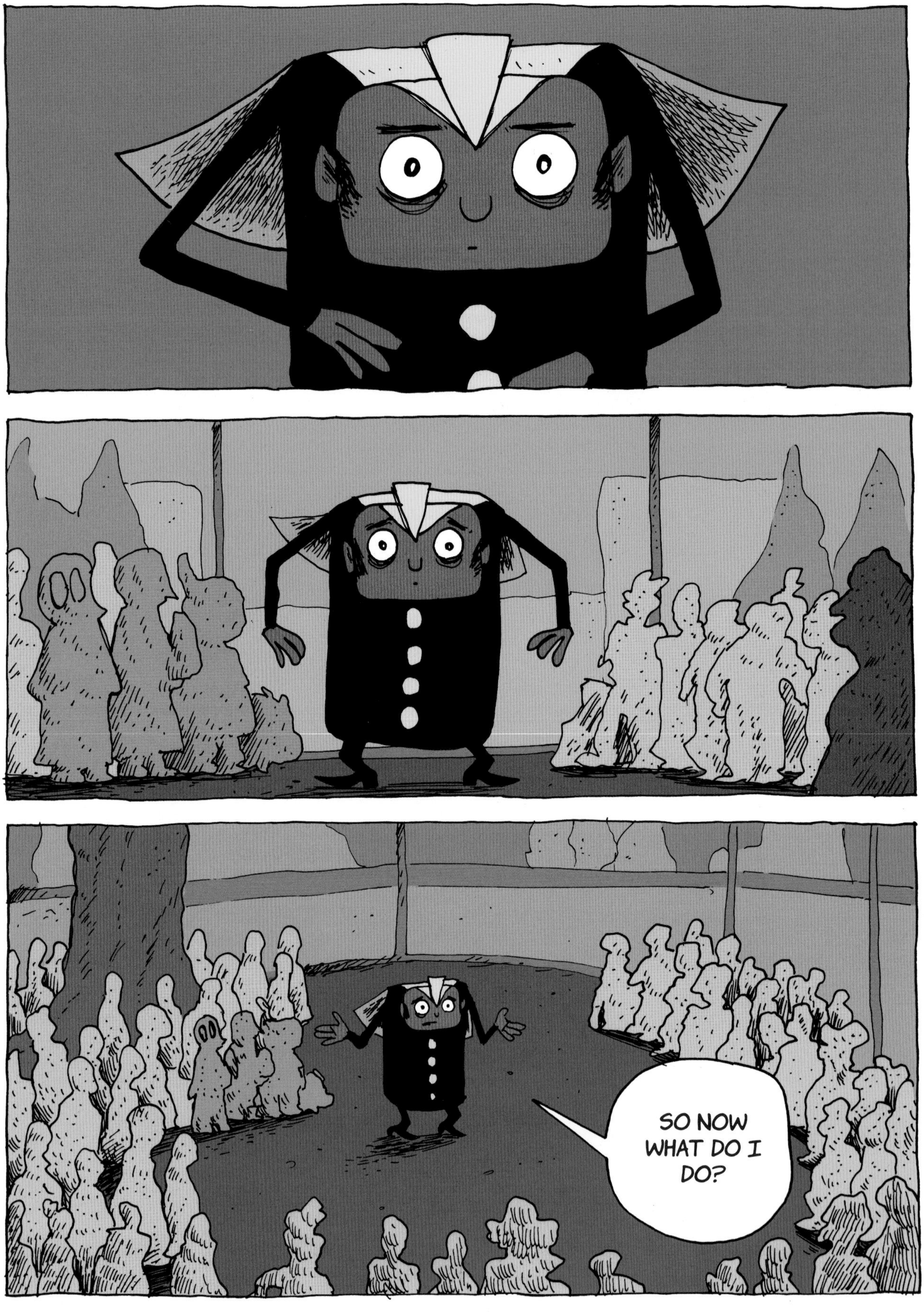
SO NOW WHAT DO I DO?

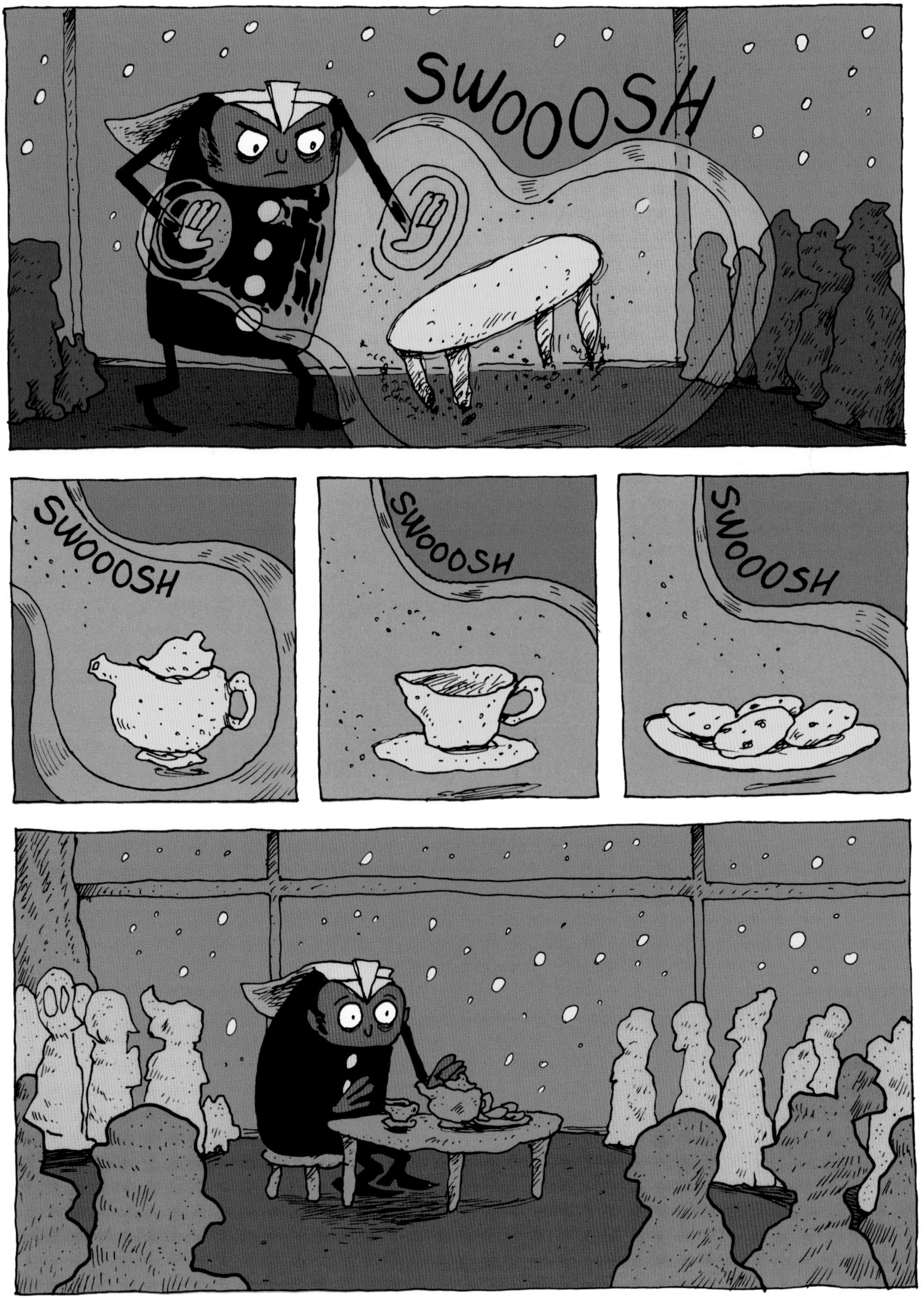
SWOOOSH
SWOOOSH
SWOOOSH
SWOOOSH

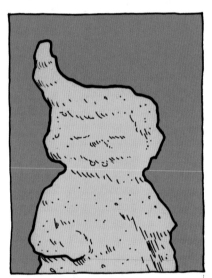

YOU'RE SO SMALL.

I TURNED YOU INTO CONCRETE AND BECAME KING OF BRATISBONA! IT WAS A JOKE!

AND NOW I'LL MAKE THE REST OF THE PLANET IMMORTAL...

...AND EVERYTHING WILL BE MINE!

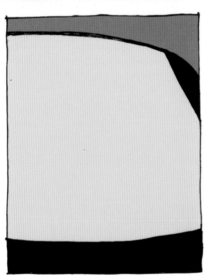

NOTHING TO SAY?

HMM, WHO KNOWS IF YOU CAN HEAR ANYTHING INSIDE THOSE SHELLS...

AND TO THINK... ALL OF THIS COULD HAVE BEEN AVOIDED.

I MEAN, ALL I WANTED WAS THE GREEN THUMB...

...LIKE THAT LITTLE FOOL OF YOURS...

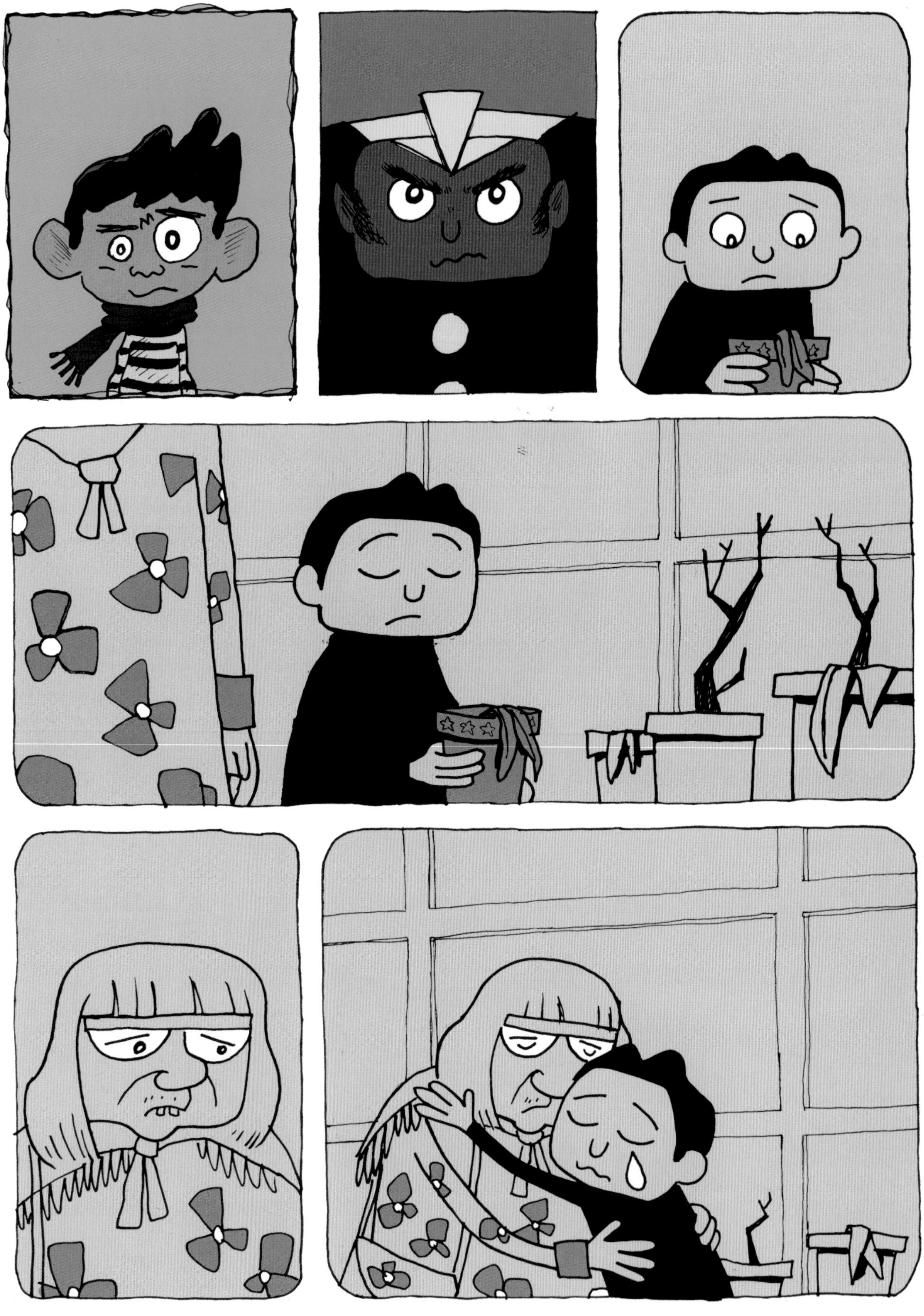

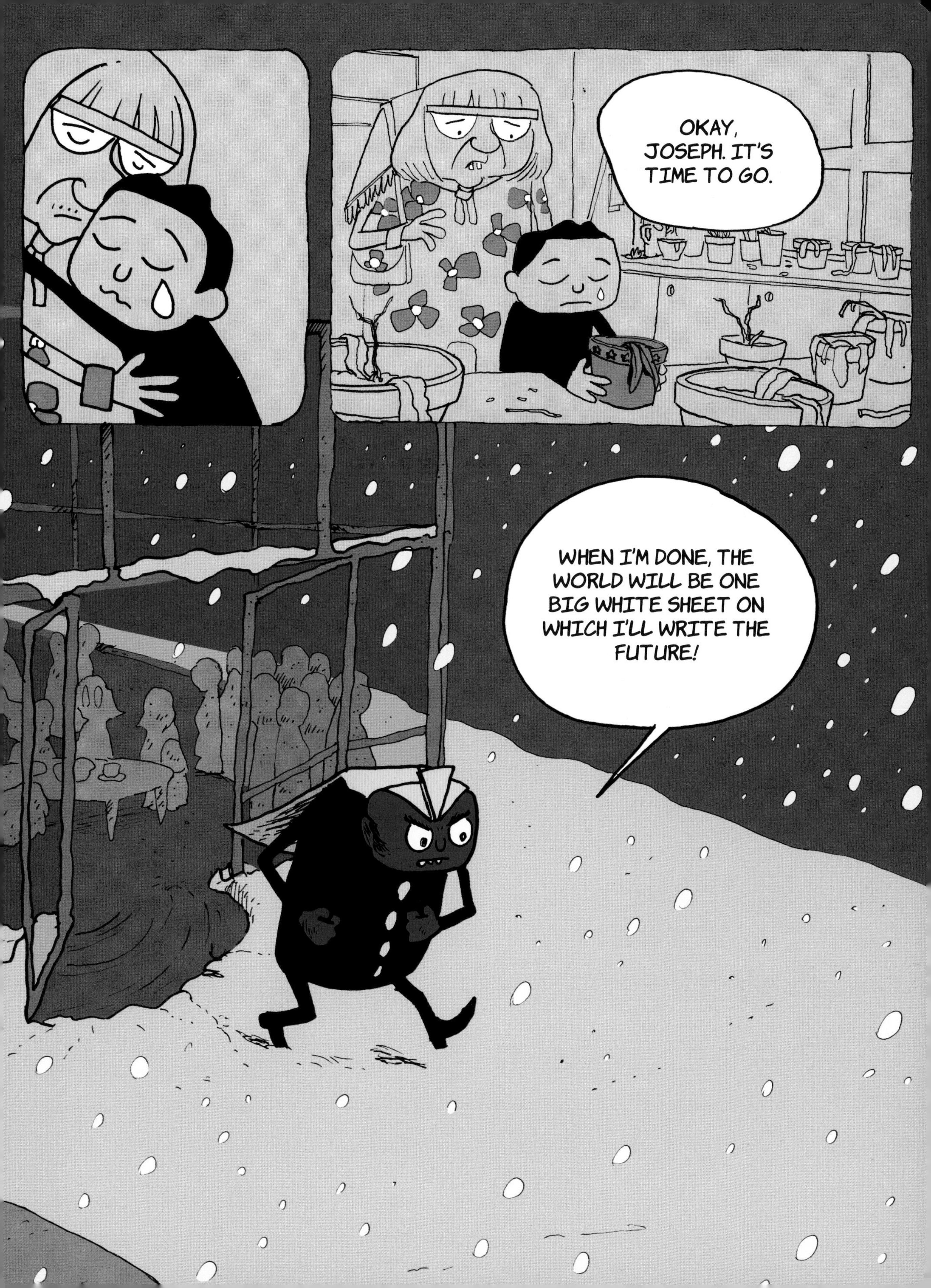
OKAY, JOSEPH. IT'S TIME TO GO.
WHEN I'M DONE, THE WORLD WILL BE ONE BIG WHITE SHEET ON WHICH I'LL WRITE THE FUTURE!

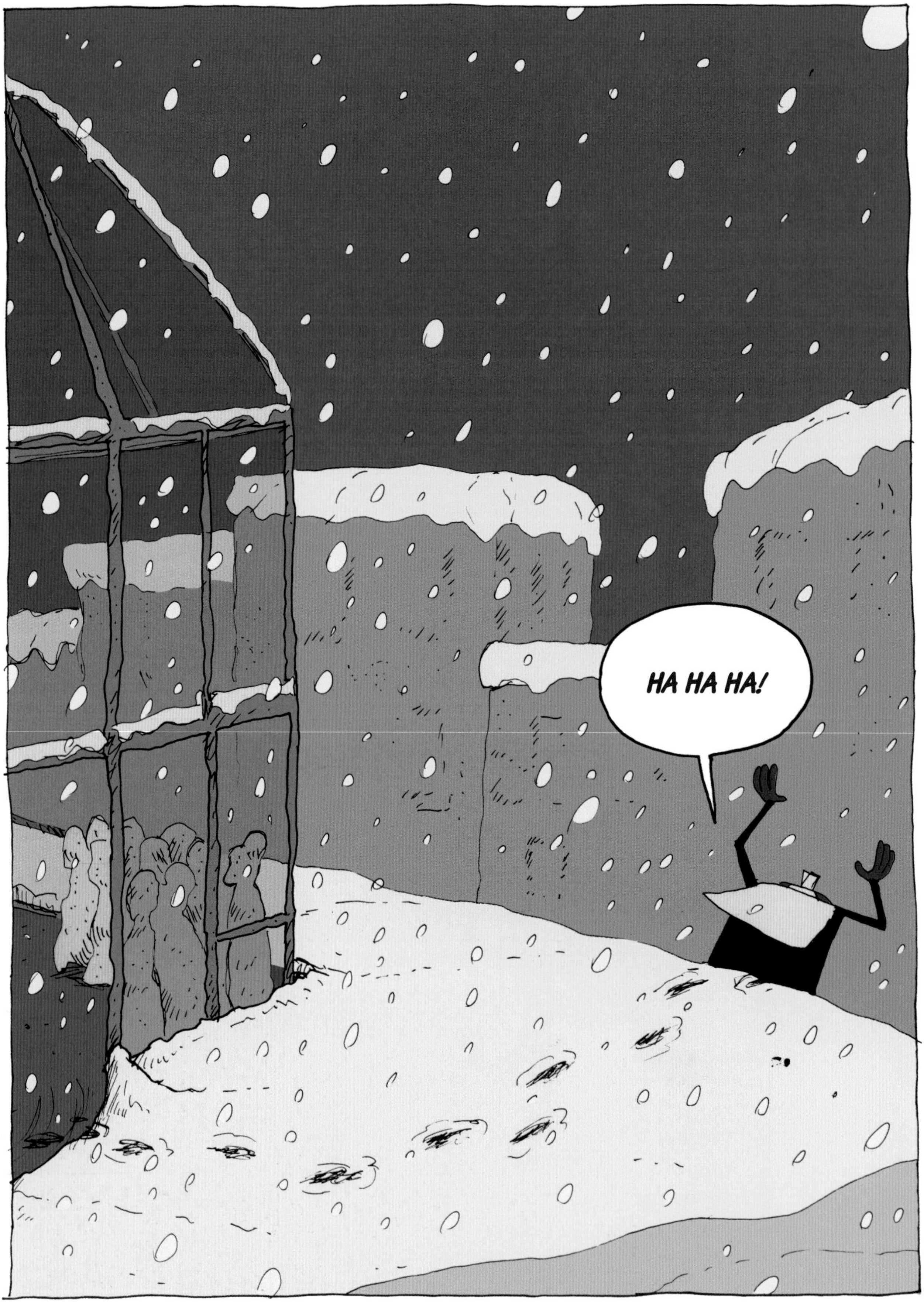
HA HA HA!

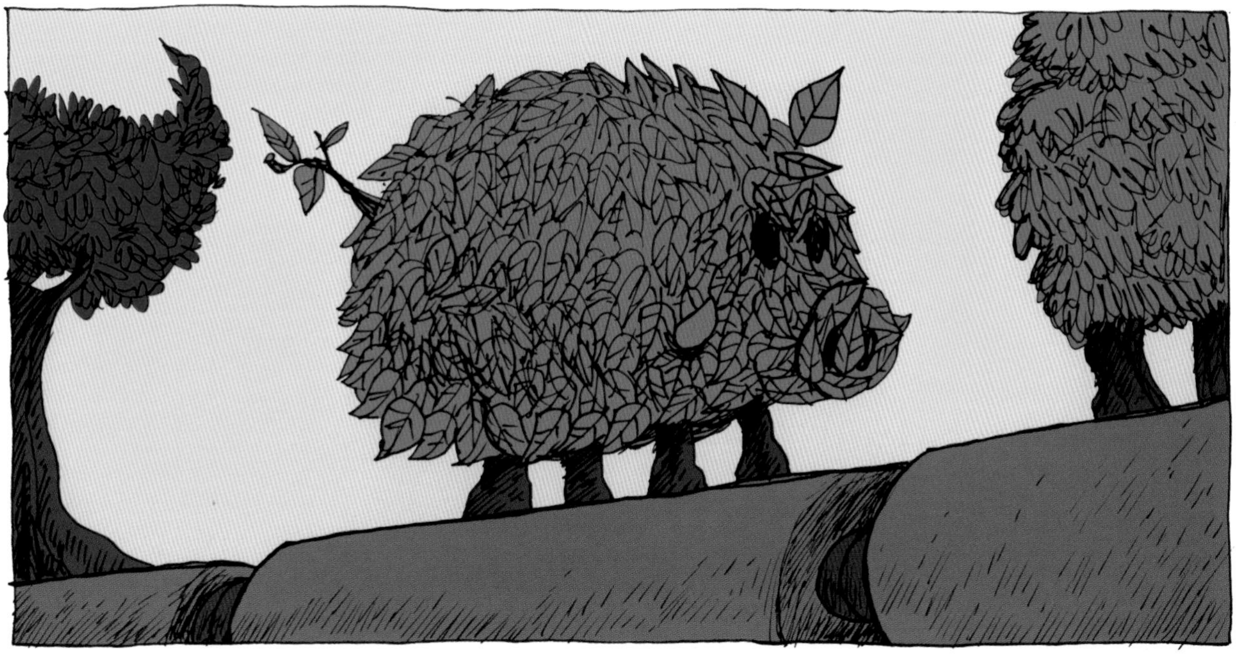

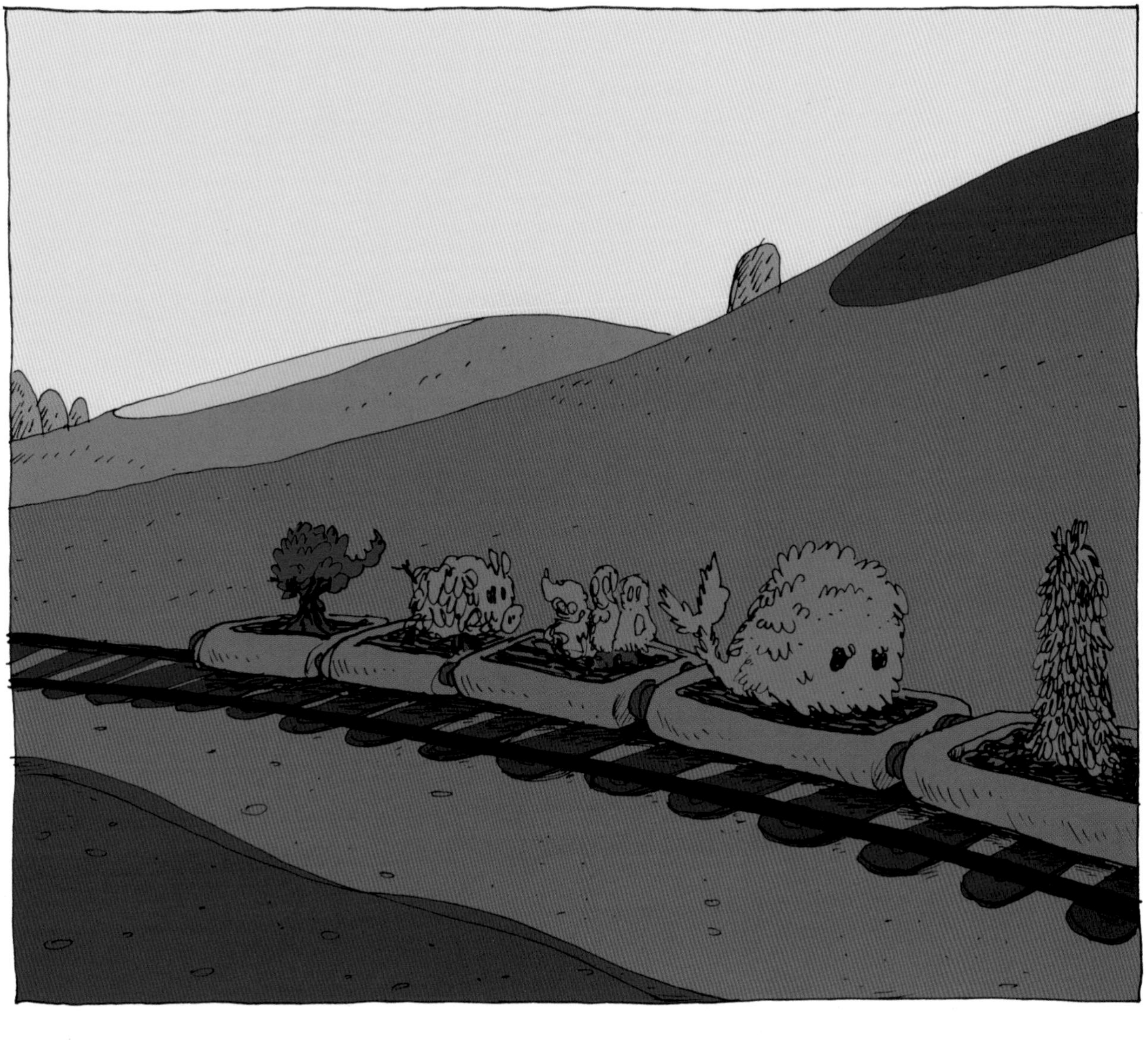

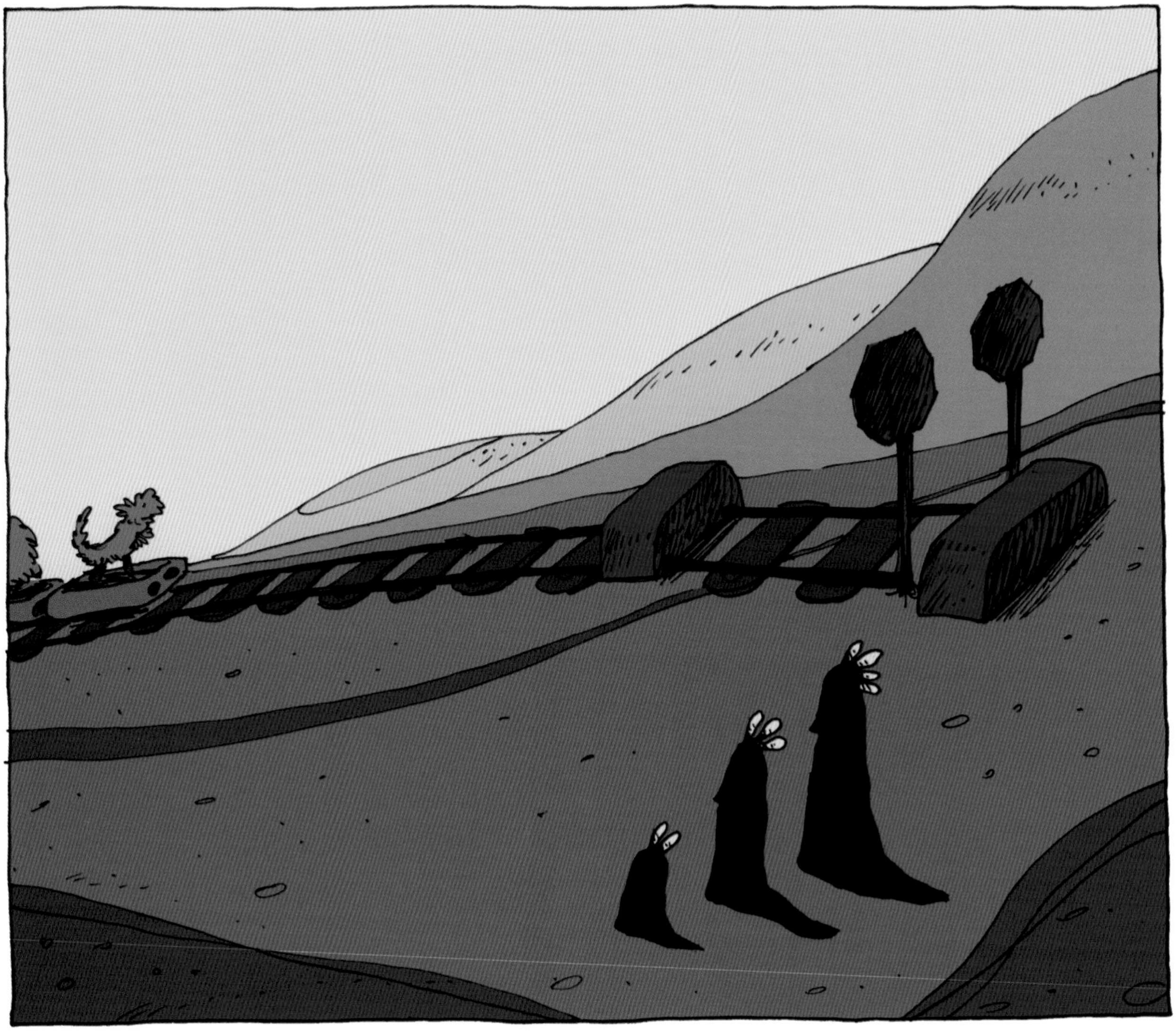

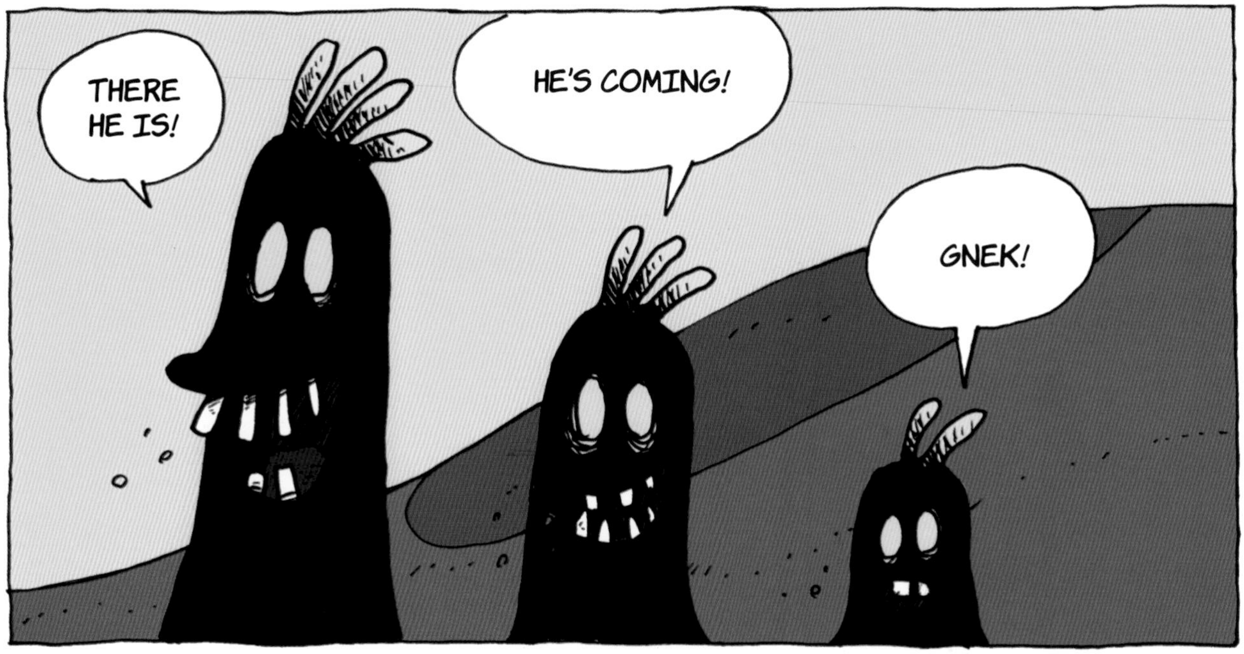
THERE HE IS!
HE'S COMING!
GNEK!

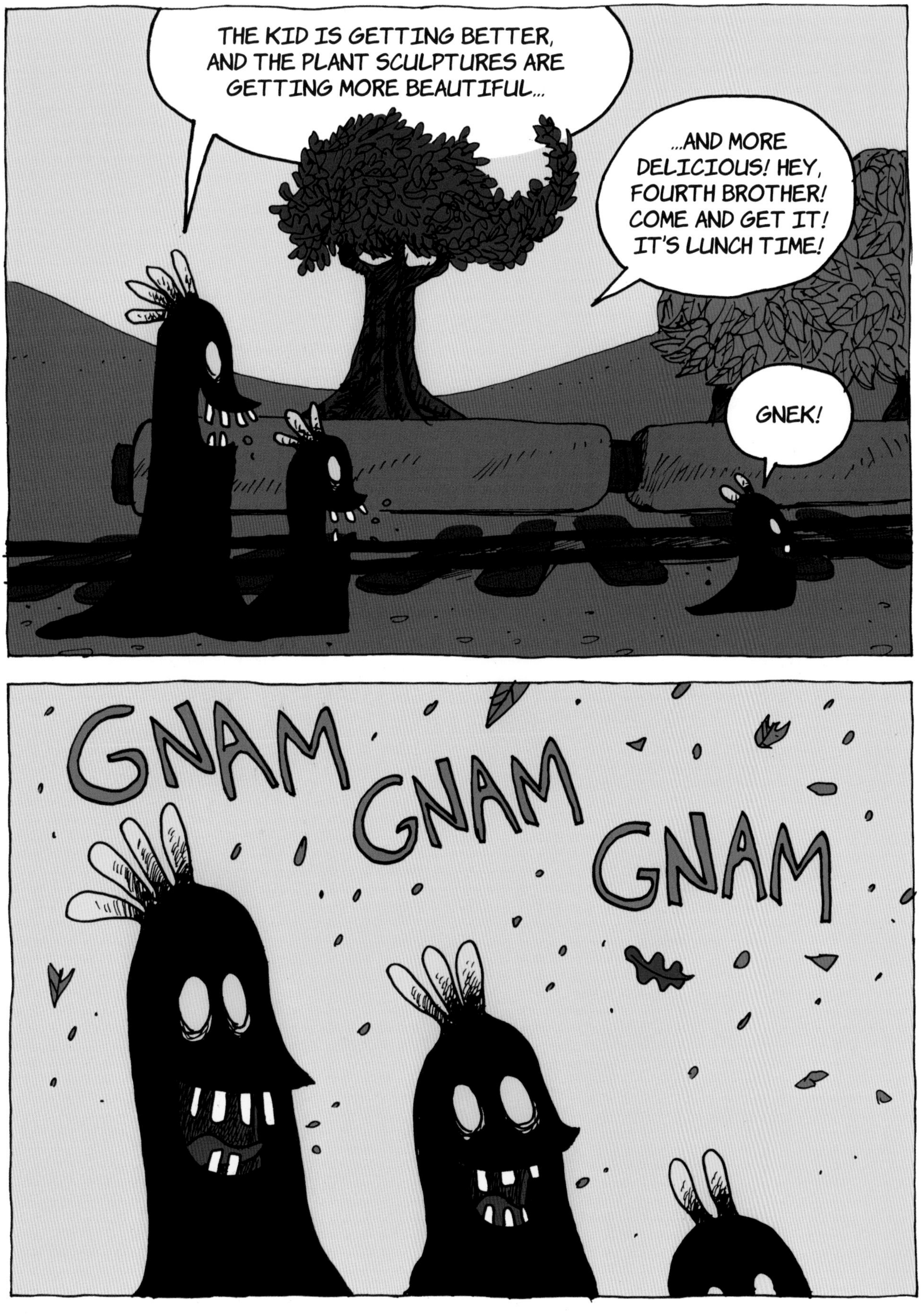
THE KID IS GETTING BETTER, AND THE PLANT SCULPTURES ARE GETTING MORE BEAUTIFUL...
...AND MORE DELICIOUS! HEY, FOURTH BROTHER! COME AND GET IT! IT'S LUNCH TIME!
GNEK!
GNAM GNAM GNAM

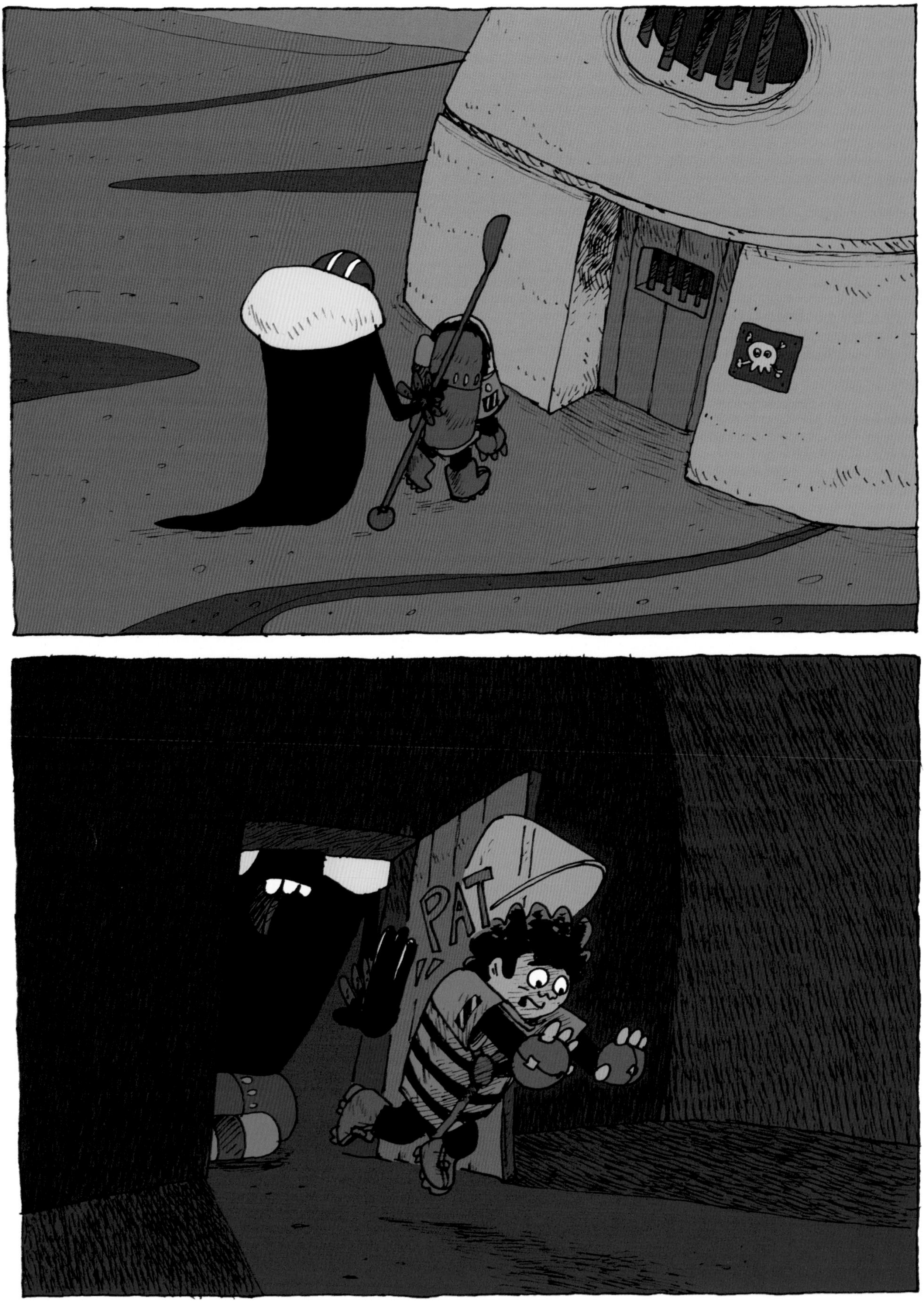
PAT

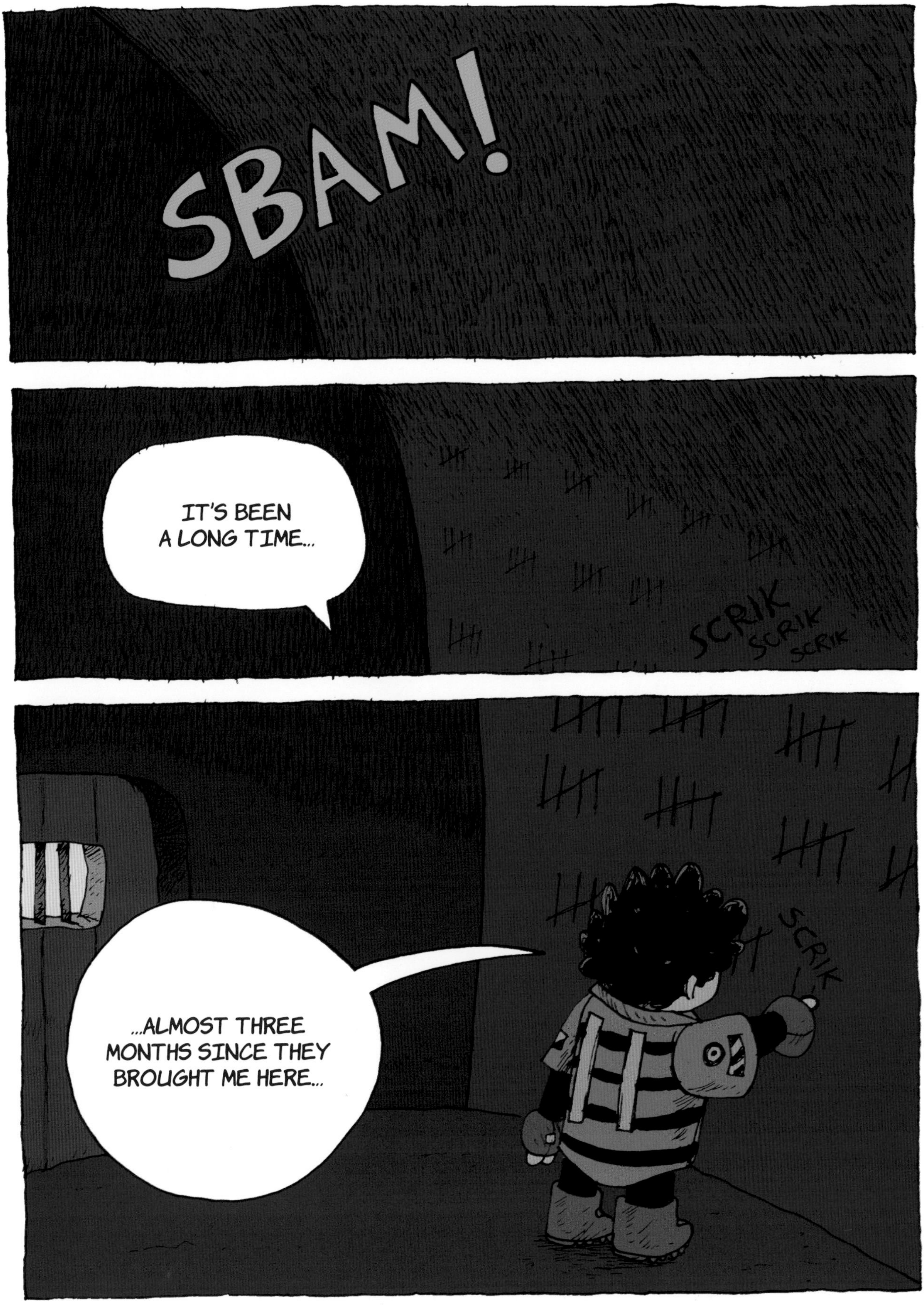
SBAM!
IT'S BEEN A LONG TIME...
SCRIK SCRIK SCRIK
...ALMOST THREE MONTHS SINCE THEY BROUGHT ME HERE...
SCRIK

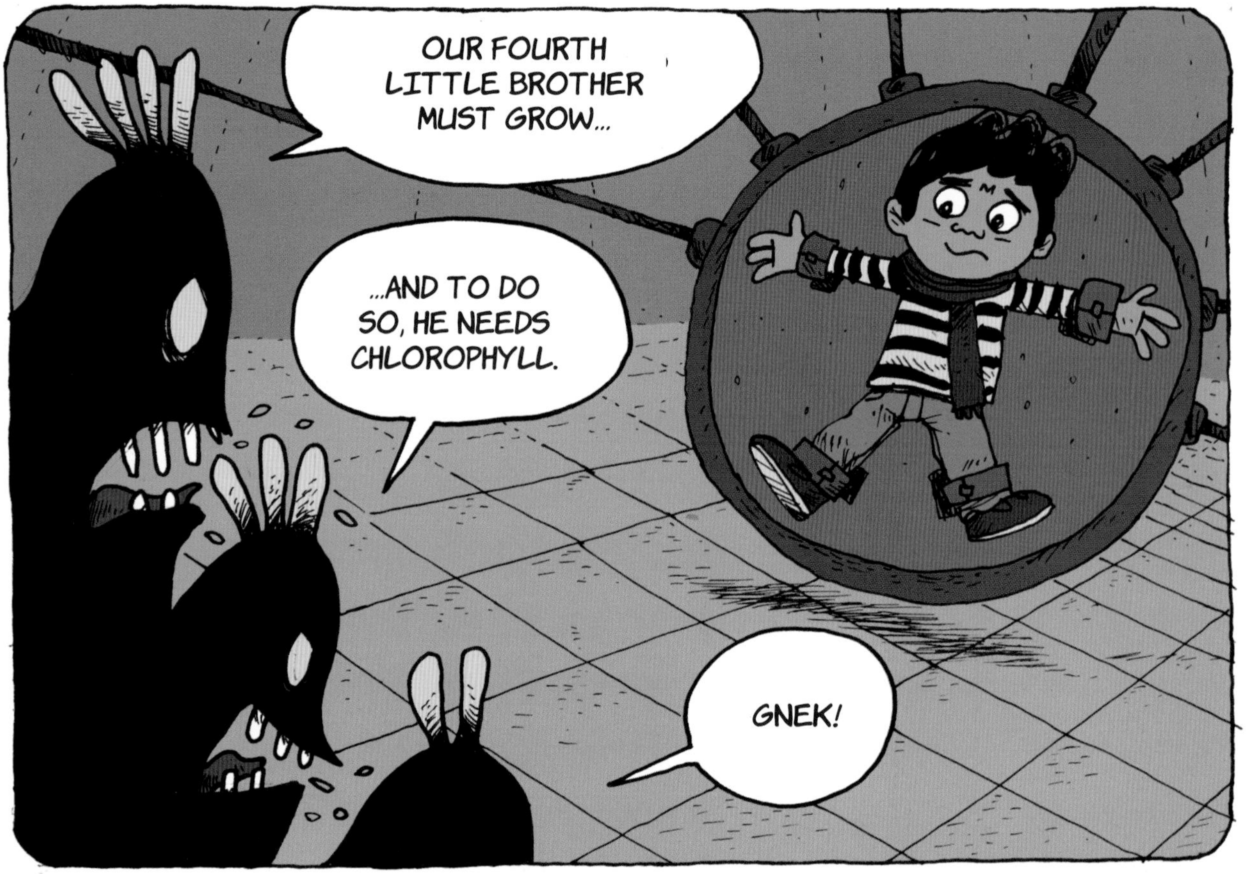
OUR FOURTH LITTLE BROTHER MUST GROW...
...AND TO DO SO, HE NEEDS CHLOROPHYLL.
GNEK!

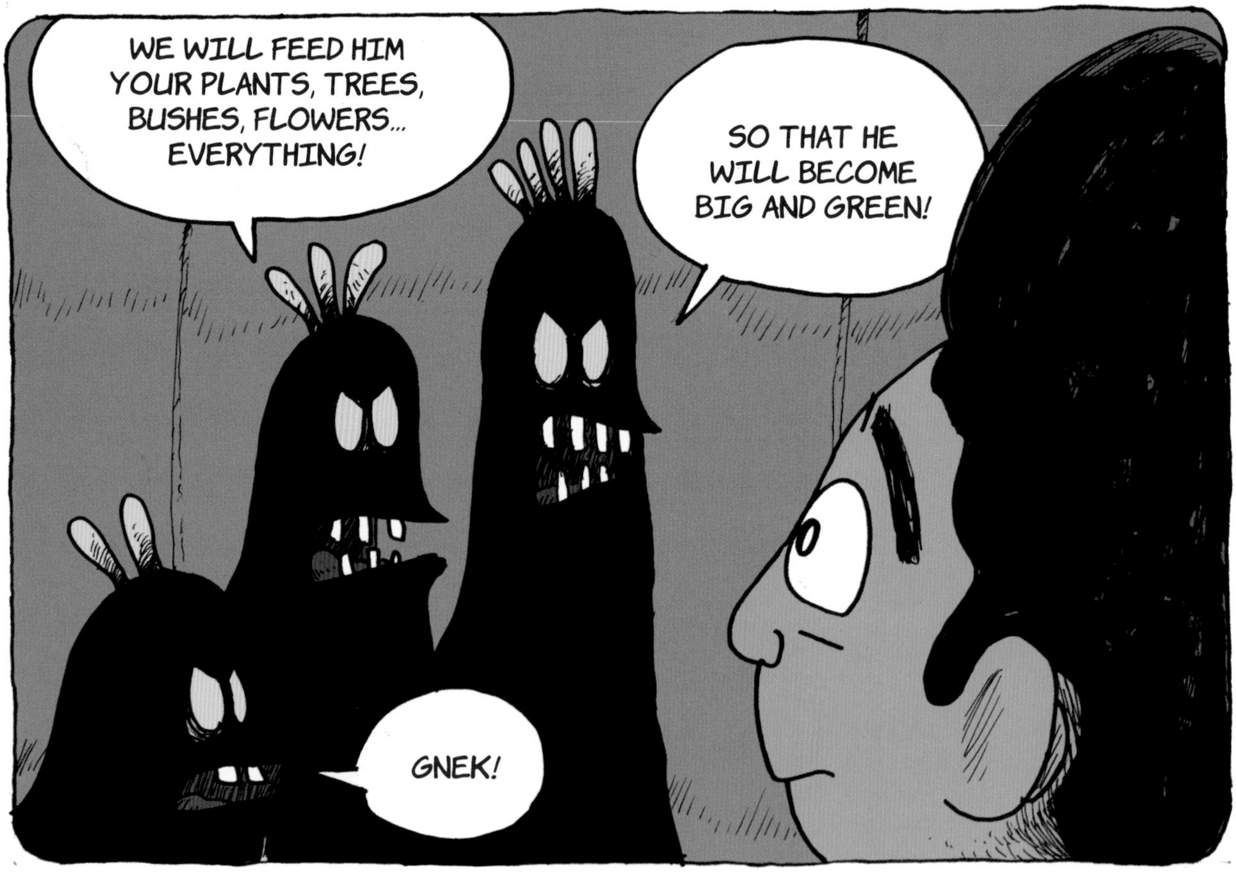
WE WILL FEED HIM YOUR PLANTS, TREES, BUSHES, FLOWERS... EVERYTHING!
SO THAT HE WILL BECOME BIG AND GREEN!
GNEK!

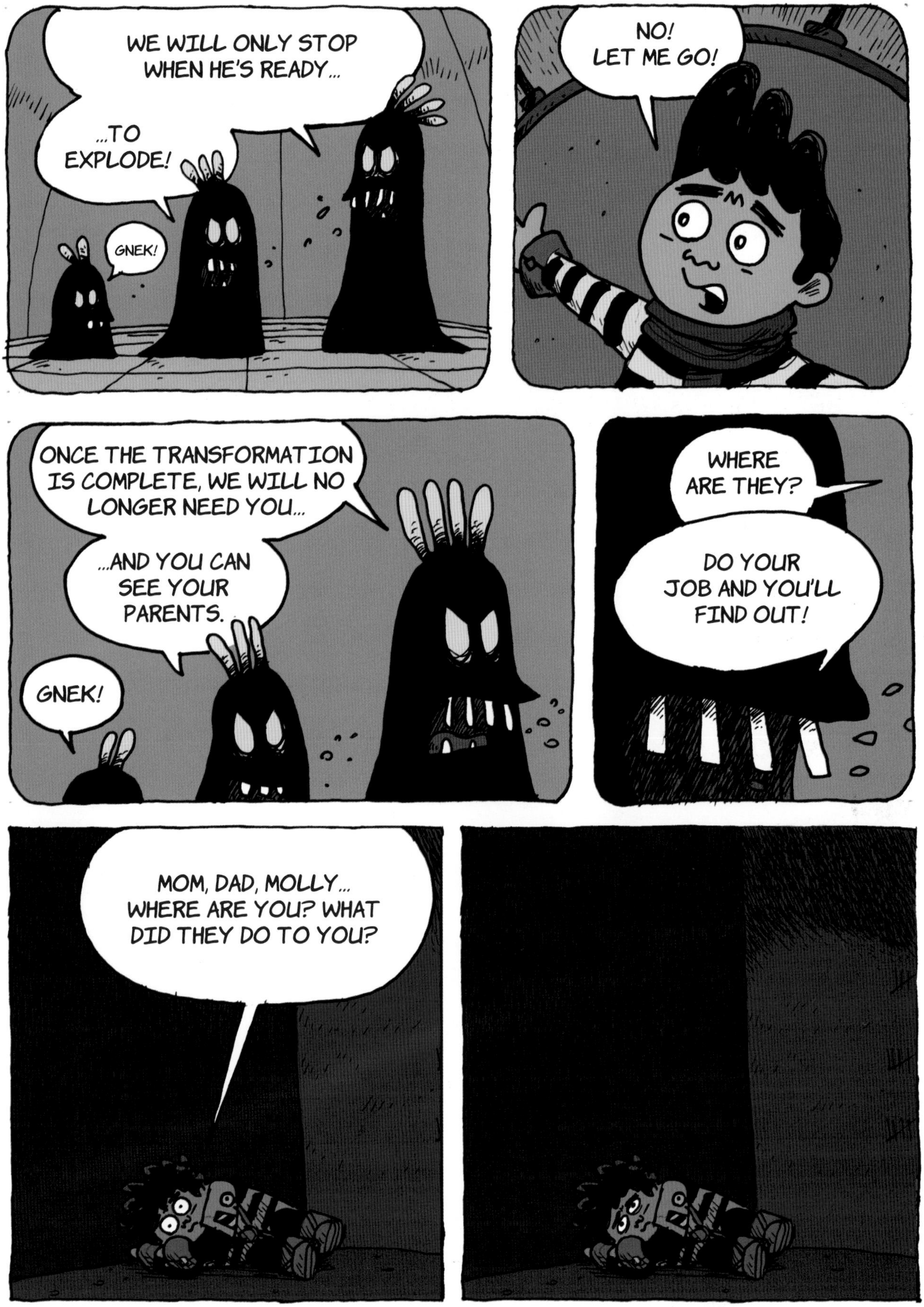
WE WILL ONLY STOP WHEN HE'S READY...
...TO EXPLODE!
GNEK!
NO! LET ME GO!
ONCE THE TRANSFORMATION IS COMPLETE, WE WILL NO LONGER NEED YOU...
...AND YOU CAN SEE YOUR PARENTS.
GNEK!
WHERE ARE THEY?
DO YOUR JOB AND YOU'LL FIND OUT!
MOM, DAD, MOLLY... WHERE ARE YOU? WHAT DID THEY DO TO YOU?

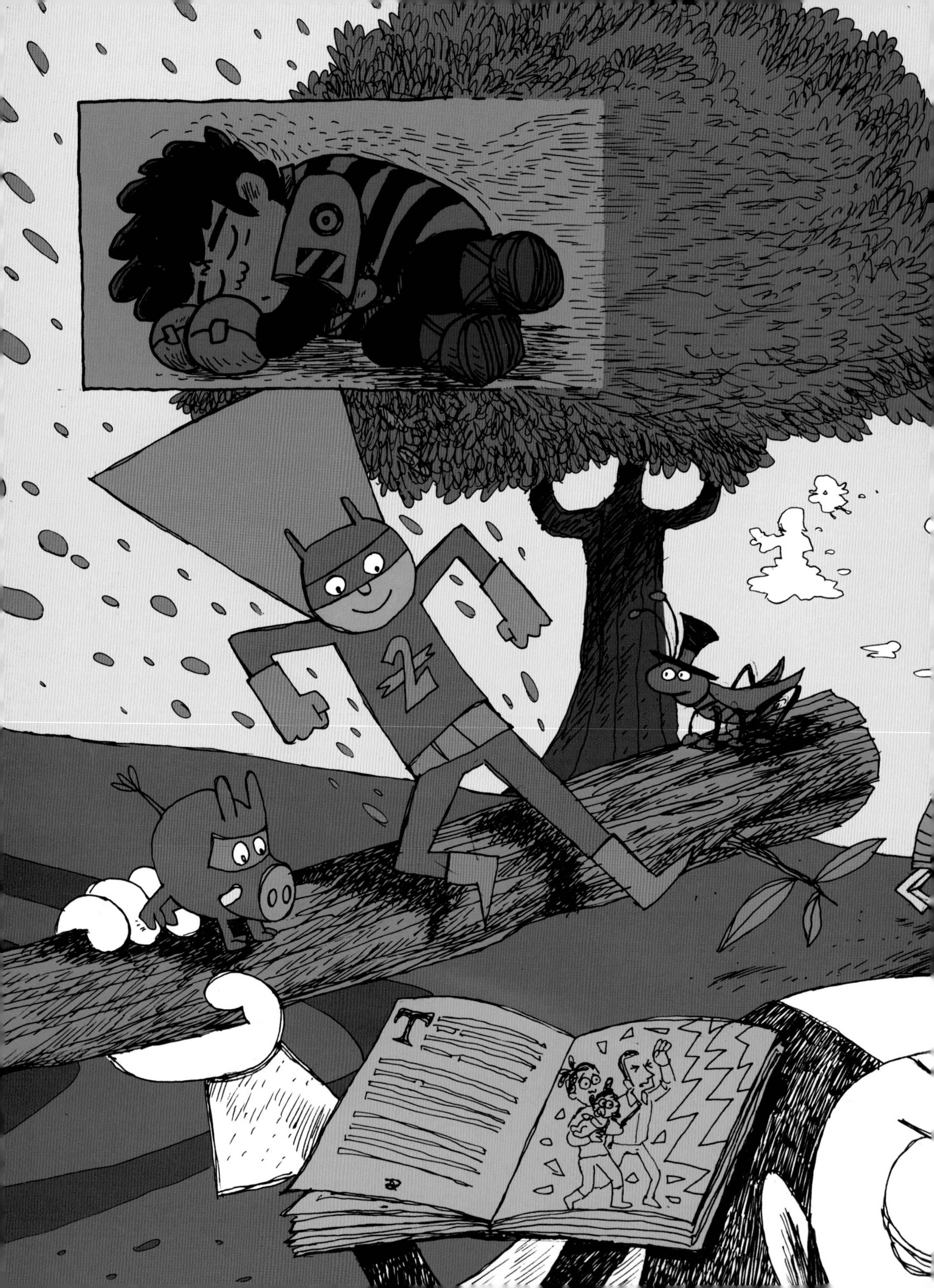

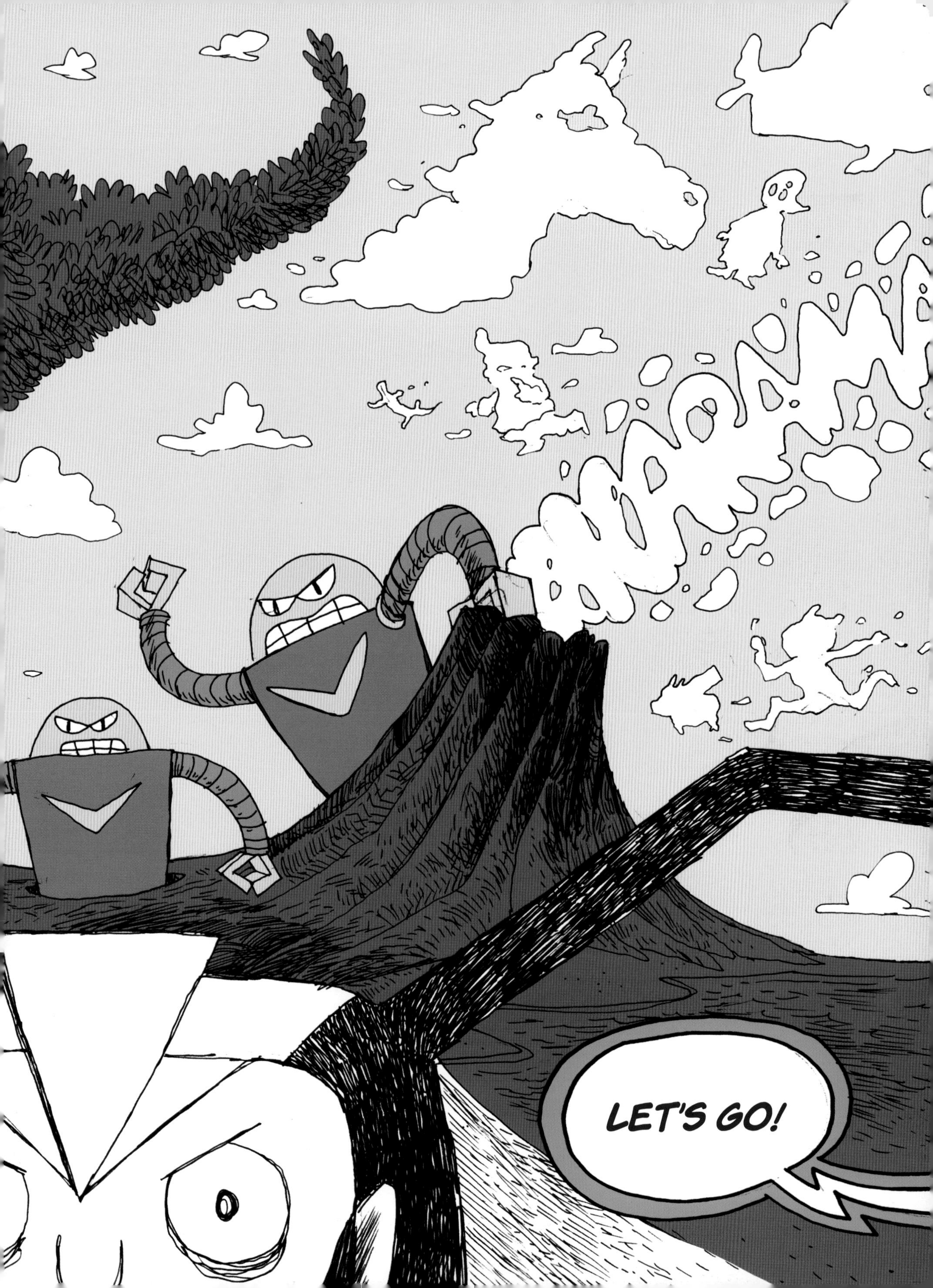
LET'S GO!

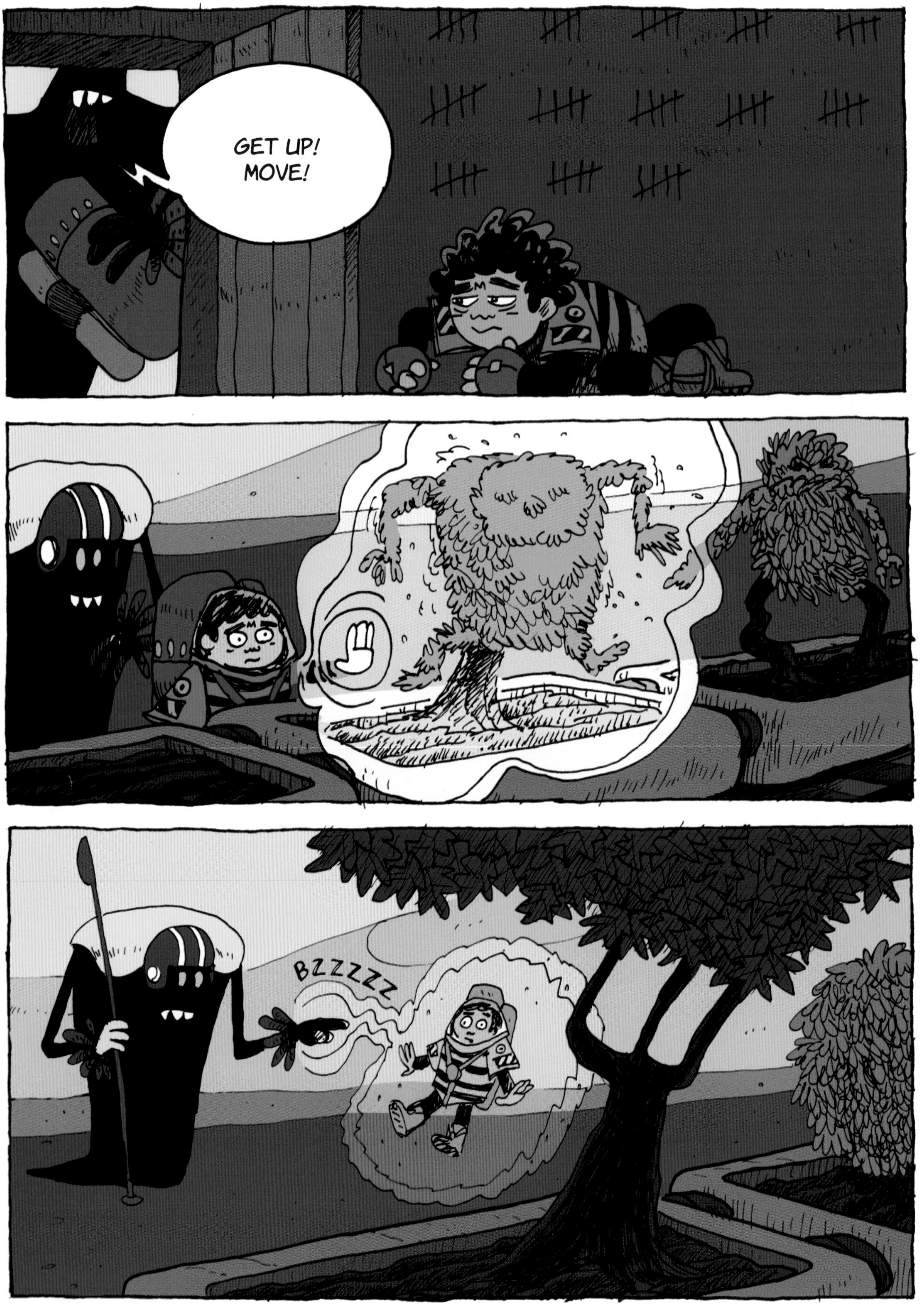
GET UP!
MOVE!
BZZZZZ

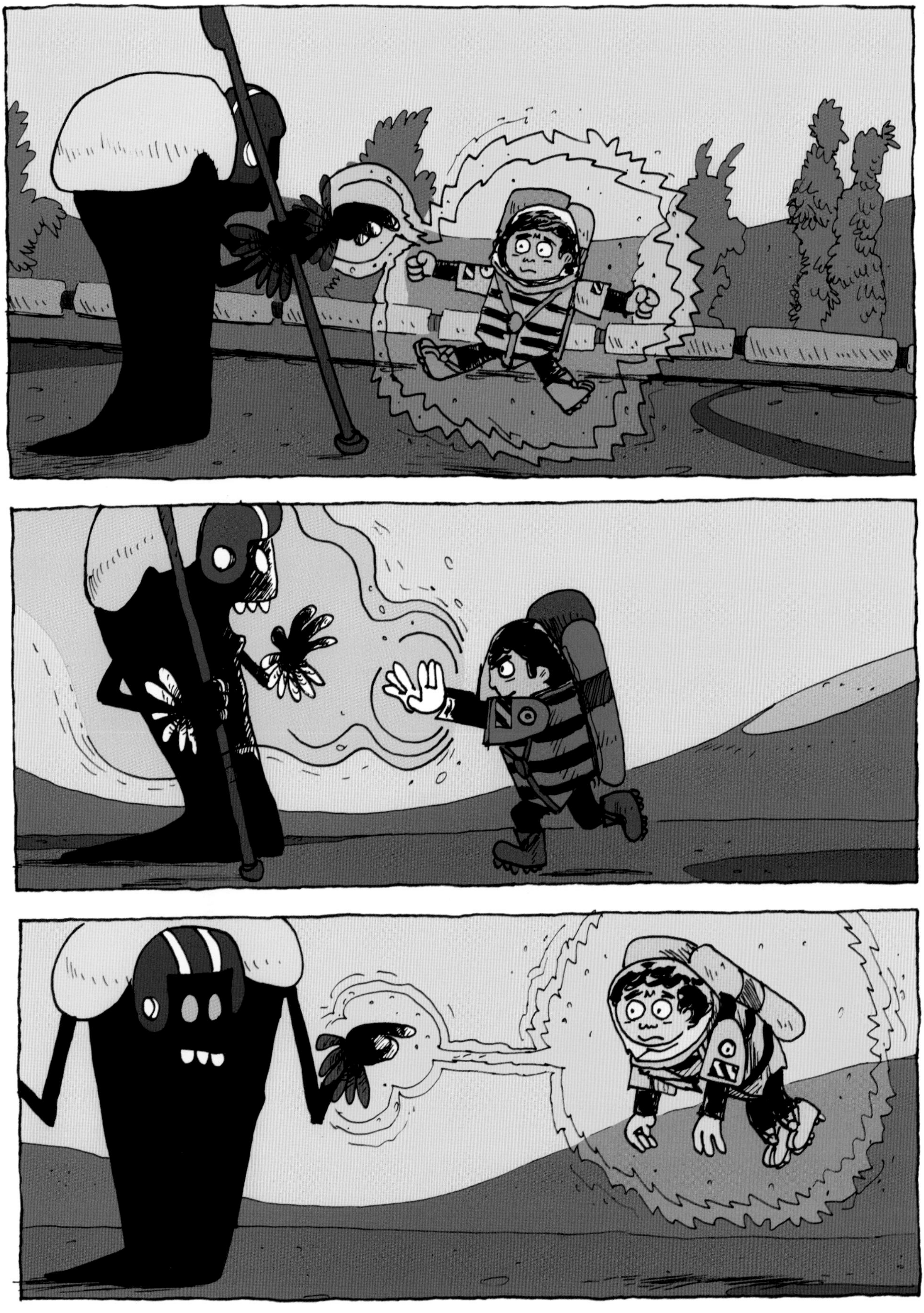

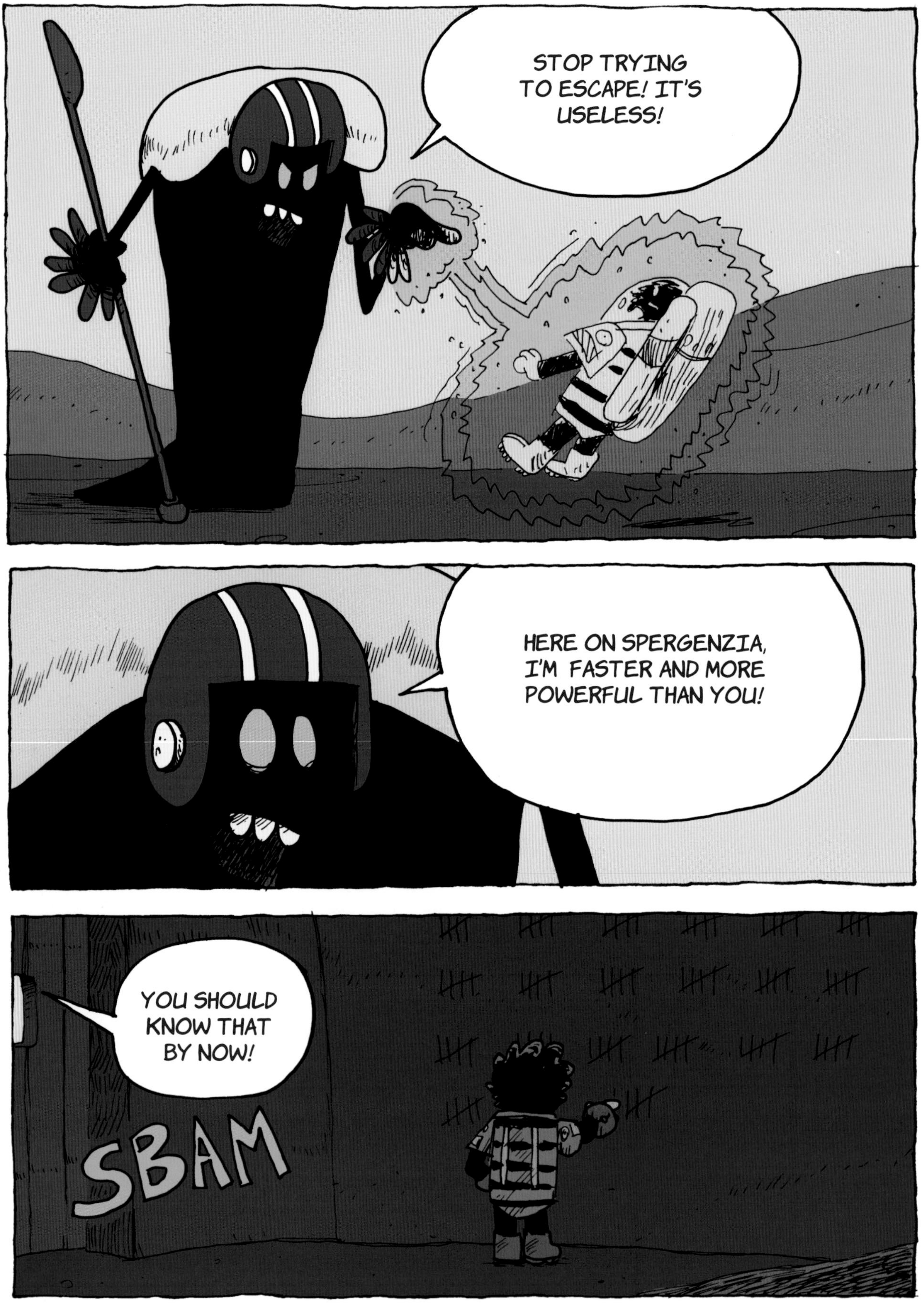
STOP TRYING TO ESCAPE! IT'S USELESS!
HERE ON SPERGENZIA, I'M FASTER AND MORE POWERFUL THAN YOU!
YOU SHOULD KNOW THAT BY NOW!
SBAM

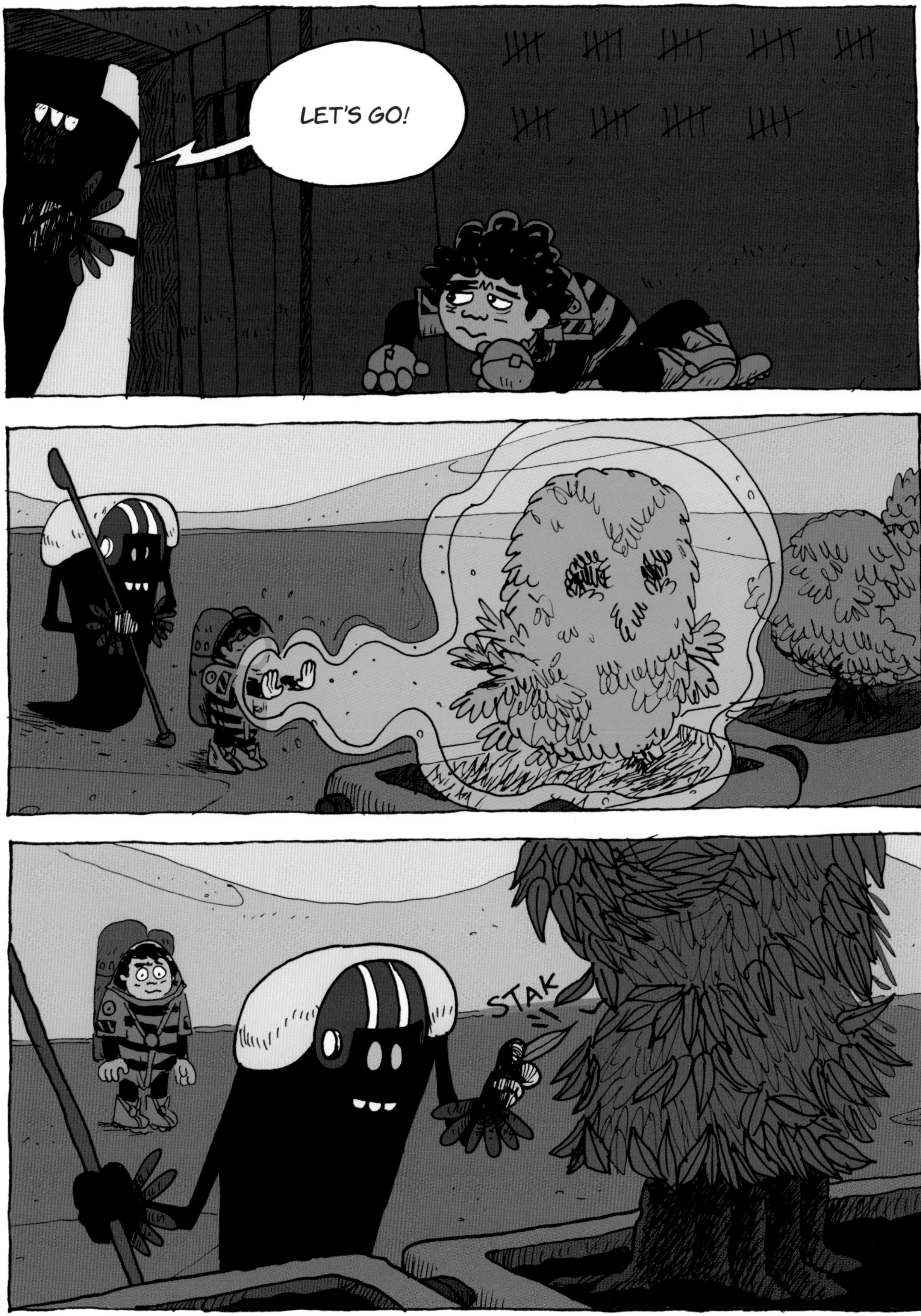
LET'S GO!
STAK

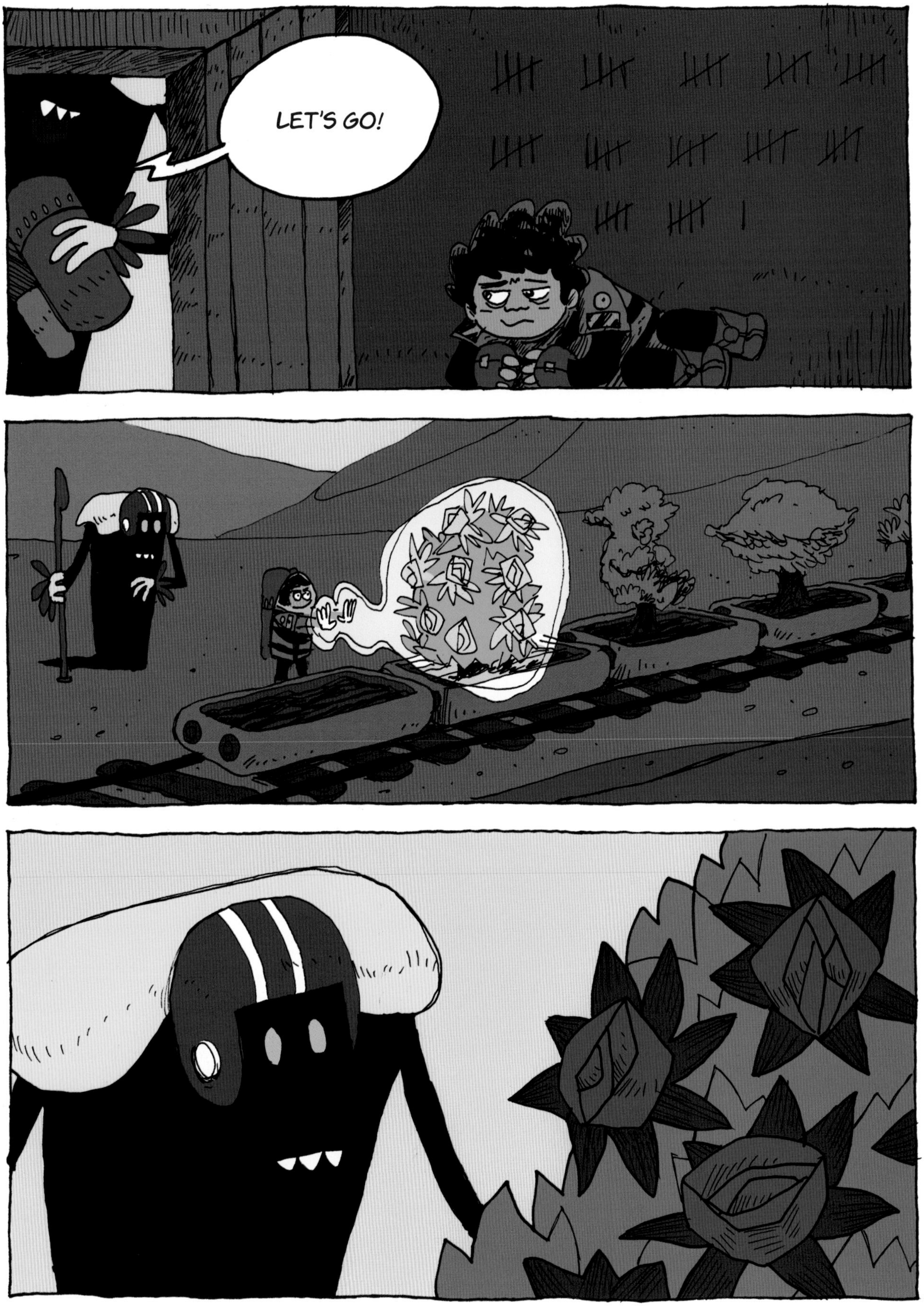
LET'S GO!

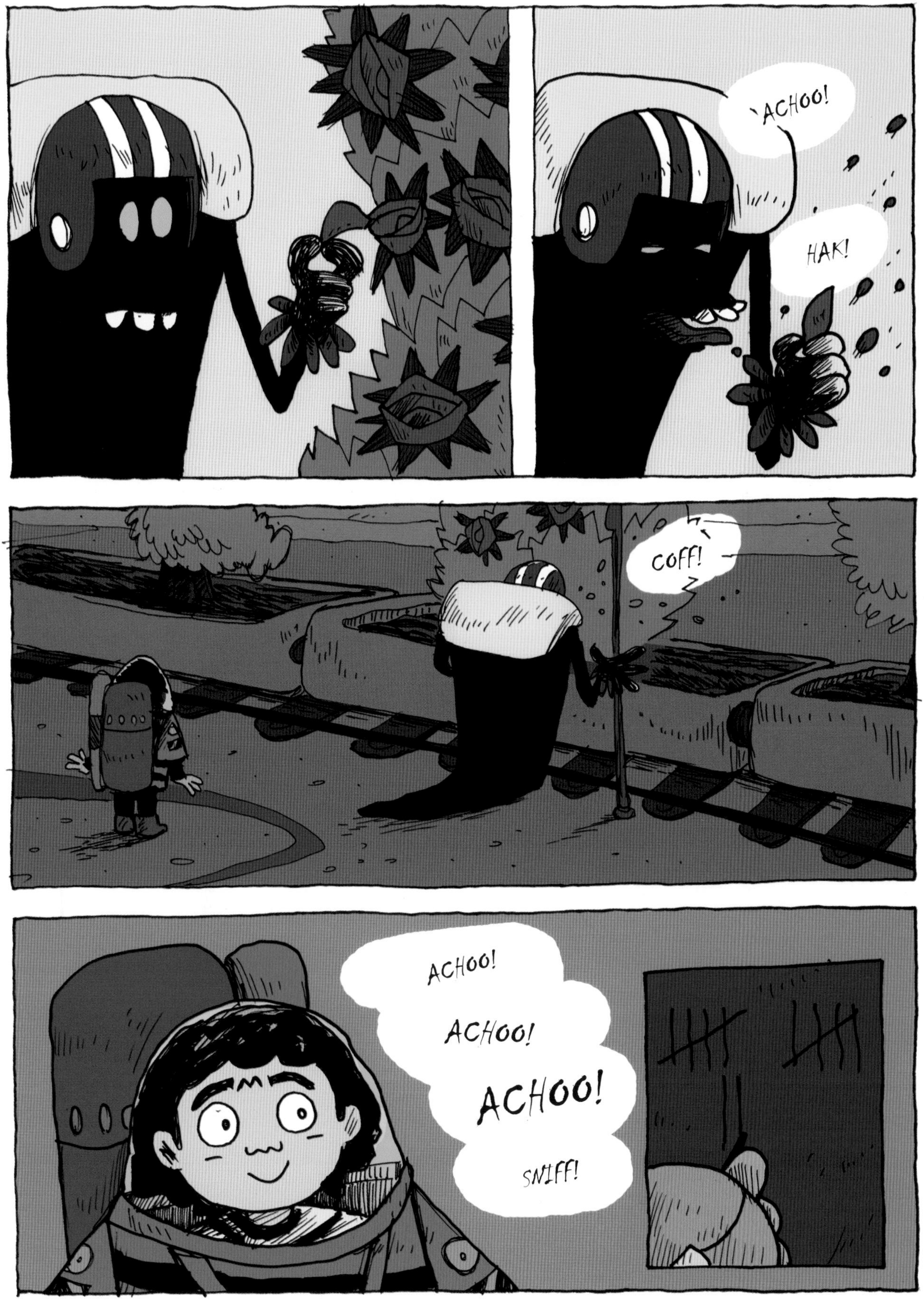
ACHOO!
HAK!
COFF!
ACHOO!
ACHOO!
ACHOO!
SNIFF!

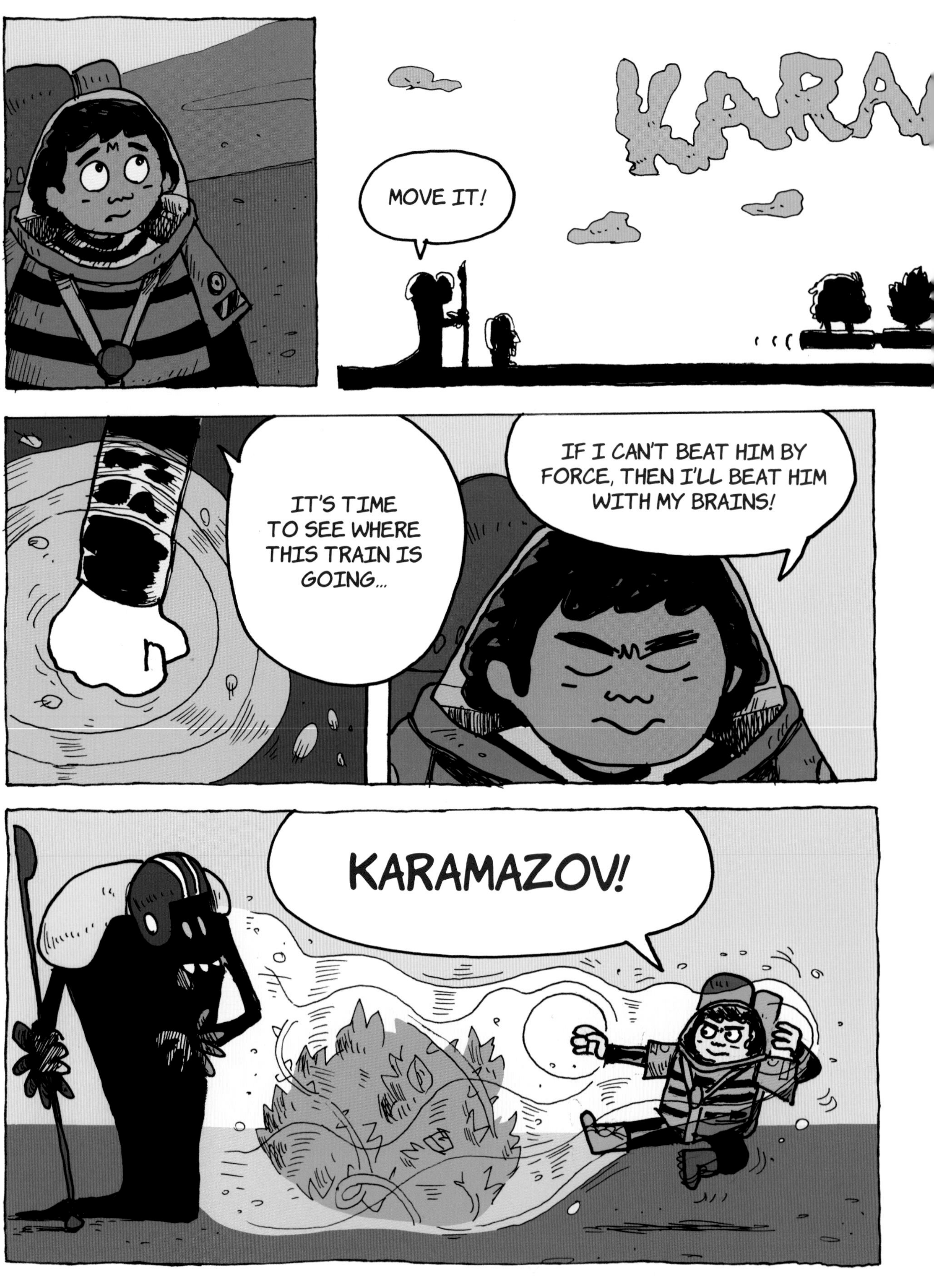
KARA
MOVE IT!
IT'S TIME TO SEE WHERE THIS TRAIN IS GOING...
IF I CAN'T BEAT HIM BY FORCE, THEN I'LL BEAT HIM WITH MY BRAINS!
KARAMAZOV!

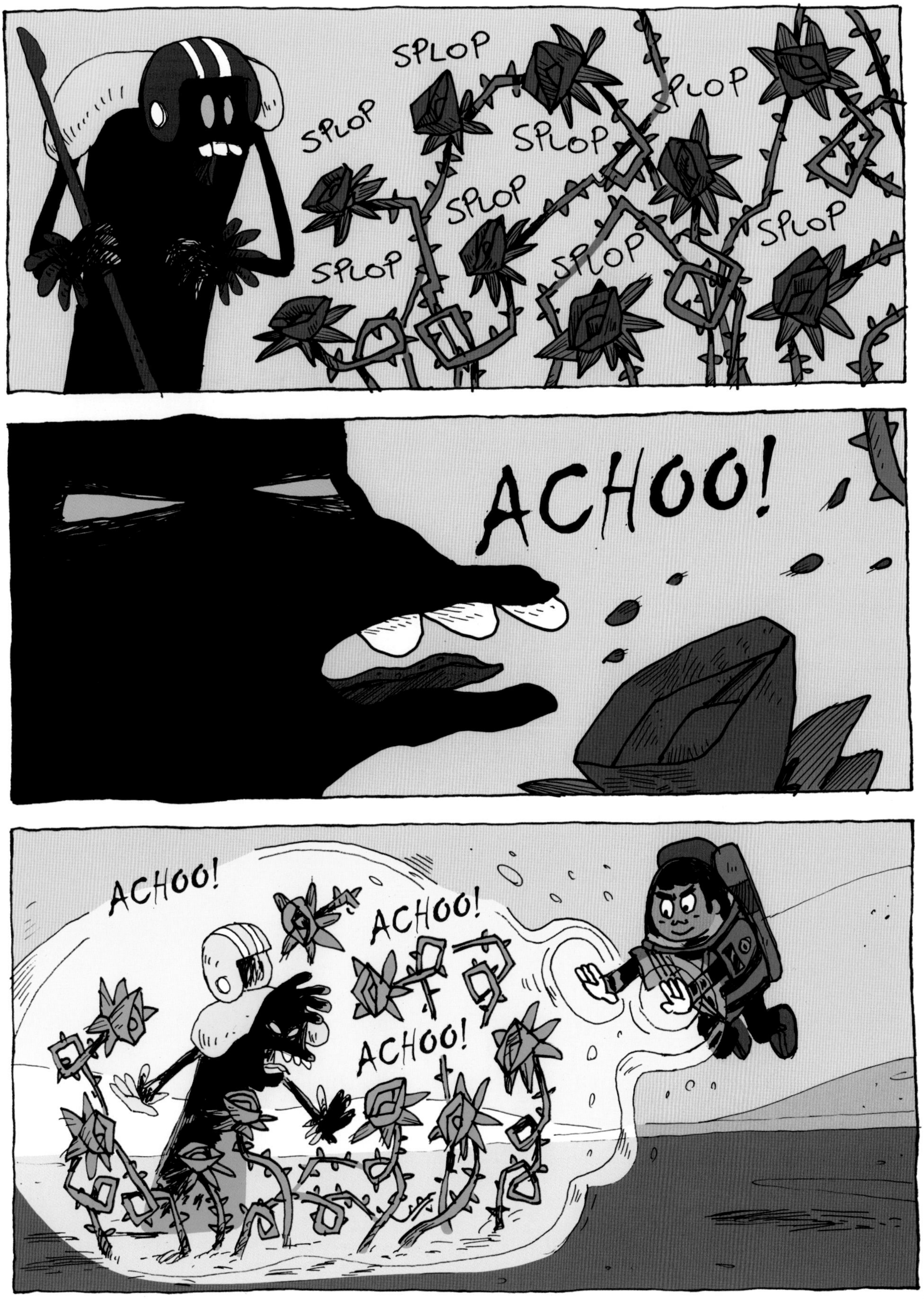
SPLOP
SPLOP
SPLOP
SPLOP
SPLOP
SPLOP
SPLOP
SPLOP
ACHOO!
ACHOO!
ACHOO!
ACHOO!

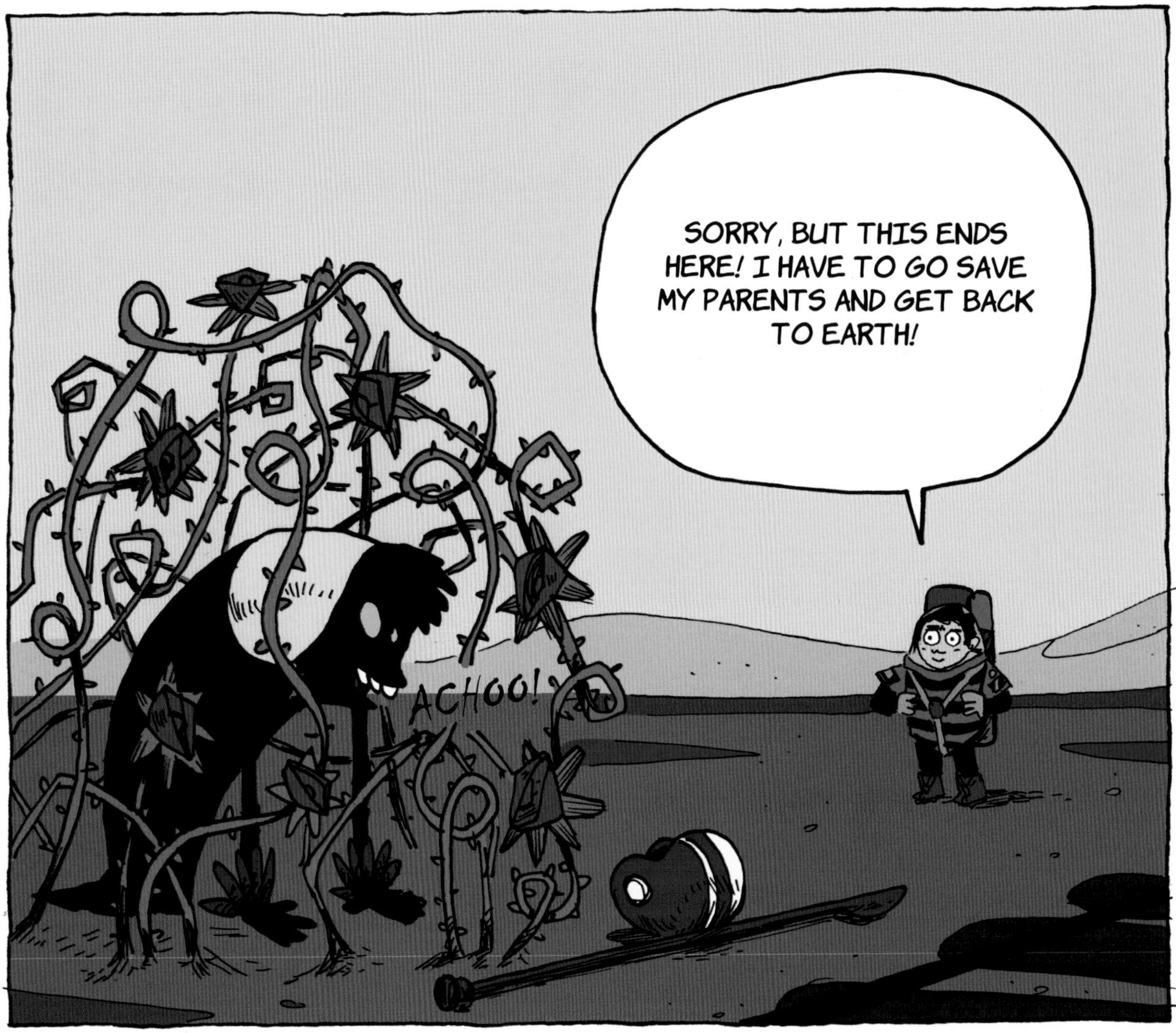
SORRY, BUT THIS ENDS HERE! I HAVE TO GO SAVE MY PARENTS AND GET BACK TO EARTH!
ACHOO!

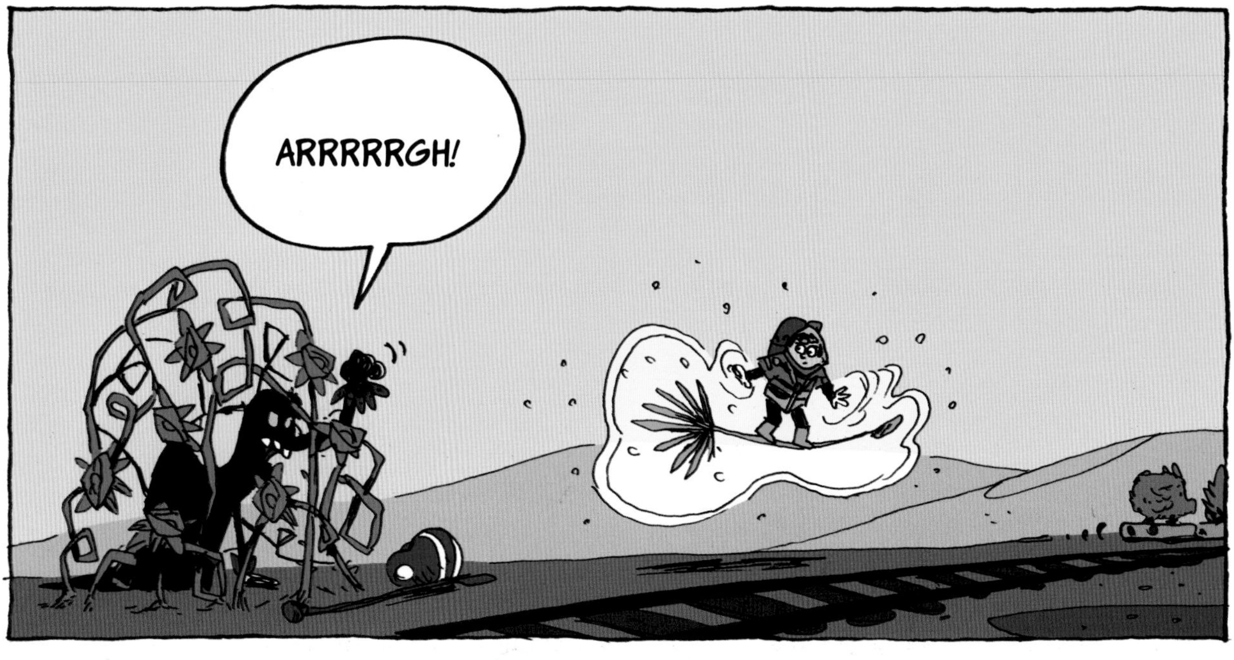
ARRRRRGH!

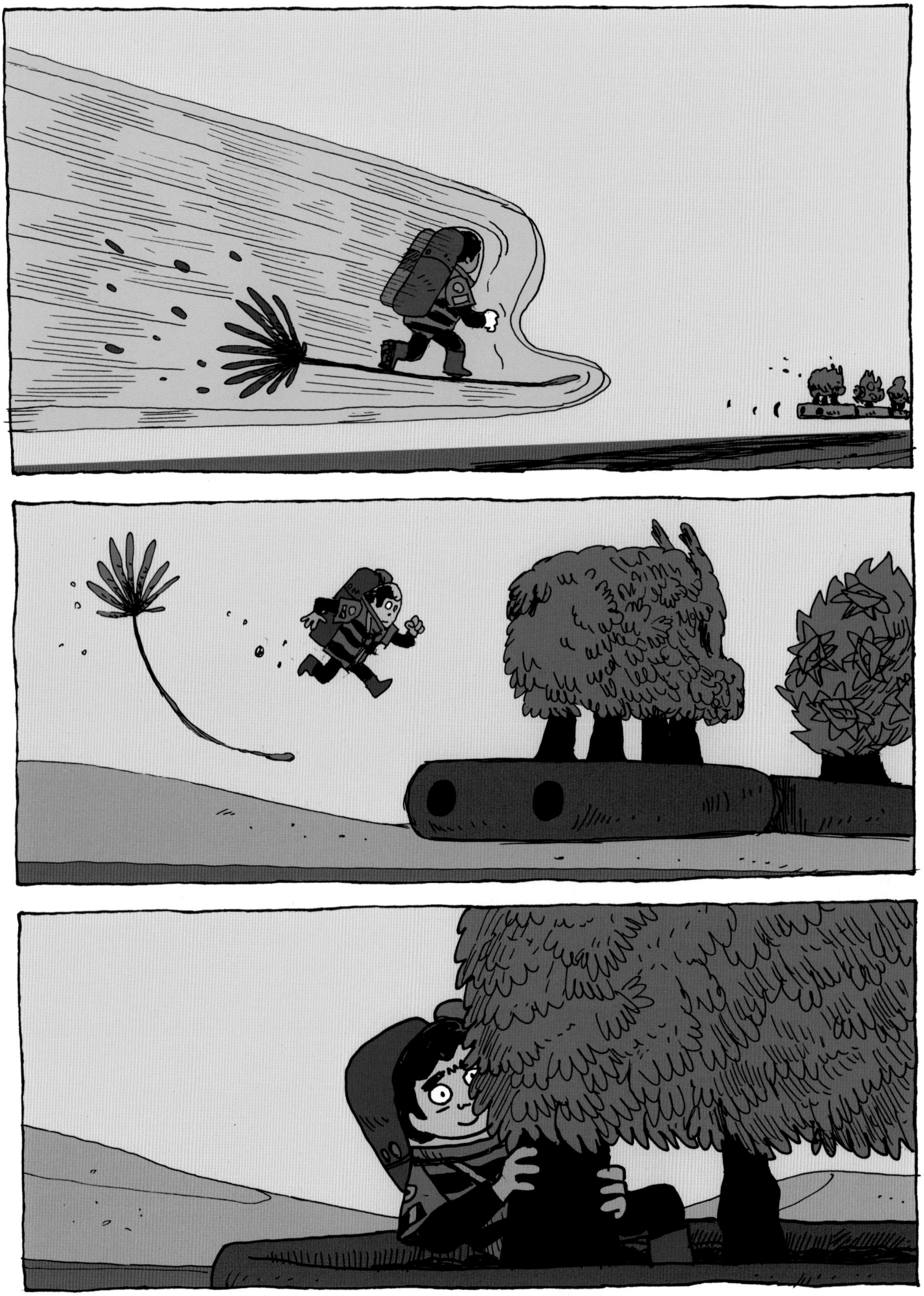

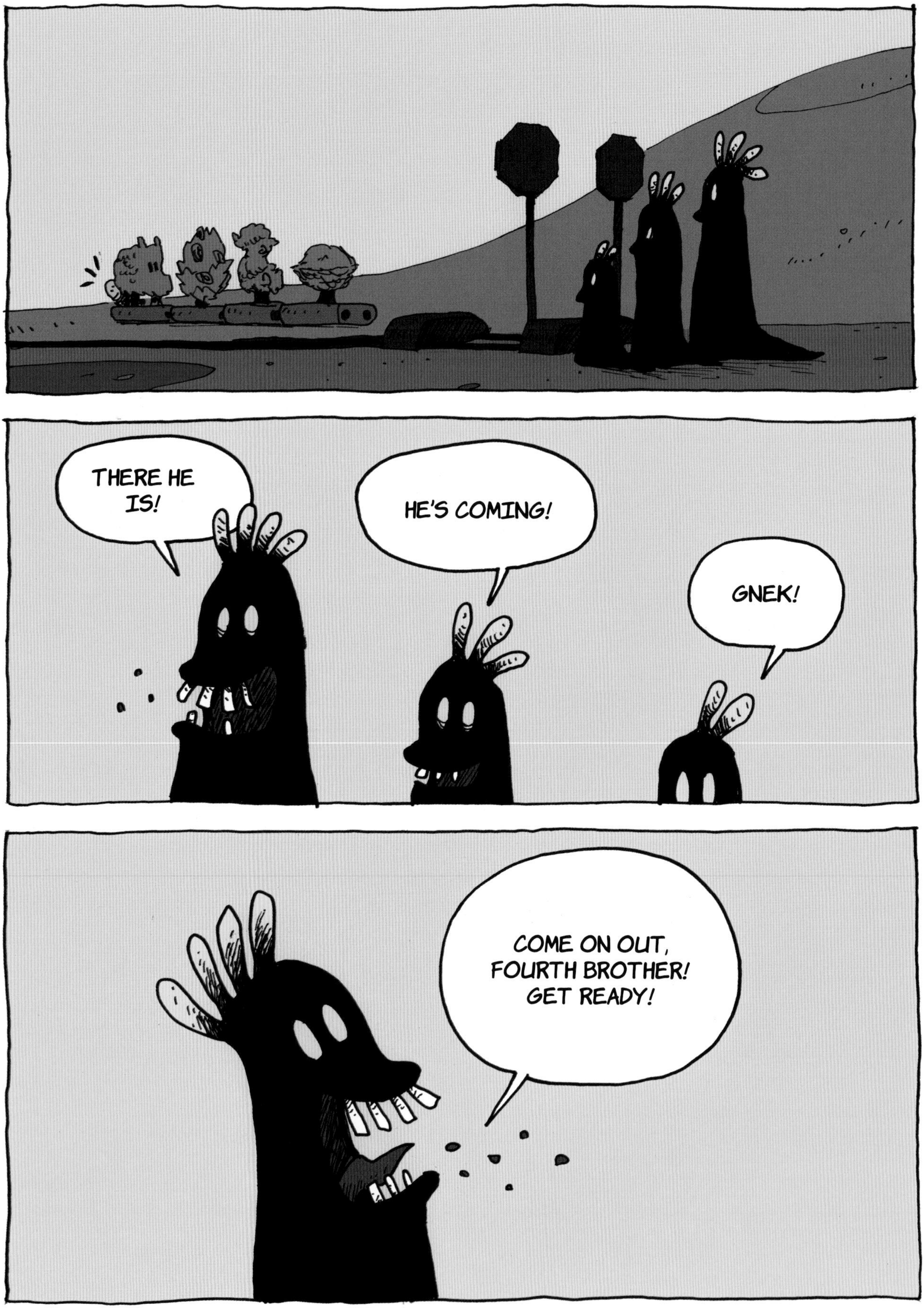
THERE HE IS!
HE'S COMING!
GNEK!
COME ON OUT, FOURTH BROTHER! GET READY!

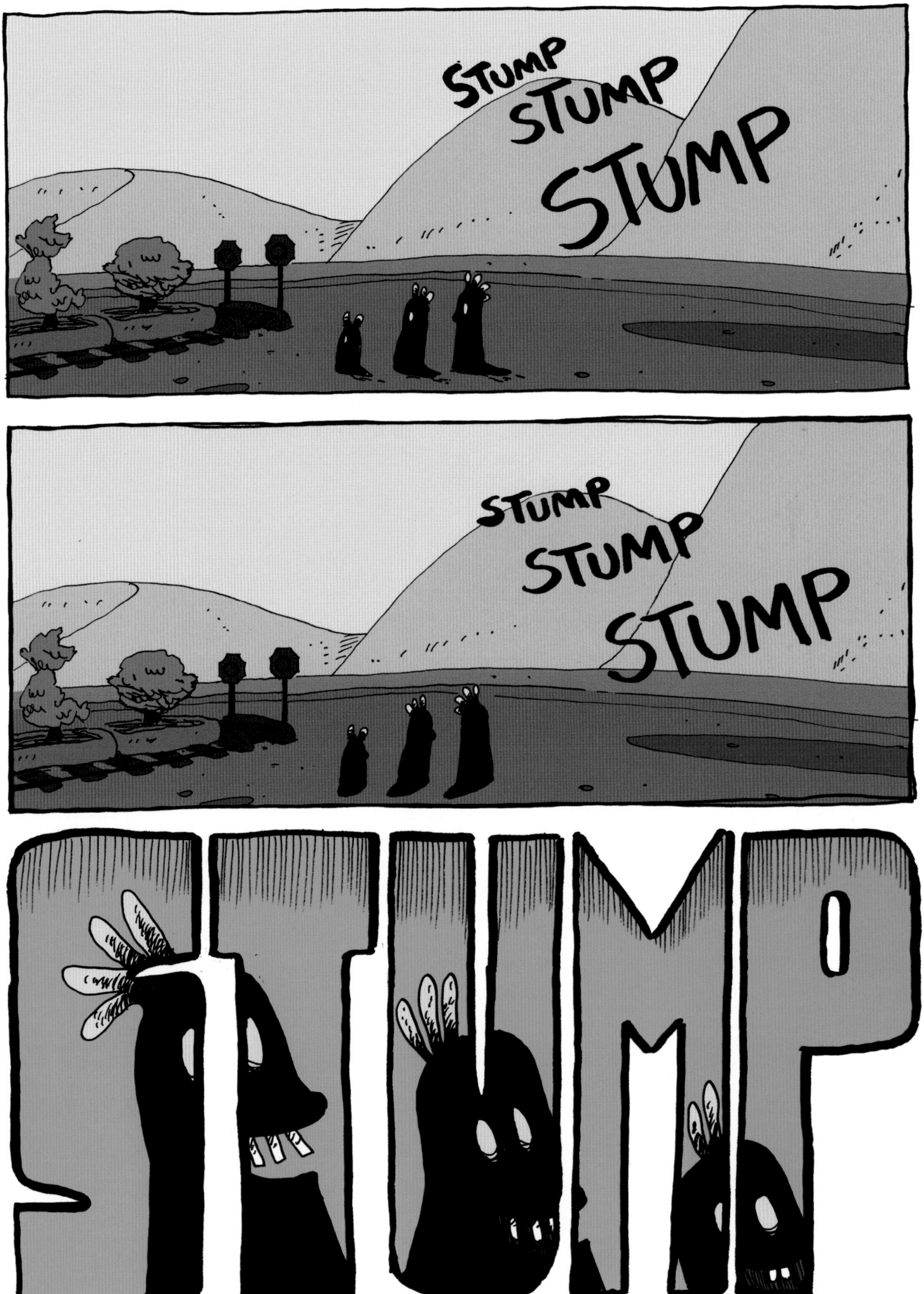
STUMP
STUMP
STUMP
STUMP
STUMP
STUMP
STUMP

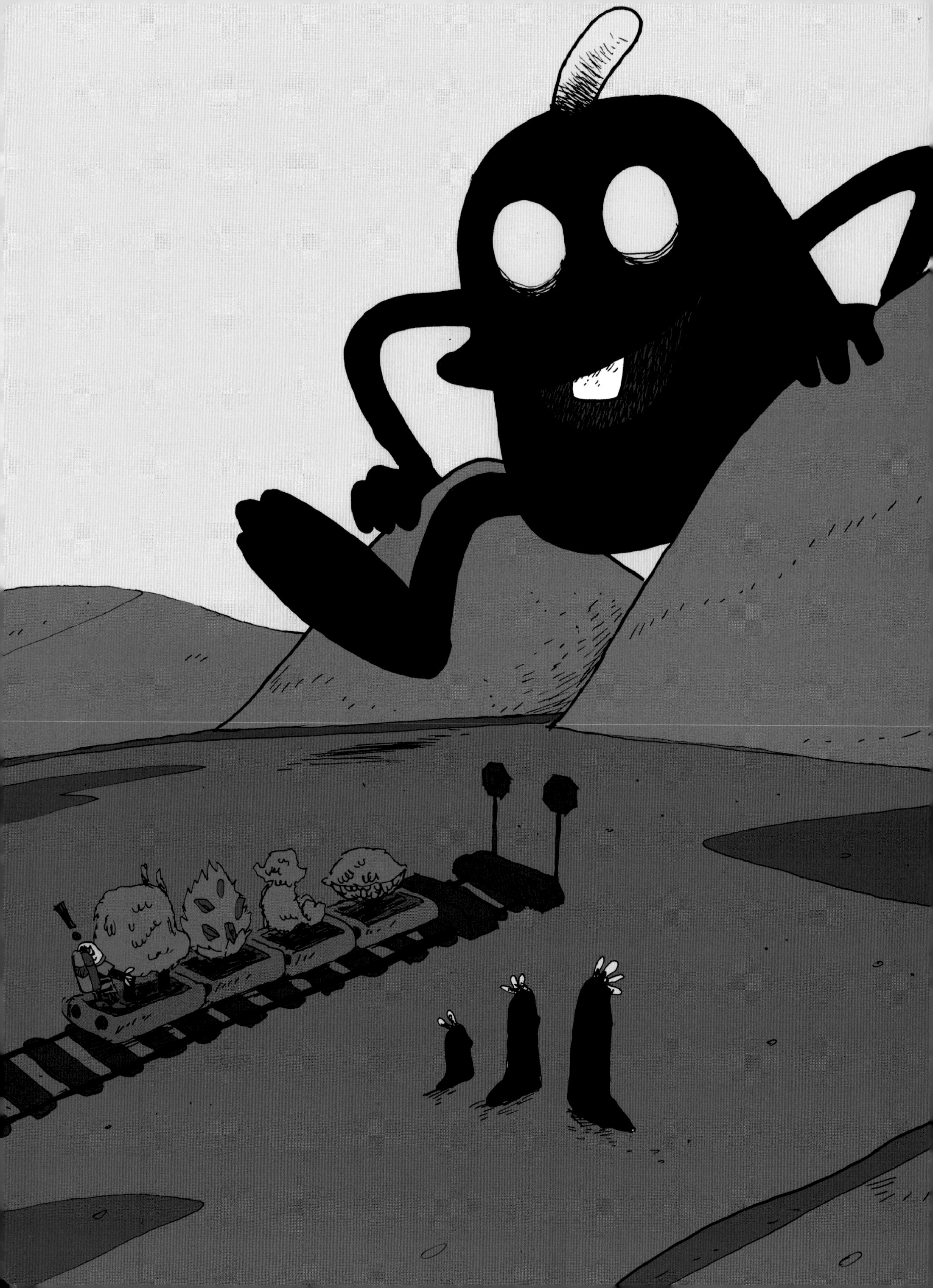

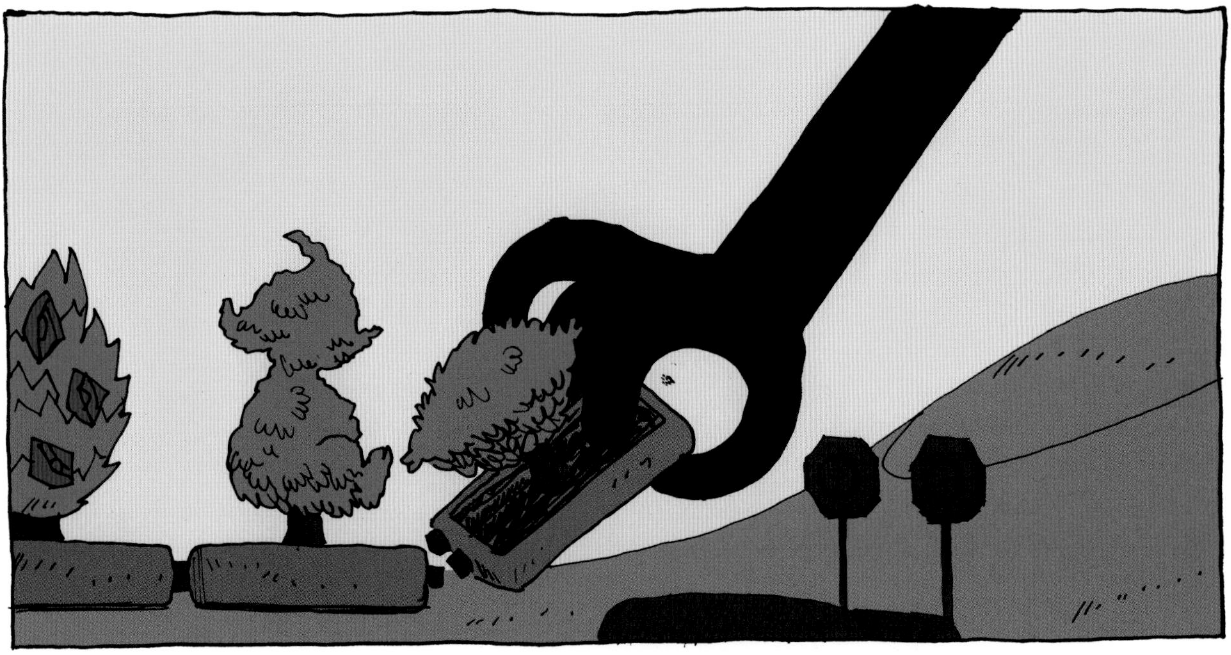

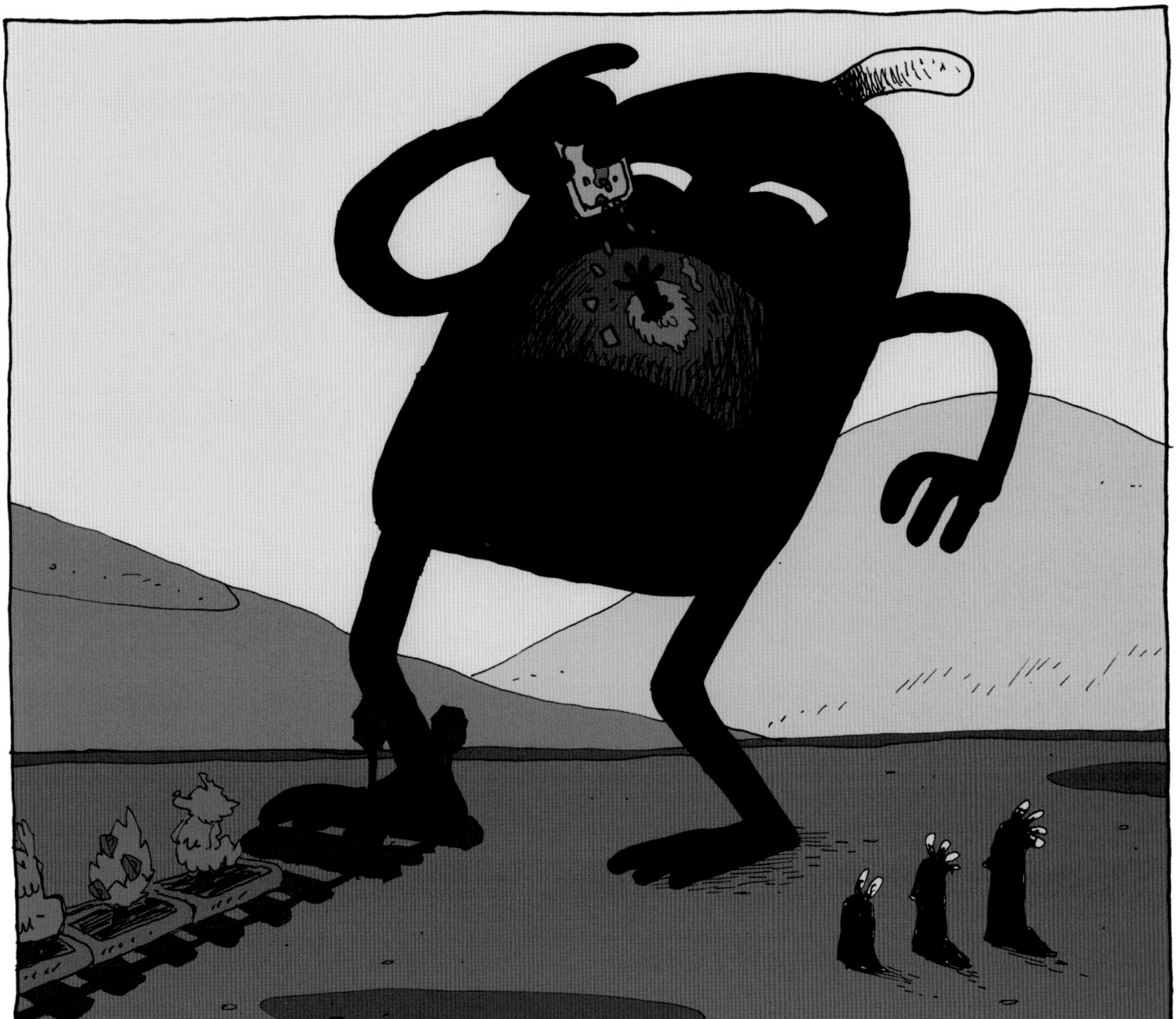

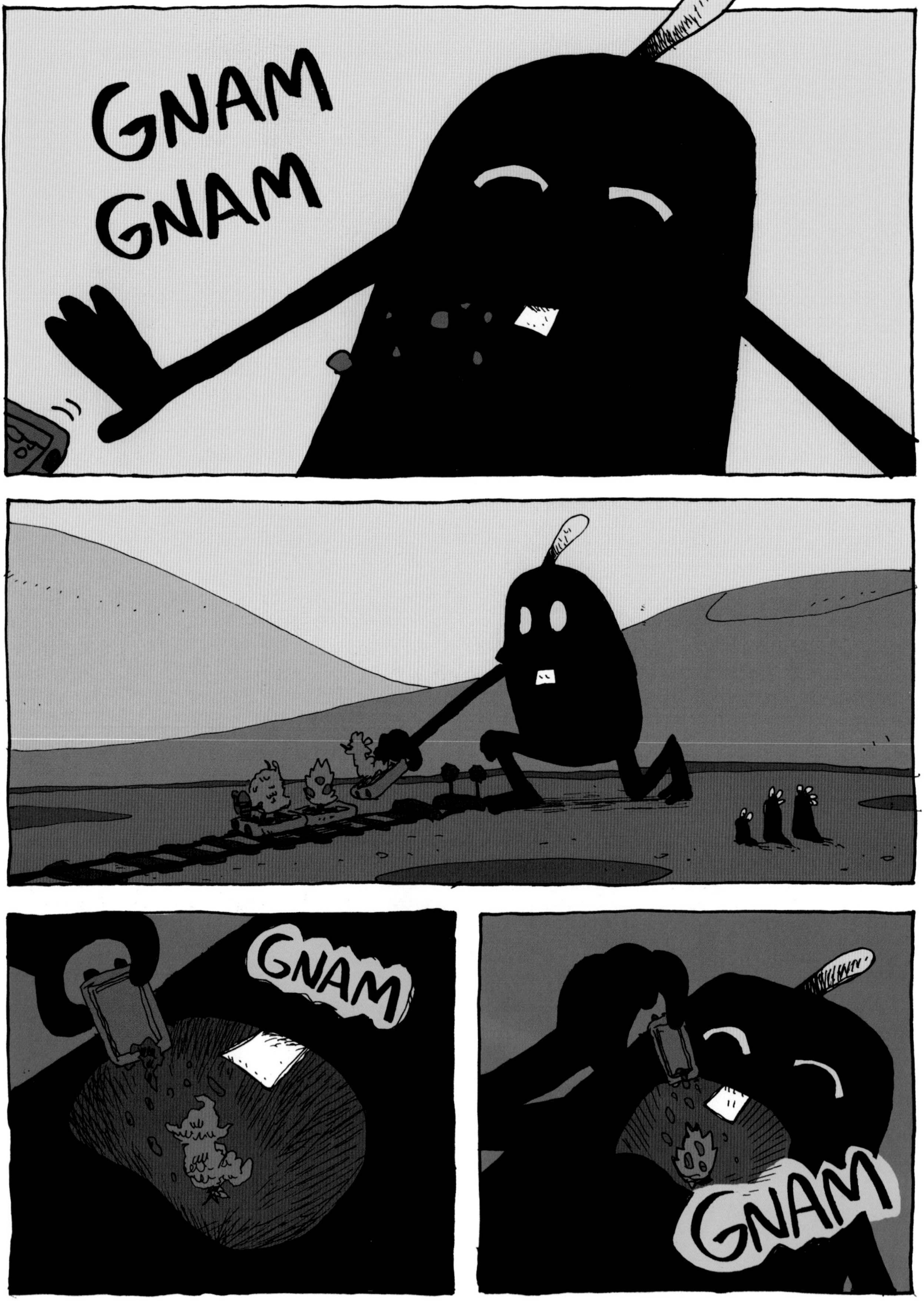
GNAM
GNAM
GNAM
GNAM

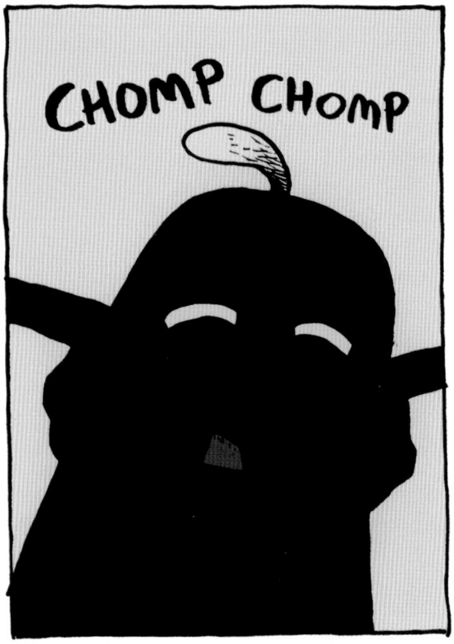
CHOMP CHOMP
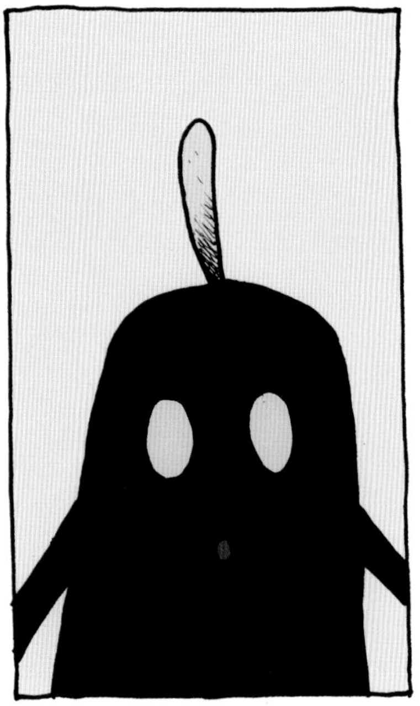
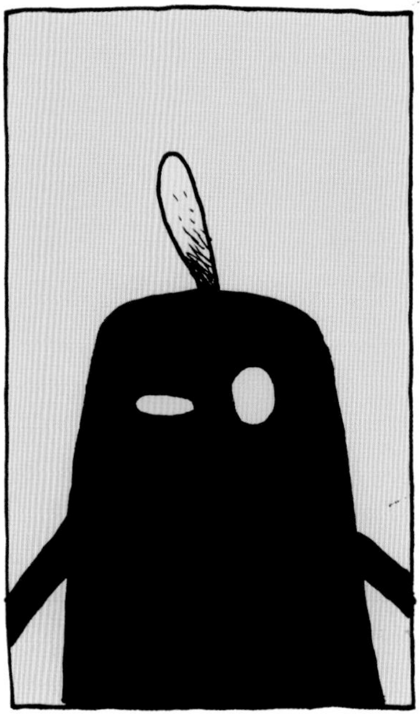
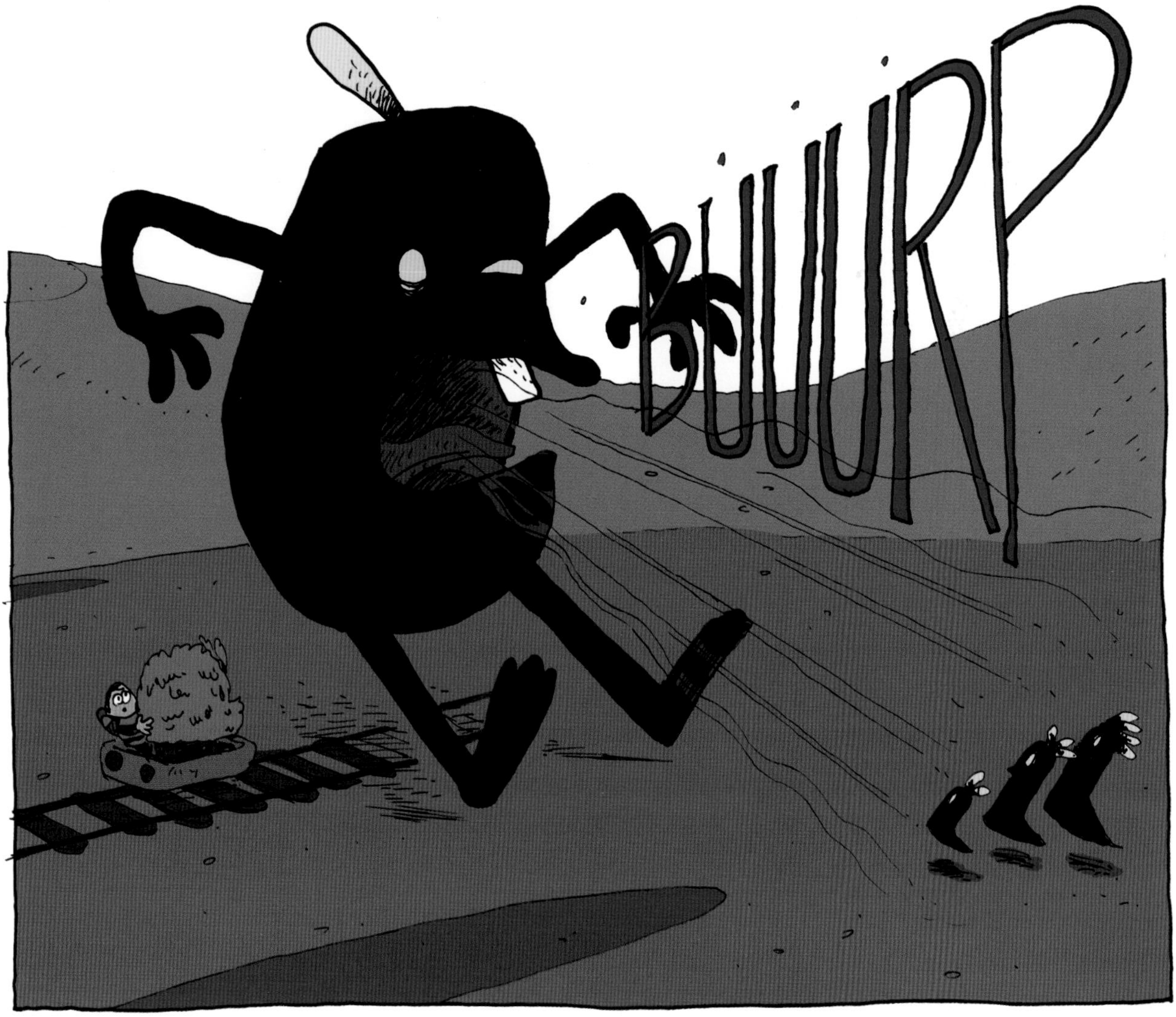
BUUURP

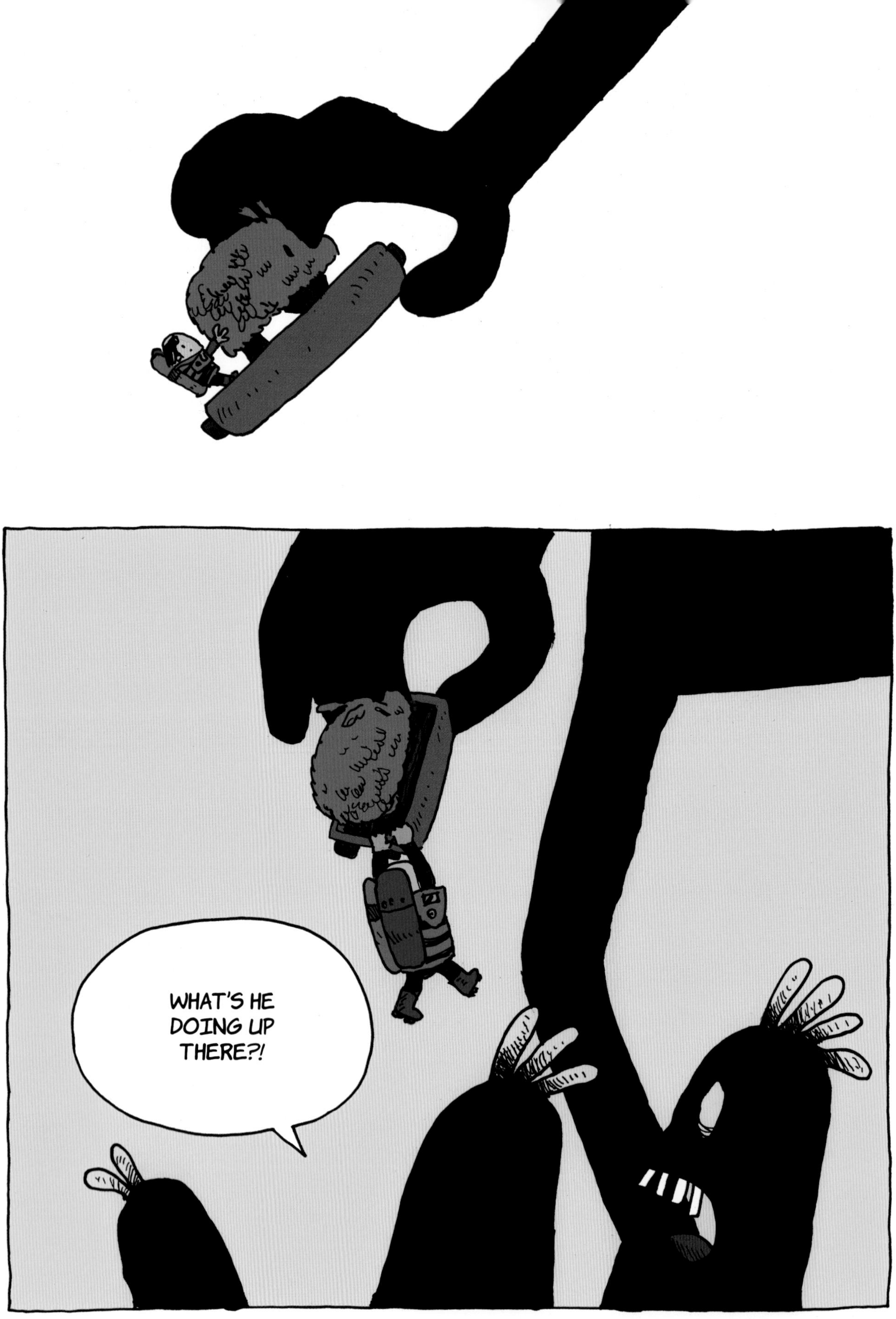
WHAT'S HE DOING UP THERE?!

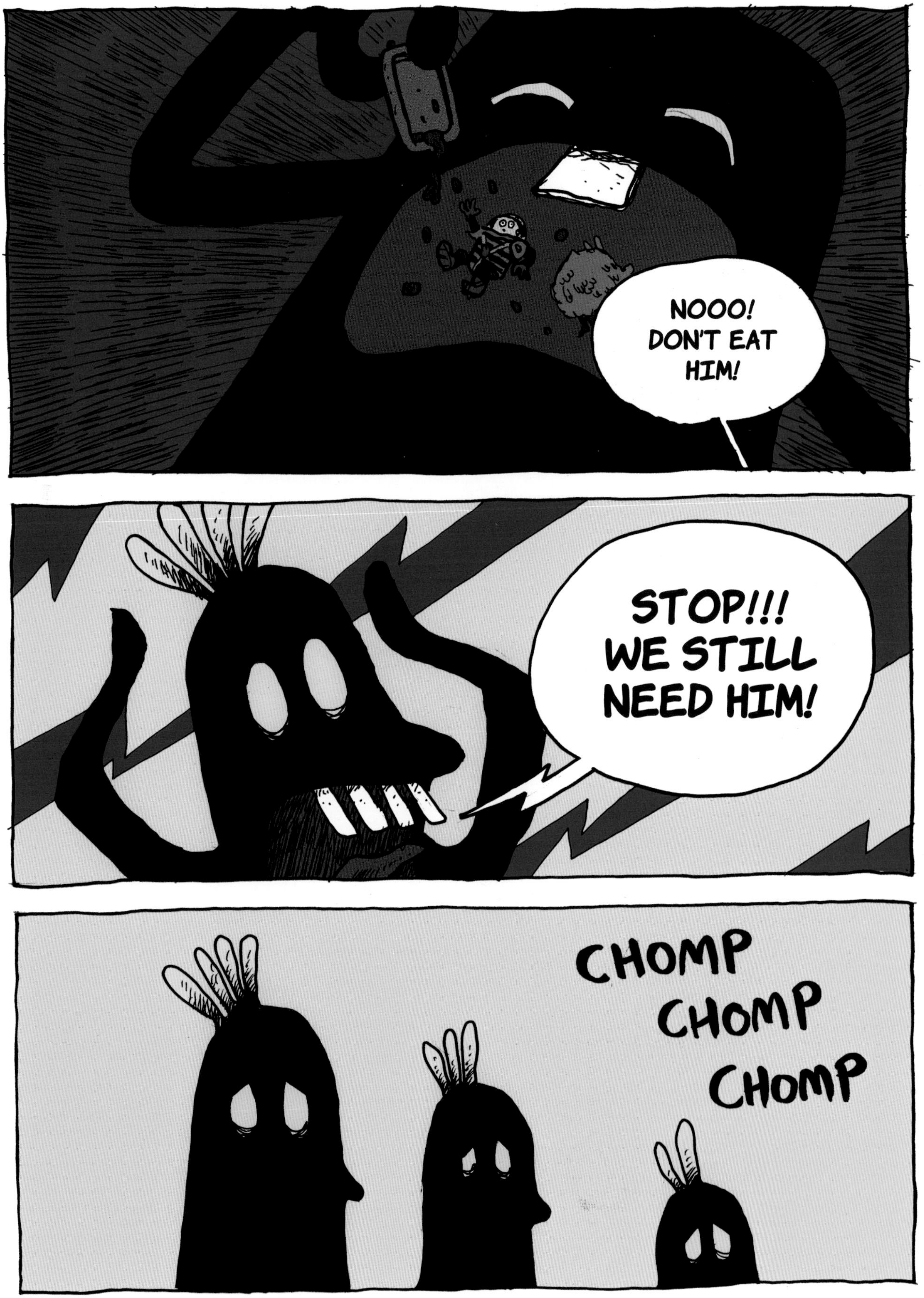
NOOO! DON'T EAT HIM!
STOP!!! WE STILL NEED HIM!
CHOMP CHOMP CHOMP

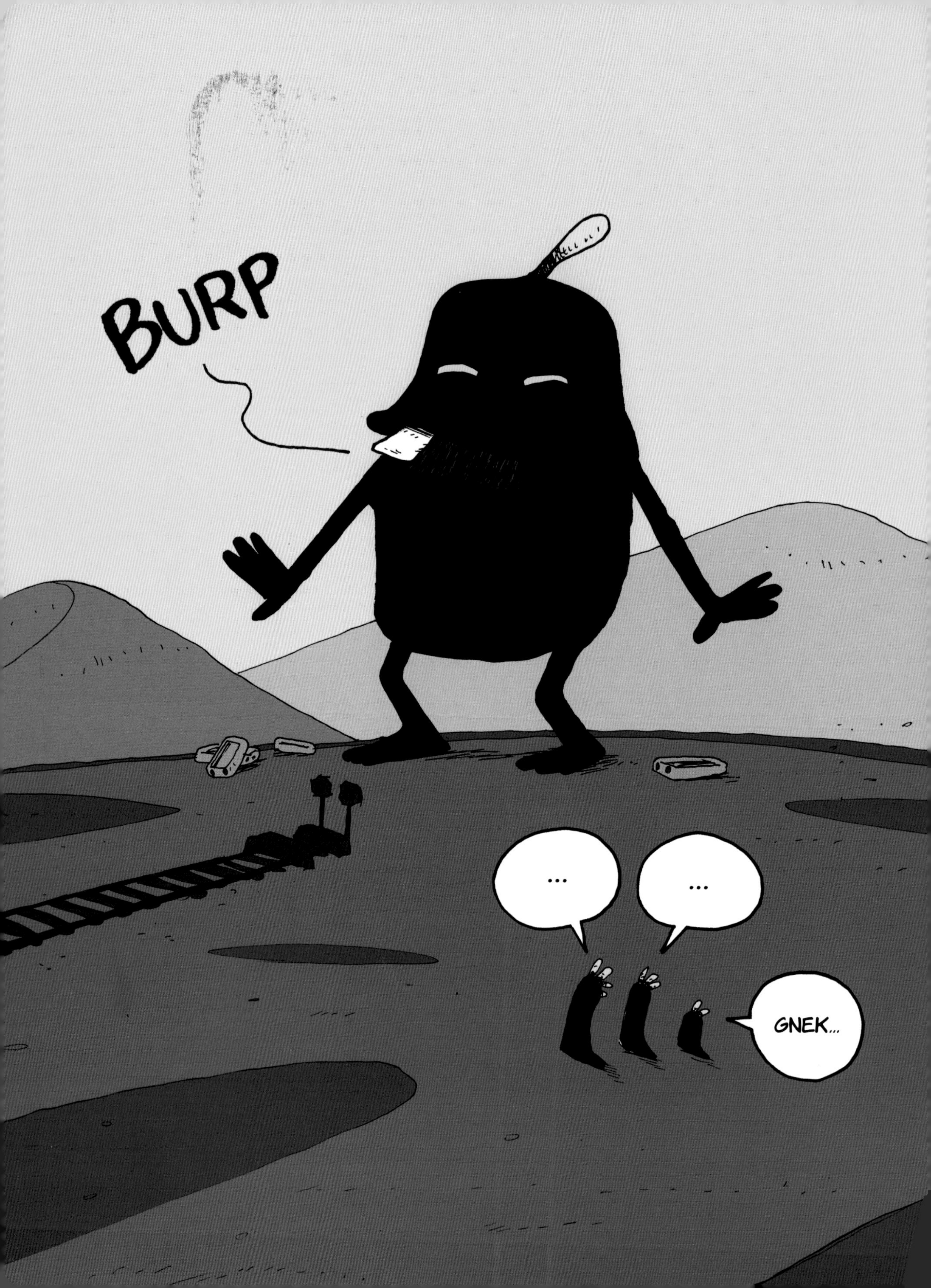
BURP
...
...
GNEK...

CHAPTER TWO
PUNCHES

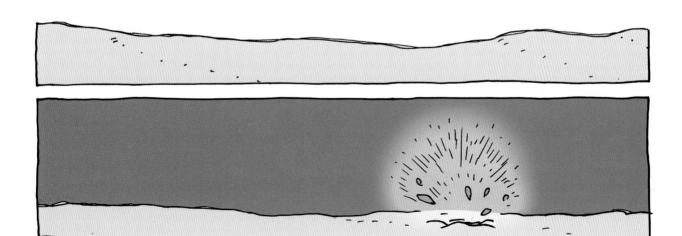

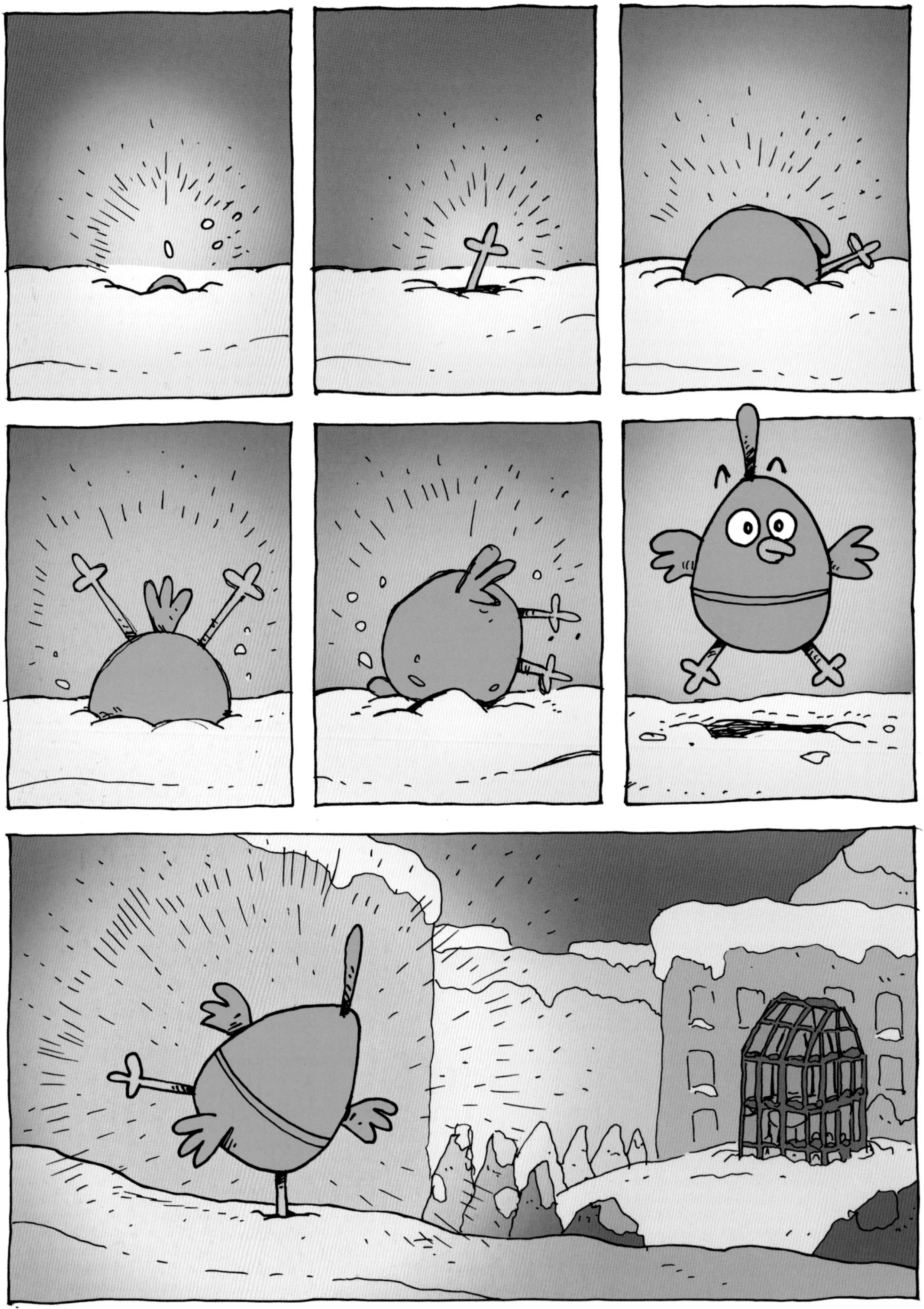

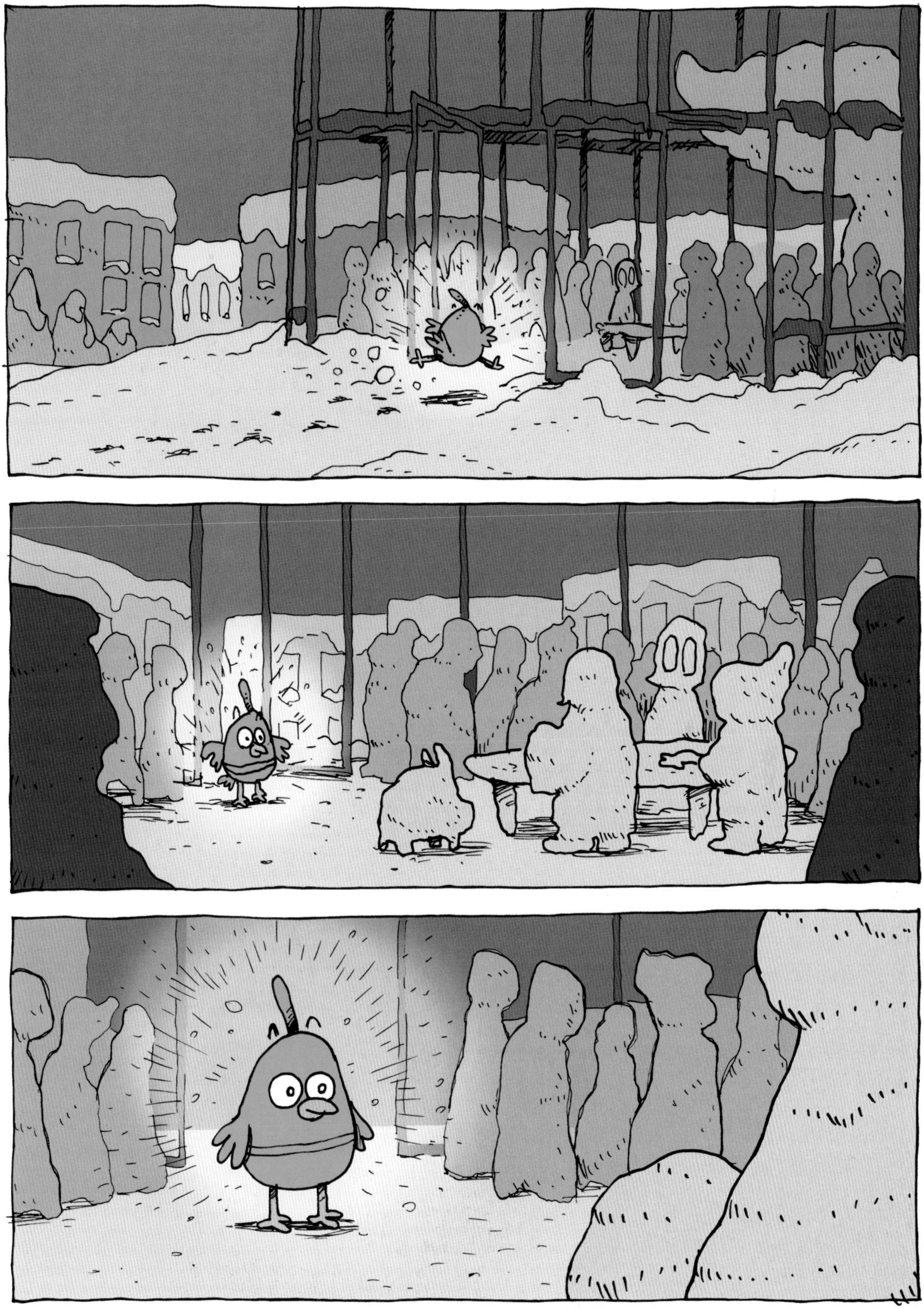

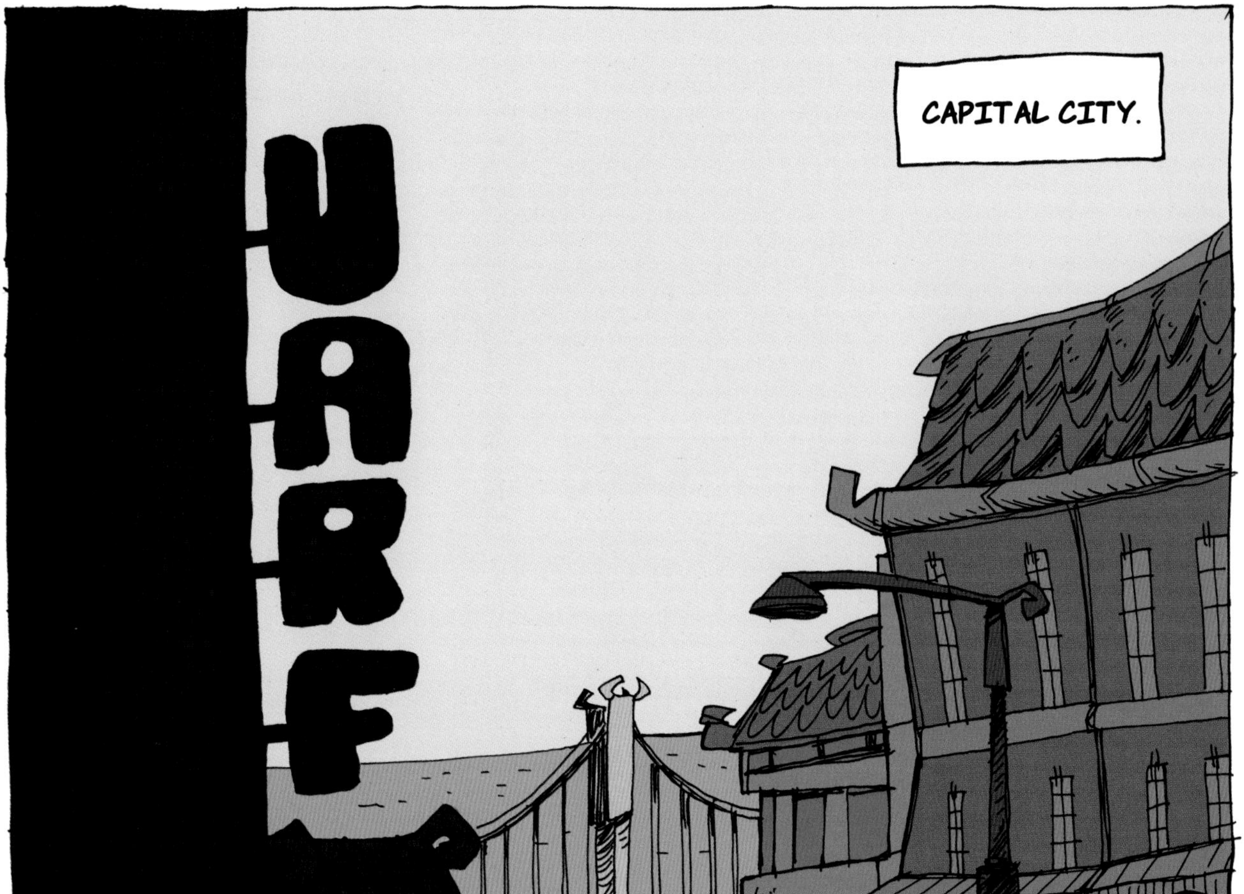
CAPITAL CITY.
UARF
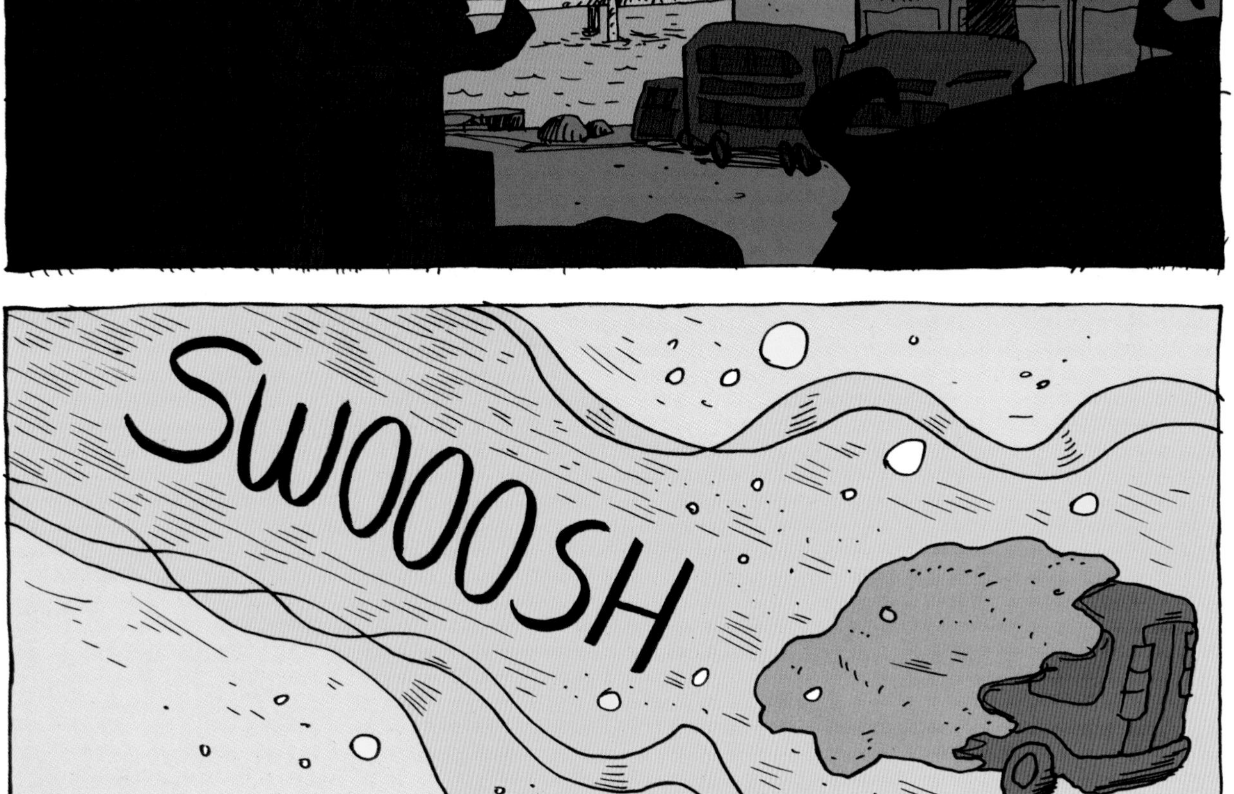
SWOOOSH

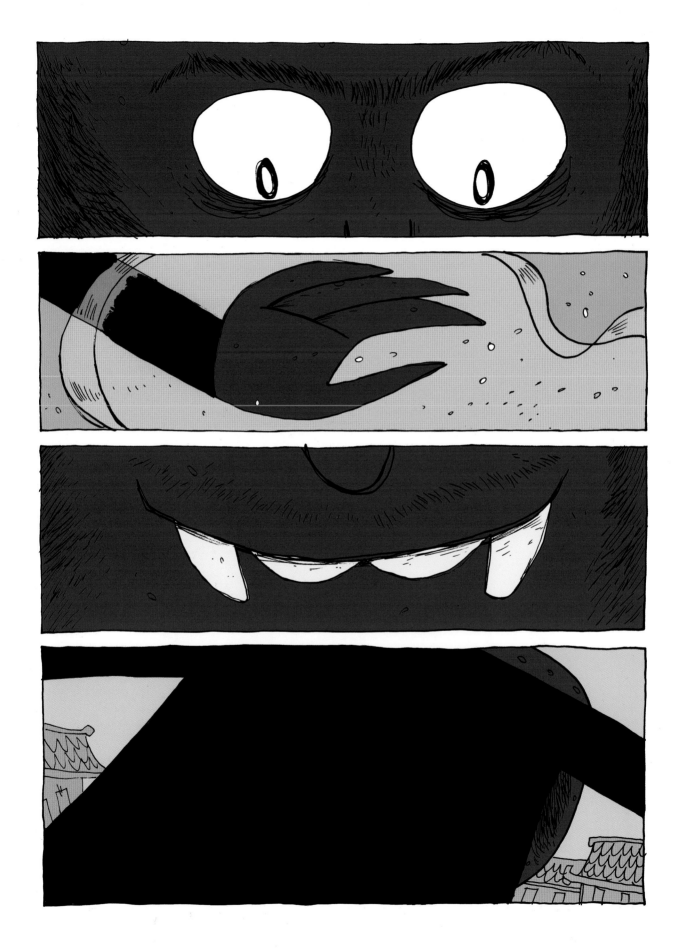

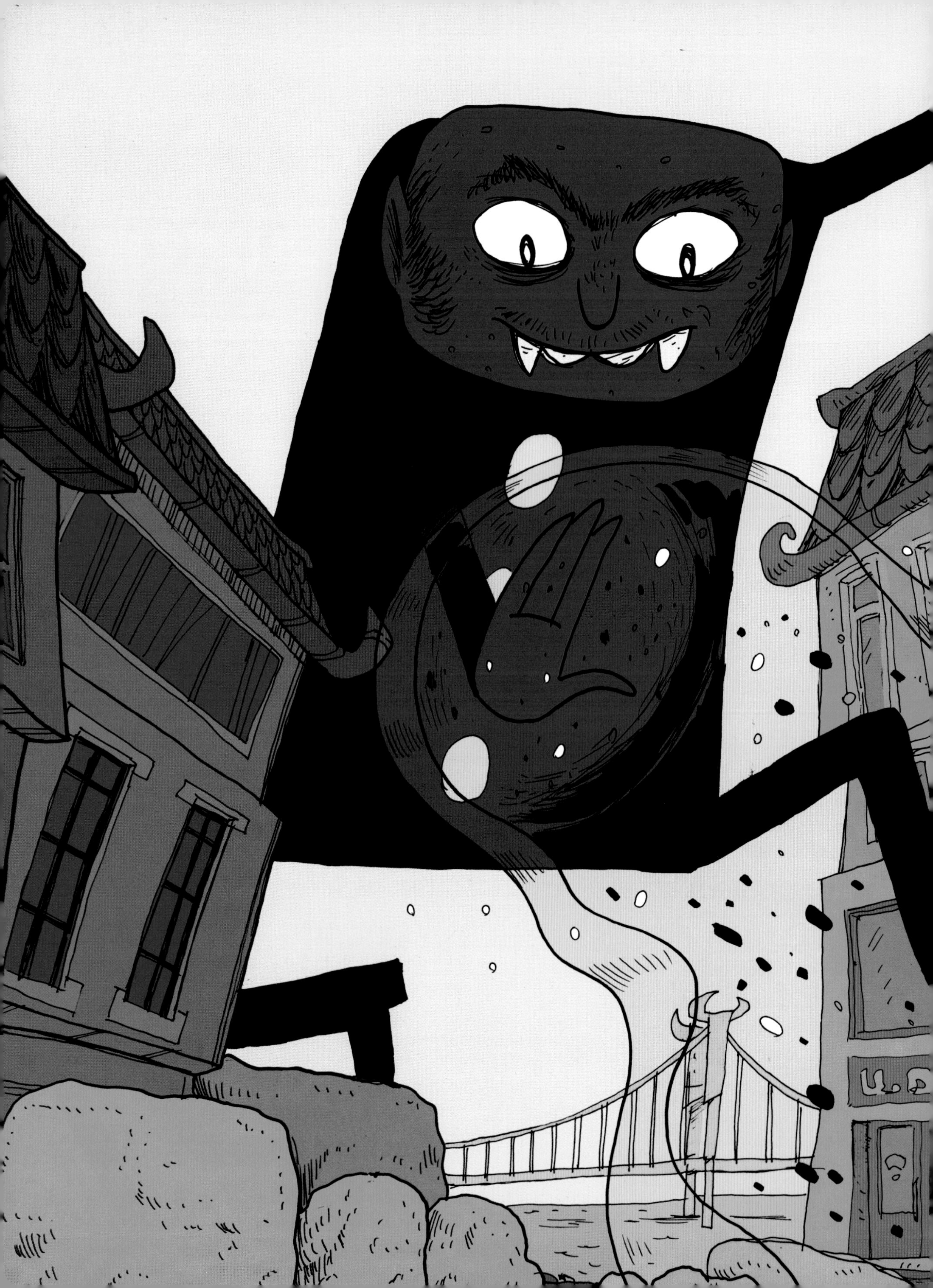

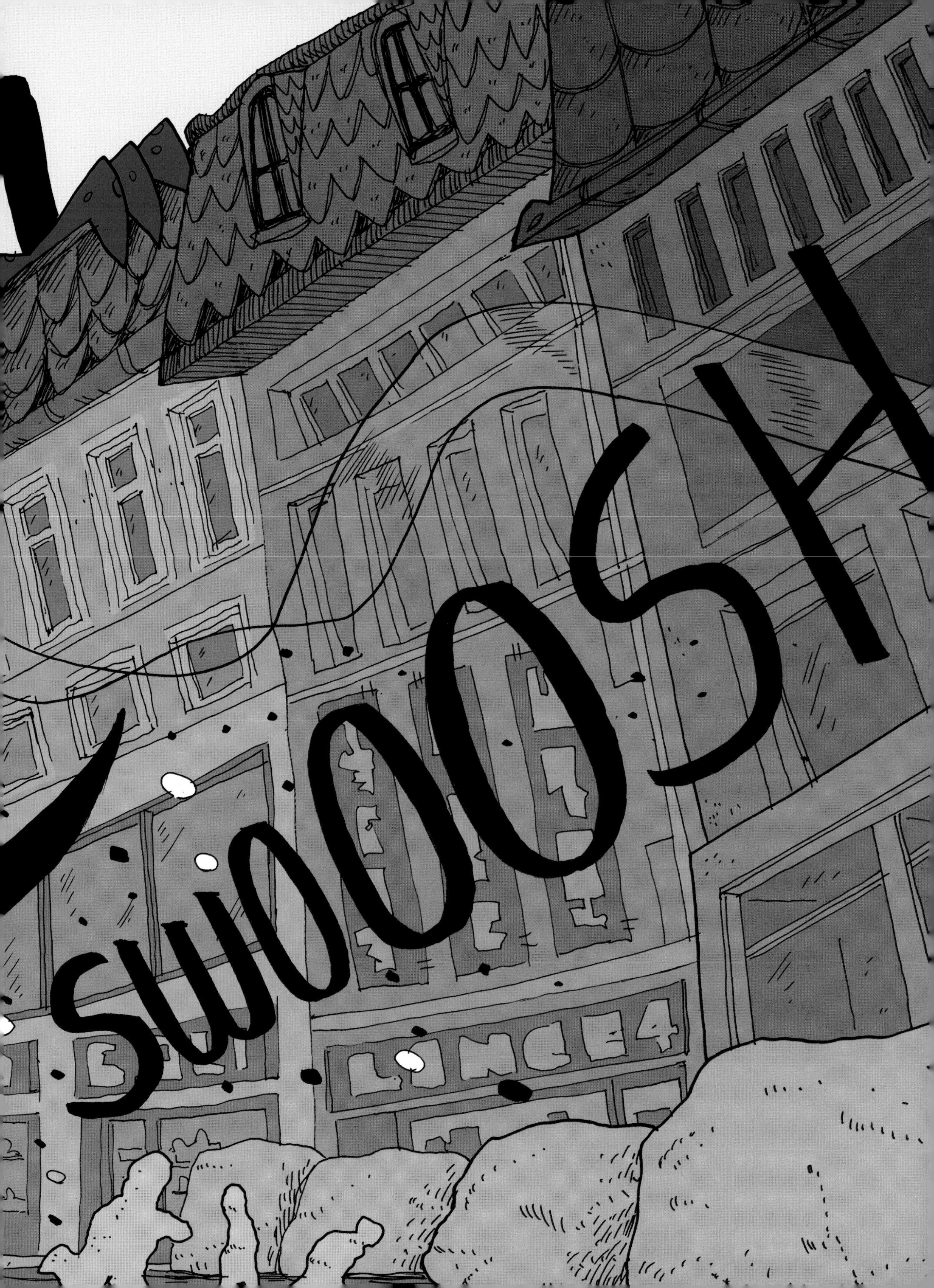
SWOOOSH

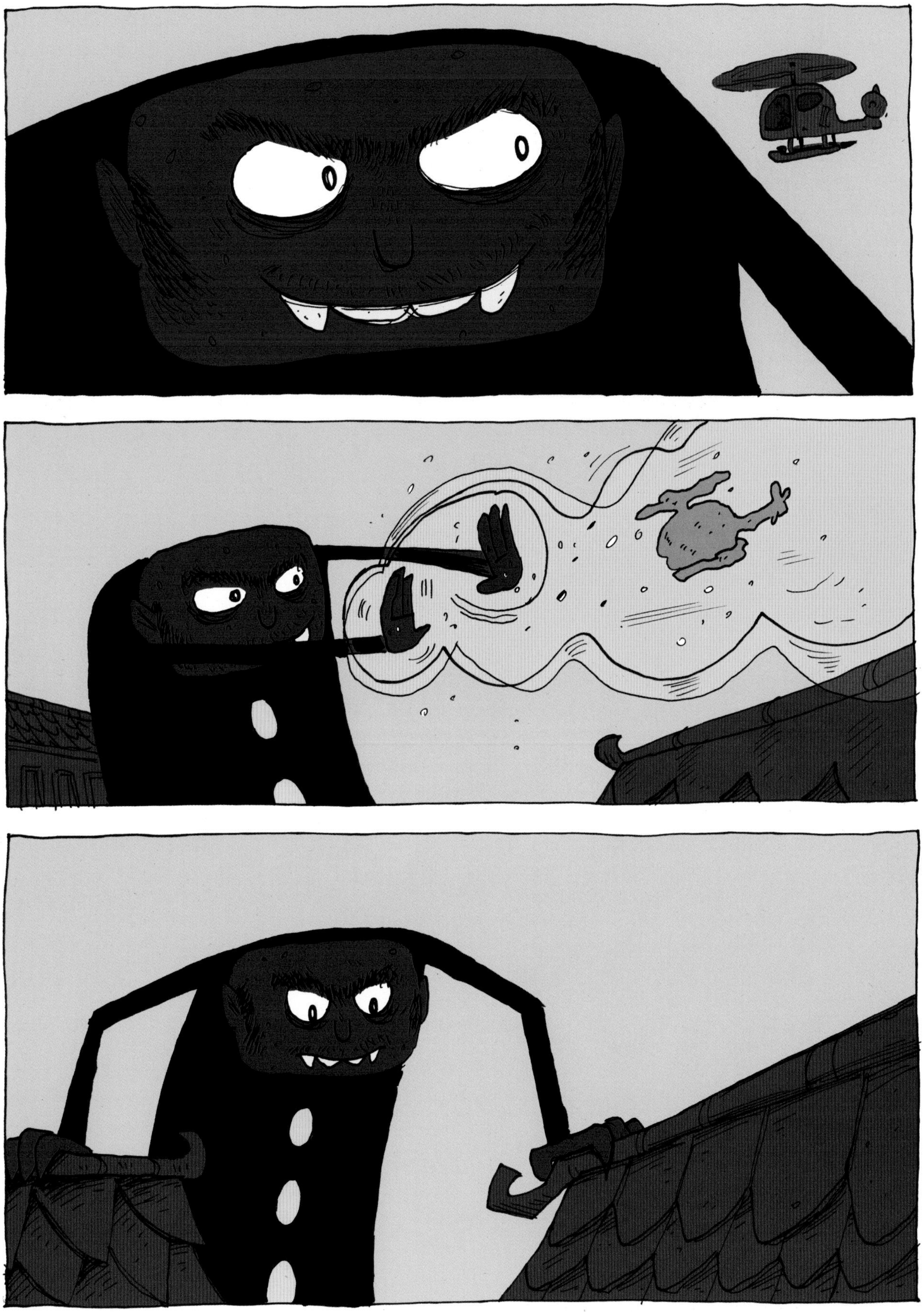

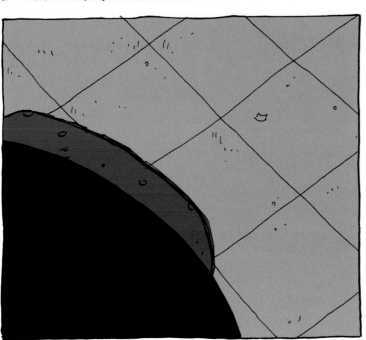

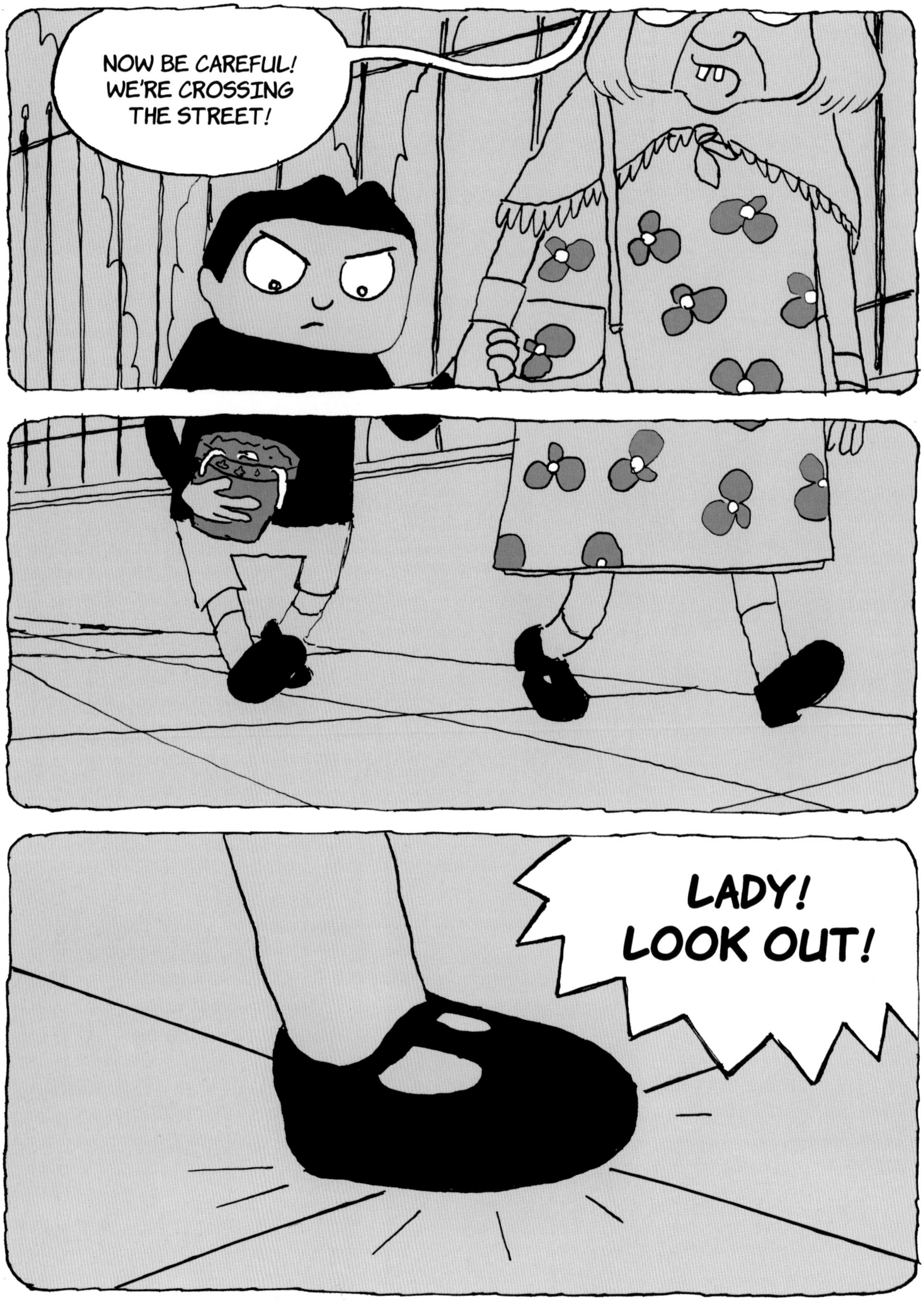
NOW BE CAREFUL! WE'RE CROSSING THE STREET!
LADY! LOOK OUT!

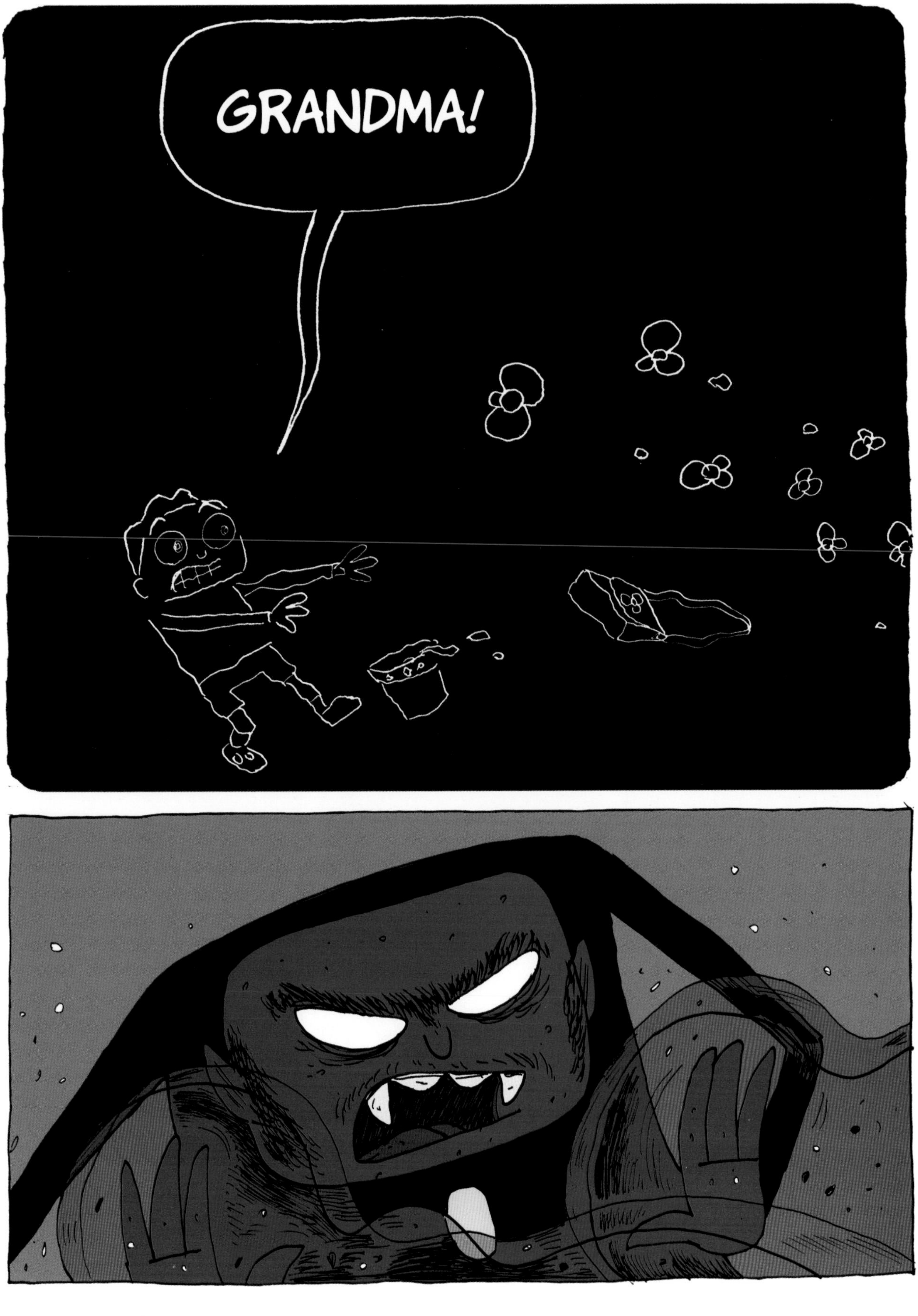
GRANDMA!

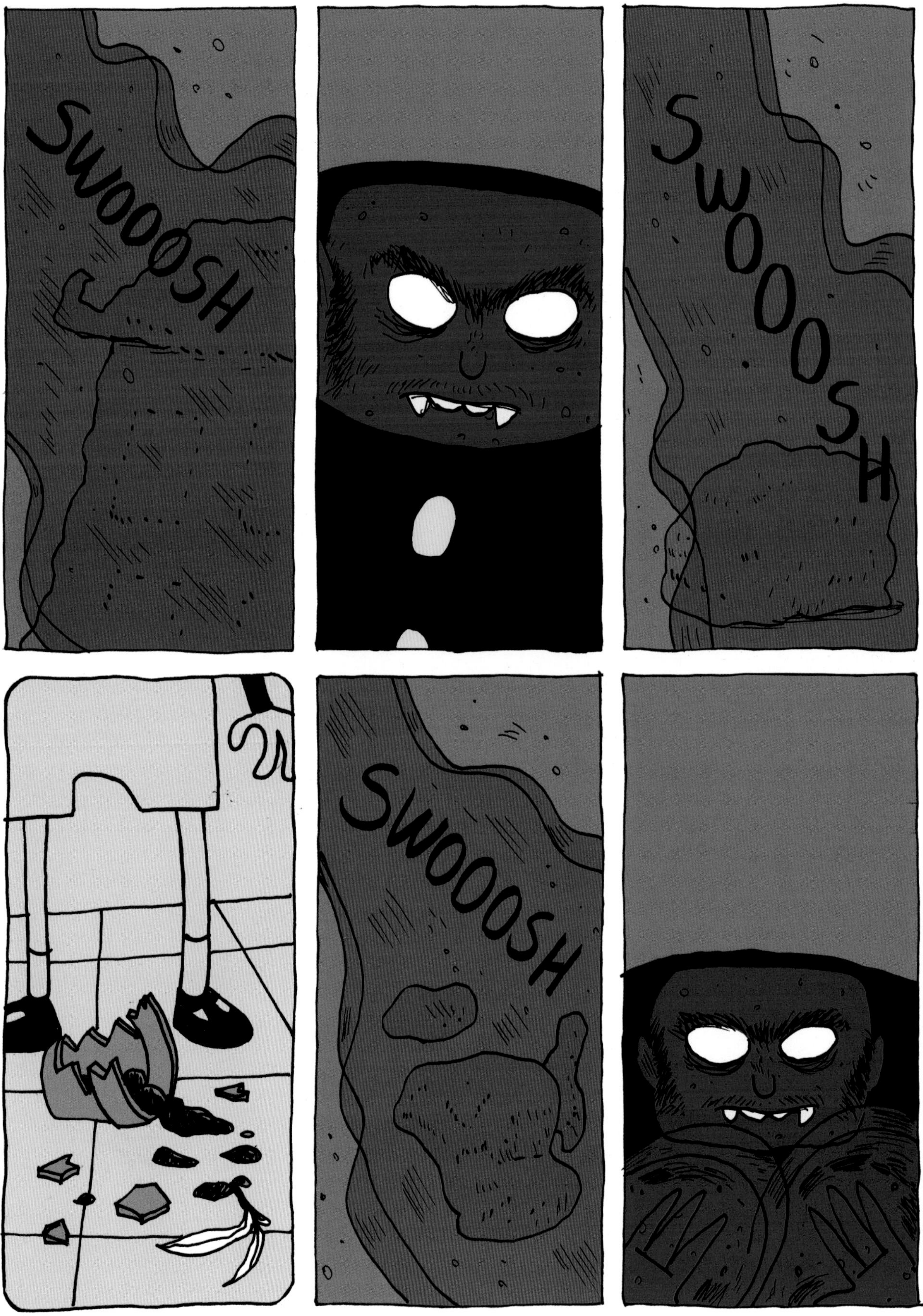
SWOOOSH
SWOOOSH
SWOOOSH

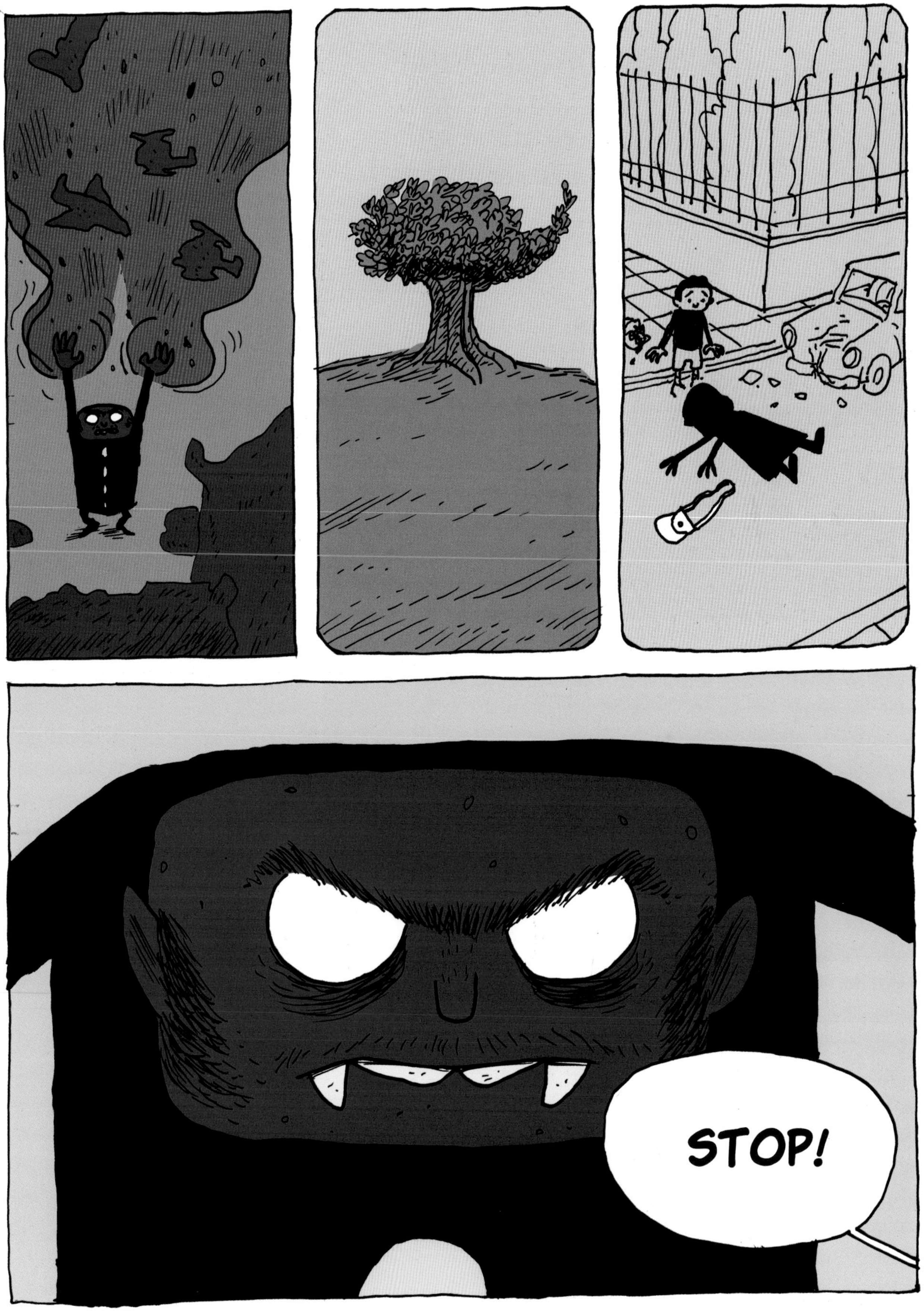
STOP!

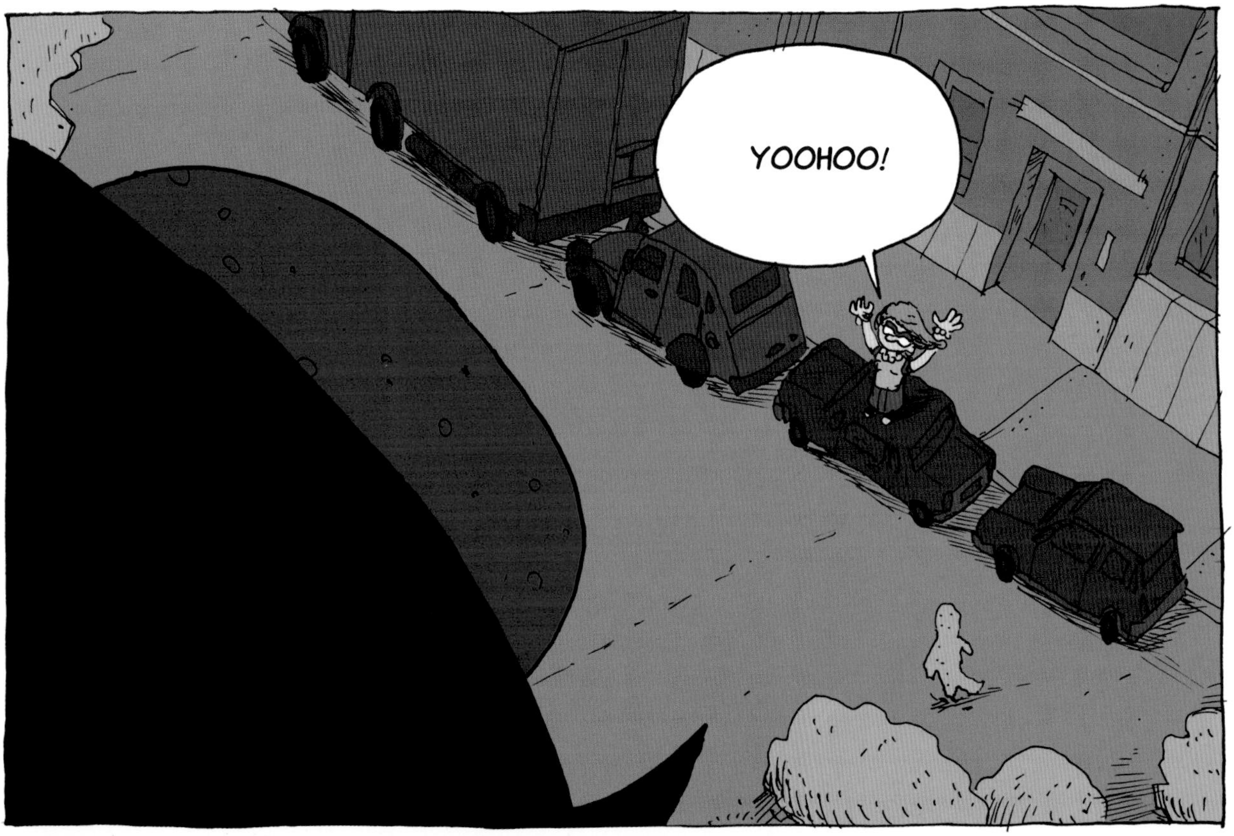
YOOHOO!

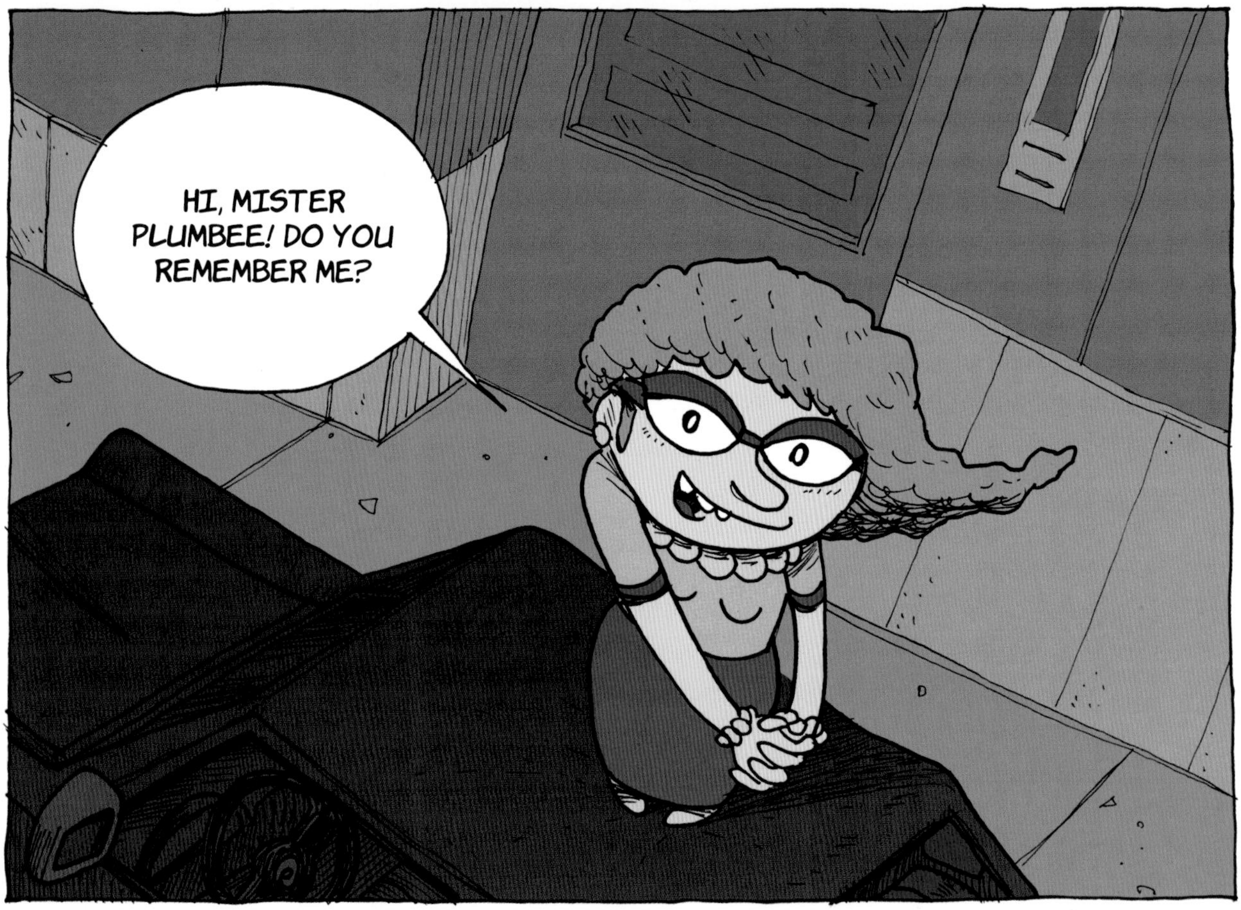
HI, MISTER PLUMBEE! DO YOU REMEMBER ME?

IT'S ME, MISS PINKETT!

WE MET LAST YEAR, REMEMBER? YOU CAME TO MY SCHOOL TO PRESENT THE NEW PARK PROJECT...

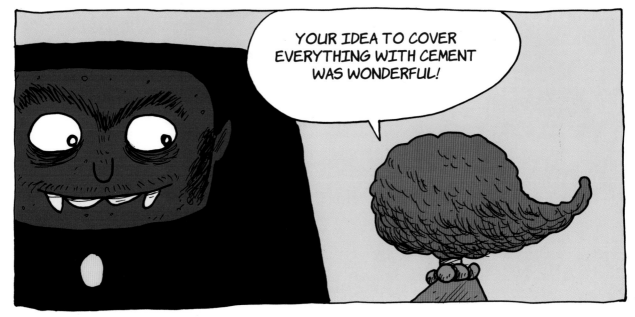

YOUR IDEA TO COVER EVERYTHING WITH CEMENT WAS WONDERFUL!

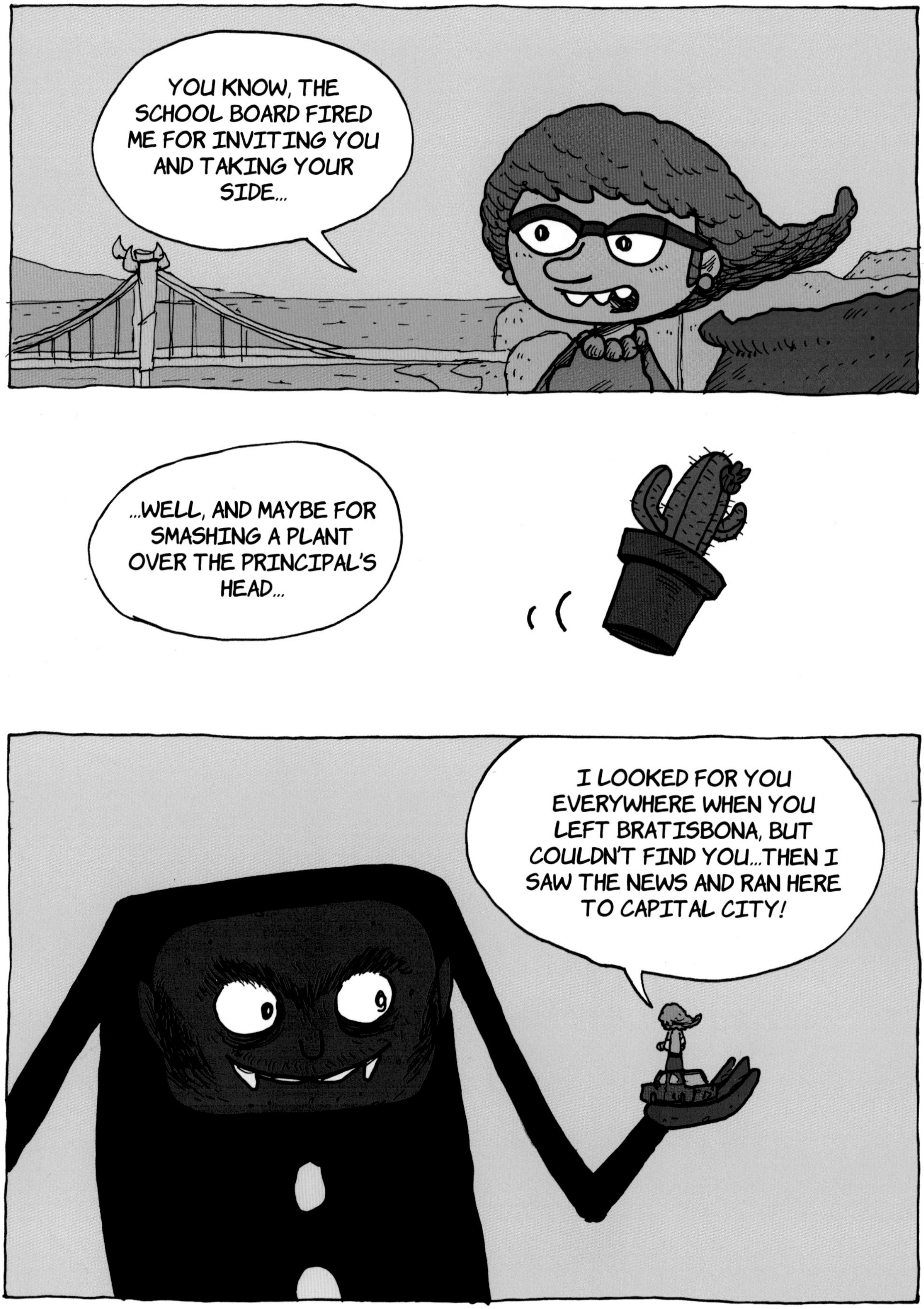
YOU KNOW, THE SCHOOL BOARD FIRED ME FOR INVITING YOU AND TAKING YOUR SIDE...
...WELL, AND MAYBE FOR SMASHING A PLANT OVER THE PRINCIPAL'S HEAD...
I LOOKED FOR YOU EVERYWHERE WHEN YOU LEFT BRATISBONA, BUT COULDN'T FIND YOU...THEN I SAW THE NEWS AND RAN HERE TO CAPITAL CITY!

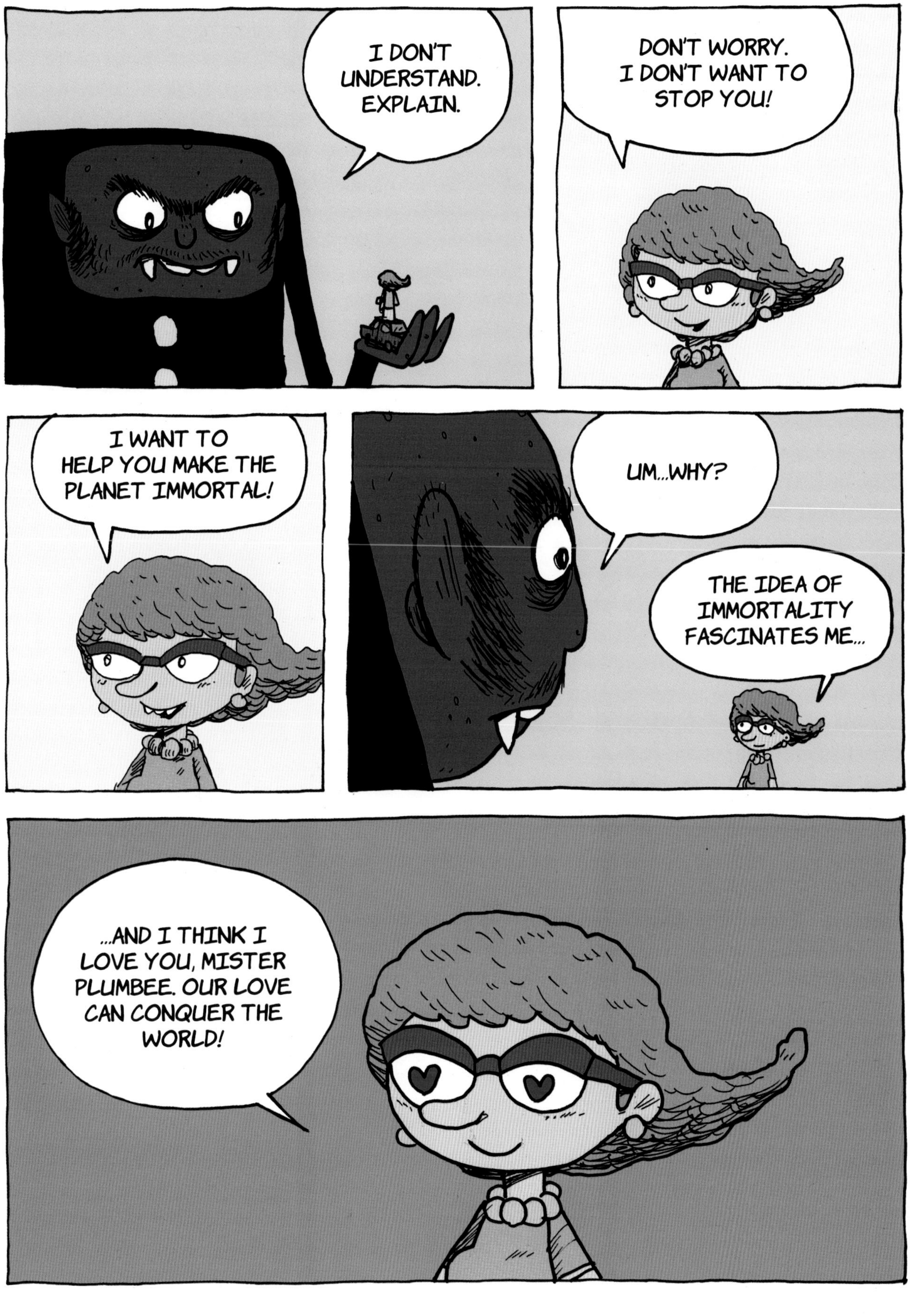
I DON'T UNDERSTAND. EXPLAIN.
DON'T WORRY. I DON'T WANT TO STOP YOU!
I WANT TO HELP YOU MAKE THE PLANET IMMORTAL!
UM...WHY?
THE IDEA OF IMMORTALITY FASCINATES ME...
...AND I THINK I LOVE YOU, MISTER PLUMBEE. OUR LOVE CAN CONQUER THE WORLD!

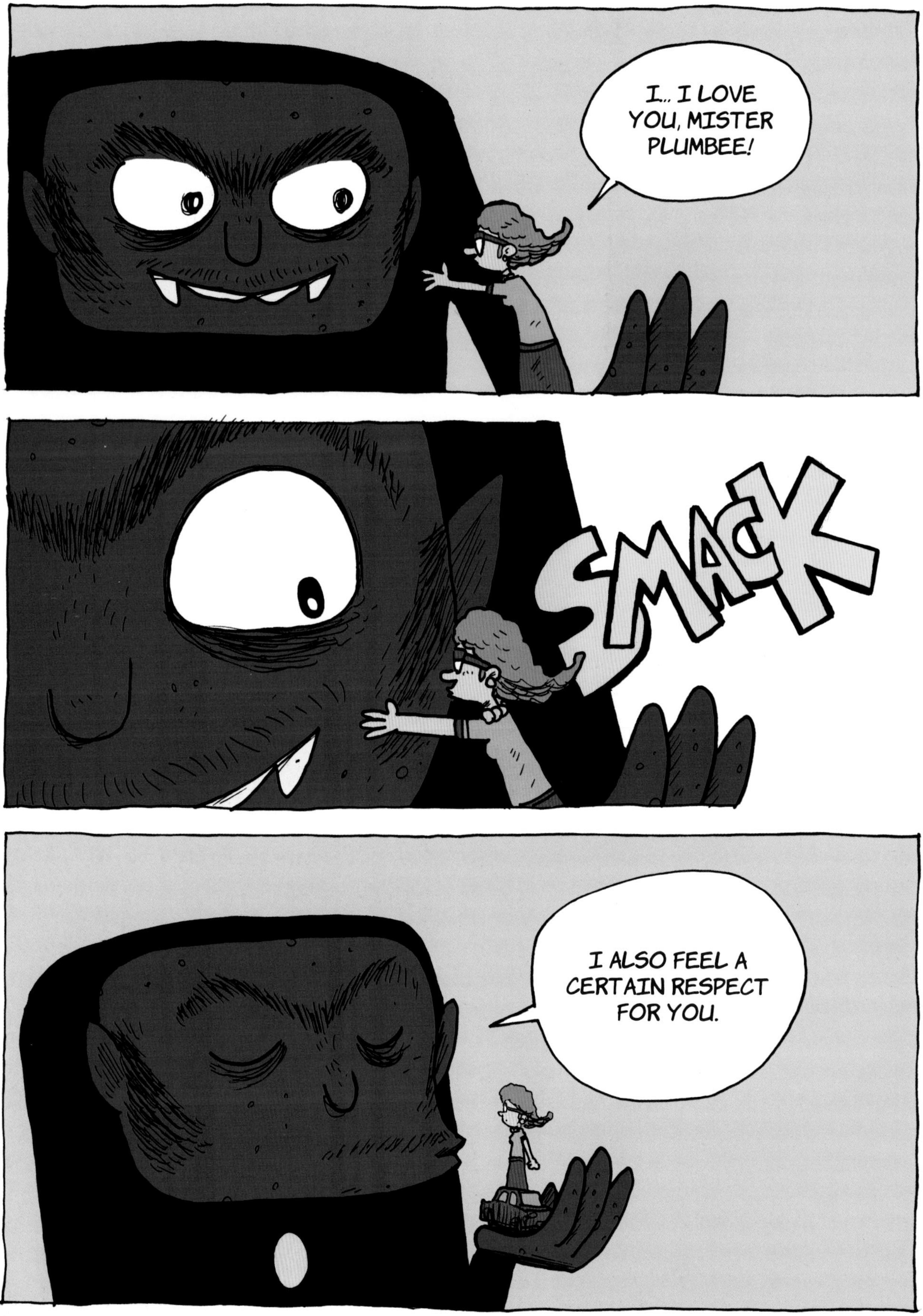
I... I LOVE YOU, MISTER PLUMBEE!
SMACK
I ALSO FEEL A CERTAIN RESPECT FOR YOU.

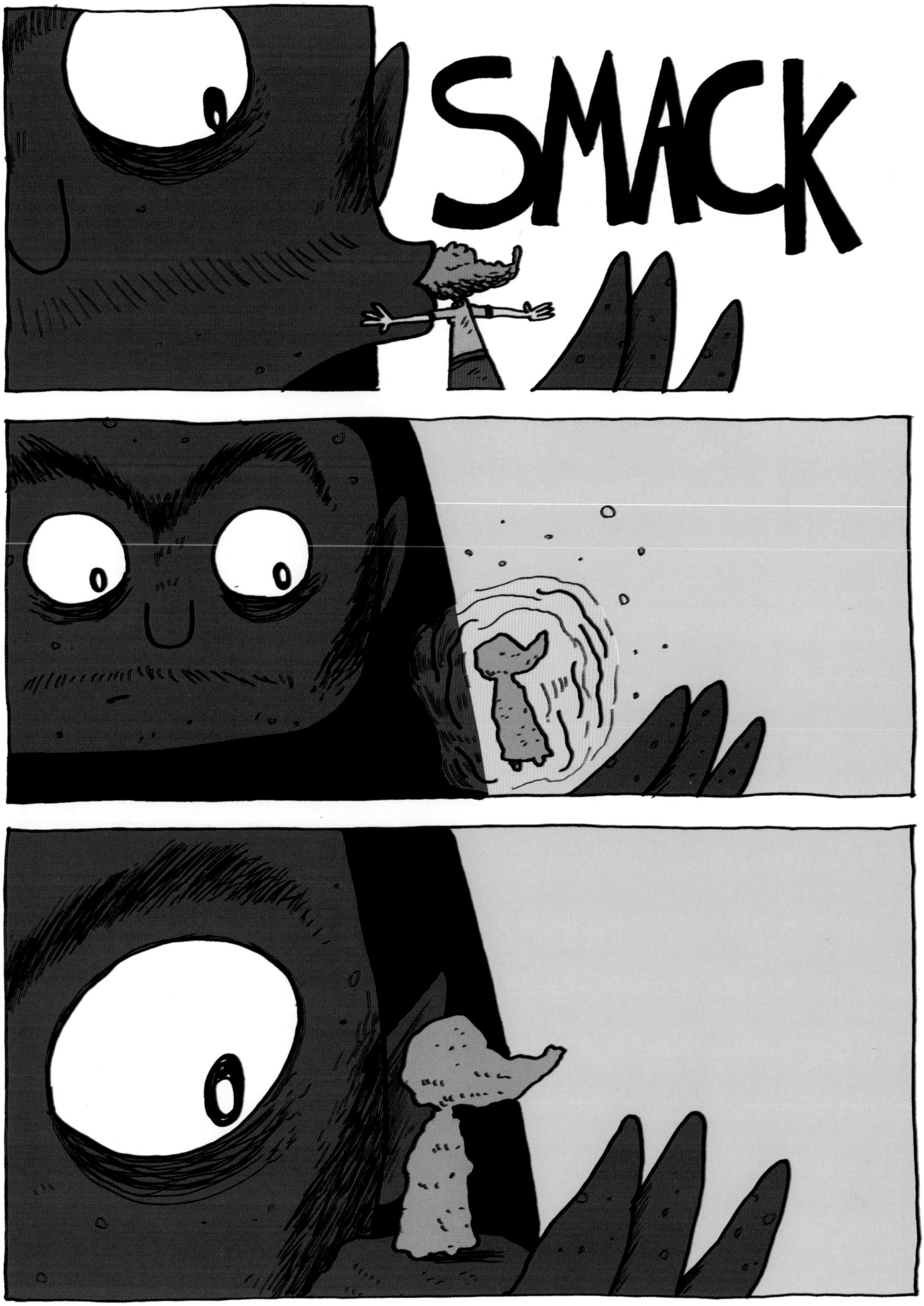
SMACK

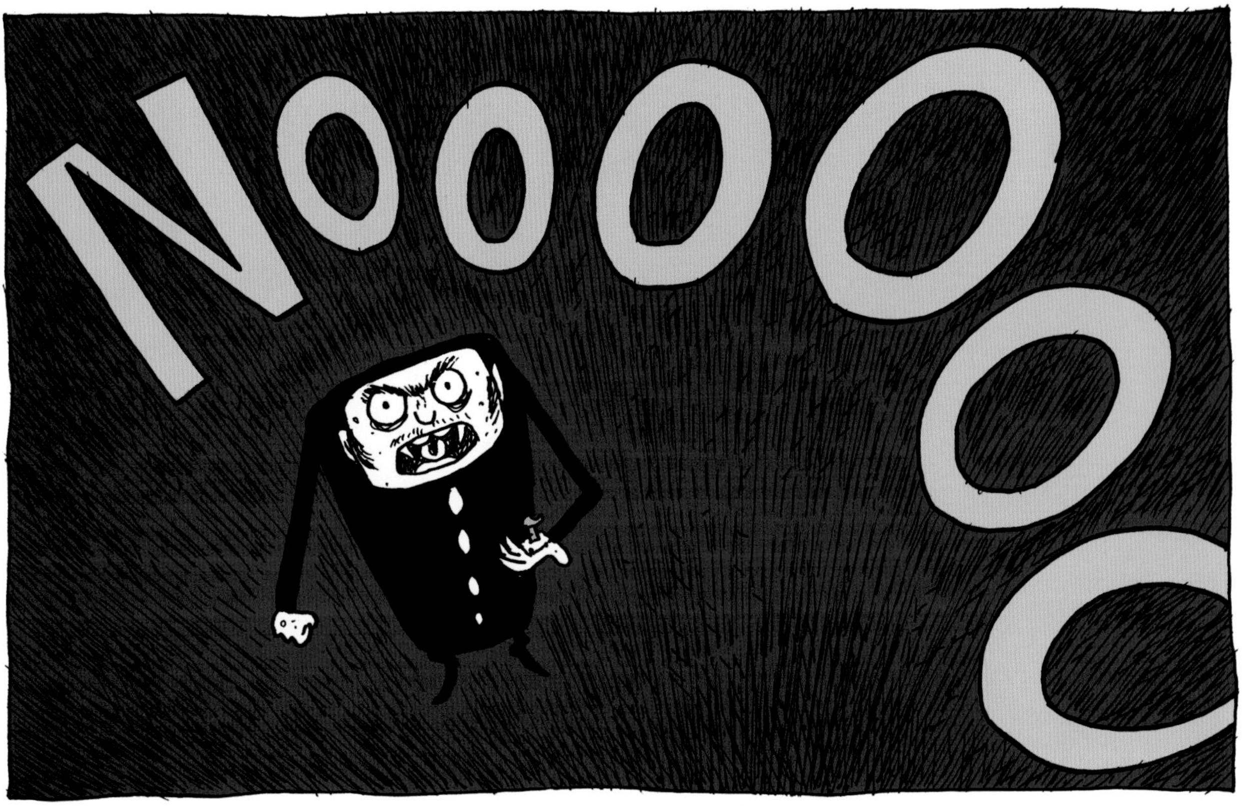
NOOOOOO

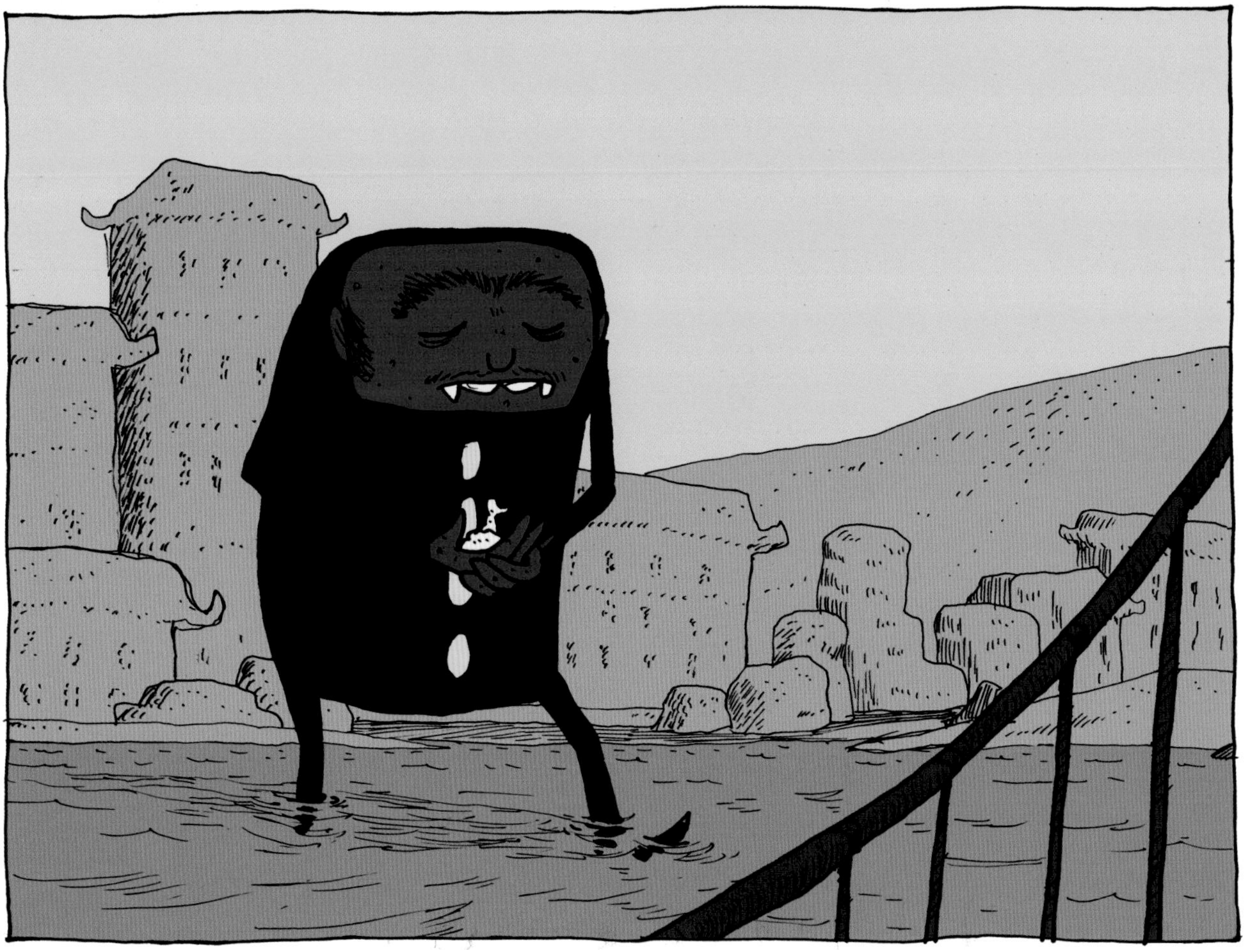

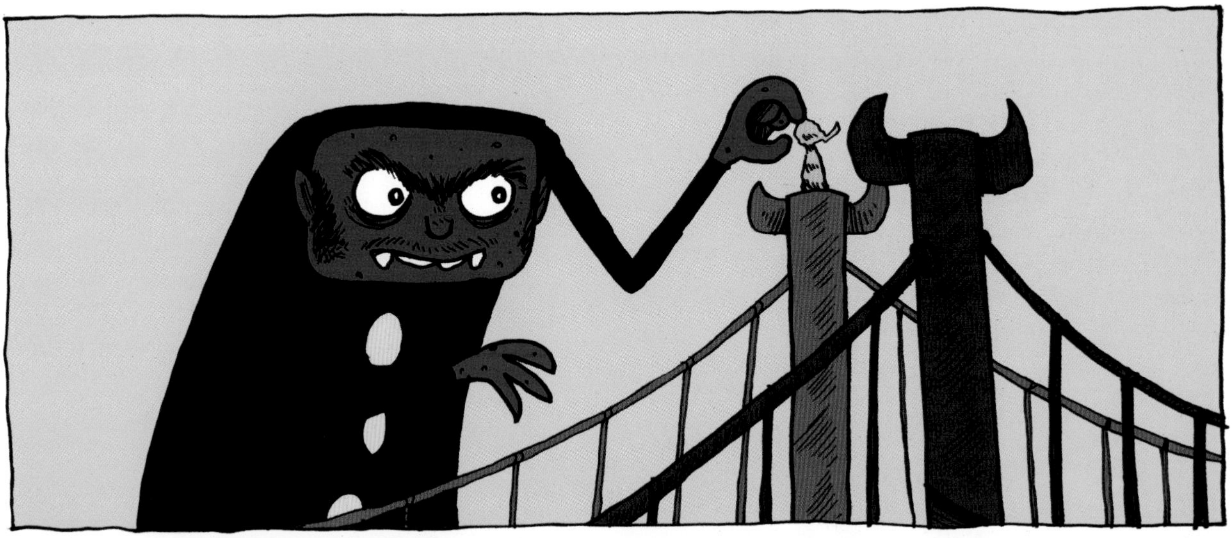

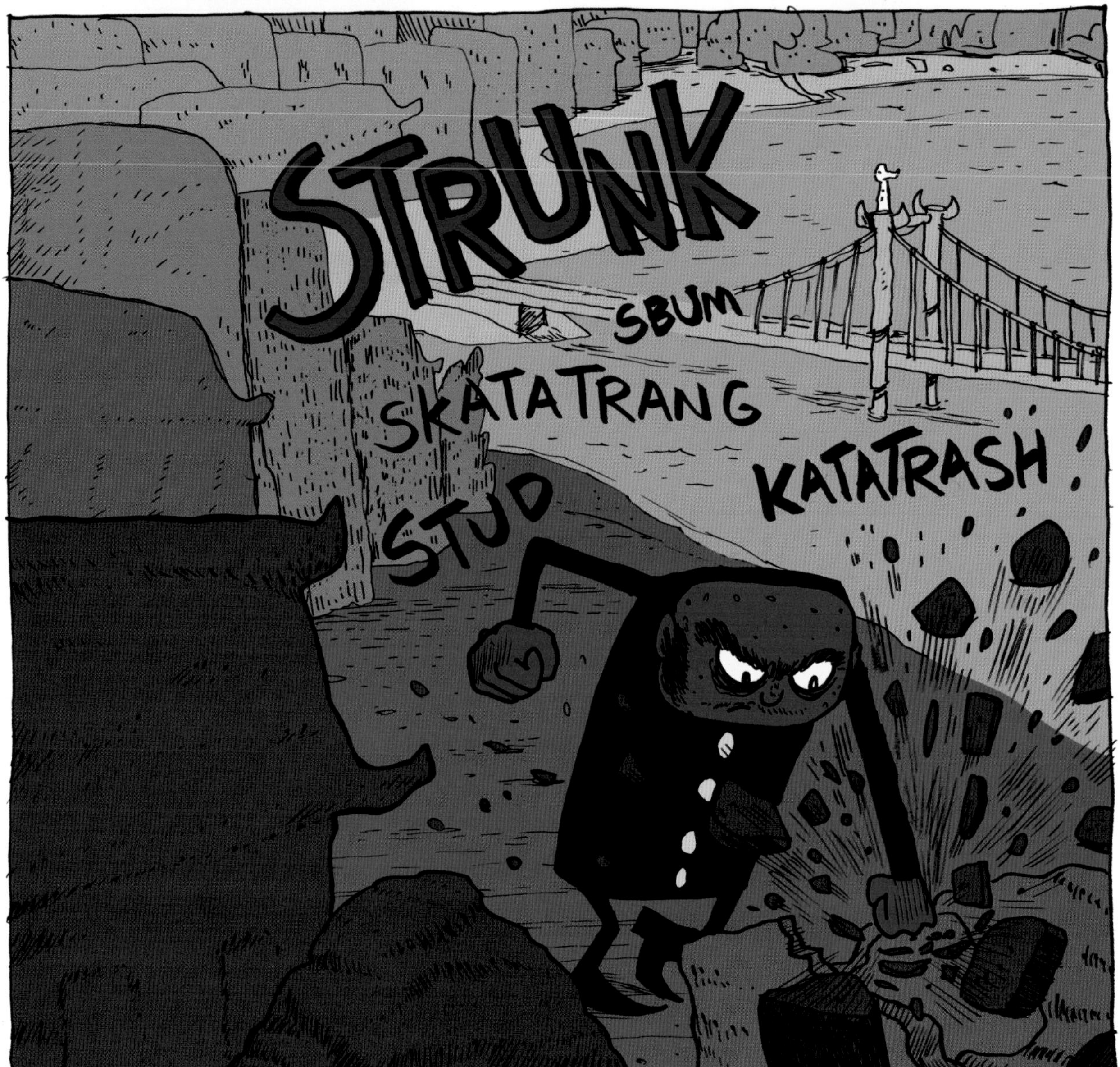
STRUNK
SBUM
SKATATRANG
KATATRASH
STUD

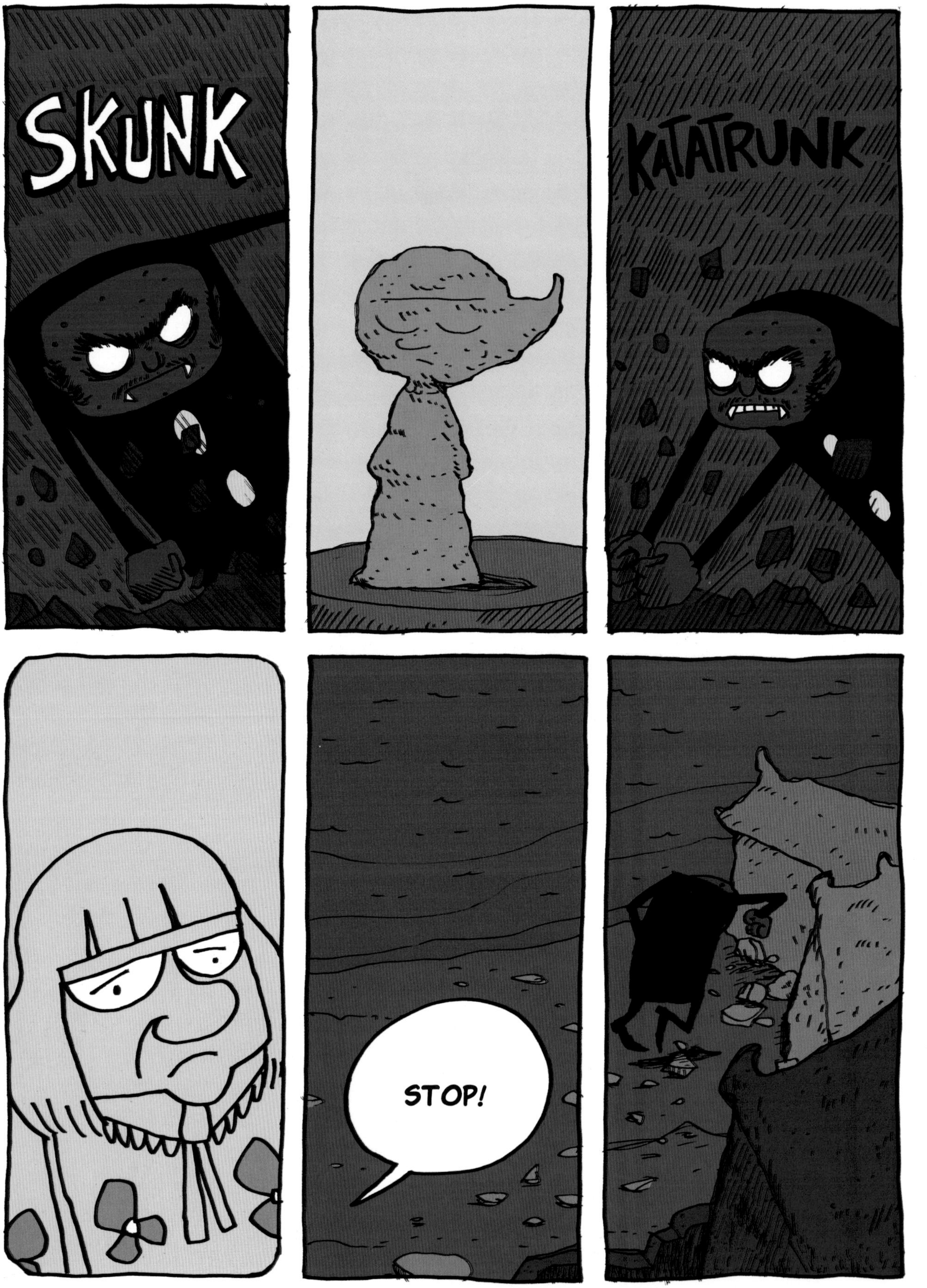
SKUNK
KATATRUNK
STOP!

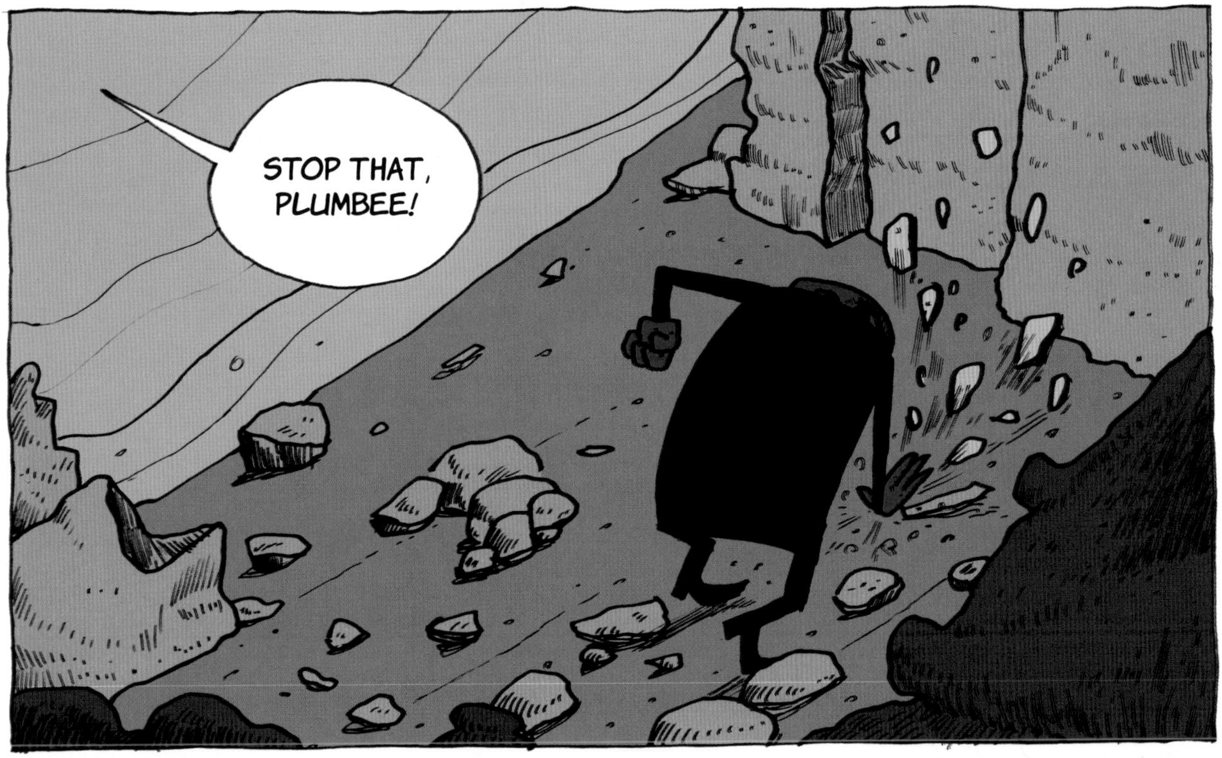
STOP THAT, PLUMBEE!

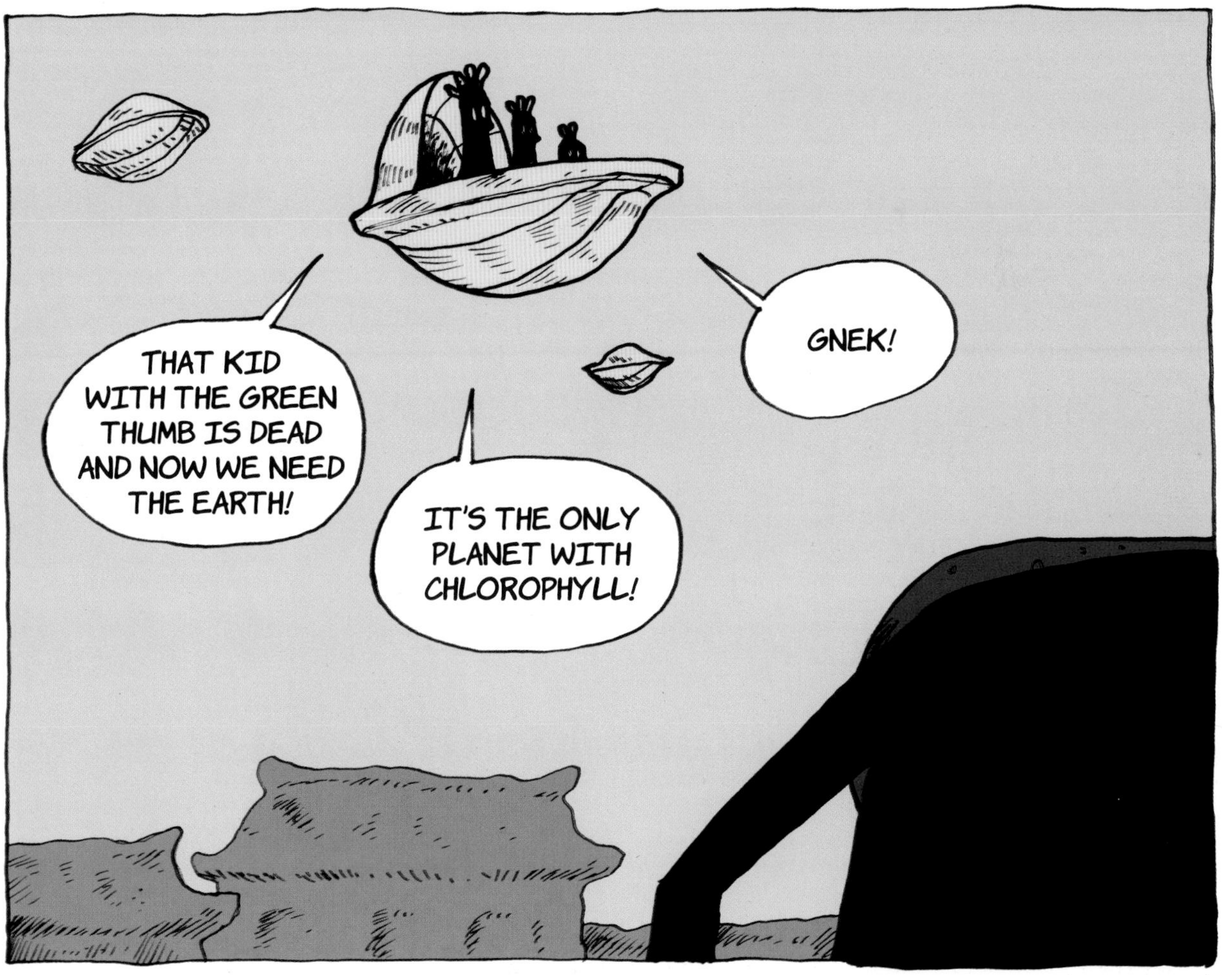
THAT KID WITH THE GREEN THUMB IS DEAD AND NOW WE NEED THE EARTH!
IT'S THE ONLY PLANET WITH CHLOROPHYLL!
GNEK!

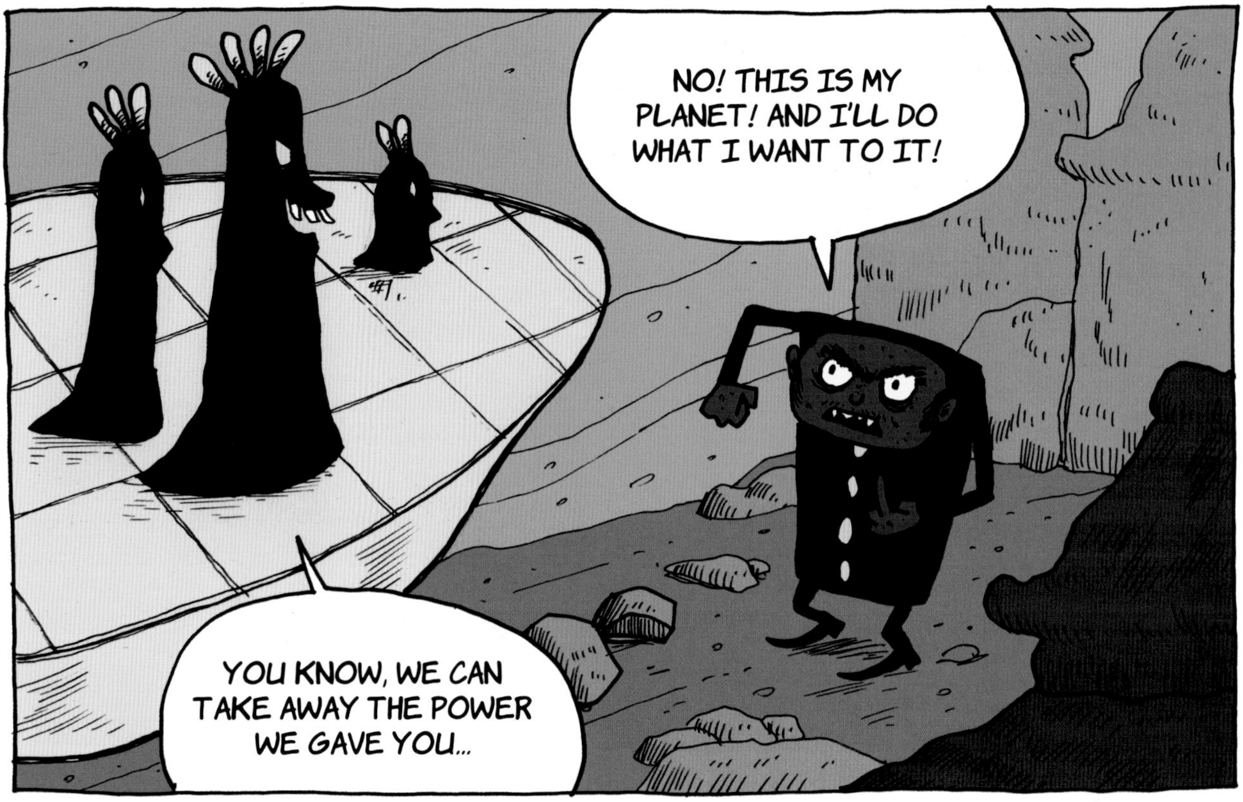
NO! THIS IS MY PLANET! AND I'LL DO WHAT I WANT TO IT!
YOU KNOW, WE CAN TAKE AWAY THE POWER WE GAVE YOU...

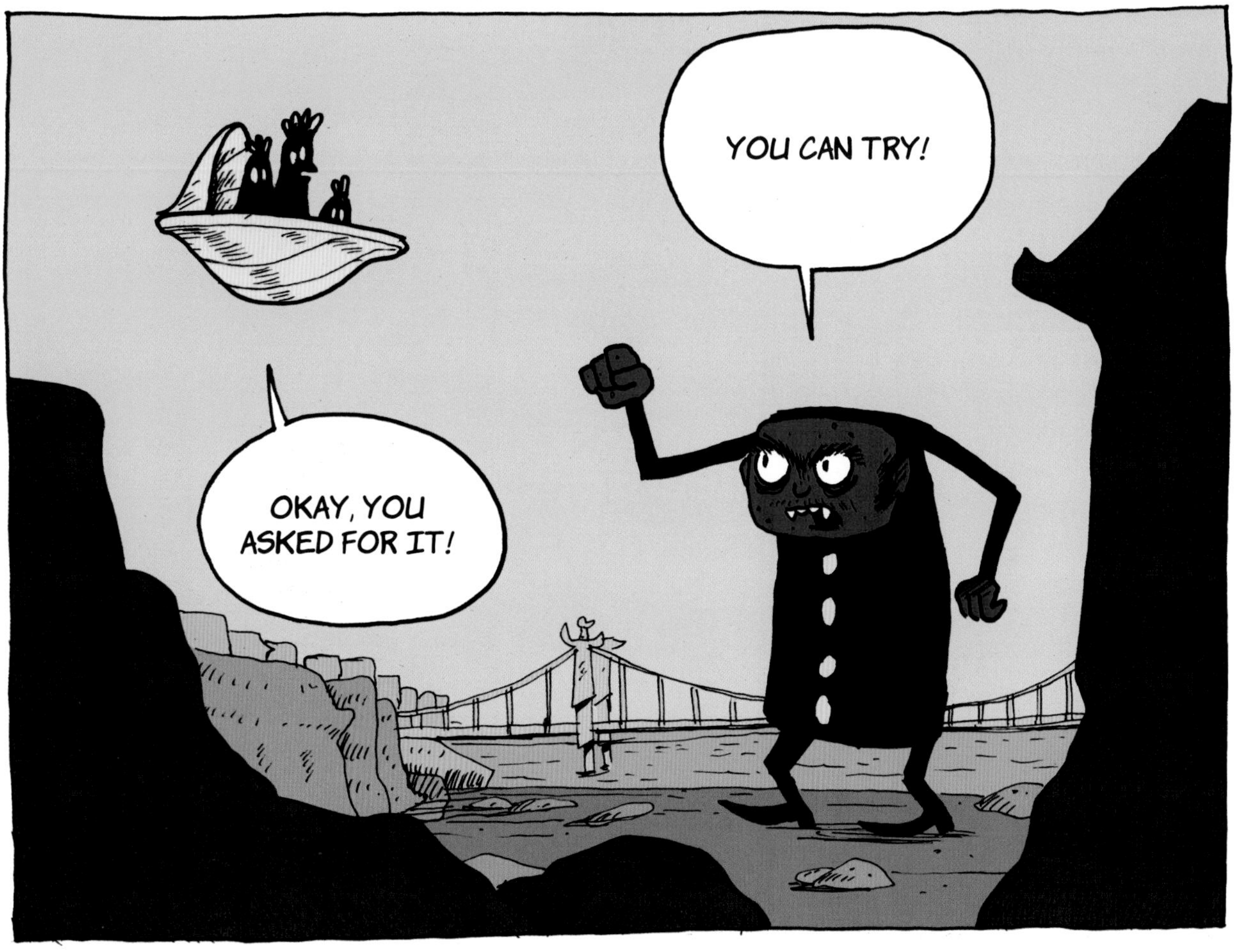
YOU CAN TRY!
OKAY, YOU ASKED FOR IT!

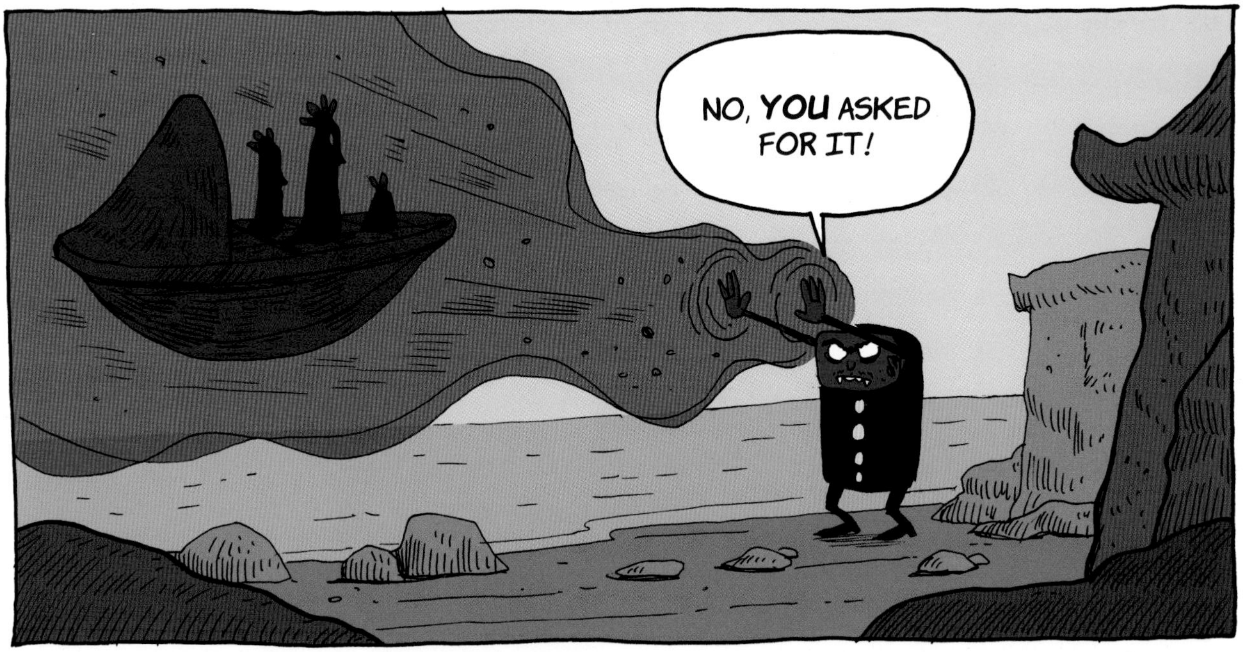
NO, YOU ASKED FOR IT!

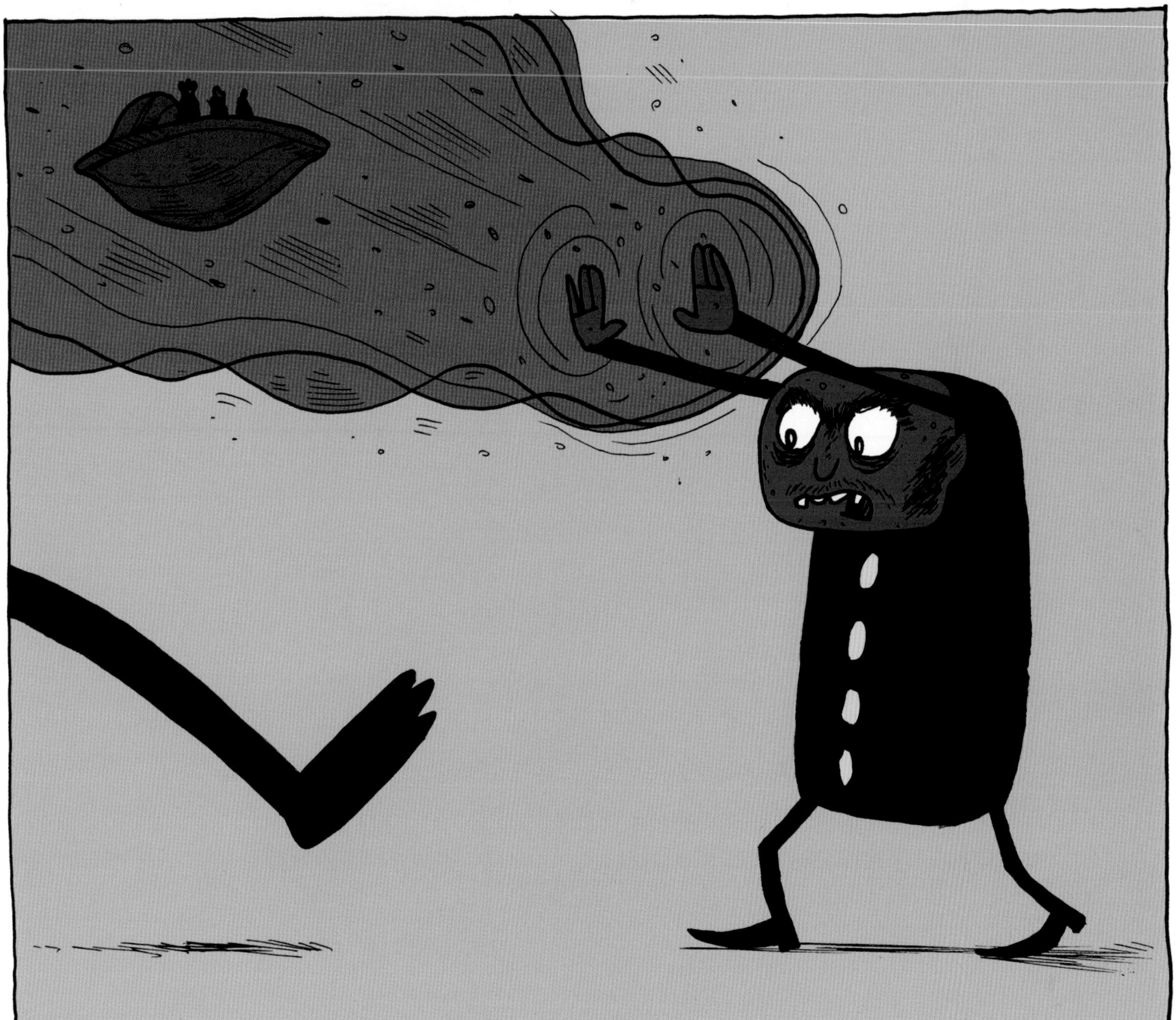

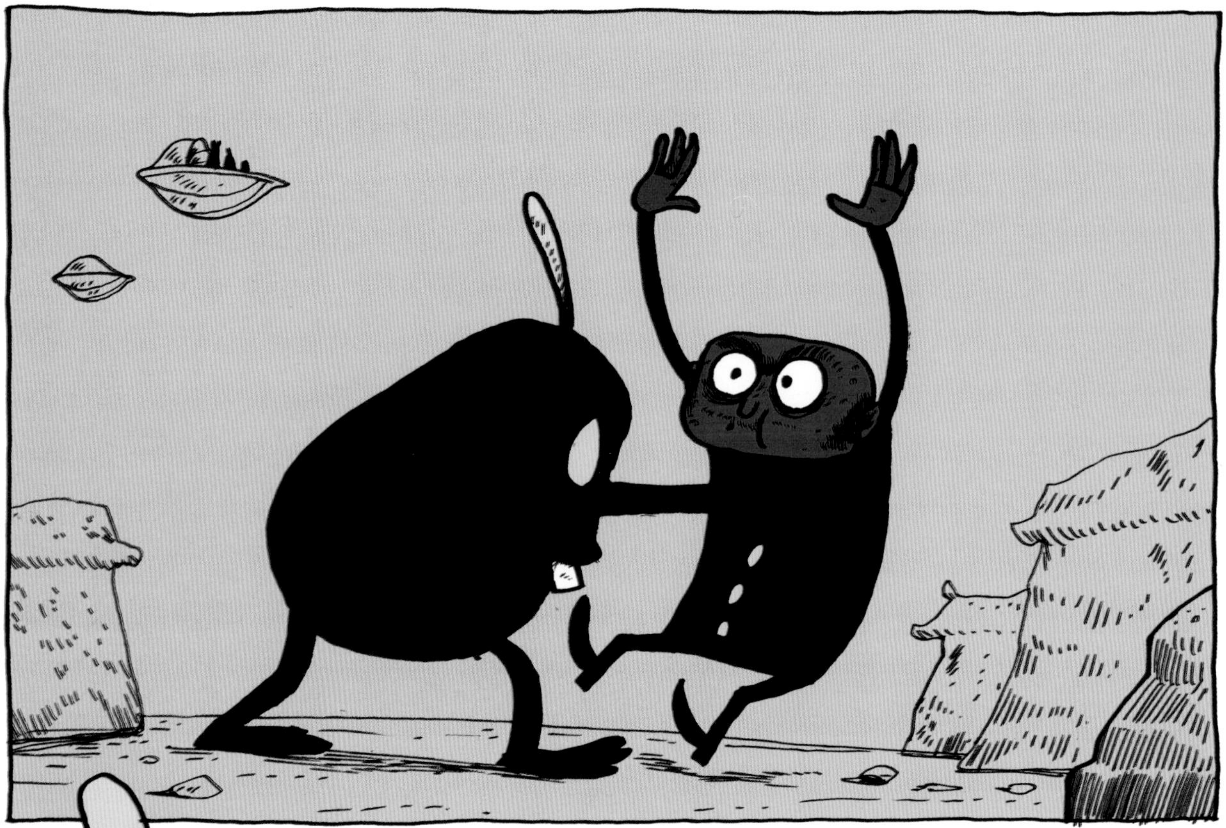

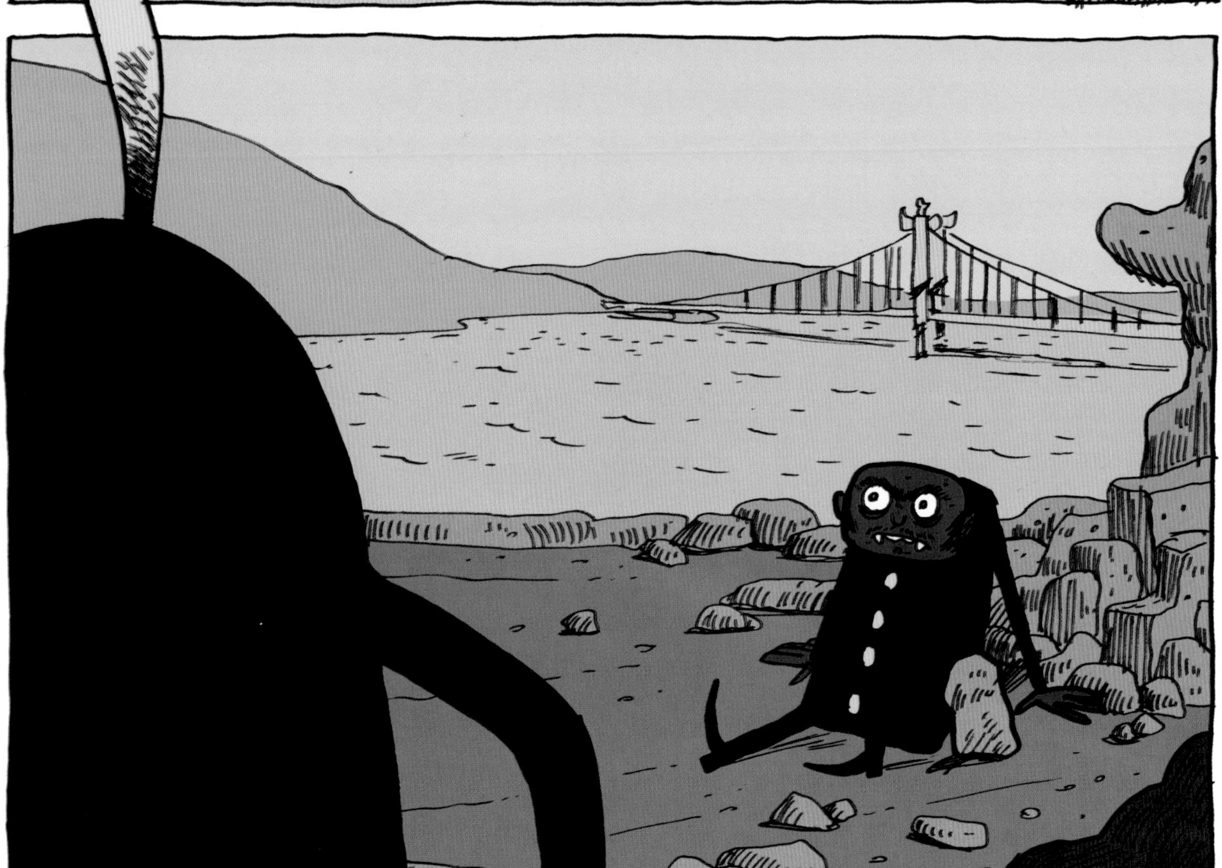

PUGN

SCHIAF

CALC

STUK

ZZOTT

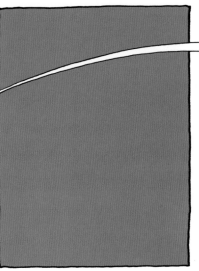

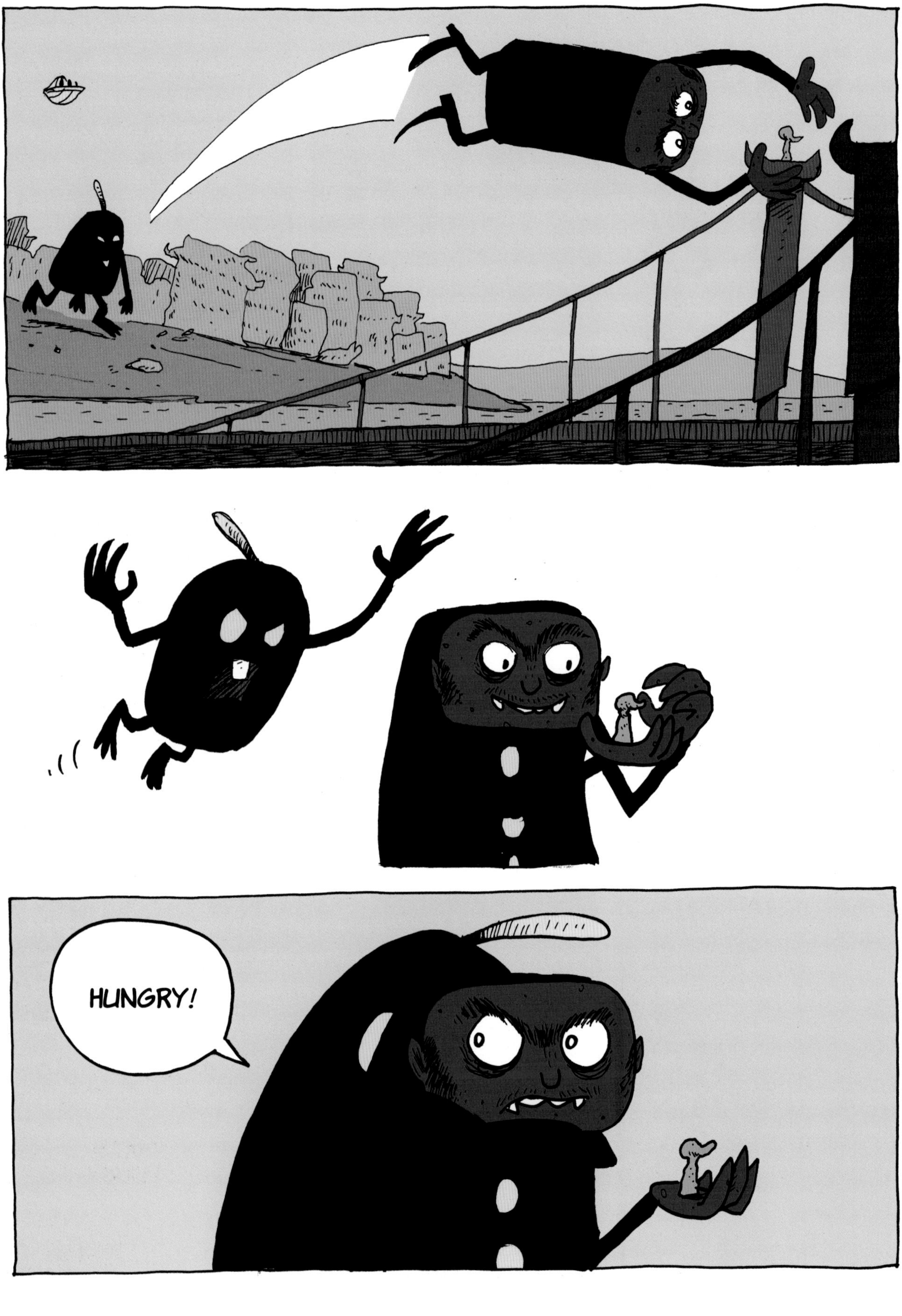
HUNGRY!

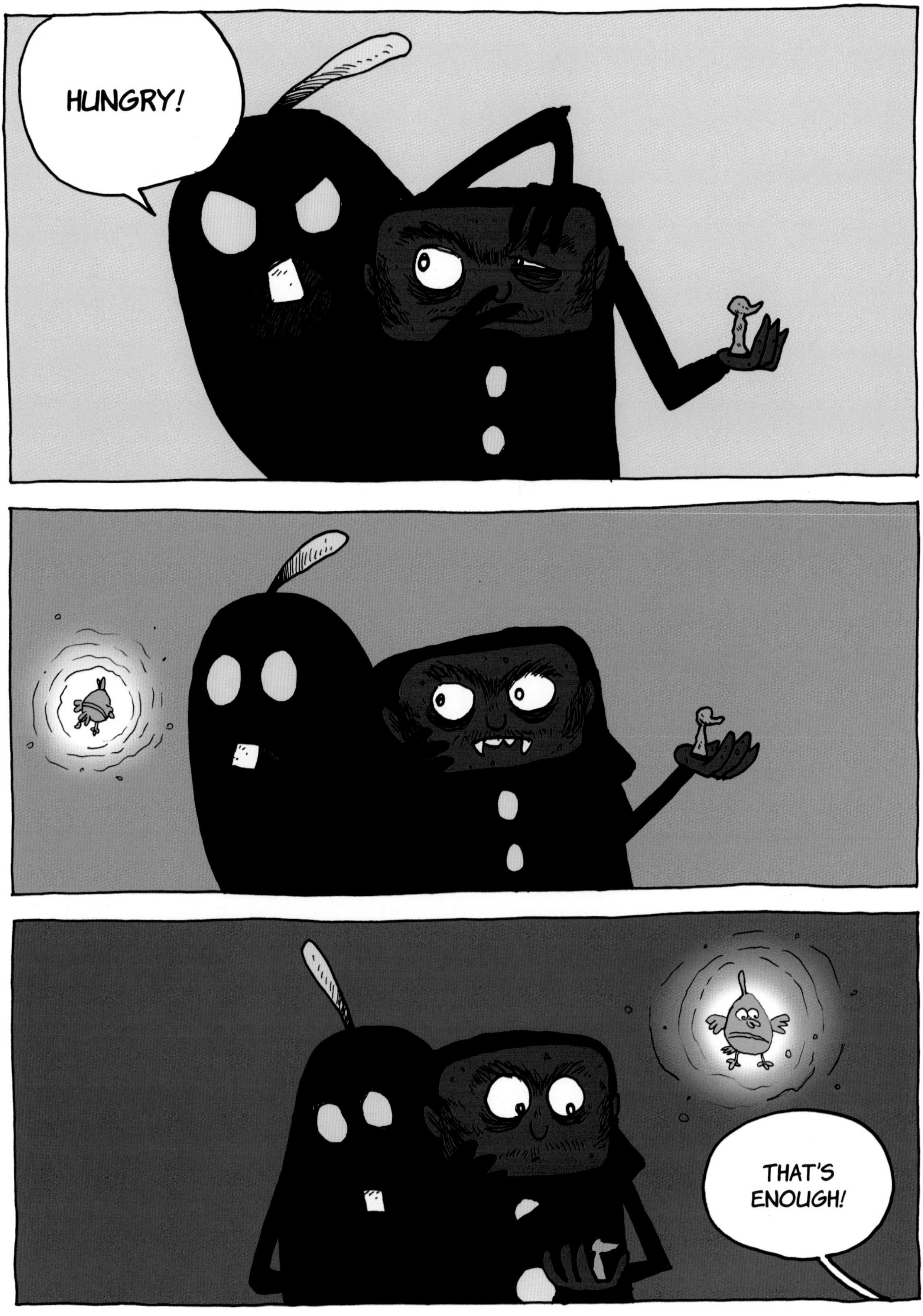
HUNGRY!
THAT'S ENOUGH!

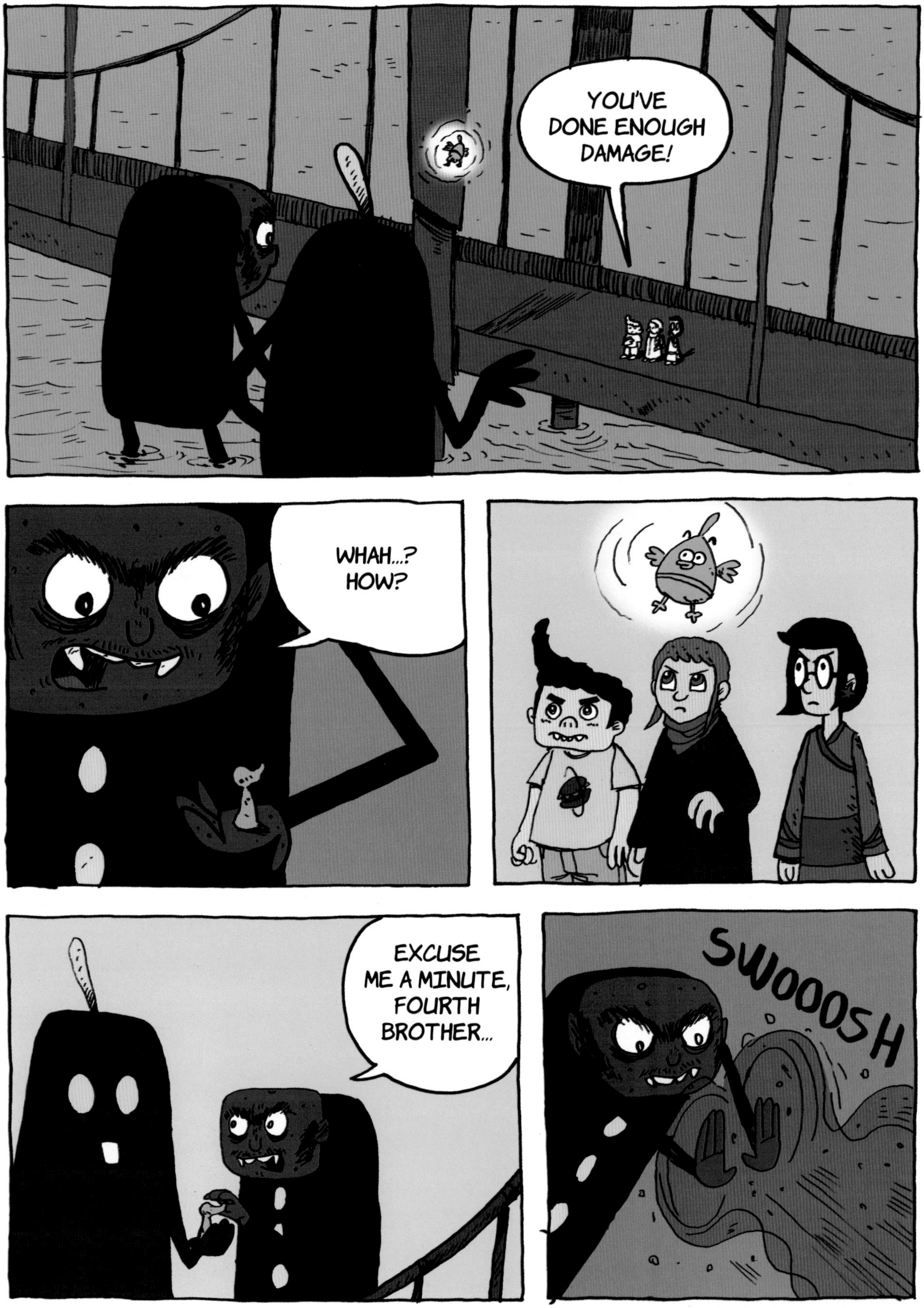
YOU'VE DONE ENOUGH DAMAGE!
WHAH...? HOW?
EXCUSE ME A MINUTE, FOURTH BROTHER...
SWOOOSH

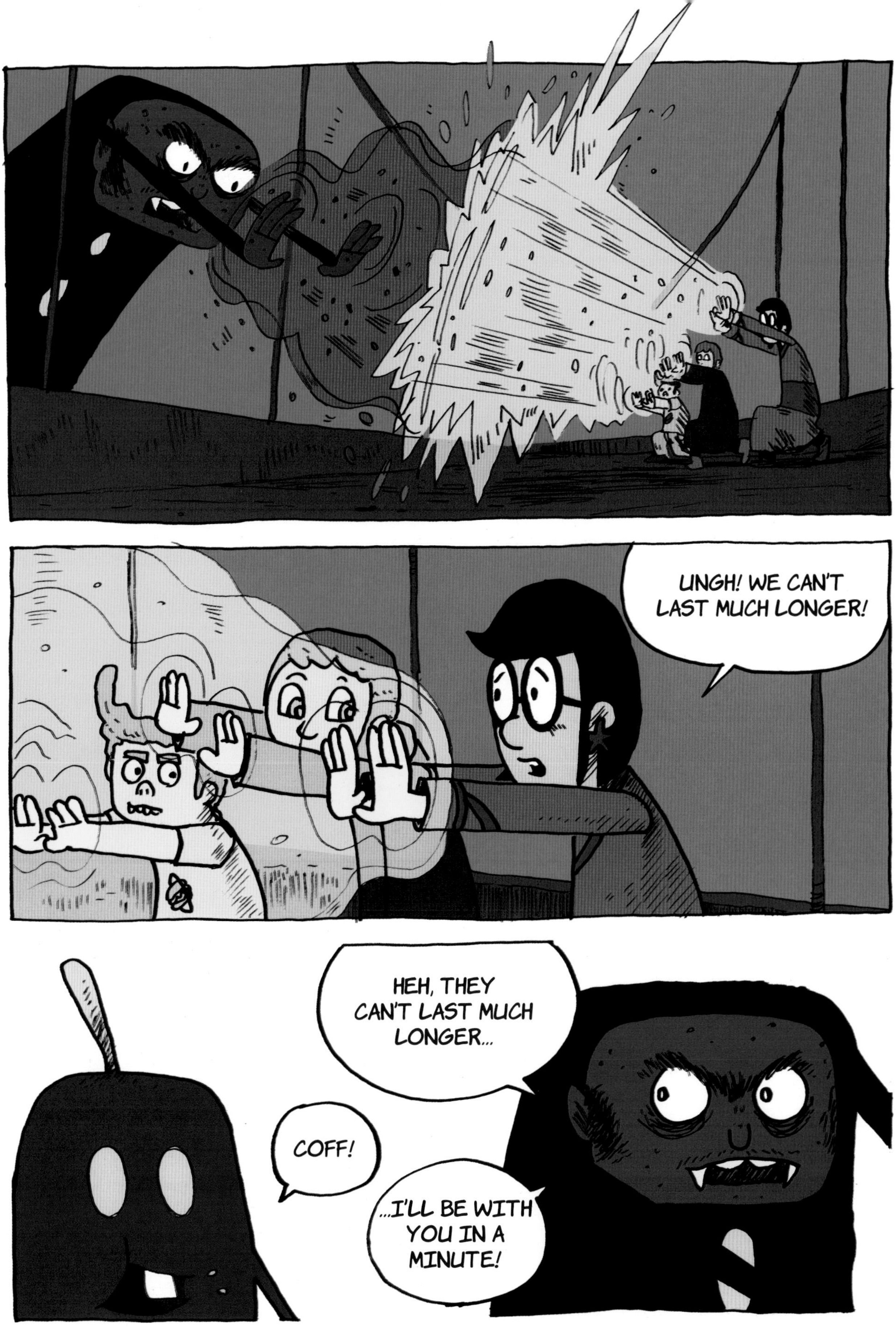
UNGH! WE CAN'T LAST MUCH LONGER!
HEH, THEY CAN'T LAST MUCH LONGER...
COFF!
...I'LL BE WITH YOU IN A MINUTE!

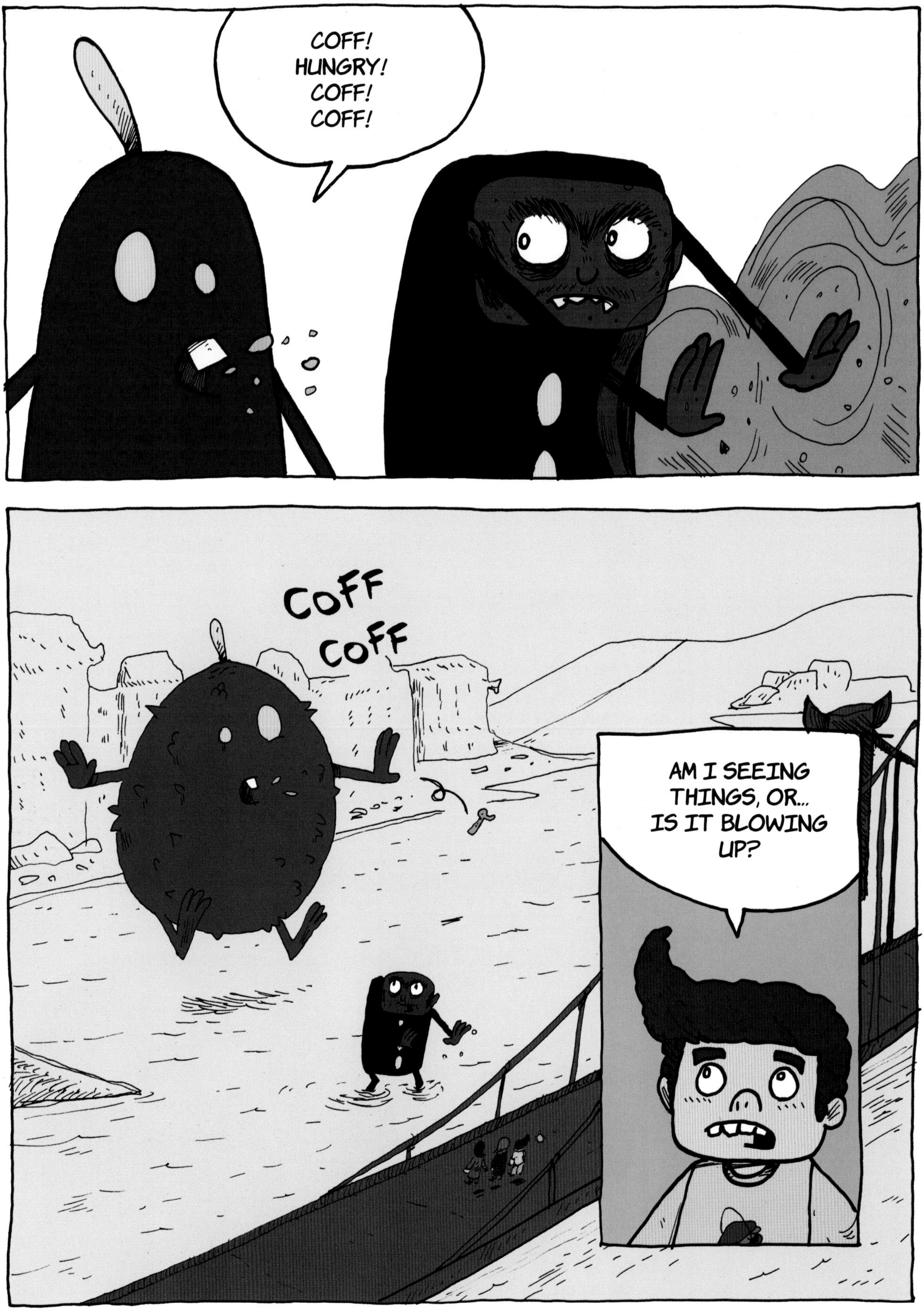
COFF! HUNGRY! COFF! COFF!
COFF COFF
AM I SEEING THINGS, OR... IS IT BLOWING UP?

CHAPTER THREE

THE GREEN
PLANET

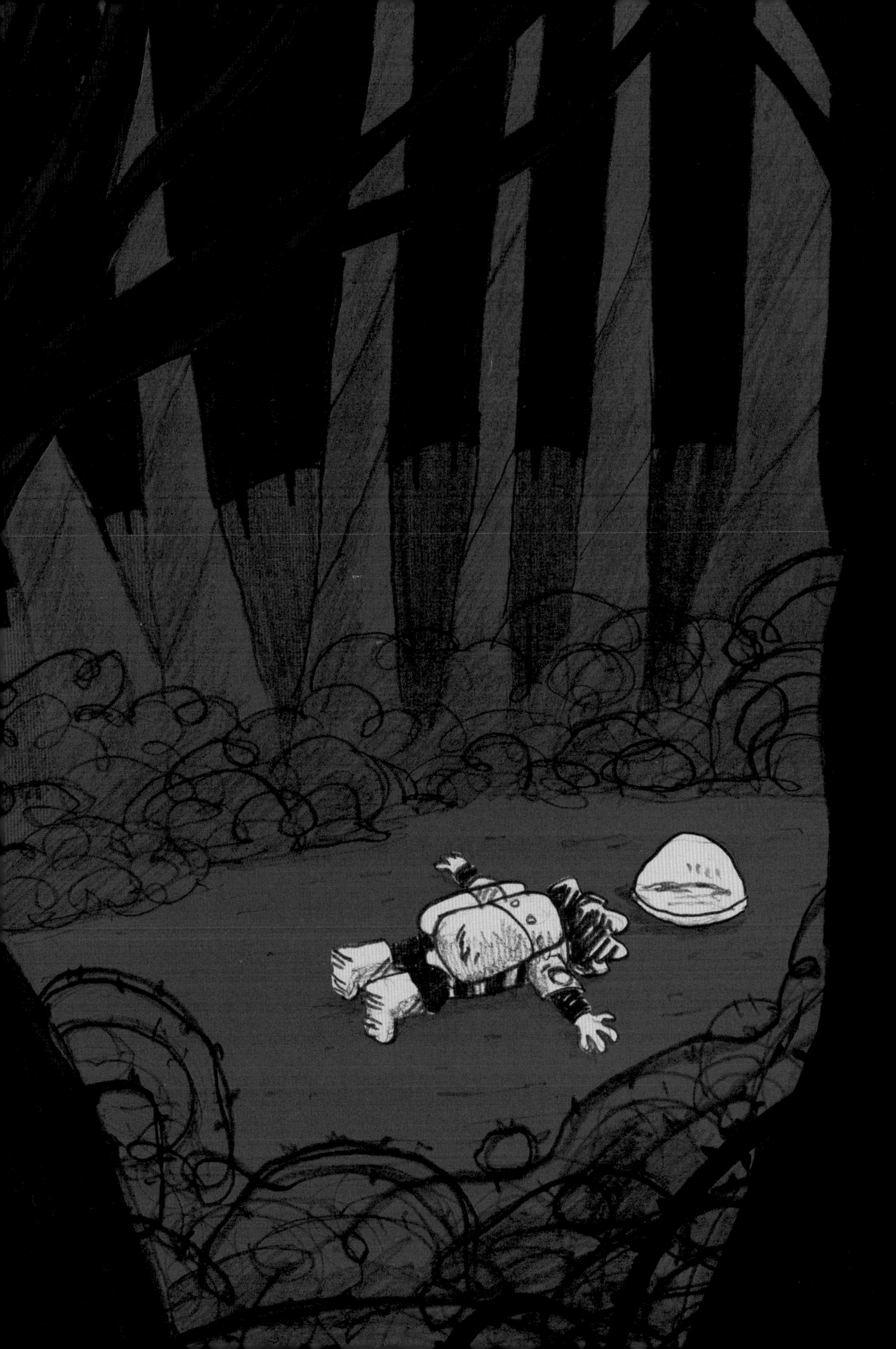

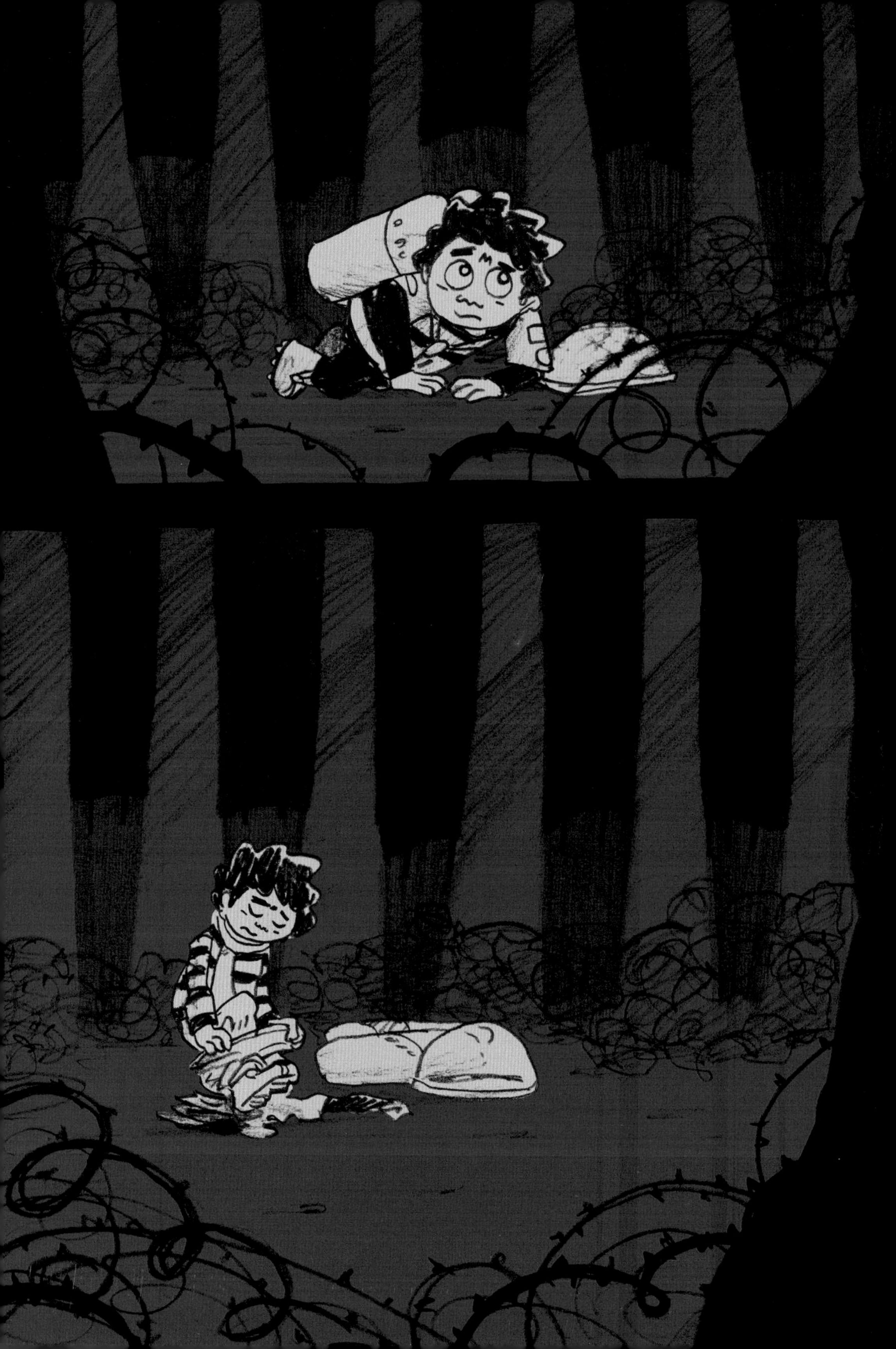

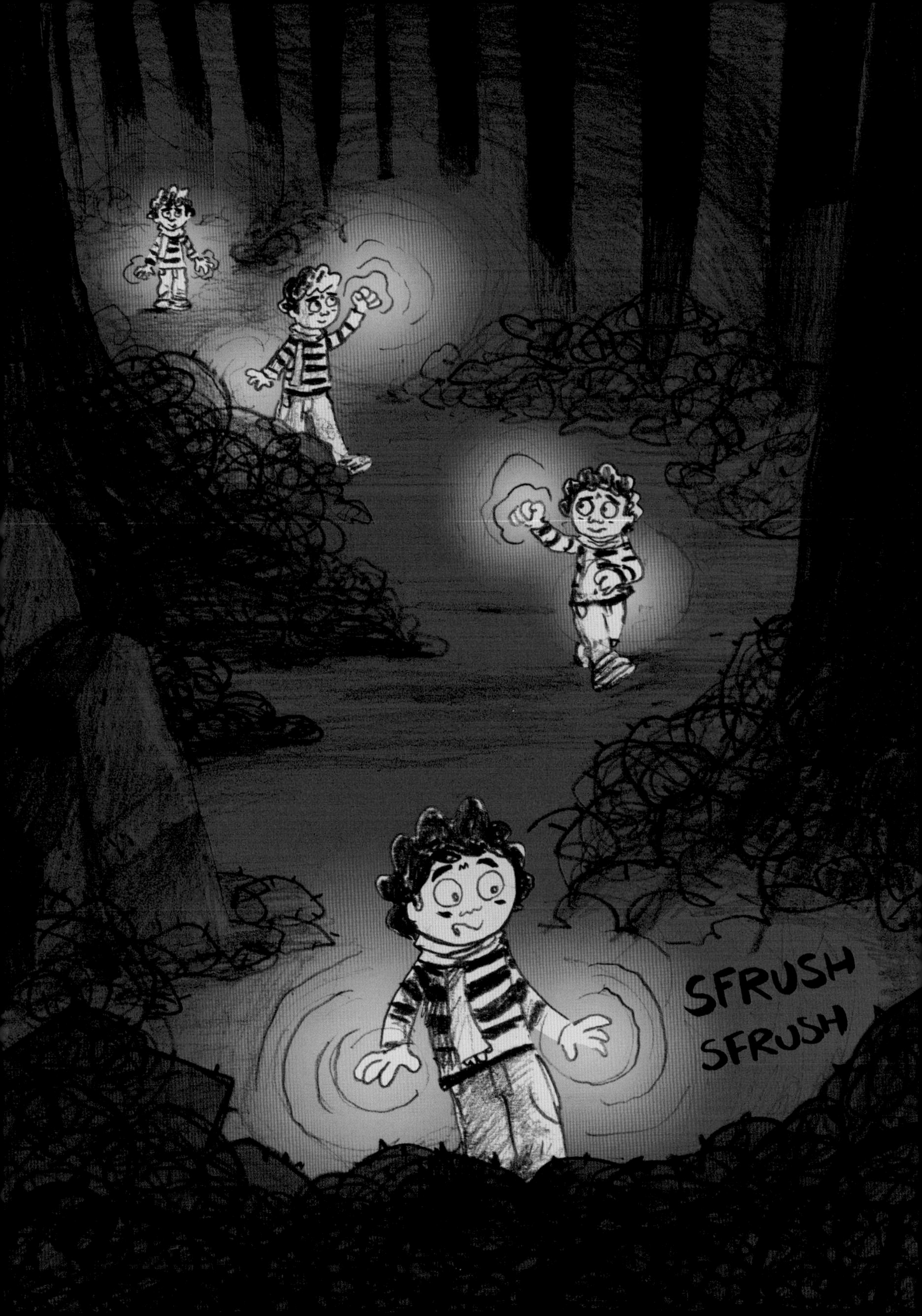
SFRUSH
SFRUSH

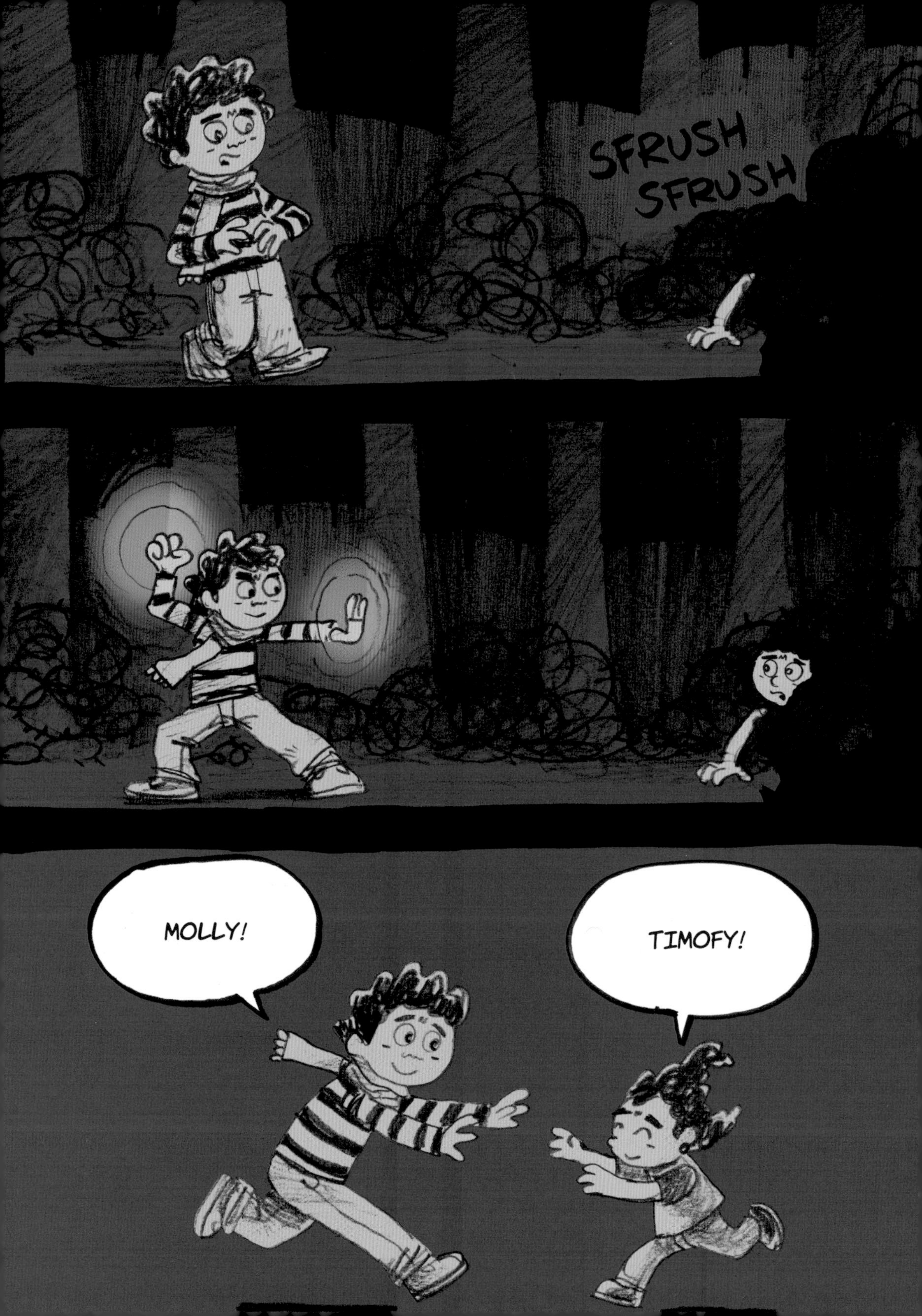
SFRUSH
SFRUSH
MOLLY!
TIMOFY!

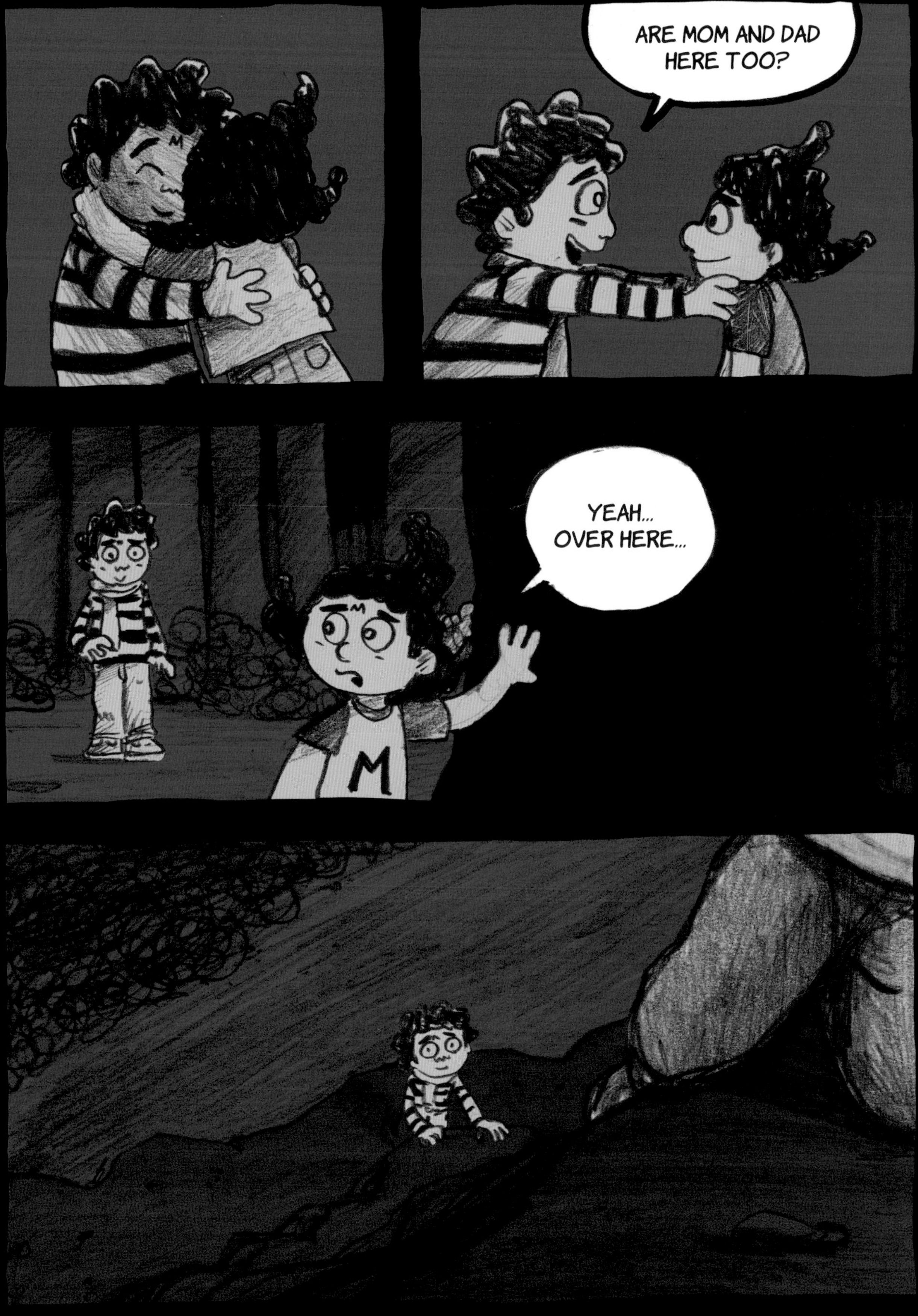
ARE MOM AND DAD HERE TOO?
YEAH... OVER HERE...

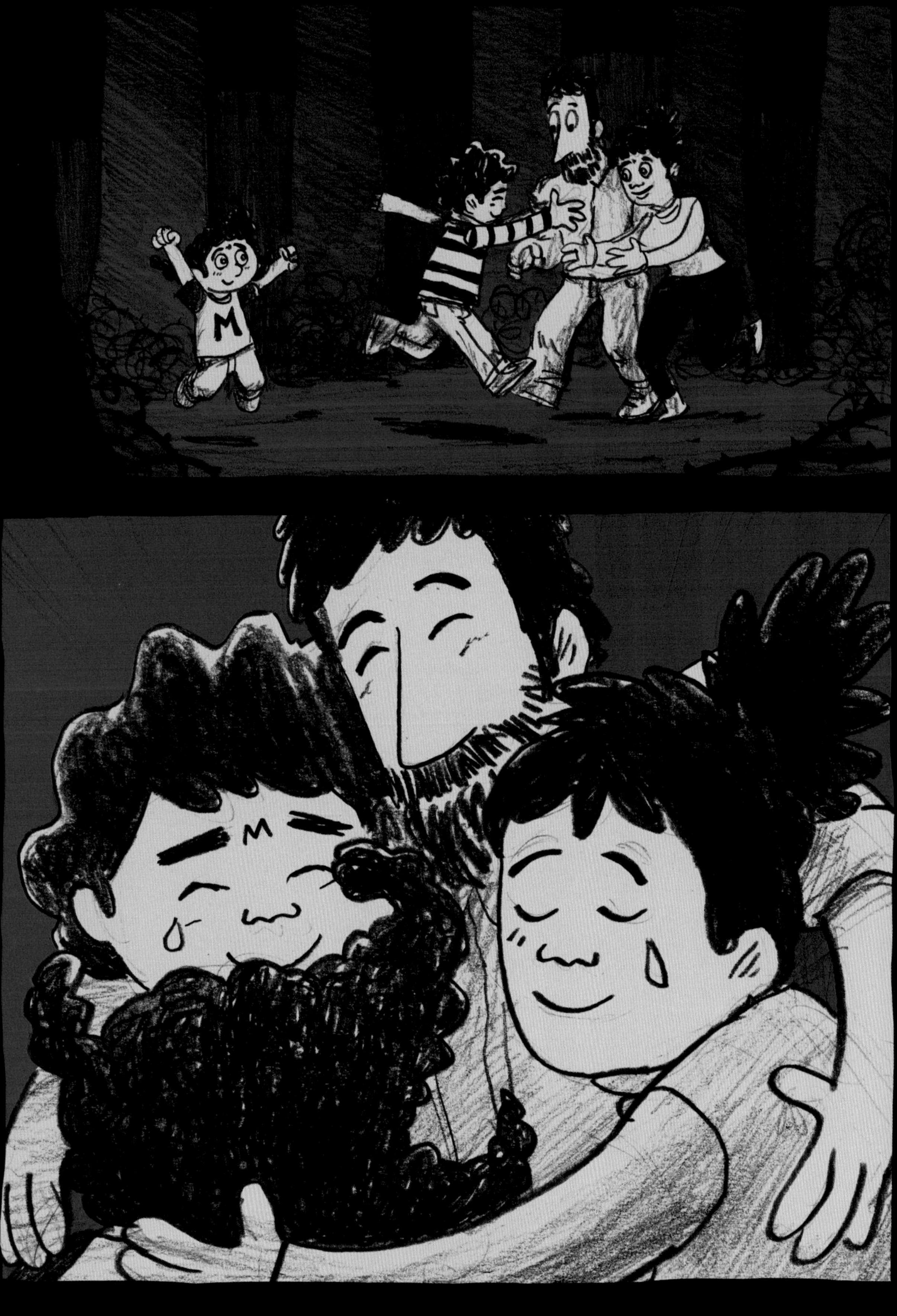

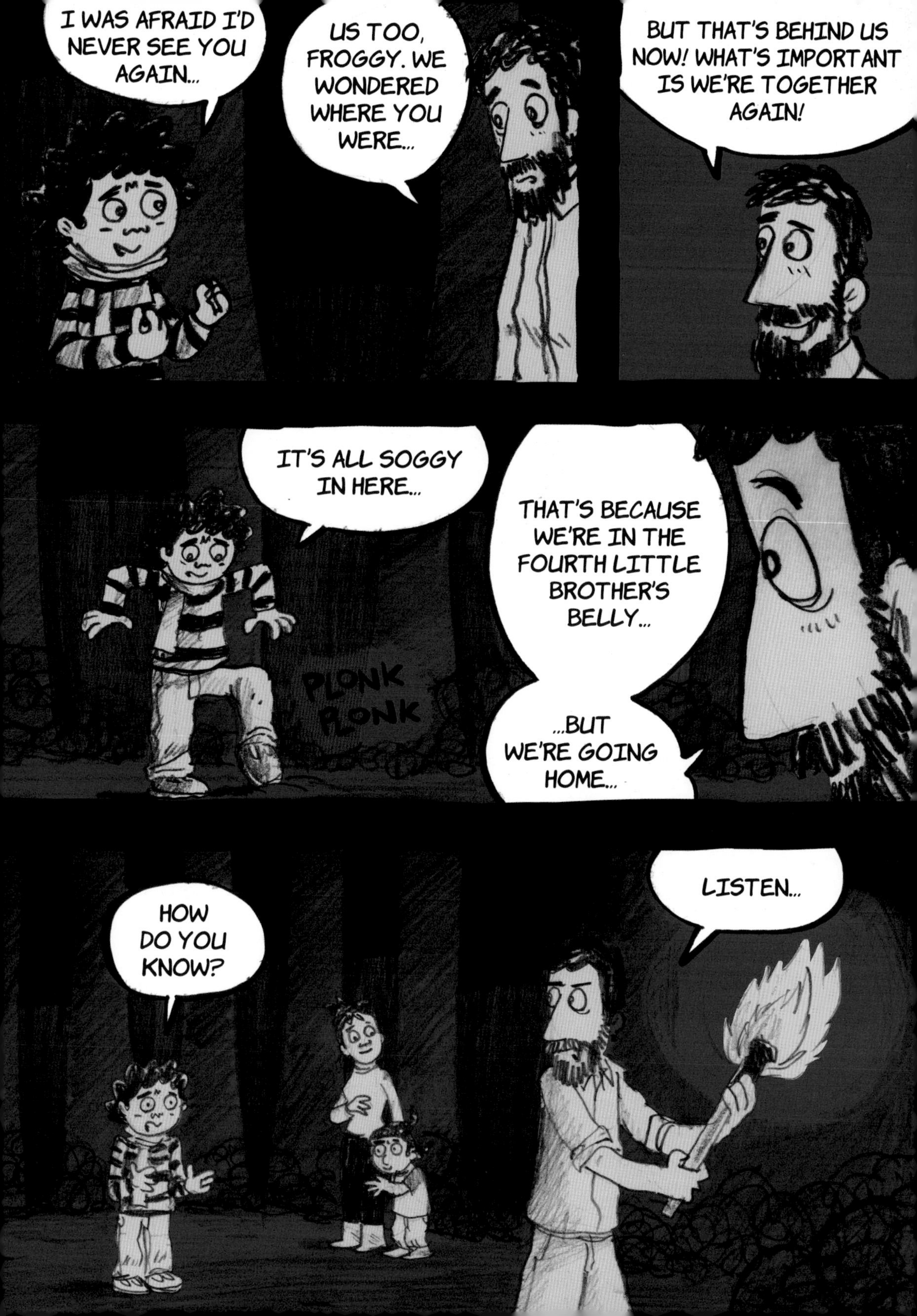
I WAS AFRAID I'D NEVER SEE YOU AGAIN...
US TOO, FROGGY. WE WONDERED WHERE YOU WERE...
BUT THAT'S BEHIND US NOW! WHAT'S IMPORTANT IS WE'RE TOGETHER AGAIN!
IT'S ALL SOGGY IN HERE...
PLONK PLONK
THAT'S BECAUSE WE'RE IN THE FOURTH LITTLE BROTHER'S BELLY...
...BUT WE'RE GOING HOME...
HOW DO YOU KNOW?
LISTEN...

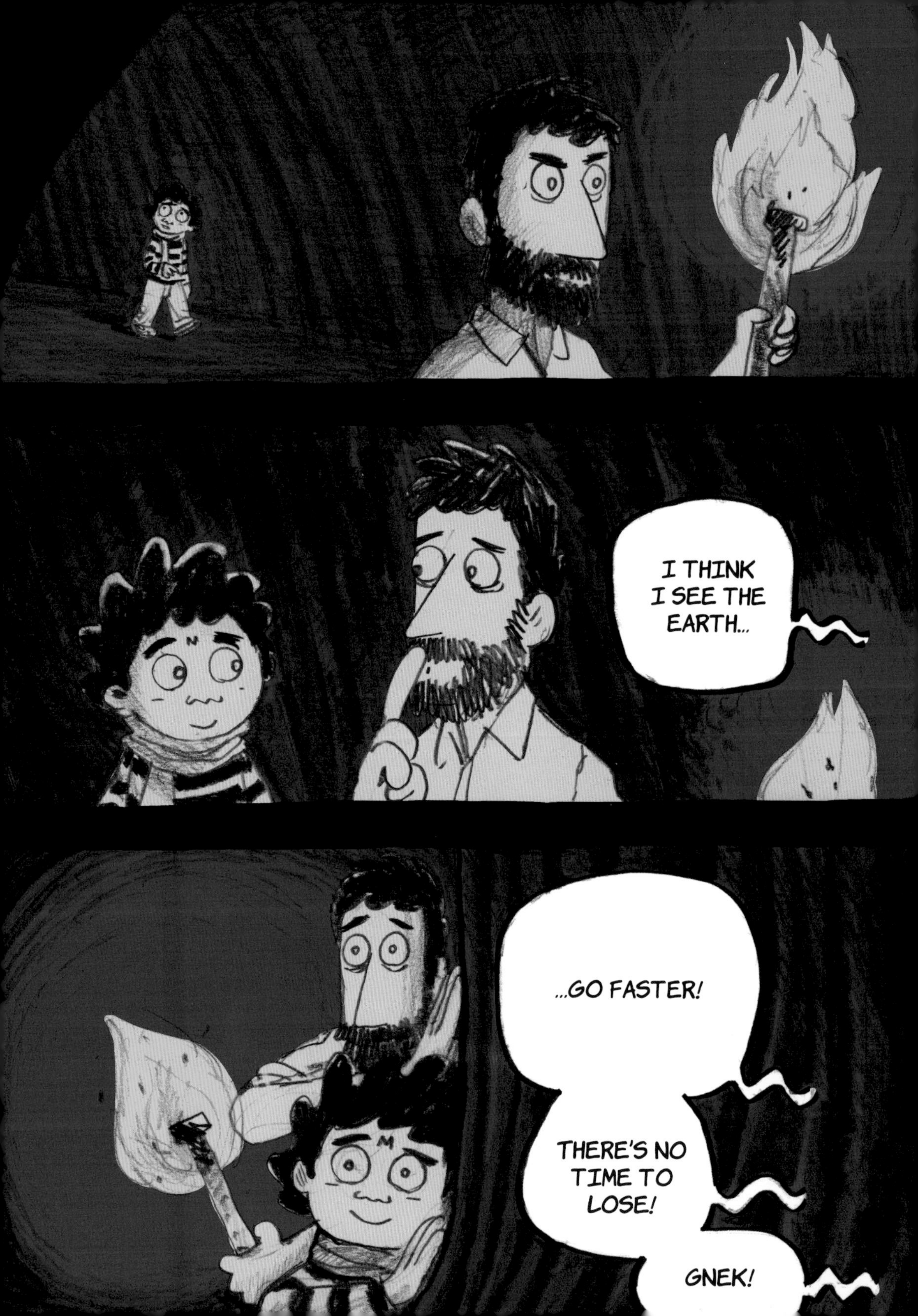
I THINK I SEE THE EARTH...
...GO FASTER!
THERE'S NO TIME TO LOSE!
GNEK!

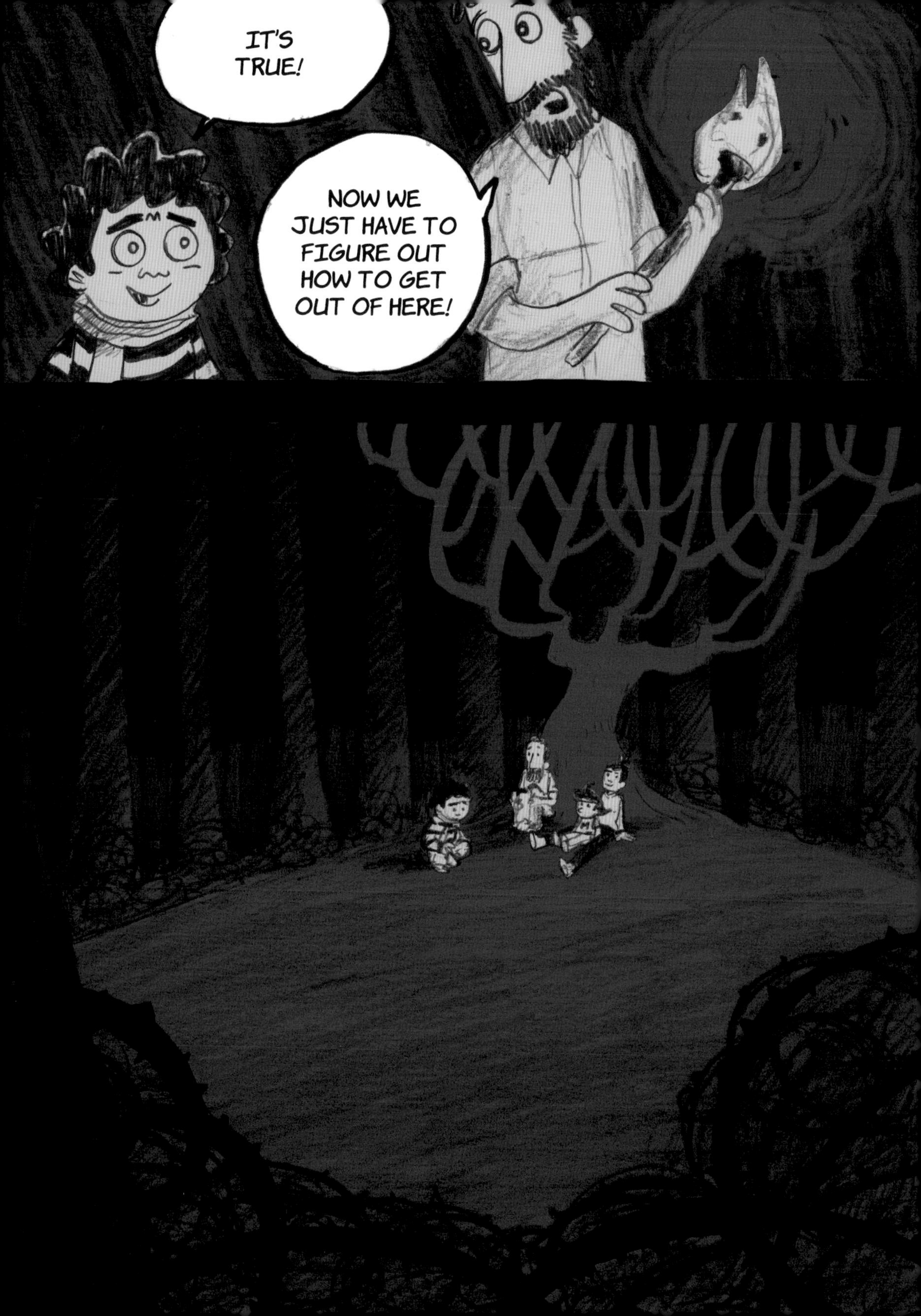
IT'S TRUE!
NOW WE JUST HAVE TO FIGURE OUT HOW TO GET OUT OF HERE!

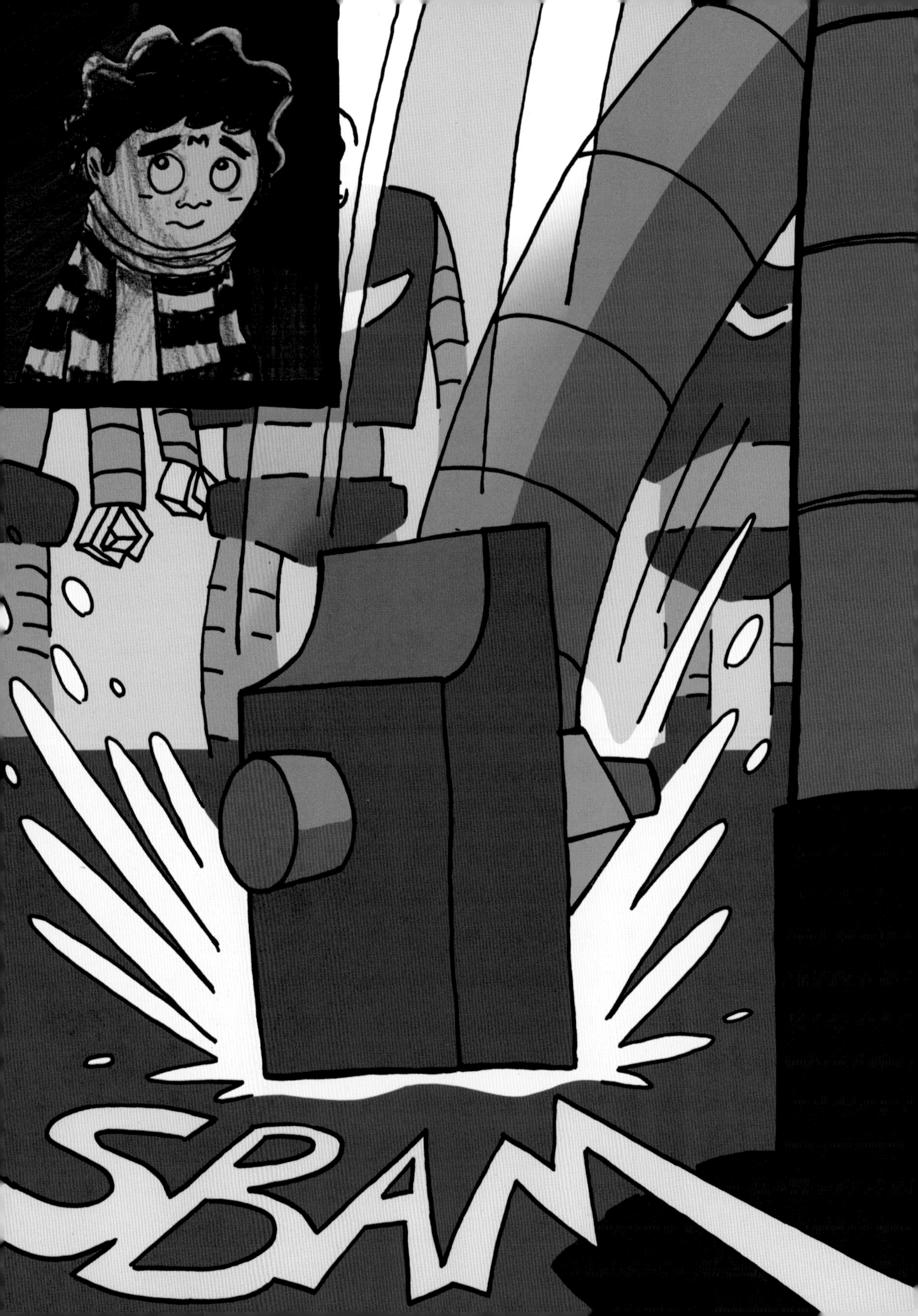
SPAM

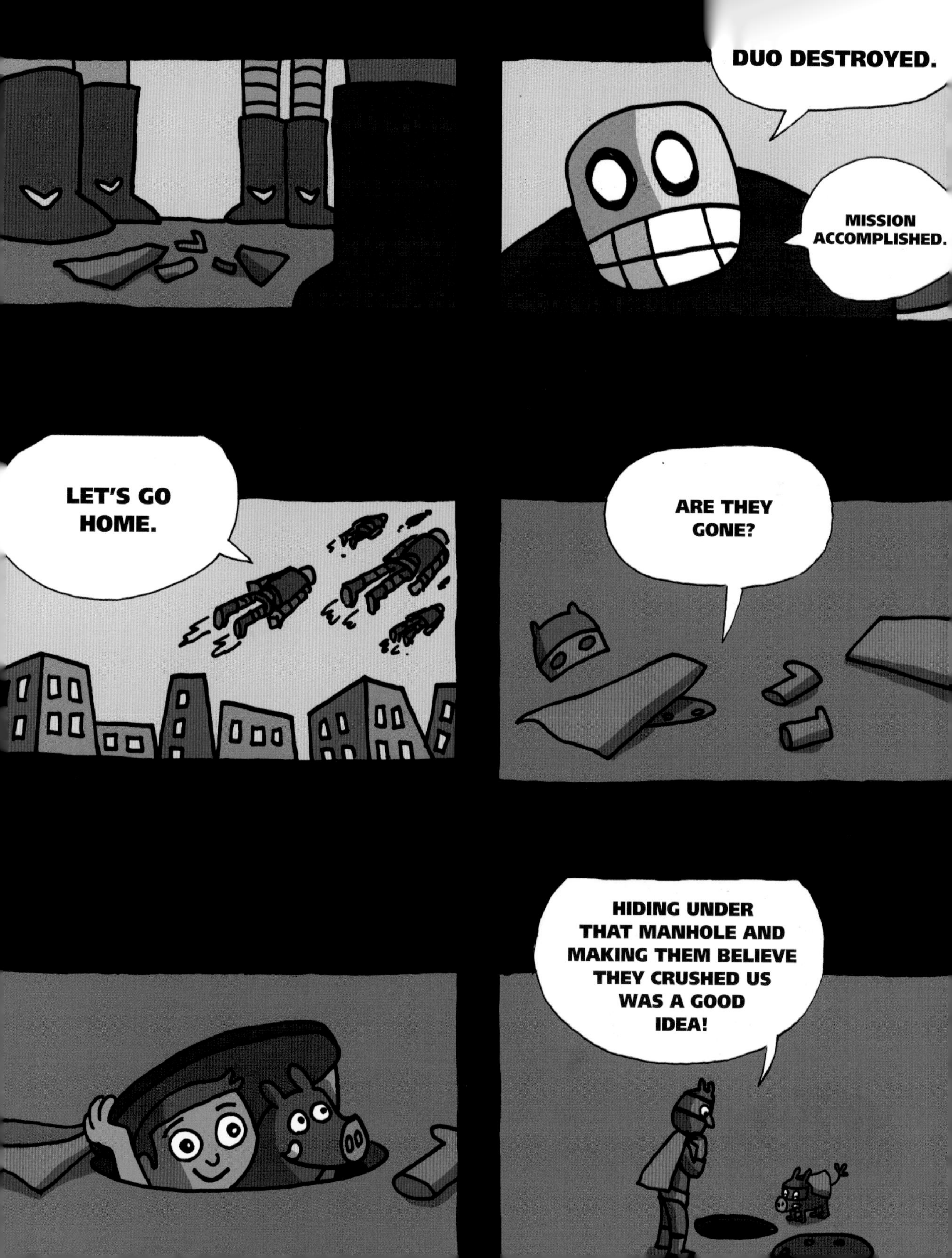
DUO DESTROYED.
MISSION ACCOMPLISHED.
LET'S GO HOME.
ARE THEY GONE?
HIDING UNDER THAT MANHOLE AND MAKING THEM BELIEVE THEY CRUSHED US WAS A GOOD IDEA!

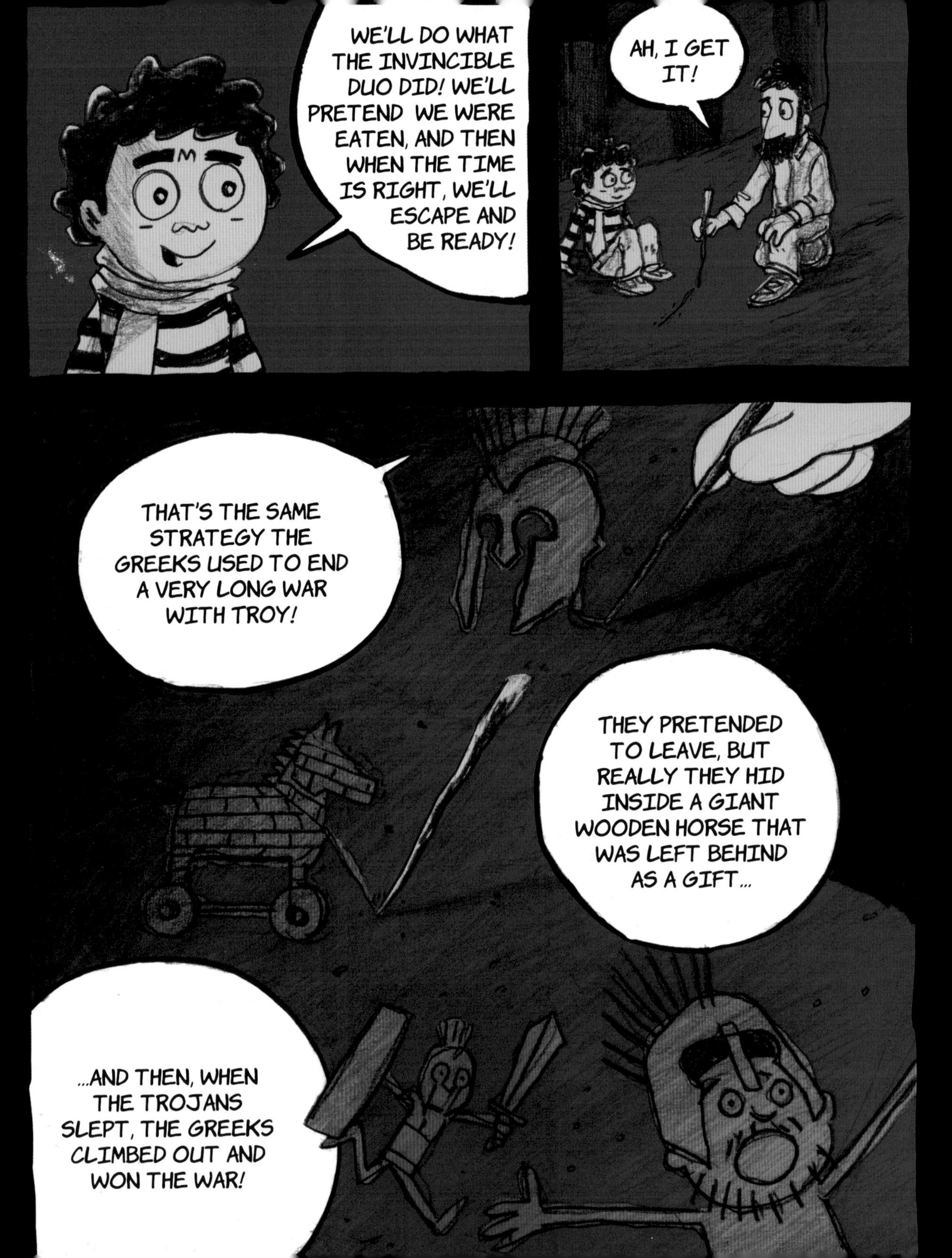
WE'LL DO WHAT THE INVINCIBLE DUO DID! WE'LL PRETEND WE WERE EATEN, AND THEN WHEN THE TIME IS RIGHT, WE'LL ESCAPE AND BE READY!
AH, I GET IT!
THAT'S THE SAME STRATEGY THE GREEKS USED TO END A VERY LONG WAR WITH TROY!
THEY PRETENDED TO LEAVE, BUT REALLY THEY HID INSIDE A GIANT WOODEN HORSE THAT WAS LEFT BEHIND AS A GIFT...
...AND THEN, WHEN THE TROJANS SLEPT, THE GREEKS CLIMBED OUT AND WON THE WAR!

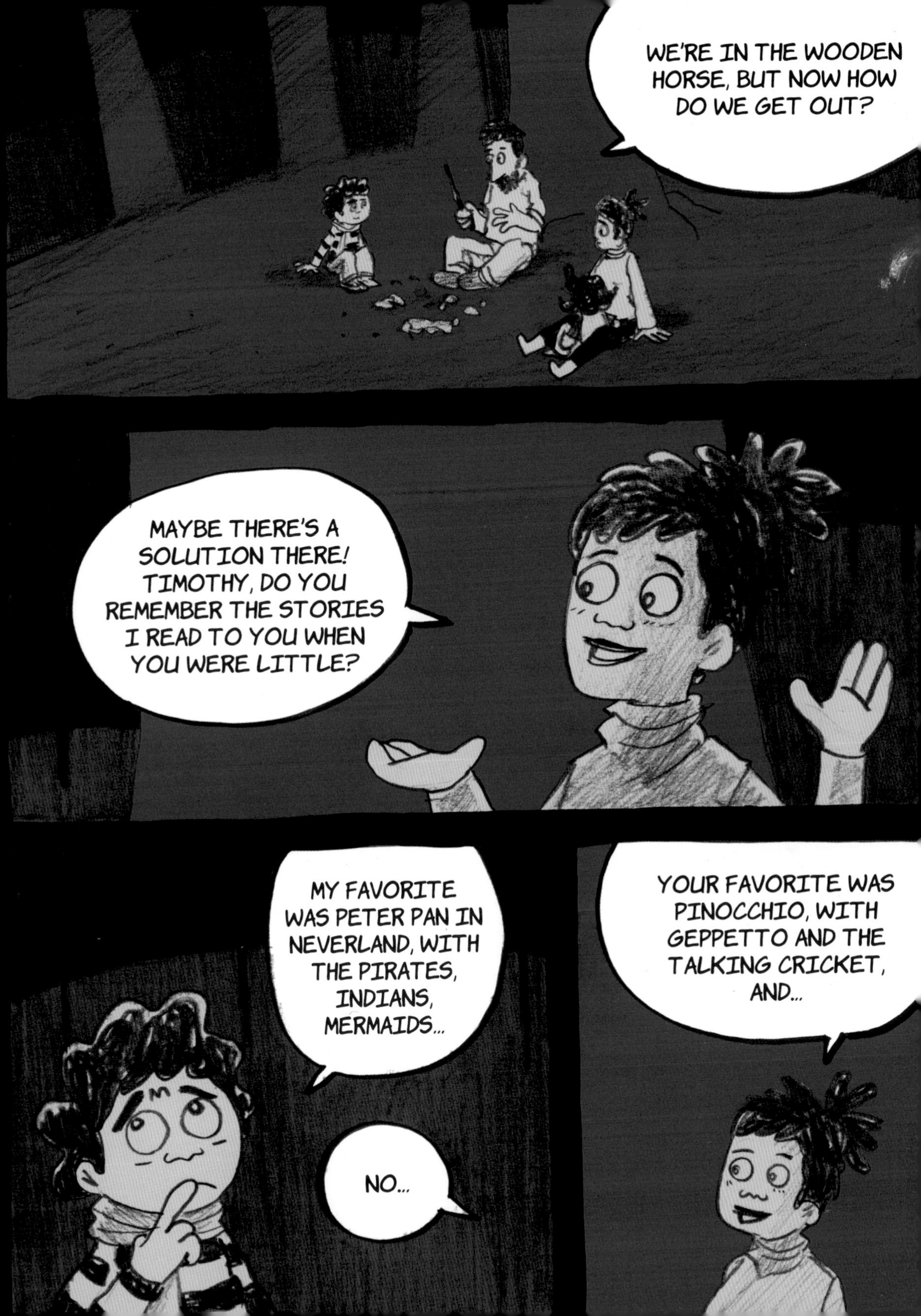
WE'RE IN THE WOODEN HORSE, BUT NOW HOW DO WE GET OUT?
MAYBE THERE'S A SOLUTION THERE! TIMOTHY, DO YOU REMEMBER THE STORIES I READ TO YOU WHEN YOU WERE LITTLE?
MY FAVORITE WAS PETER PAN IN NEVERLAND, WITH THE PIRATES, INDIANS, MERMAIDS...
YOUR FAVORITE WAS PINOCCHIO, WITH GEPPETTO AND THE TALKING CRICKET, AND...
NO...

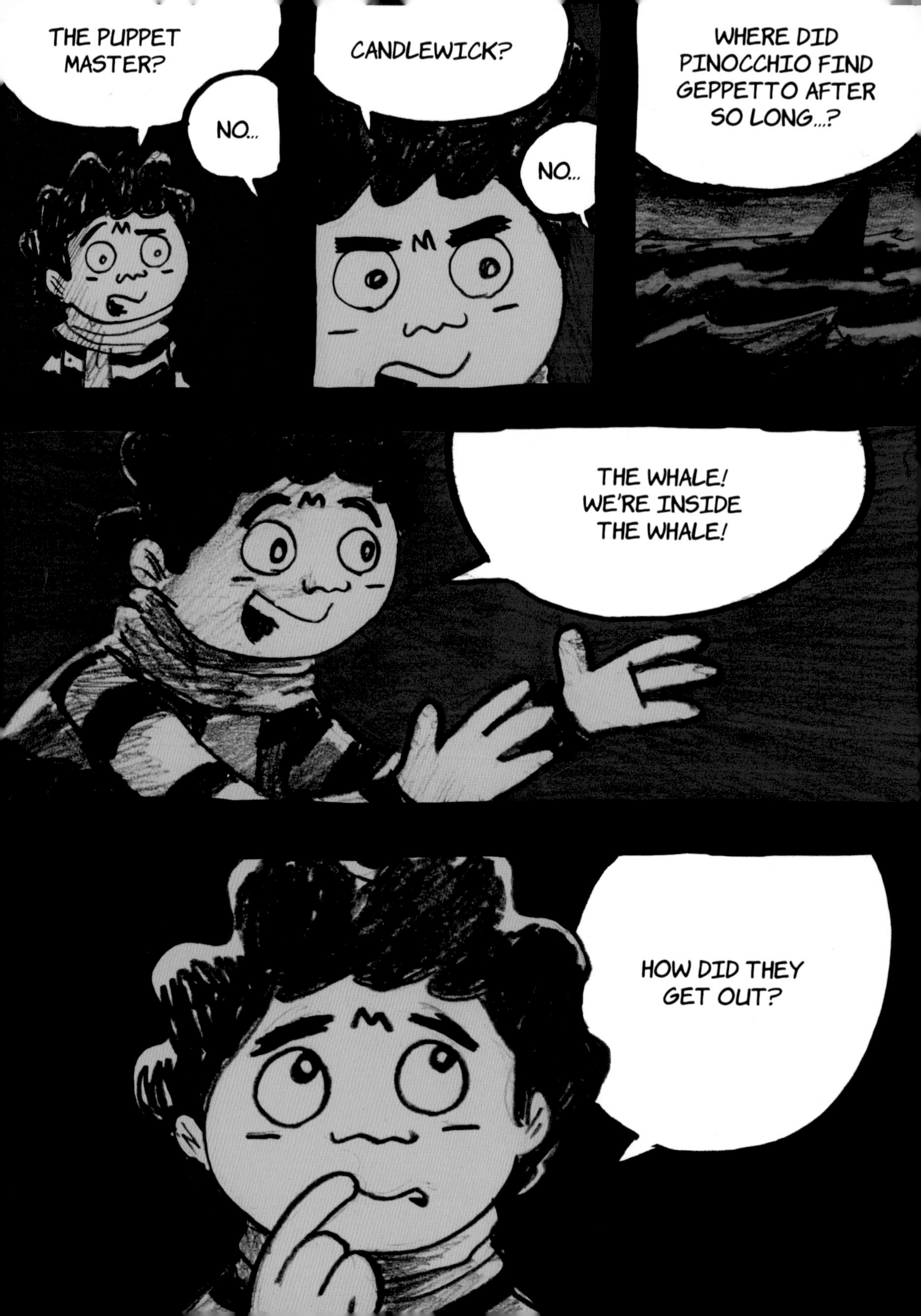
THE PUPPET MASTER?
NO...
CANDLEWICK?
NO...
WHERE DID PINOCCHIO FIND GEPPETTO AFTER SO LONG...?
THE WHALE! WE'RE INSIDE THE WHALE!
HOW DID THEY GET OUT?

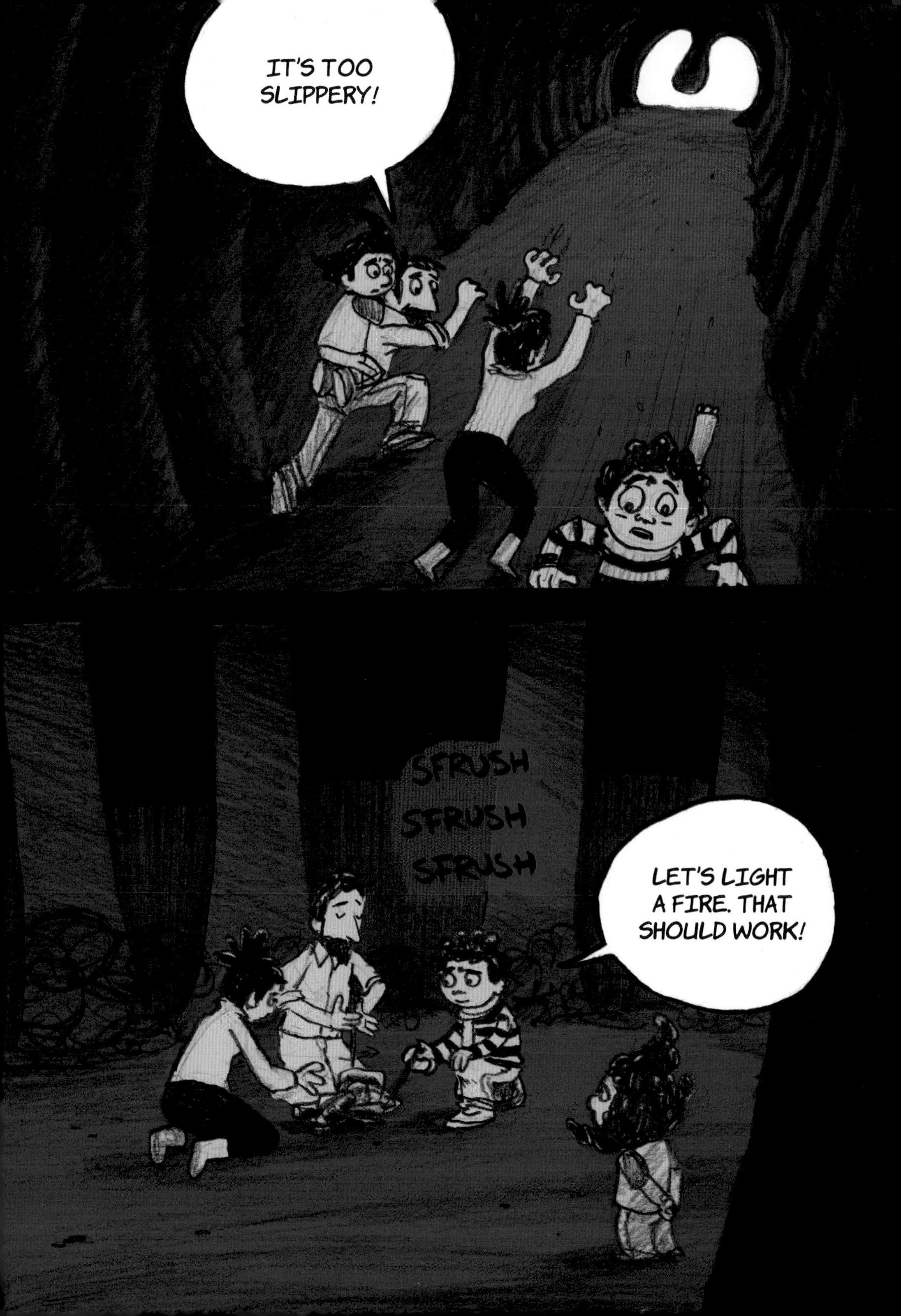
IT'S TOO SLIPPERY!
SFRUSH
SFRUSH
SFRUSH
LET'S LIGHT A FIRE. THAT SHOULD WORK!

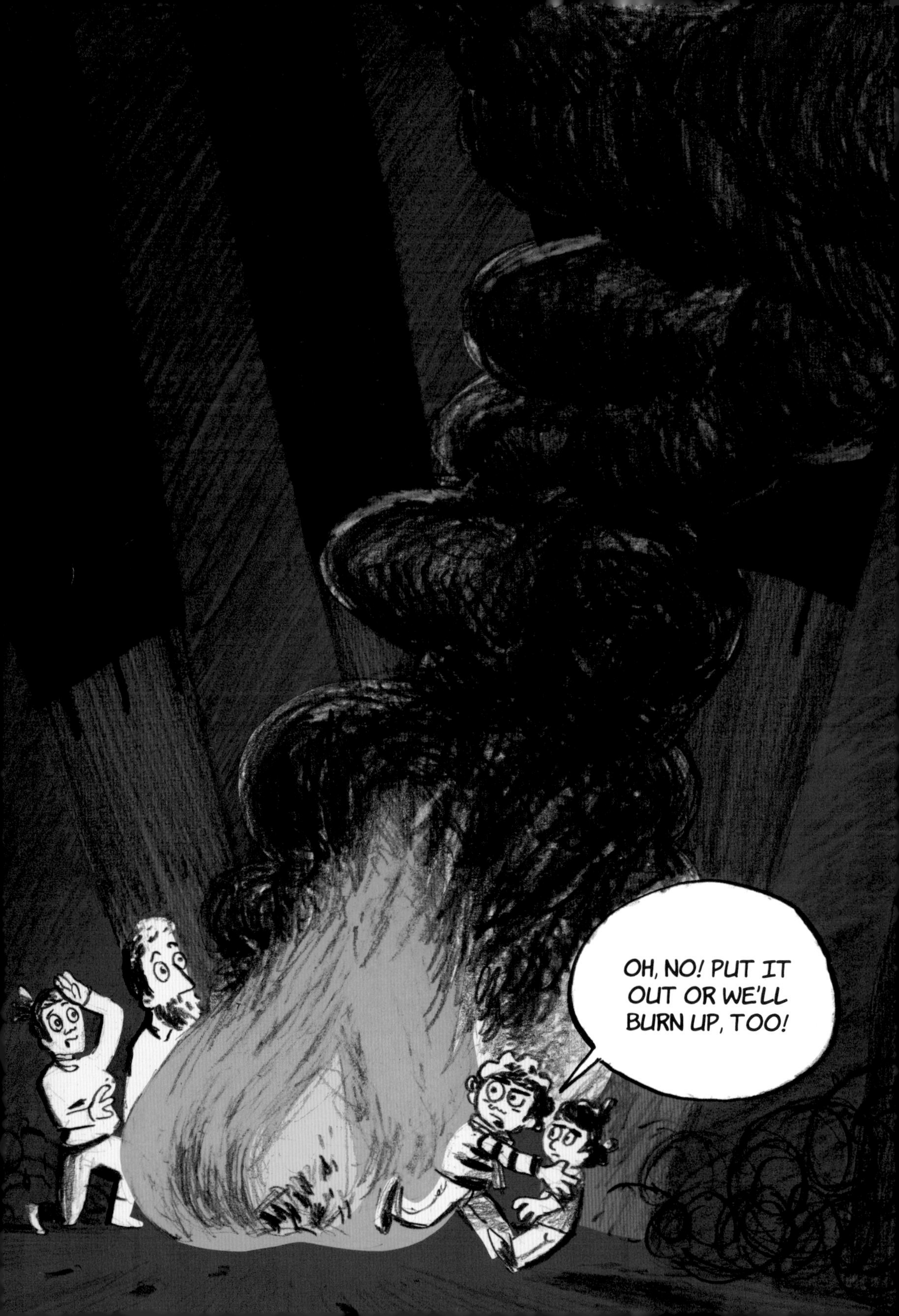
OH, NO! PUT IT OUT OR WE'LL BURN UP, TOO!

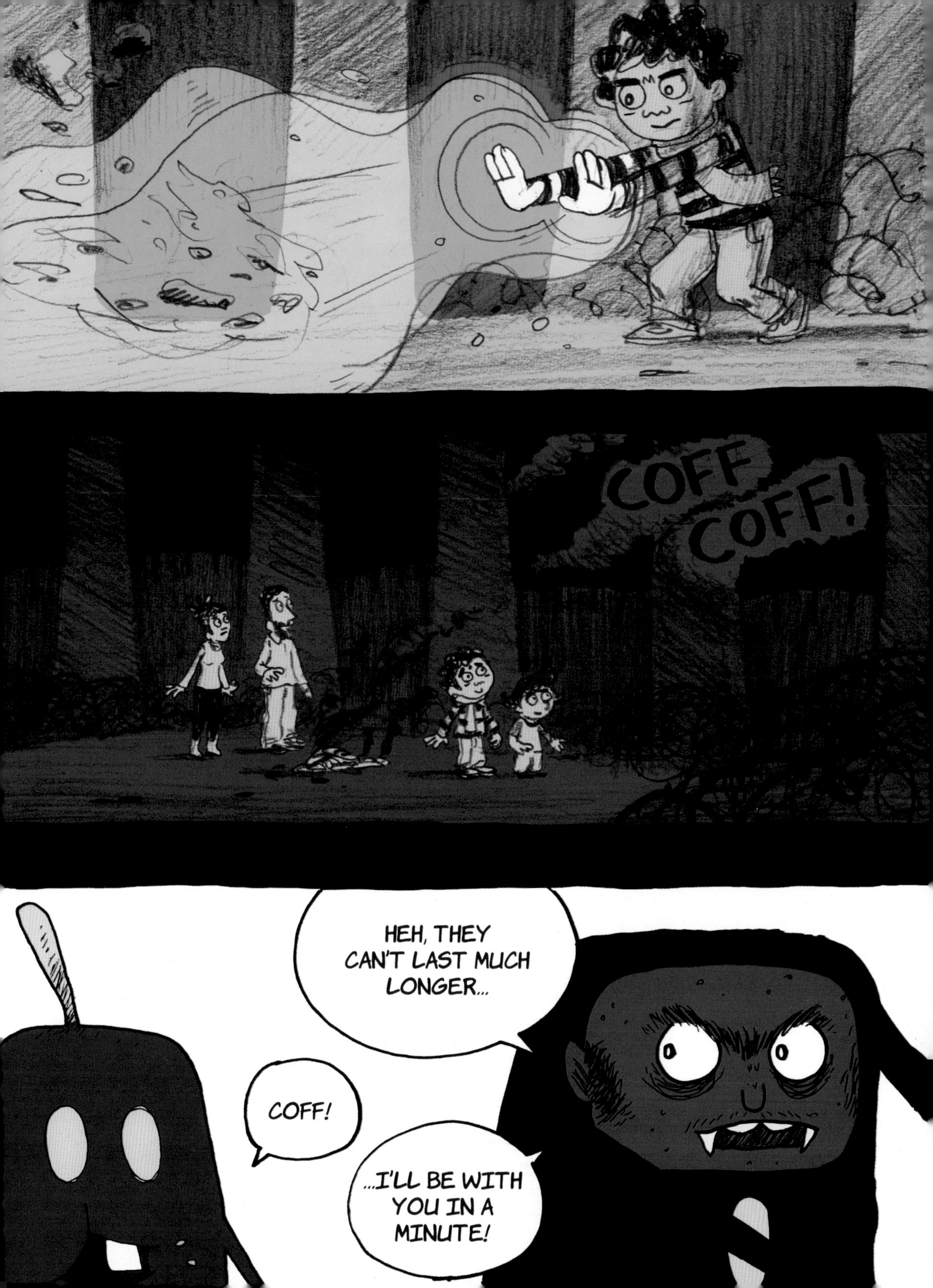
COFF COFF!
HEH, THEY CAN'T LAST MUCH LONGER...
COFF!
...I'LL BE WITH YOU IN A MINUTE!

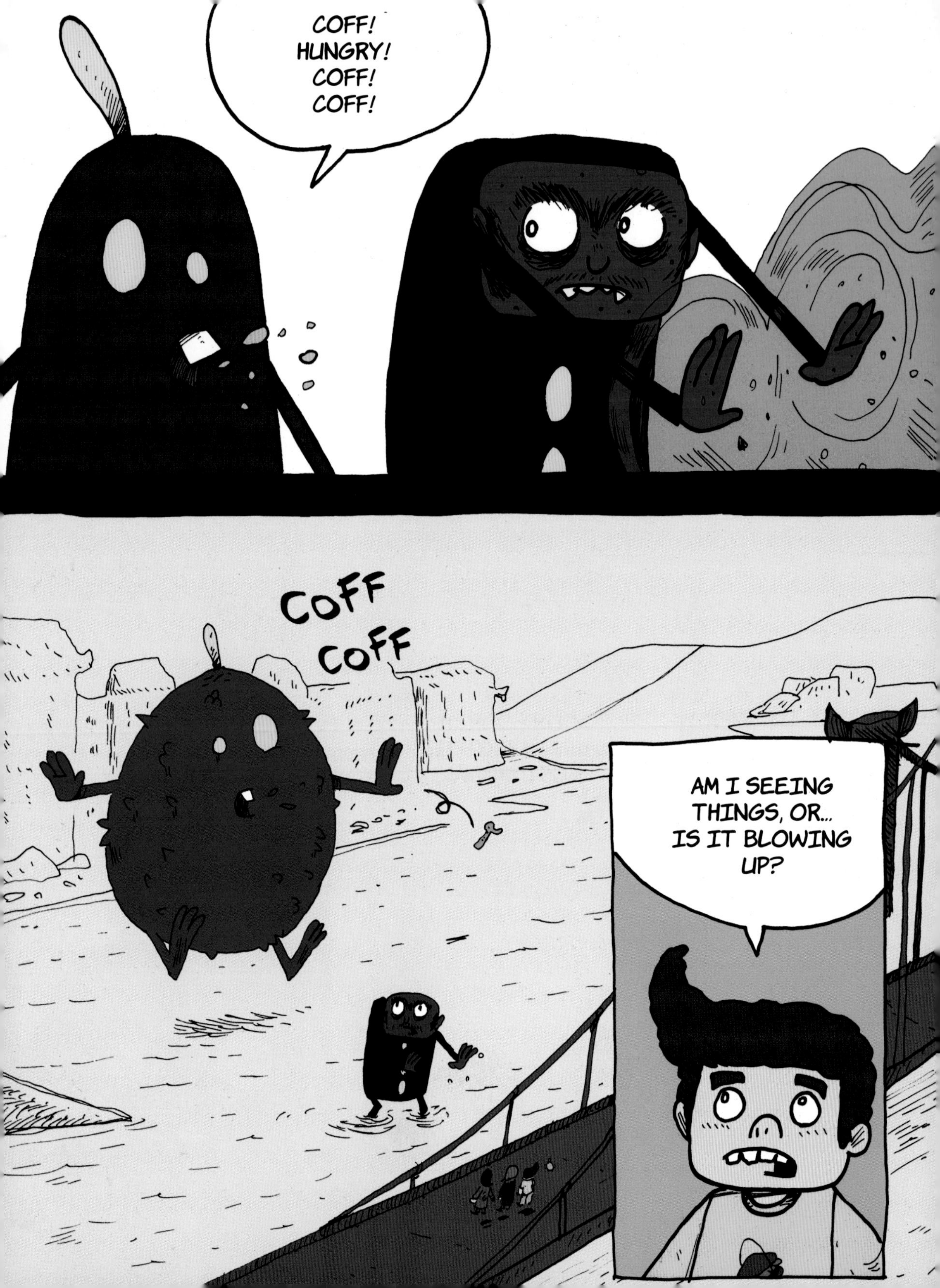
COFF! HUNGRY! COFF! COFF!
COFF COFF
AM I SEEING THINGS, OR... IS IT BLOWING UP?

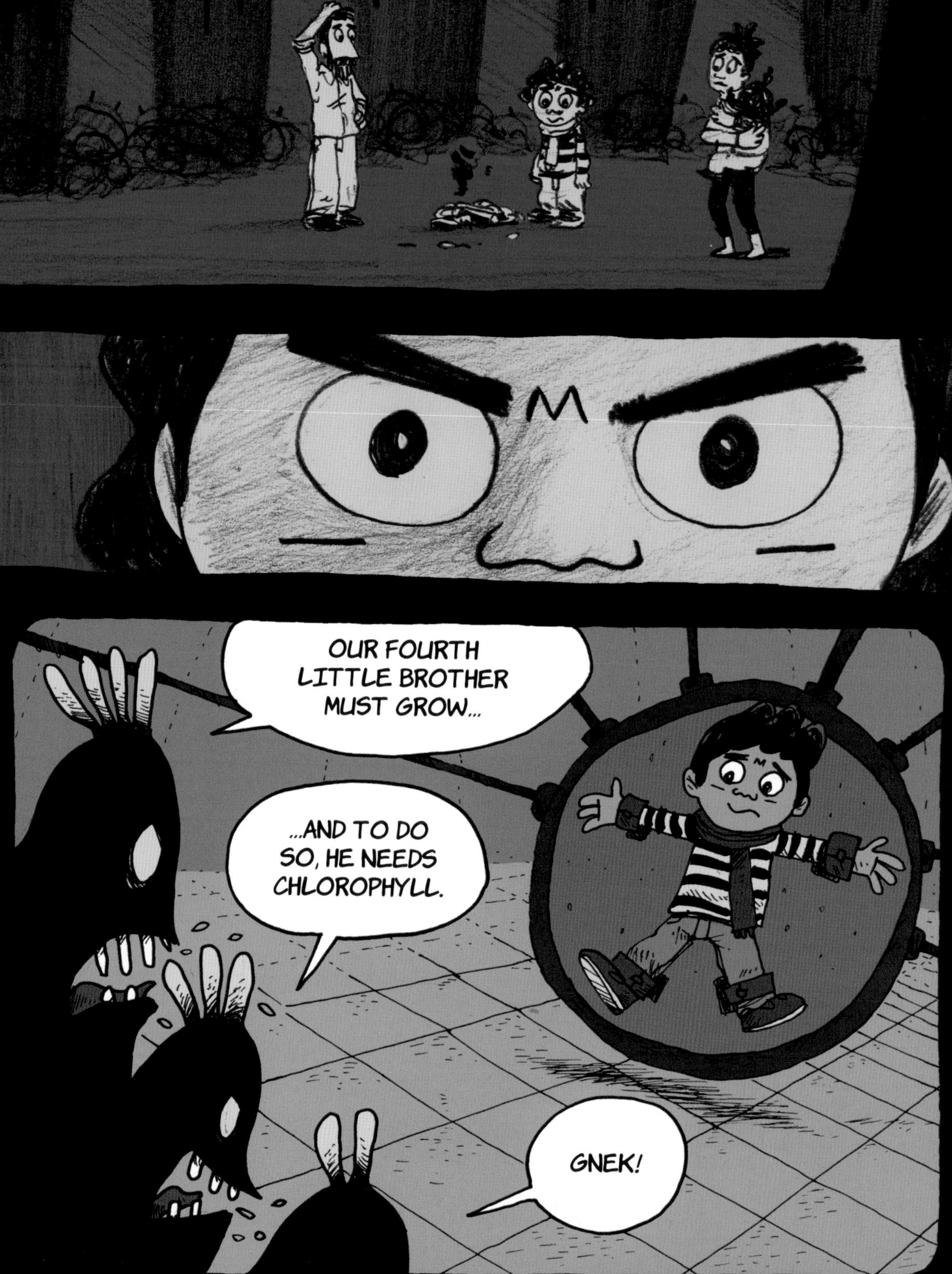

OUR FOURTH LITTLE BROTHER MUST GROW...
...AND TO DO SO, HE NEEDS CHLOROPHYLL.
GNEK!

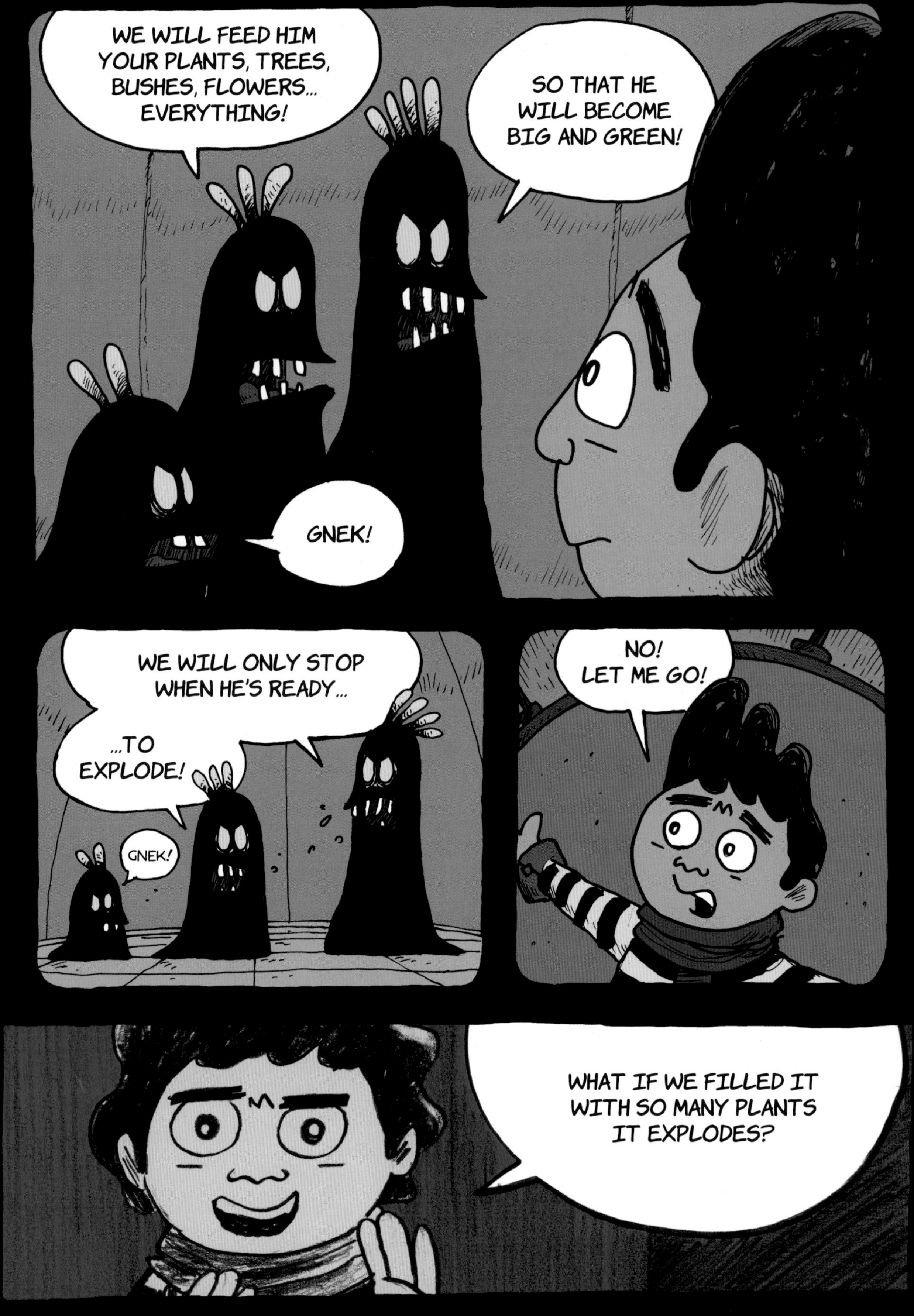
WE WILL FEED HIM YOUR PLANTS, TREES, BUSHES, FLOWERS... EVERYTHING!
SO THAT HE WILL BECOME BIG AND GREEN!
GNEK!
WE WILL ONLY STOP WHEN HE'S READY...
...TO EXPLODE!
GNEK!
NO! LET ME GO!
WHAT IF WE FILLED IT WITH SO MANY PLANTS IT EXPLODES?

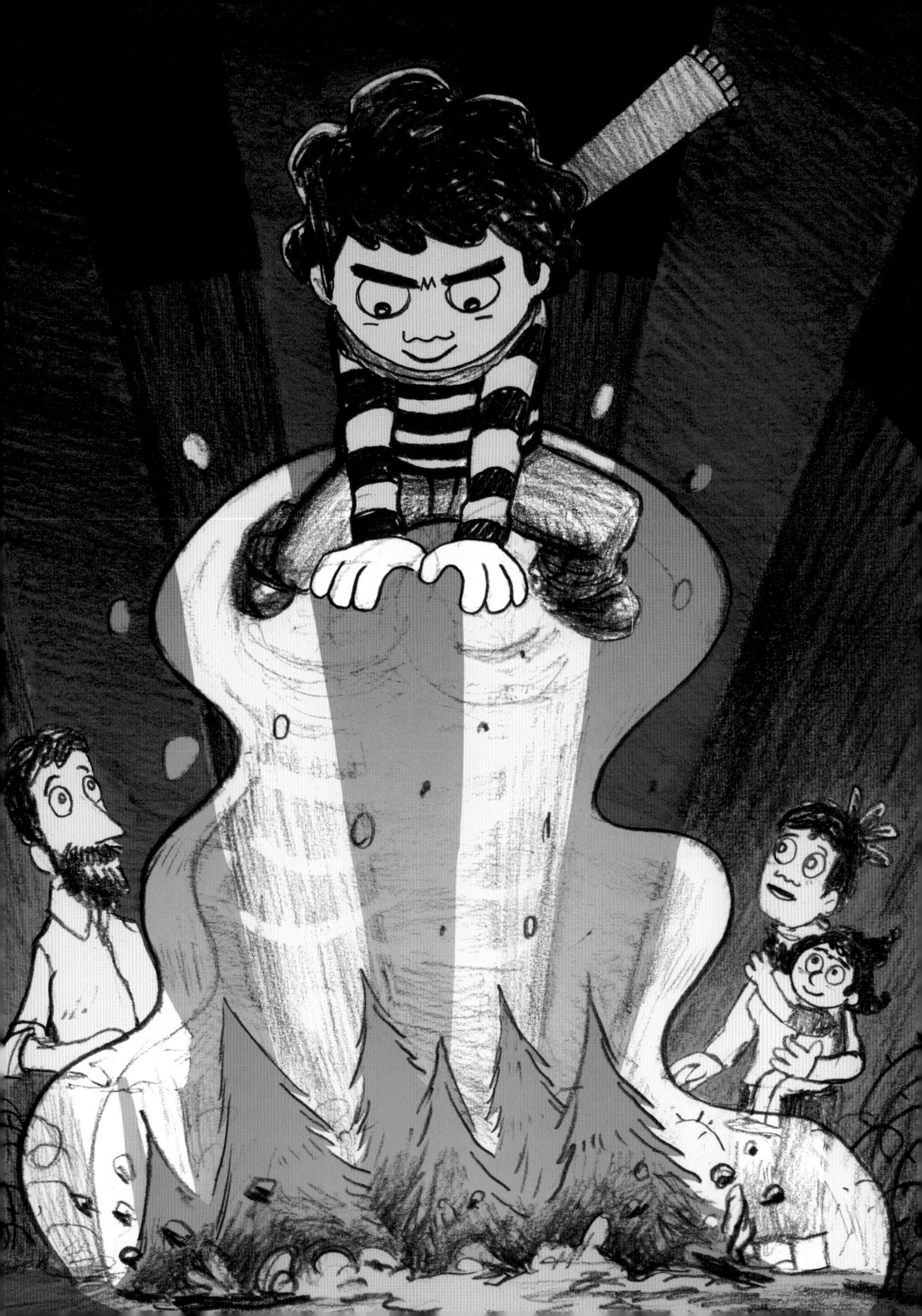

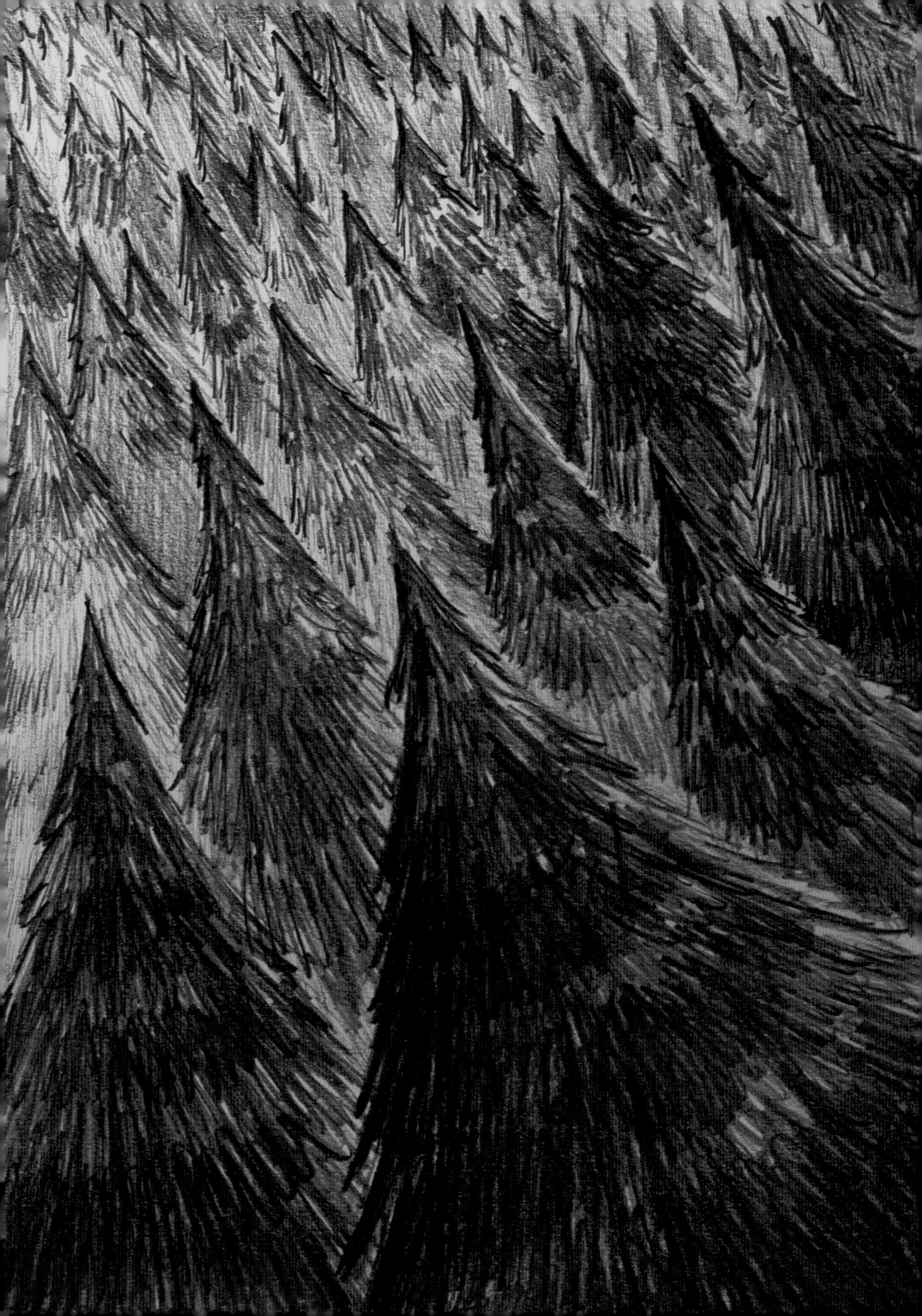

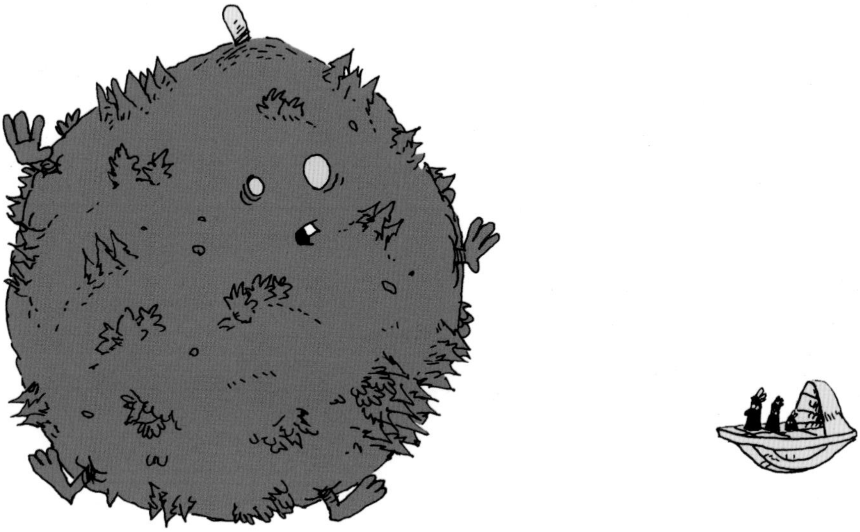

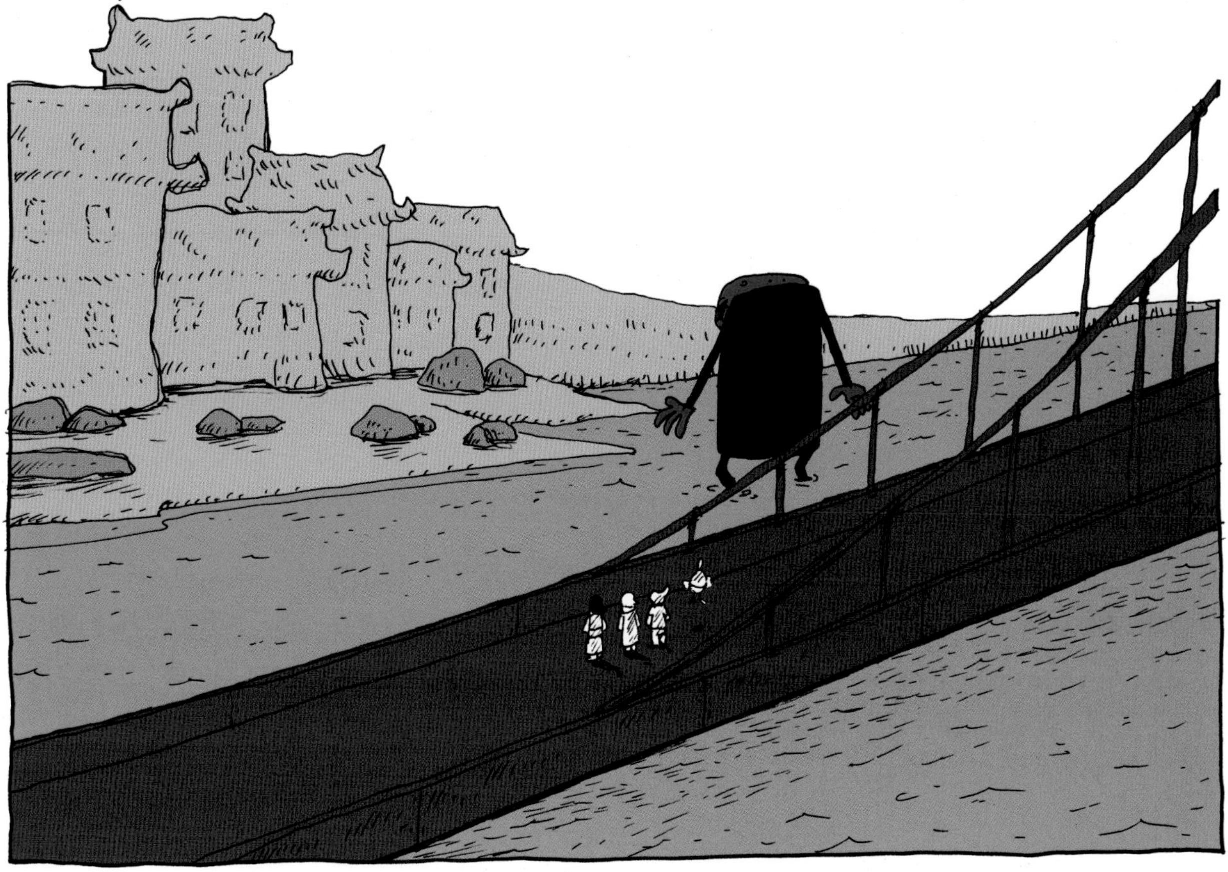

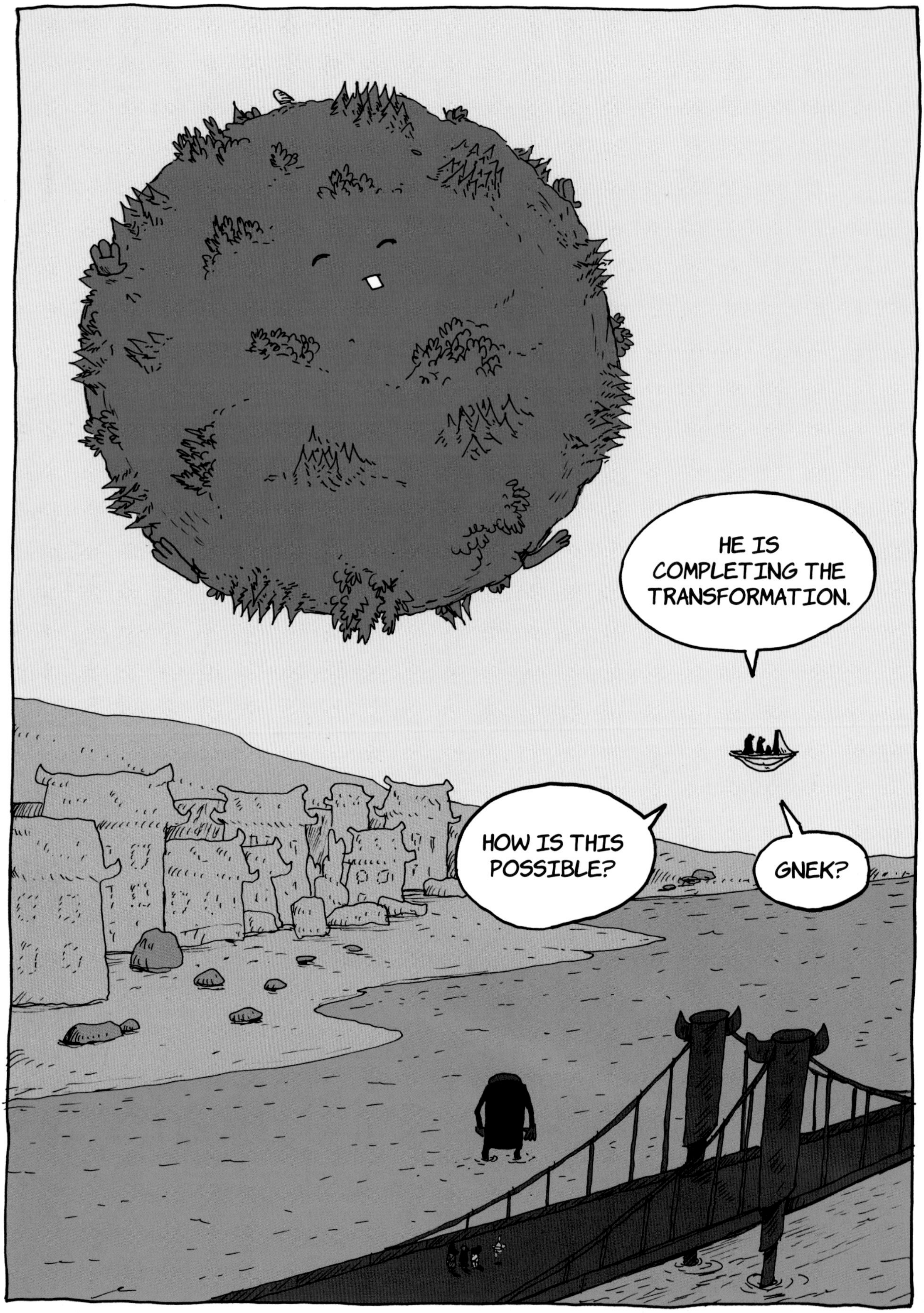
HE IS COMPLETING THE TRANSFORMATION.
HOW IS THIS POSSIBLE?
GNEK?

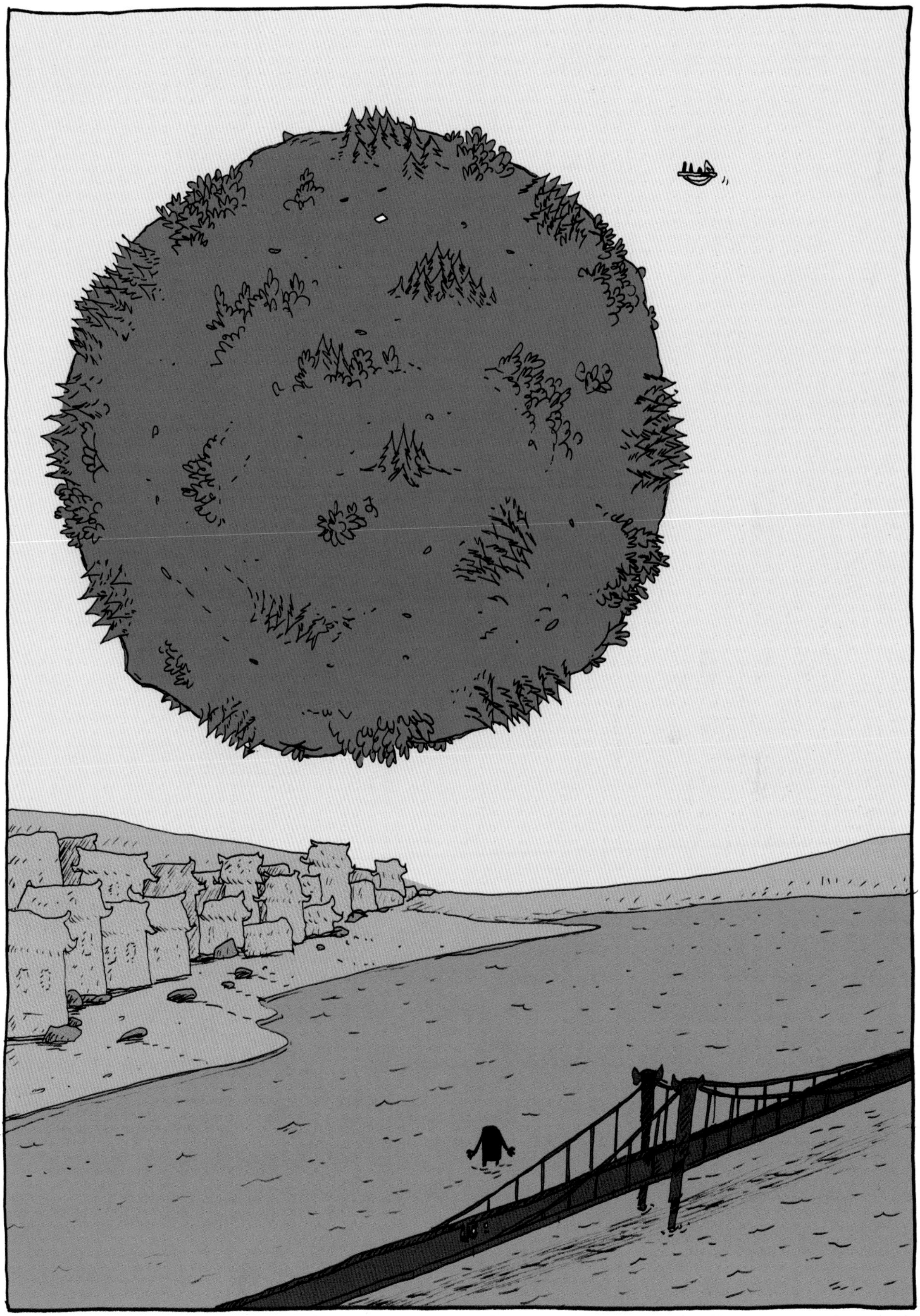

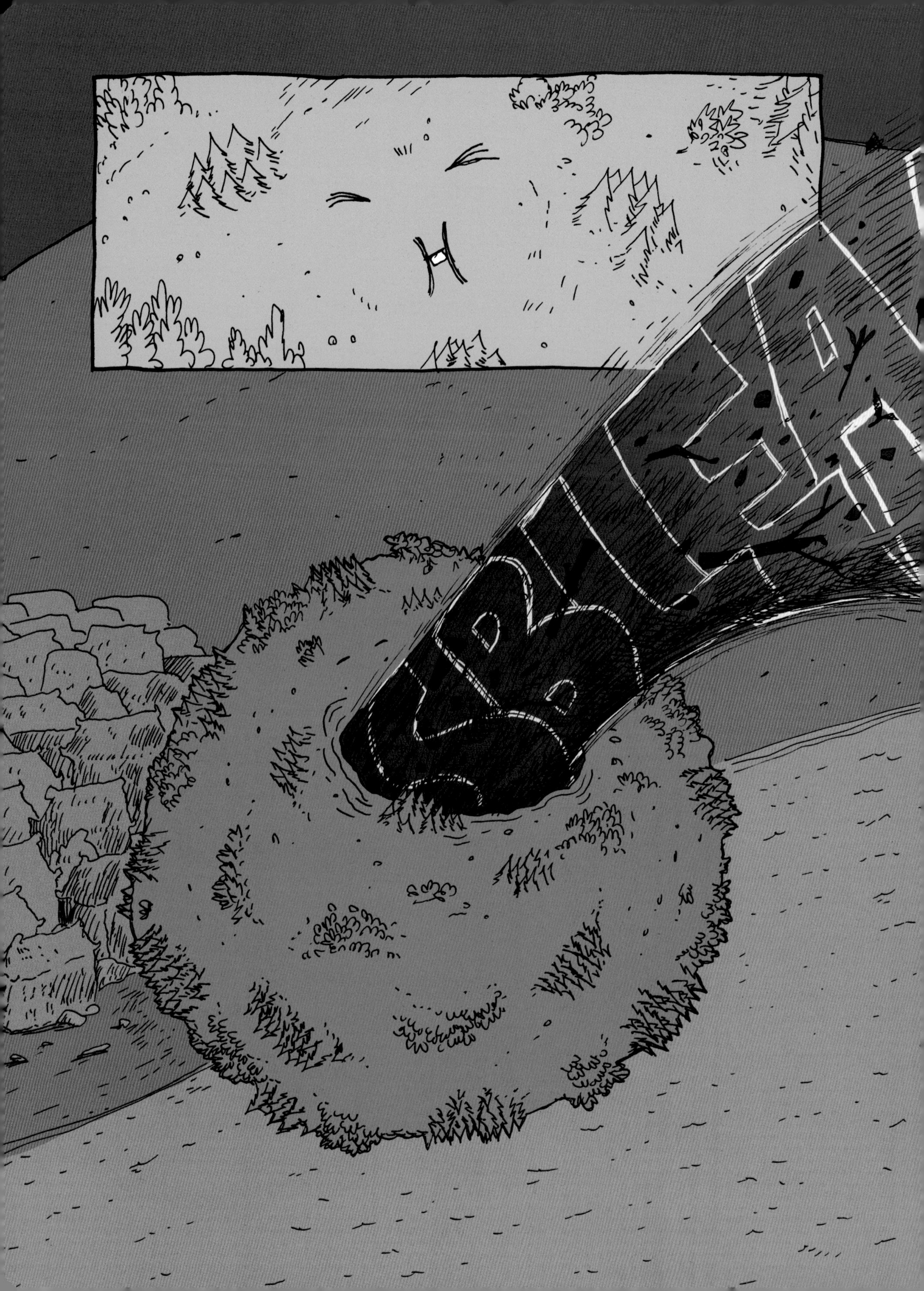

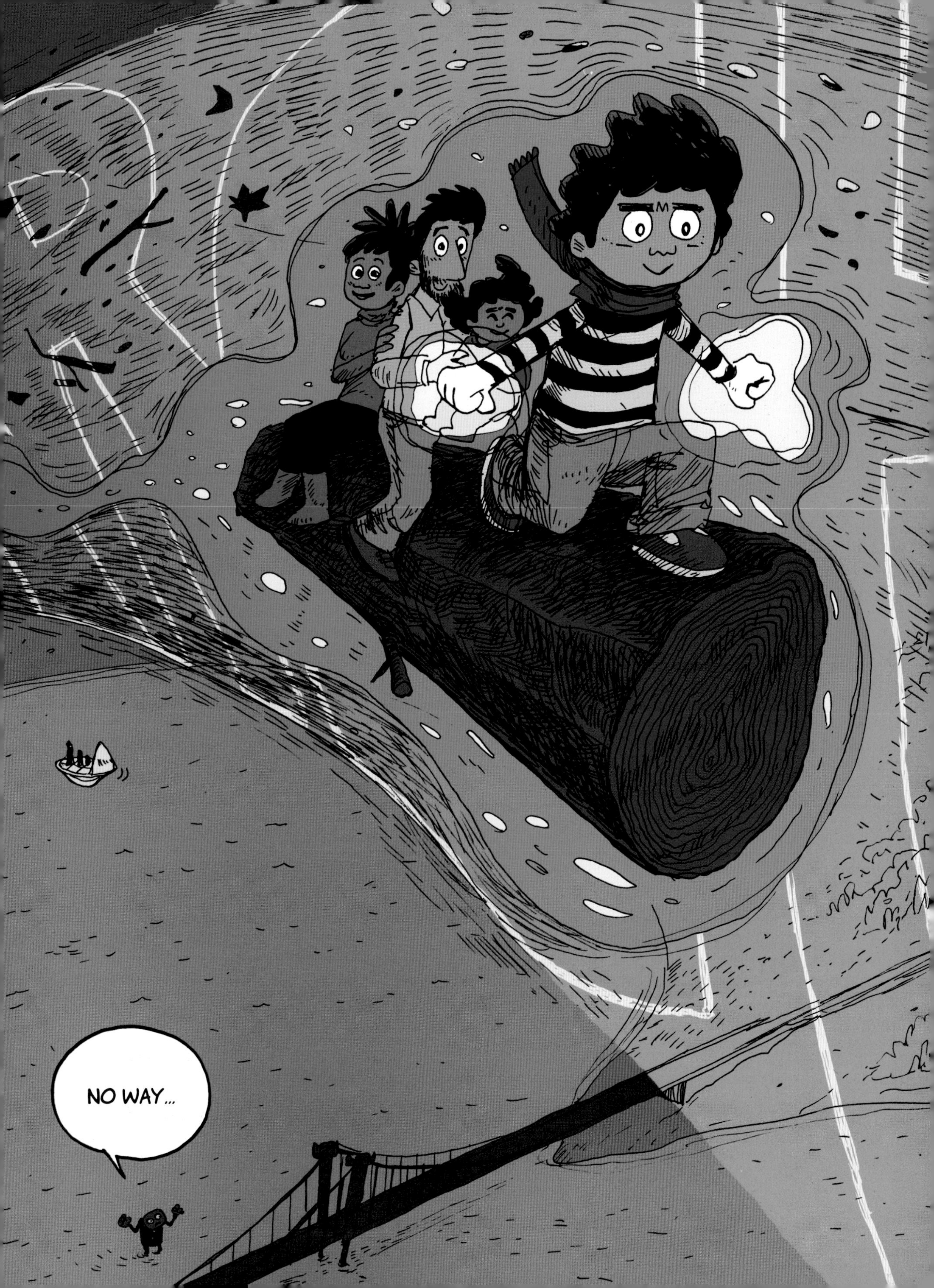
NO WAY...

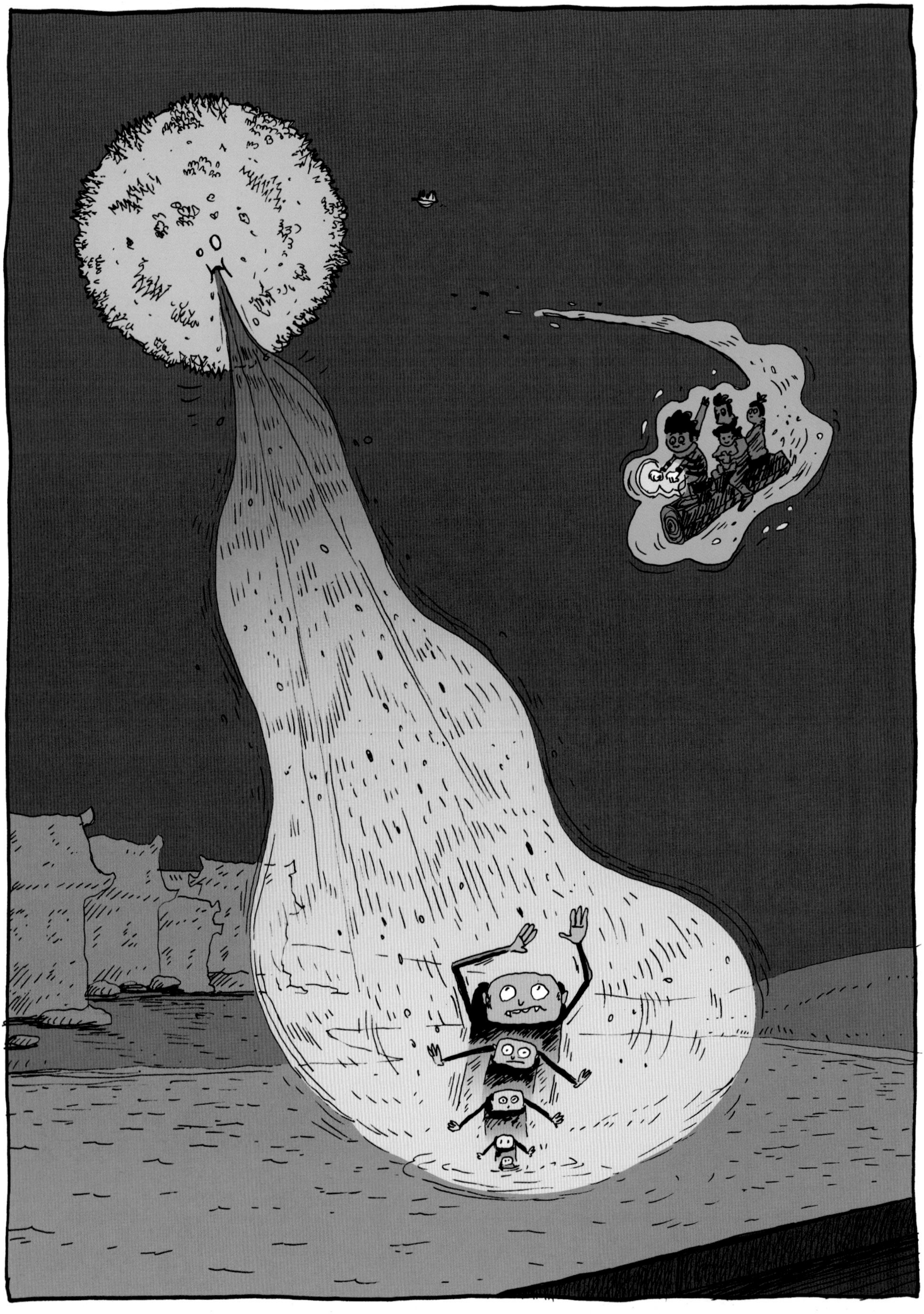

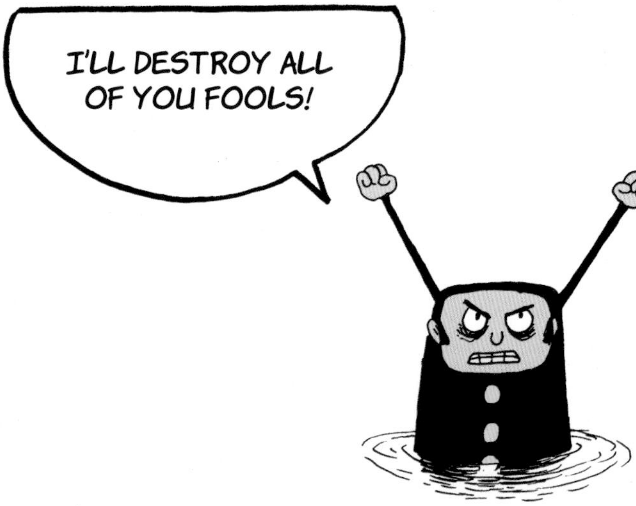
I'LL DESTROY ALL OF YOU FOOLS!

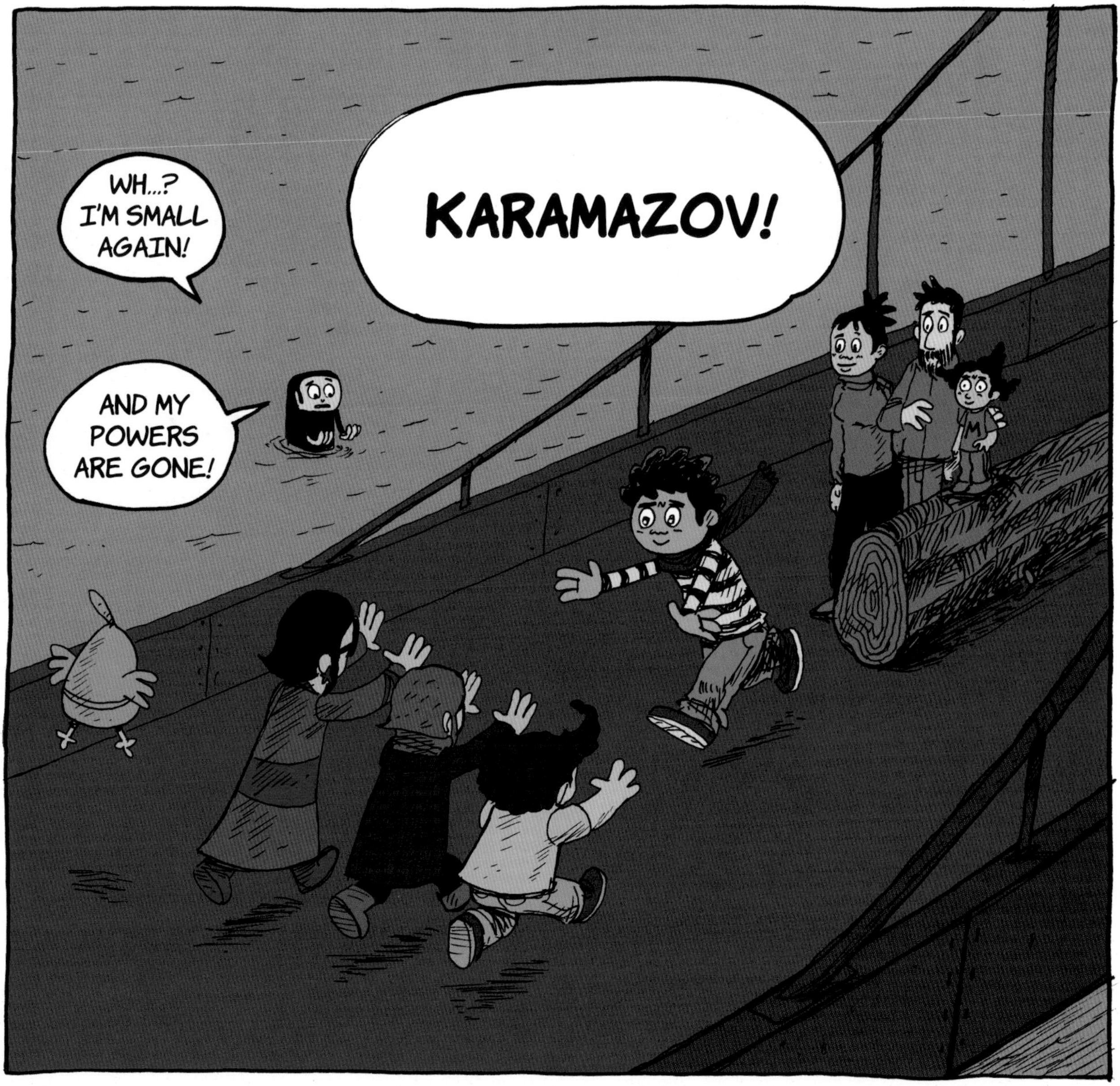
WH...? I'M SMALL AGAIN!
AND MY POWERS ARE GONE!
KARAMAZOV!

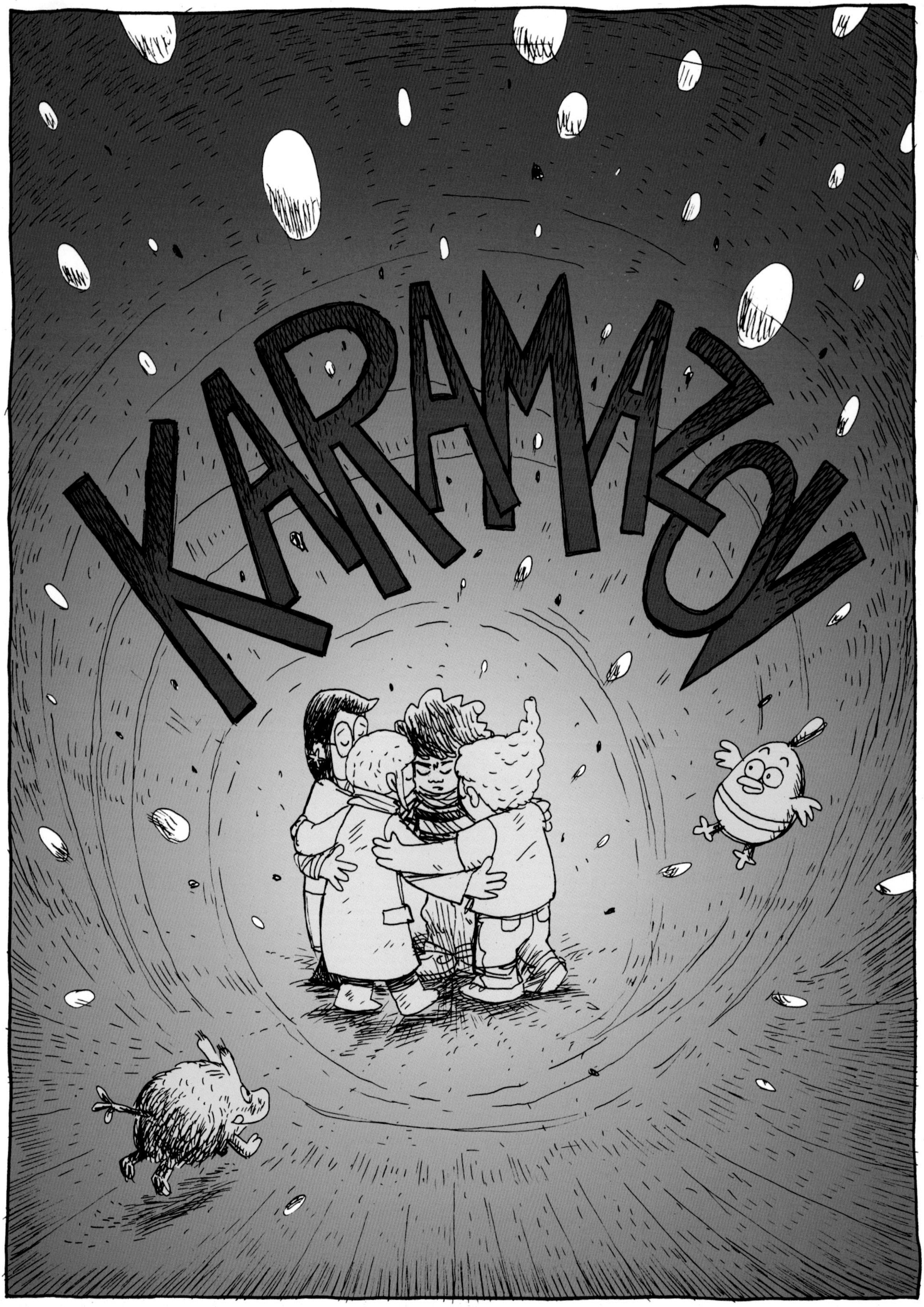
KARAMAZOV

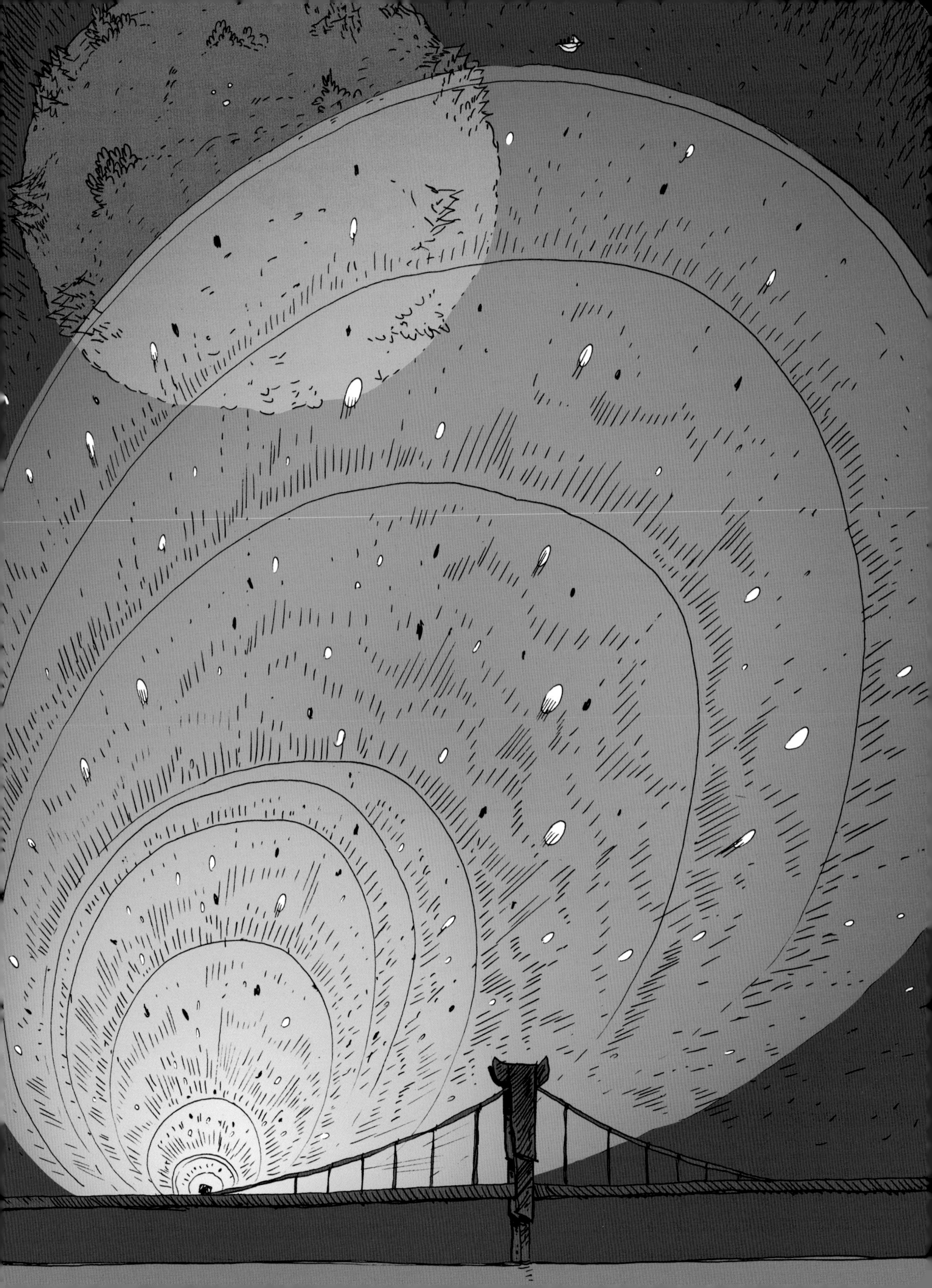

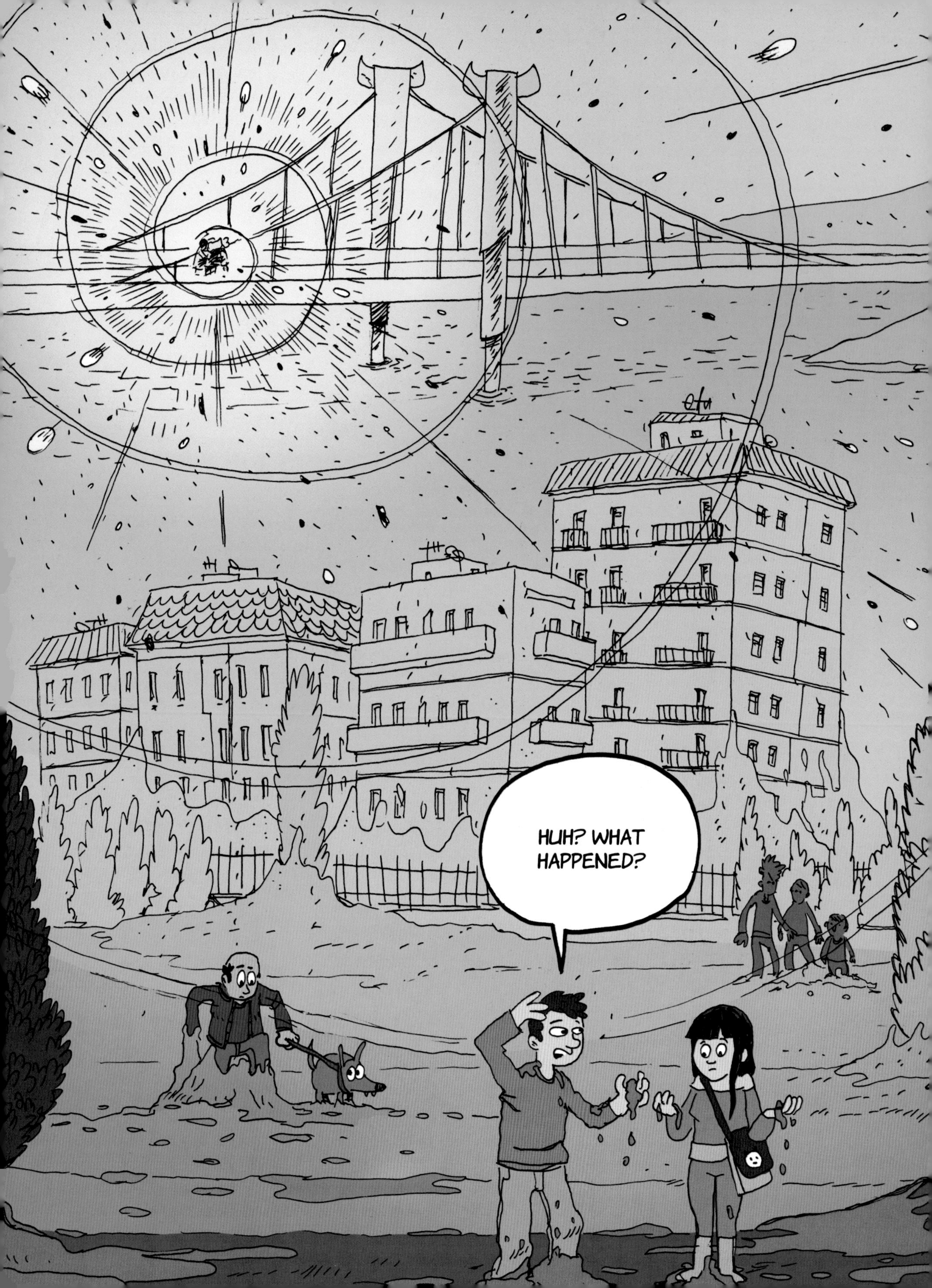
HUH? WHAT HAPPENED?

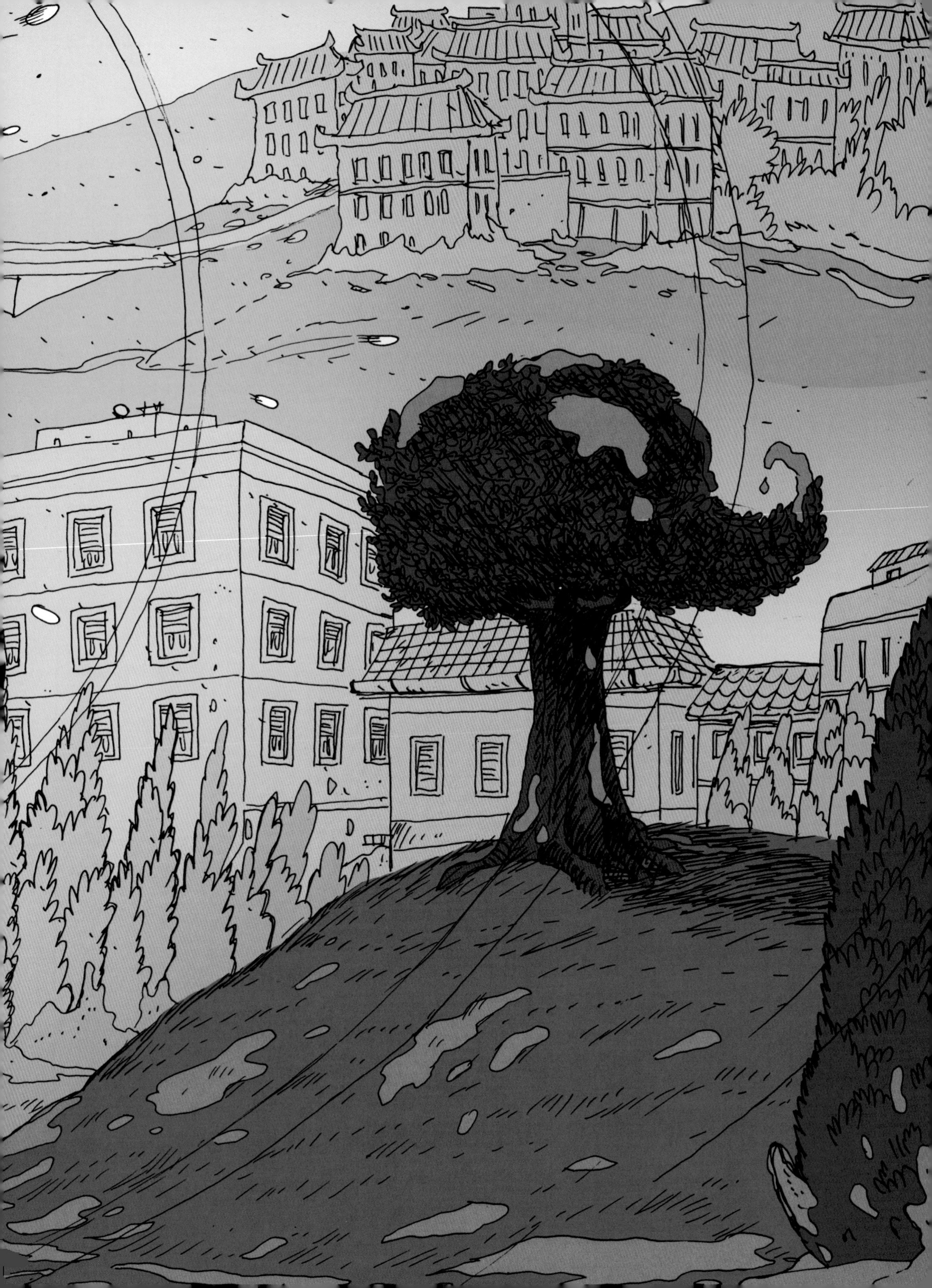

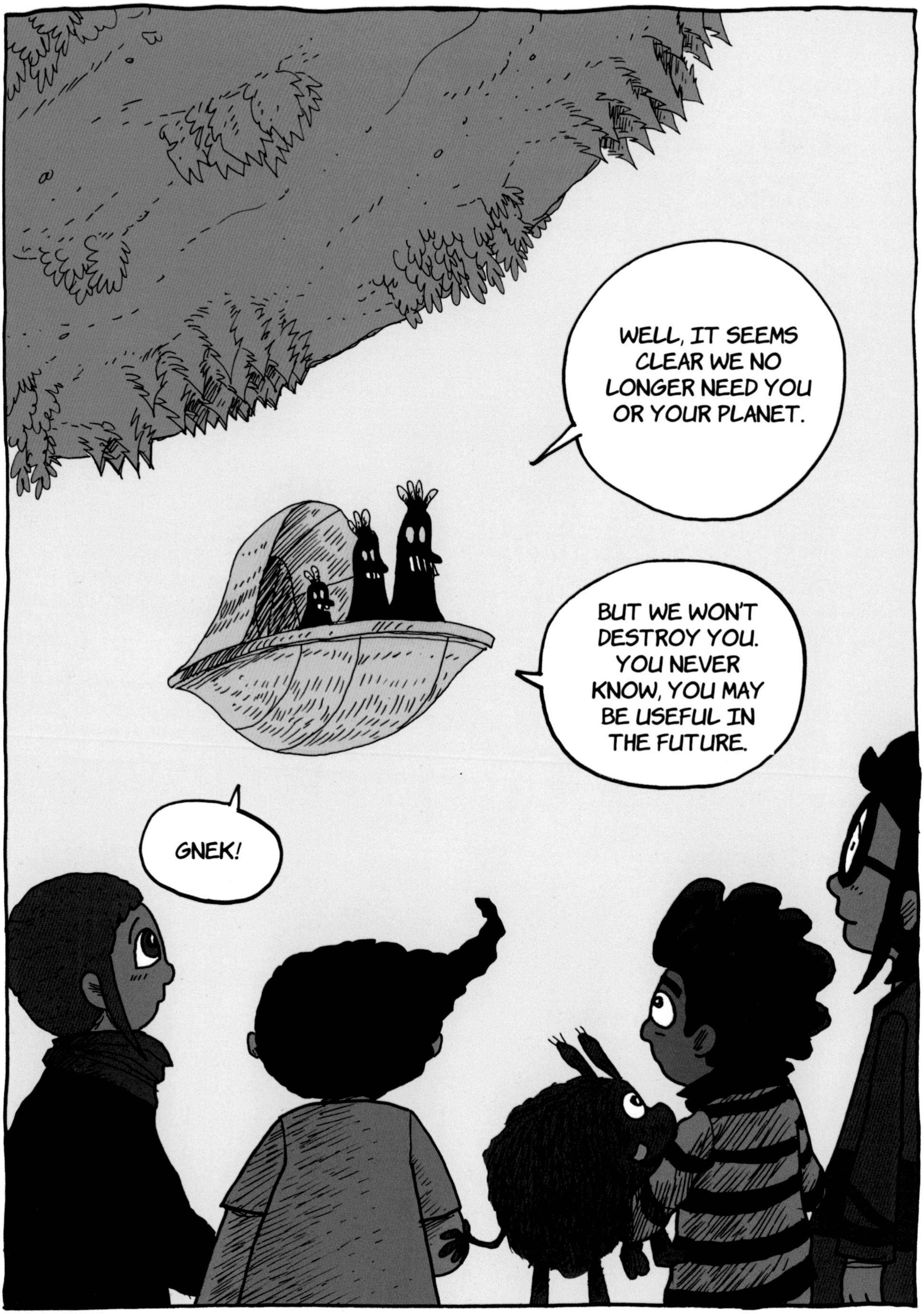
WELL, IT SEEMS CLEAR WE NO LONGER NEED YOU OR YOUR PLANET.
BUT WE WON'T DESTROY YOU. YOU NEVER KNOW, YOU MAY BE USEFUL IN THE FUTURE.
GNEK!

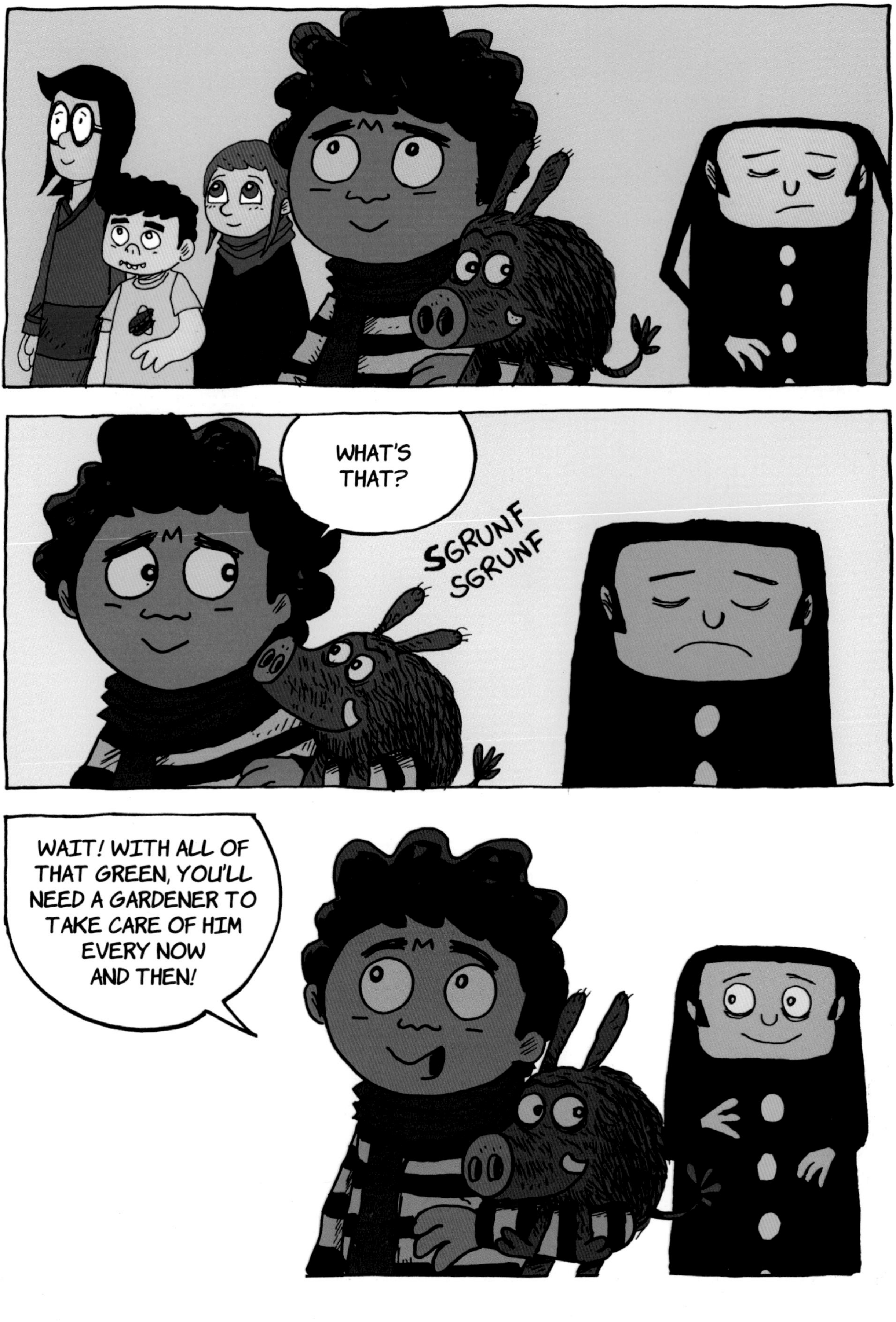
WHAT'S THAT?
SGRUNF SGRUNF
WAIT! WITH ALL OF THAT GREEN, YOU'LL NEED A GARDENER TO TAKE CARE OF HIM EVERY NOW AND THEN!

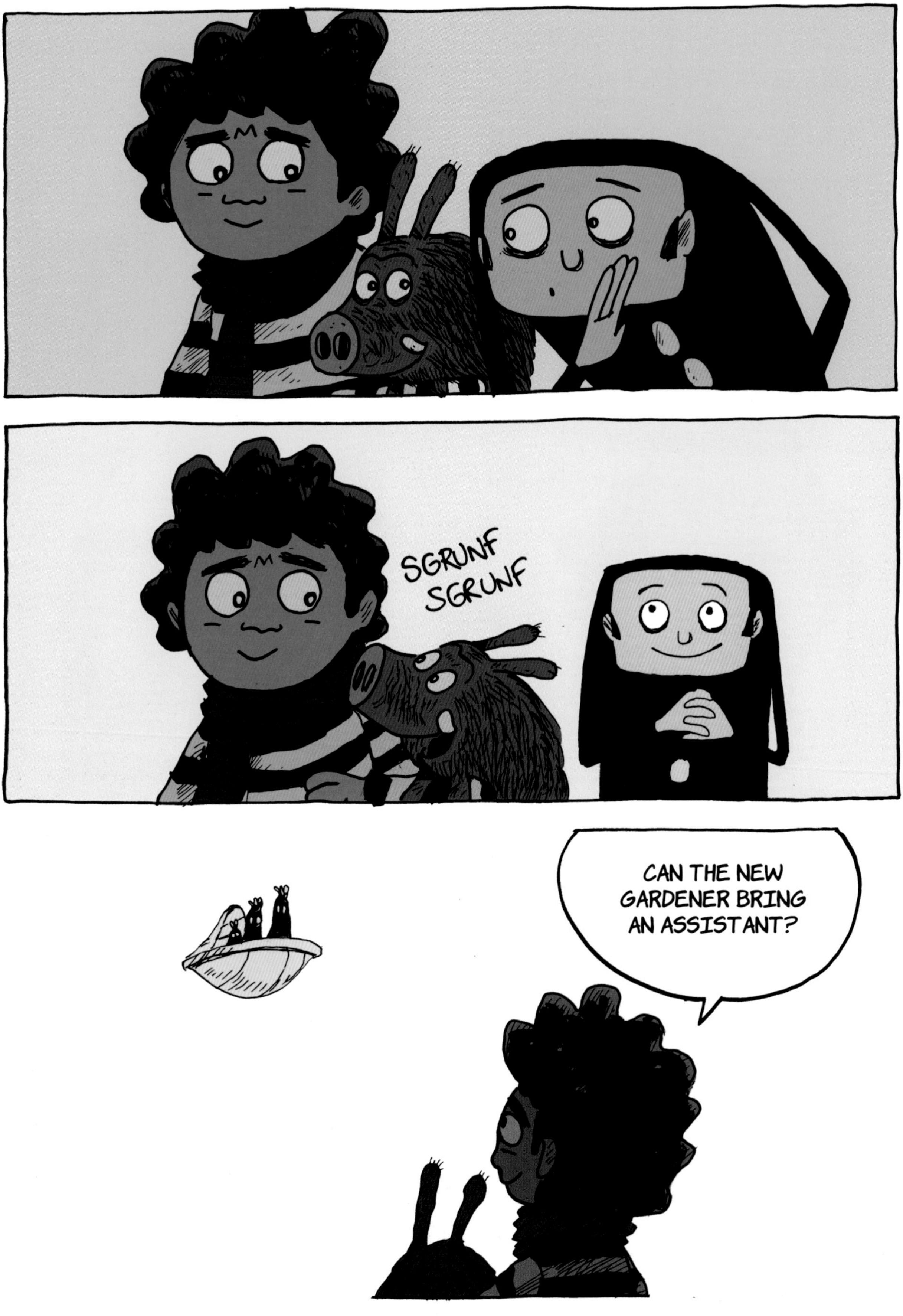
SGRUNF
SGRUNF
CAN THE NEW GARDENER BRING AN ASSISTANT?

EPILOGUE
HOMECOMING

KARAMAZOV

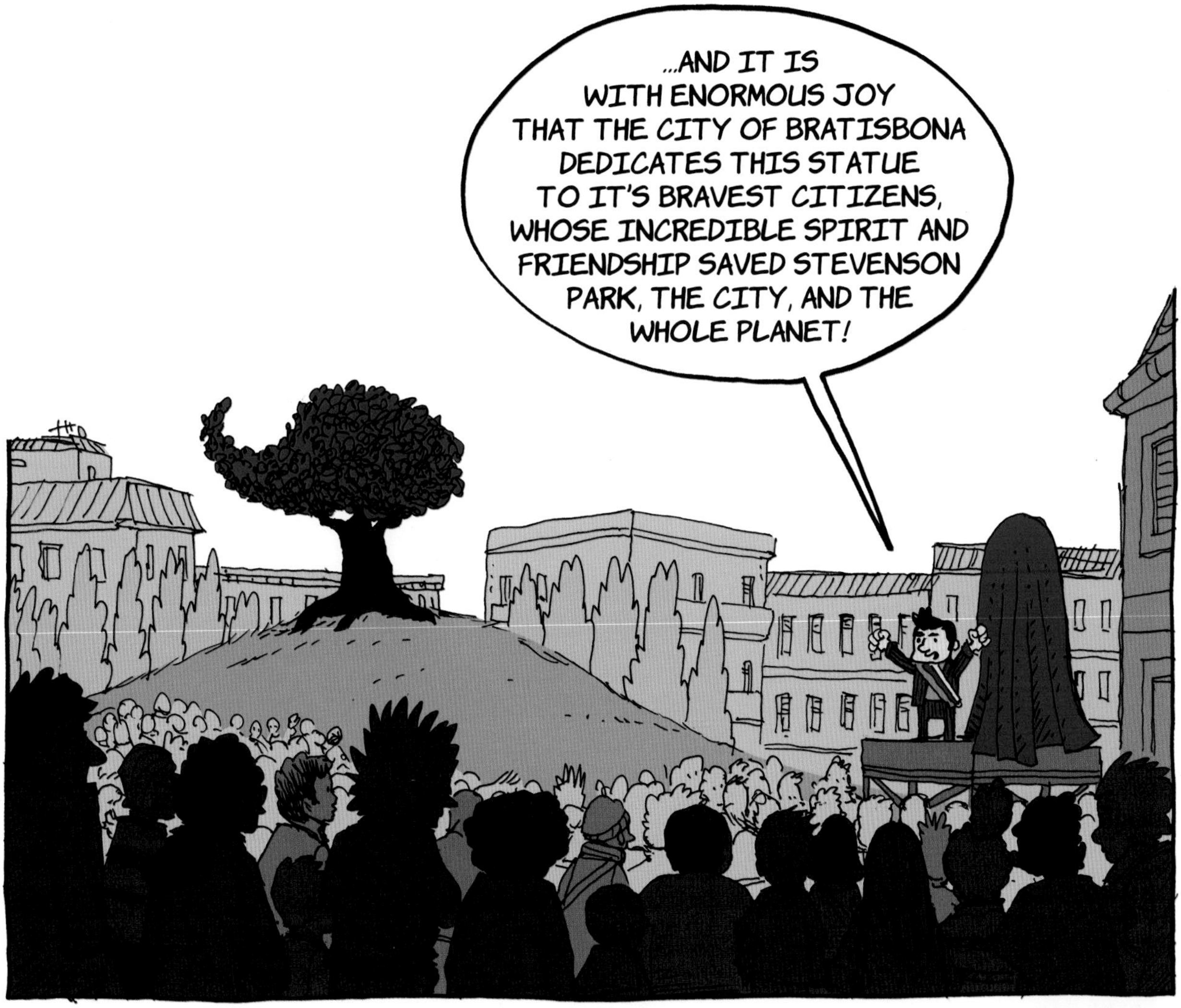
...AND IT IS WITH ENORMOUS JOY THAT THE CITY OF BRATISBONA DEDICATES THIS STATUE TO IT'S BRAVEST CITIZENS, WHOSE INCREDIBLE SPIRIT AND FRIENDSHIP SAVED STEVENSON PARK, THE CITY, AND THE WHOLE PLANET!

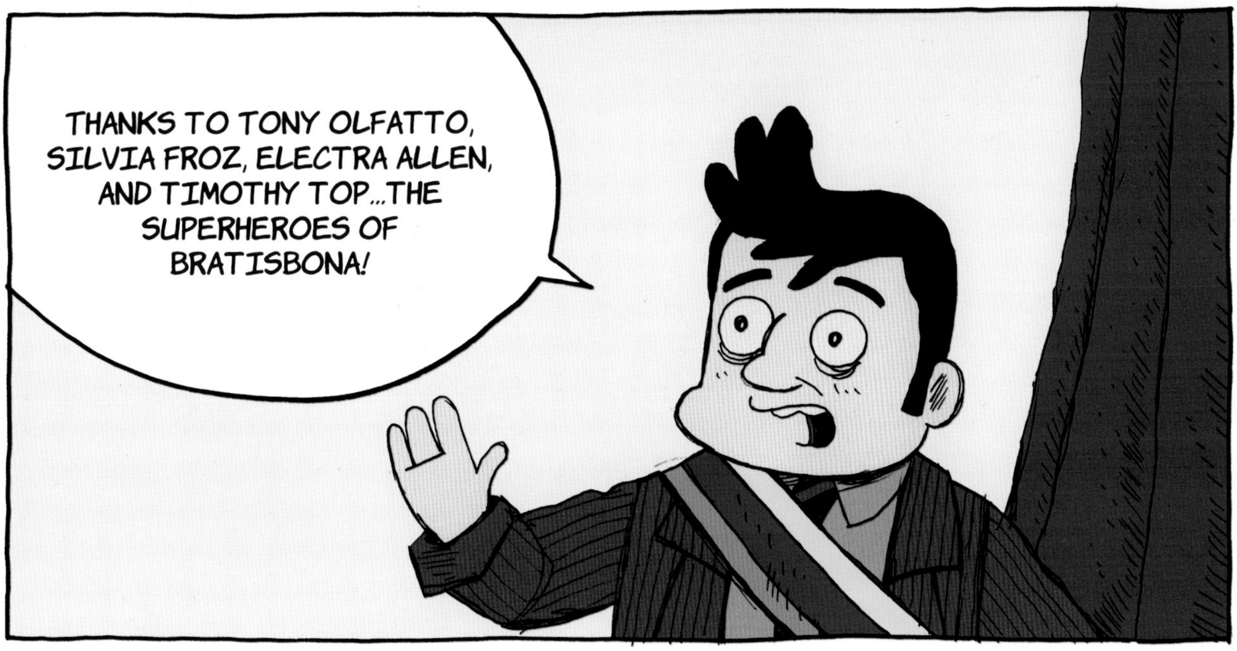
THANKS TO TONY OLFATTO, SILVIA FROZ, ELECTRA ALLEN, AND TIMOTHY TOP...THE SUPERHEROES OF BRATISBONA!

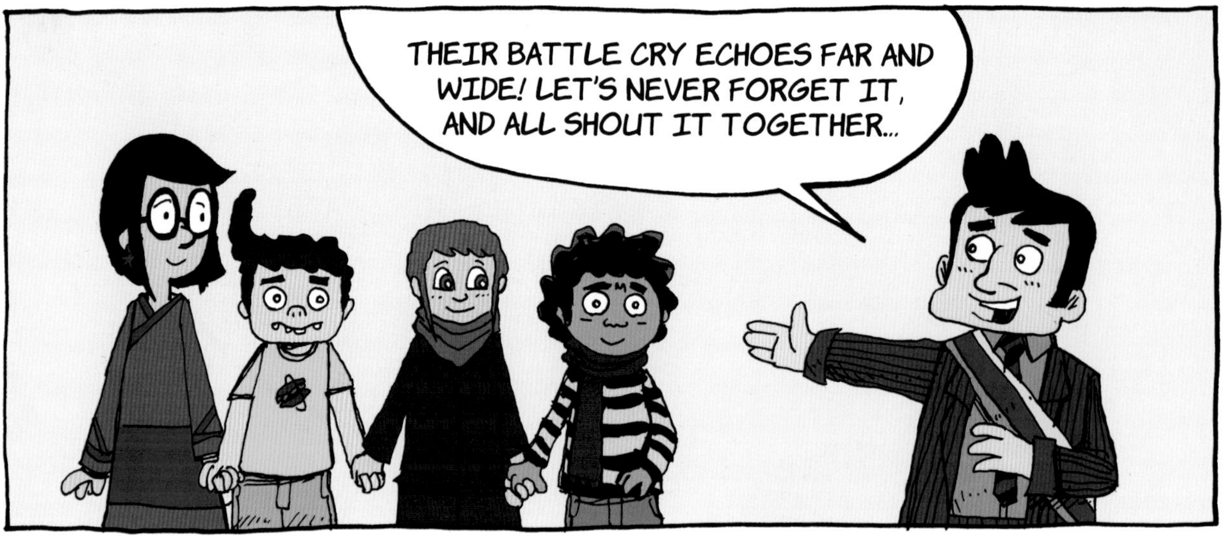
THEIR BATTLE CRY ECHOES FAR AND WIDE! LET'S NEVER FORGET IT, AND ALL SHOUT IT TOGETHER...

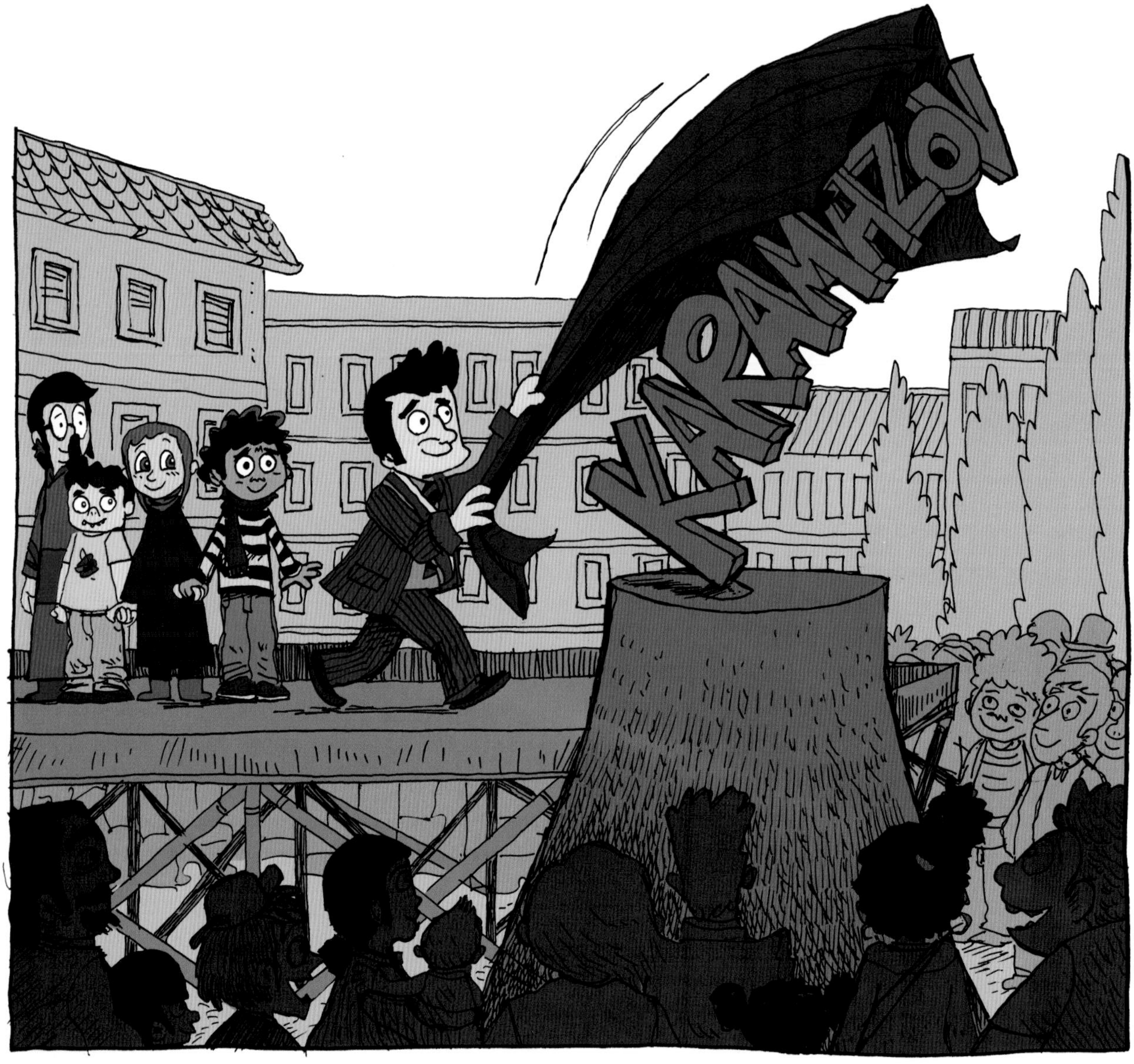
KARAMAZOV

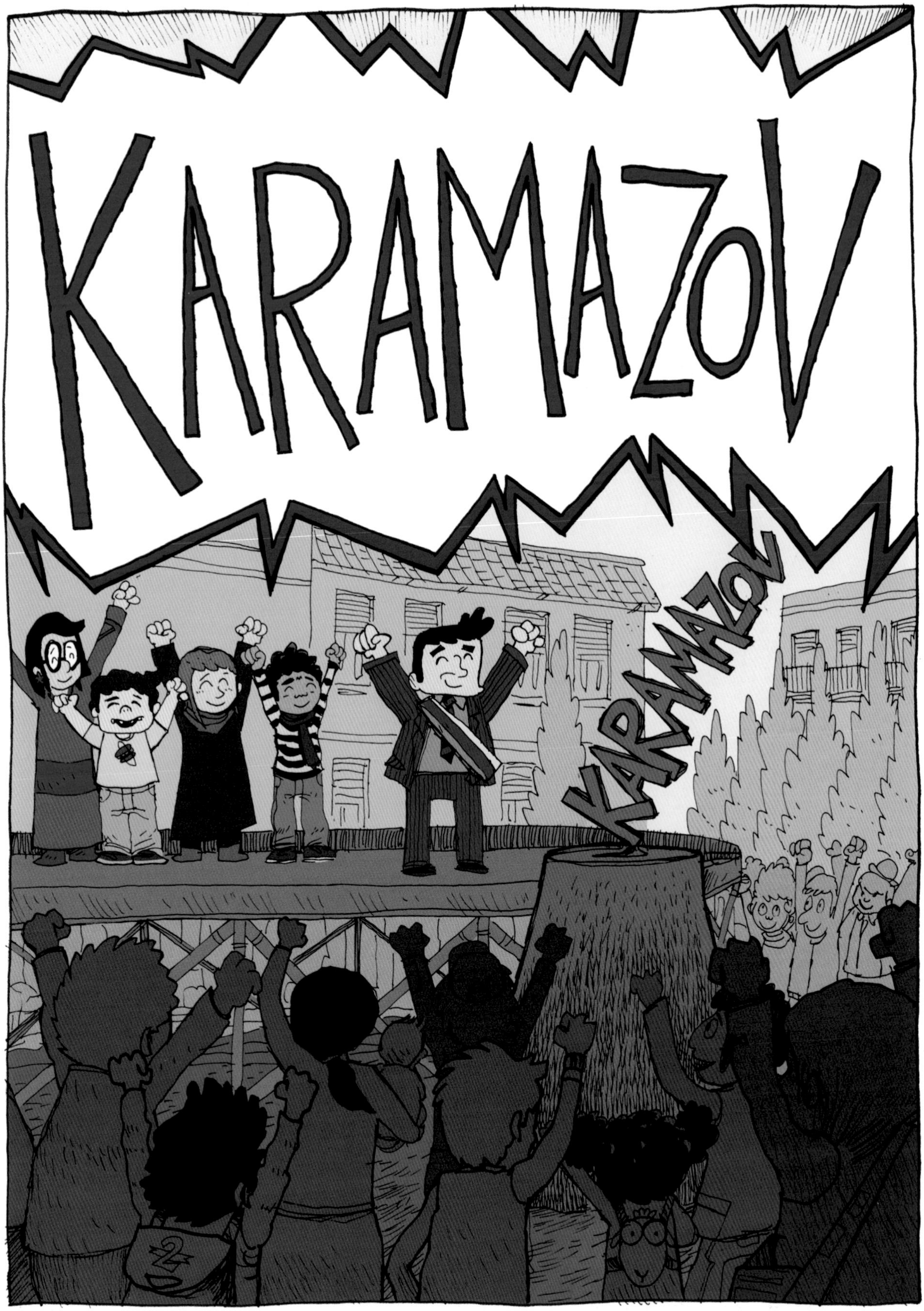
KARAMAZOV
KARAMAZOV

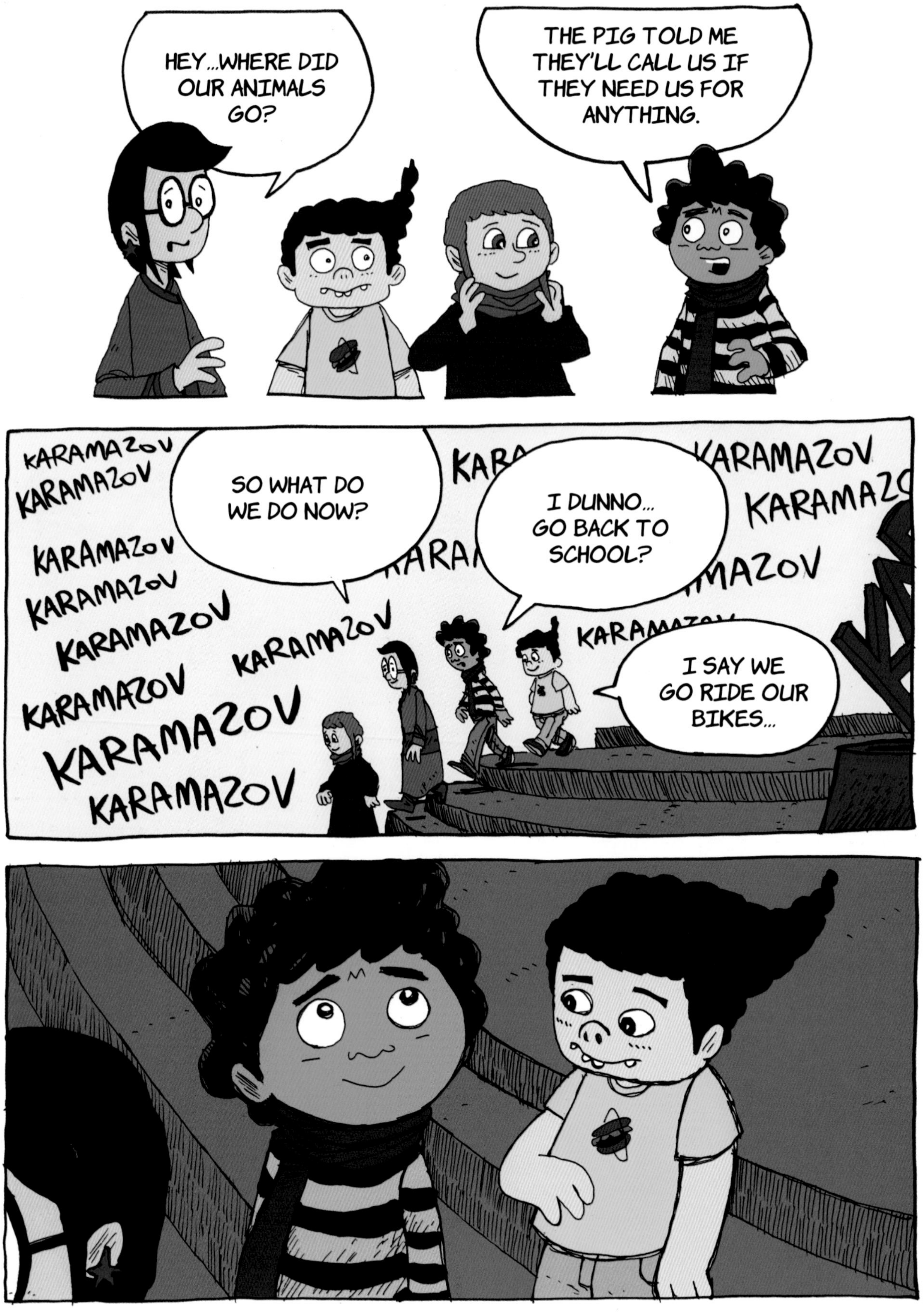
HEY...WHERE DID OUR ANIMALS GO?
THE PIG TOLD ME THEY'LL CALL US IF THEY NEED US FOR ANYTHING.
KARAMAZOV KARAMAZOV KARAMAZOV KARAMAZOV KARAMAZOV KARAMAZOV KARAMAZOV KARAMAZOV KARAMAZOV KARAMAZOV KARAMAZOV
SO WHAT DO WE DO NOW?
I DUNNO... GO BACK TO SCHOOL?
I SAY WE GO RIDE OUR BIKES...

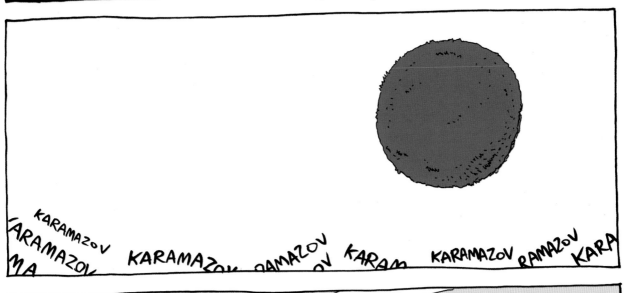

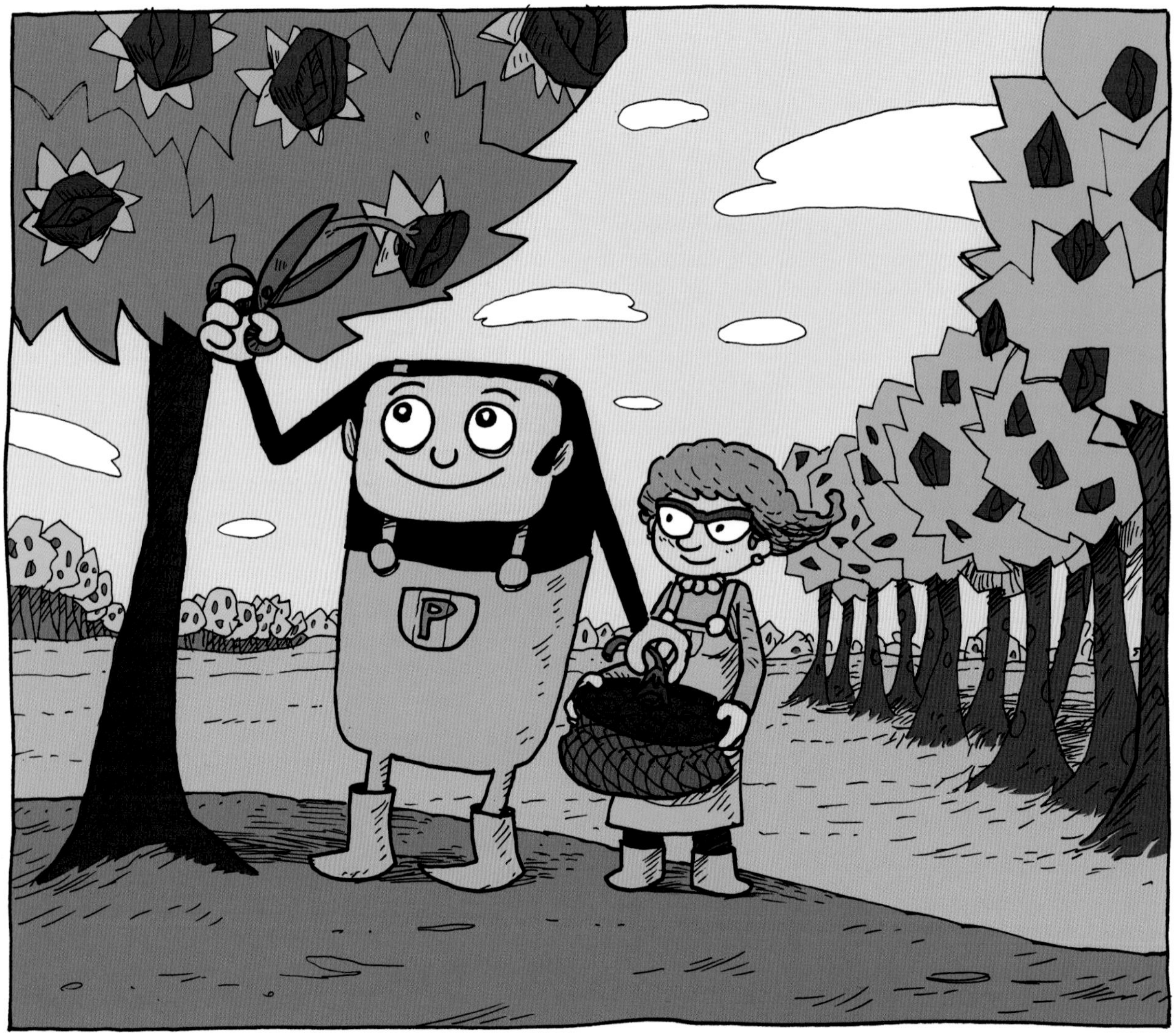

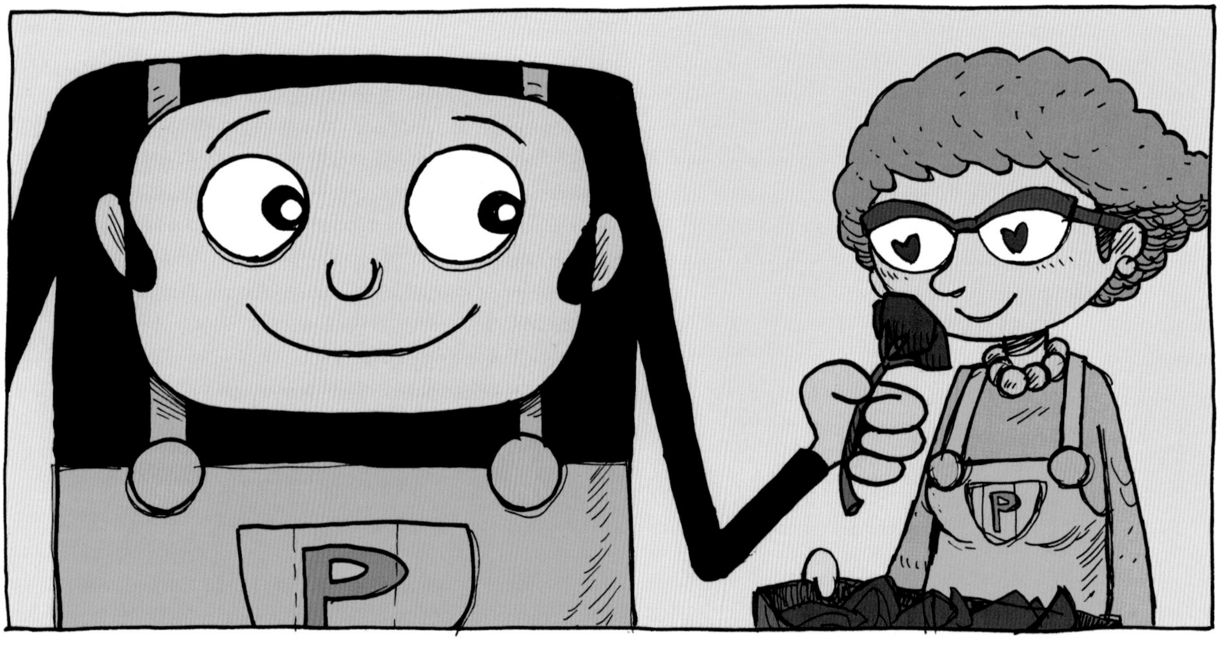

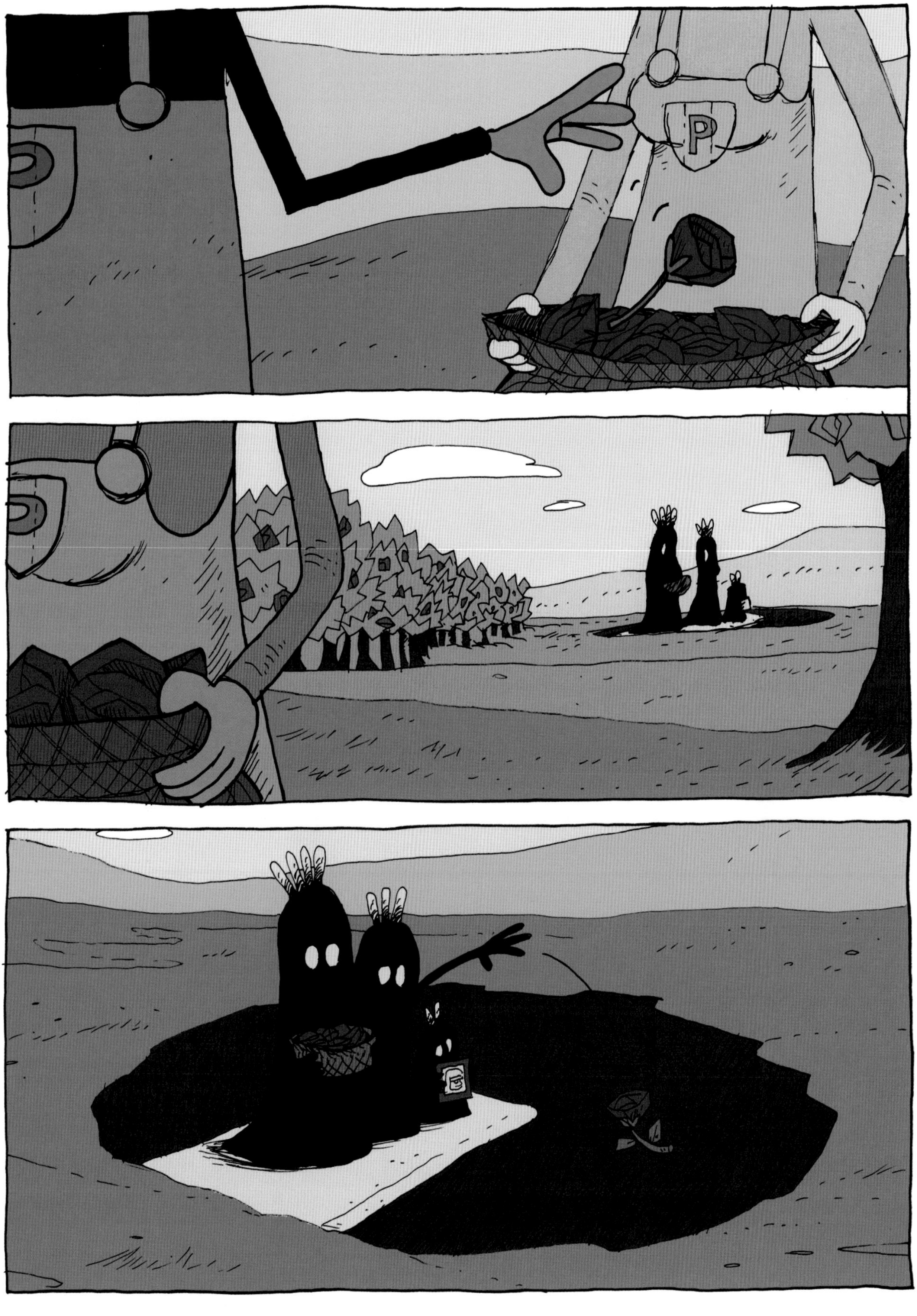

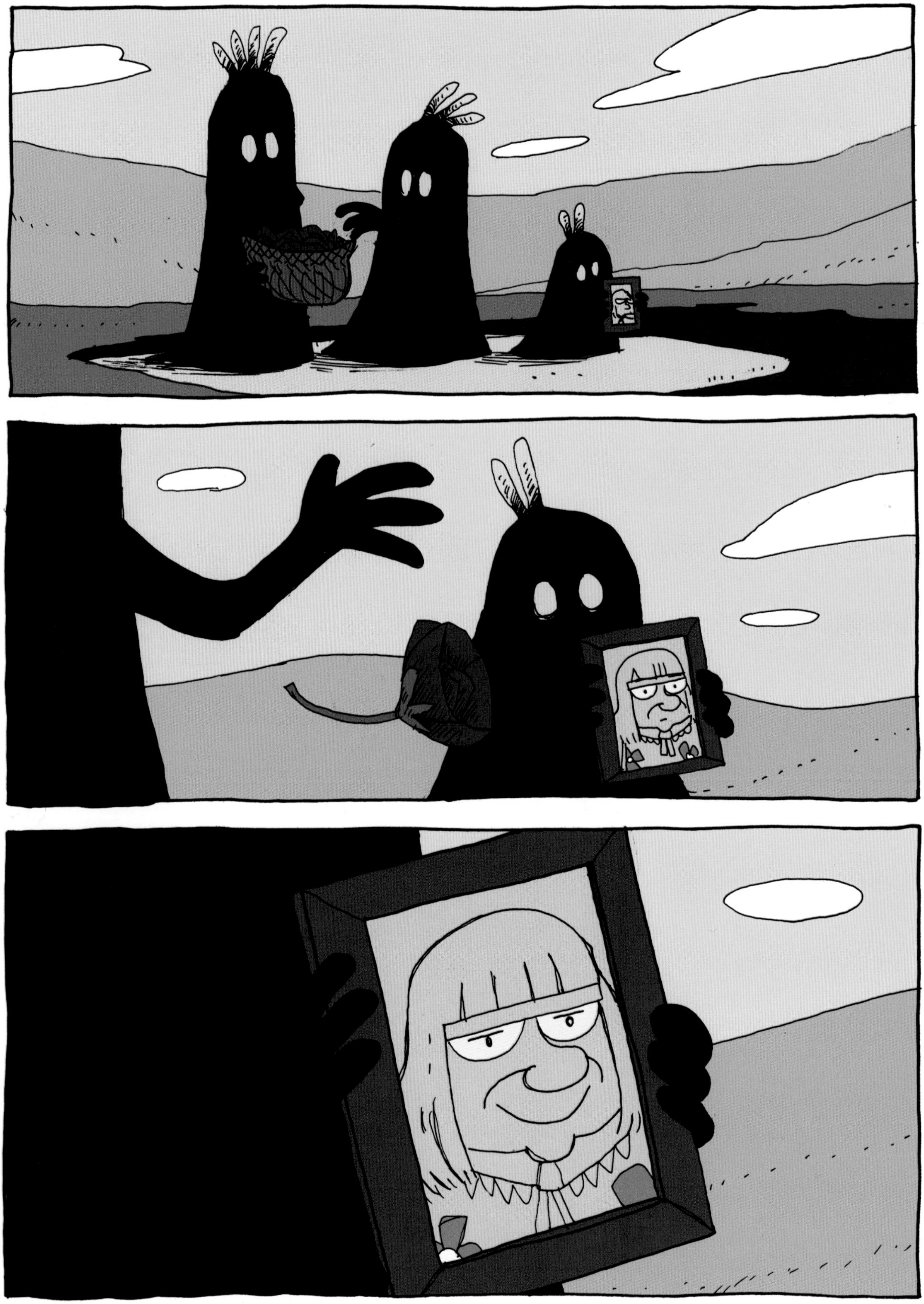

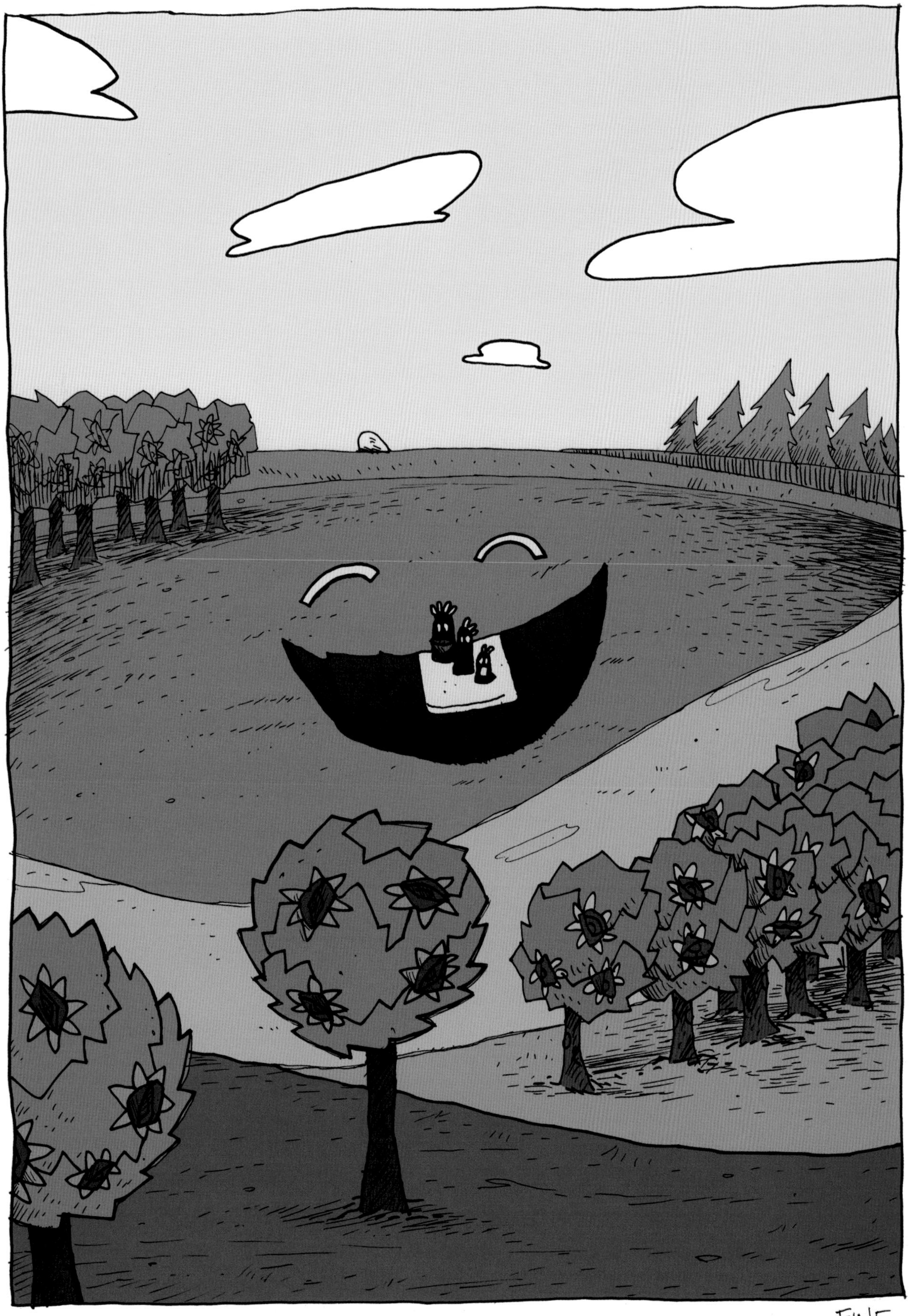

FINE